Definition of "reincarnation." *Collins English Dictionary - Complete & Unabridged 10th Edition*. HarperCollins Publishers. 22 May. 2012. <Dictionary.com http://dictionary.reference.com/browse/reincarnation>.

Whatever our souls are made of, his and mine are the same, quoted from Emily Brontë, Wuthering Heights, first published in 1847.

Cover design and manuscript layout by Amber Tanderes

Cover photo by Aleshyn Andrei/Shutterstock.com

Author photo by Jillian Saltmarsh

Lyrics from "Love Song" reprinted with the express permission of Tesla

Printed in Charleston, South Carolina

IN A GARDEN WHITE

a novel by Kathleen Ready Dayan

For my family—in this world and the next—
for the role each of you
played in the telling of this story.
And for Richard, who inspired me to write it.

re·in·car·na·tion [ree-in-kahr-**ney**-sh*uh*n]

1. the belief that the soul, upon death of the body, comes back to earth in another body or form.

2. rebirth of the soul in a new body.

3. a new <u>incarnation</u> or embodiment, as of a person.

There is nothing in your world or mine that can part those
whom love has united.
Love, like life, is stronger than death.
Love, like life, is the spirit,
and the spirit cannot be destroyed—
Silver Birch

The White Garden

It was no small request, to be reborn into yet another human form. And although he might speak out against it, already he knew that he would relent. He would follow Kalli anywhere, even to Earth and back…again.

Her voice was like wind chimes, as ethereal as the first utterances of a newborn baby. Elia listened carefully, a skill that had taken many lifetimes to master. The argument was a familiar one. Her mother was on Earth and she couldn't bear the separation. How could he oppose her when separation was his biggest obstacle as well? It was everyone's. No one wanted to part from those they loved. Whether in body or in spirit, it was the perpetual heartbreak.

Elia dug his hand into a sack of sugar and watched as the granules slipped through his fingers into the red clay cups they'd loved so much in a past life that they had recreated them at home. "There are too many people on Earth. We might not find each other," he said.

Kalli turned to face him. Her skin was as smooth and flawless as polished glass. No wrinkles revealed her history or her struggles. Unlike the physical body, with age the spirit becomes stronger, and the light exuded by the life force within—on Earth seen by some as an aura—becomes brighter. Kalli shone like a small sun, the center of Elia's universe. Her small hands brushed grounds from the coffee beans she was grinding onto the worn plank floor.

"Of course we will," she stated. "We're inseparable."

"No Kalli, we're not. Only here we are." Although he couldn't break the cycle of rebirth, he could control the *where* and *when* of it. It was a matter of free will. Heaven was his most compelling argument. There was only one thing that could prompt him to leave it now: Kalli's absence. Like he always said, *it wouldn't be Heaven without her*.

He moved to the window of the cottage that was their home and peered out at the tropical flowers, orchids and hibiscus, that lined the stone path leading to their door and at the blossoming Japanese cherry trees being utilized by a group of monkeys who had made this their Heaven, too. Elia wore only buckskin pants with no shoes on his feet, two feathers were tied into his long hair, and a bear paw was painted on his chest—remnants of his last life. But clothes and mannerisms aside, he did not look Native American. His hair was light brown with streaks of gold, and his eyes were a startling blue. Even in the Spirit World where appearance can be chosen, his drew attention. His body, as brown as an Indian's, set against the fairness of his eyes and hair was carved like an athlete's. But most remarkable was the light he emitted, a bright electric blue that had a way of transmuting with his emotions to a deep indigo.

Outside the window, two white lions, mates, were passing by. They felt Elia's gaze and nodded their heads at him respectfully. He returned the gesture, almost bowing. In his world words were unnecessary; every nuance could be expressed silently but completely. There was no need to say that his heart was grieving, that he was terrified of being separated from his own mate. They understood and commiserated. Elia sighed as the lions continued on their way. Even though not in human form, the lions—and countless other creatures—were his friends and once he was reborn would cease to be part of his life.

A mourning dove landed on the sill of the open window, its glistening black eyes inviting him to hold it. All animals, but most particularly birds, were drawn to him. They could feel his energy. And he could feel theirs, even when he was residing in a physical body. Elia was strikingly perceptive, and over many lifetimes had developed the ability to heal both people and animals with his touch. He stroked the bird's throat with the tip of his index finger, then watched it take flight from his hand before turning back to the matter before him.

There had been many lifetimes and every time he had recognized Kalli. His intuition was so attuned that he had trusted the magnetic pull he felt each time he saw her housed in new flesh, as a poor girl in the French

2

countryside, an Italian opera singer, or the daughter of a Palestinian merchant with skin as brown as cappuccino and eyes as dark as the rich coffee beans she was now grinding for their expected guests. But what if this time he didn't?

"They're here," he suddenly announced. And they were, as if his words had magically made it so. Two Native American men stood on the threshold of the cottage's open door. Elia greeted them both warmly, but the more amiable embrace was saved for Moonhawk, his brother. The man accompanying him was Running Deer, who during his last lifetime had been a Chippewa elder and whose image persisted as such.

Kalli was right behind Elia, waiting her turn to greet their friends. Moonhawk was like her brother, as well, and had served as her brother-in-law numerous times. It never failed to make him laugh when she greeted him with a kiss on both cheeks, the European way. It was as foreign to him as chocolate truffles served on a silver platter or cream mixed into his coffee. He had never been born into society as Kalli had. His desire was always for a simple life, close to the earth, an Australian Aborigine, a Tibetan monk or most recently, a Native American. And in between those lifetimes he used his wisdom to guide others reborn to the physical world.

She had both guests by the hand and was joyfully leading them into the cozy parlor that was bedecked with flickering candles and white flowers arranged in glass vases. It wasn't cold, but a fire burned in the fireplace. Perched on the mantel was an oil painting of Elia that Kalli had created. Even in the portrait, firelight danced across his cheekbones and jaw. Firelight. *Once an Indian always an Indian,* Elia liked to say. And fire to Indians was a sacred thing. He sat next to it and waited. He would not speak of the matter until she was beside him.

Kalli brought coffee to their guests in the red clay cups and filled the room with her golden light just by moving through it. Her long skirt swished along the floor and Elia listened. Her eyes became spellbound by the wildflowers offered to her by Running Deer and Elia watched. When it was

3

empathy or compassion that he mused upon, it was Kalli who came to mind, Kalli who would rush in to ease the suffering of any creature. But mostly when he pondered the miracle of love, it was Kalli that he envisioned. There had never been another whom he had loved like her.

She handed him the cup before she sat beside him. His eyes took in the hot liquid as he tried to remember what it tasted like when he was made of flesh. They had recreated it because they loved it; not because they needed liquid, or food for that matter. It existed only if they desired it. But the experience was different now than in a human body. In Spirit the contrast didn't exist. He pondered the word *warm* and how it had a different meaning when compared to freezing cold fingers that came from walking through a snowstorm.

Elia raised his eyes to meet the ebony eyes of his brother. There was no need to vocalize any of his thoughts, emotions or reservations about the rebirth, save for the politeness and respect he wished to show. Moonhawk could hear them all. "Kalli's mother..." he began.

"Will bear another child," his brother finished. "Perhaps she could bear two?" Elia shook his head. "It's the safest way," Moonhawk pressed. "The only guaranty you'll be together."

"I'm not her brother," Elia replied. He had no intention of being Kalli's twin.

Moonhawk's healing green light permeated the room. The energy spun around Elia as he'd felt it countless times before, and he noticed the familiar quieting of his thoughts, but this time it could not go deep enough to lighten the anguish in his heart. Too much was at stake. There was no tribe to be born into, no guaranteed way of being in his wife's proximity long enough for soul recognition. Elia hadn't felt so trapped since that moment more than a hundred years prior in Earth time when the filthy soldier in the tattered blue jacket had pulled the trigger and forced him away from Kalli.

"My mother's name is Mary," Kalli offered. "This time it's Mary."

4

Elia spoke slowly, "There's a woman who lives near Mary, on the same little street…"

Kalli's eyes grew wide at the realization of his intent. She had heard his thought beforehand but had interpreted it as a passing reflection, not one so deeply embedded that it might prompt him to take action. The woman he was referring to was an alcoholic and drug abuser. Her mind, body and spirit were all tainted by it.

"We could grow up near each other," he argued. "You would *know* me Kalli."

"Choose another woman," Running Deer stated quietly.

"You could be born sick," Kalli argued, vocalizing all of their concerns. "Even if you're healthy your life will be affected by her choices…by her manner of living."

"It makes no difference to me, don't you see?" her husband threw out desperately.

"Elia," Moonhawk calmly interjected. "It's you who doesn't see. The woman you choose as a mother will impact the entire lifetime. This decision shouldn't be made impulsively."

Kalli crept onto Elia's lap like a cat who fit the space perfectly. Together they blended like the colors of a sunset. It was hard to decipher where one ended and the other began. He stroked her curls. Even hair made of light feels remarkably physical when felt with fingers made of light. *I can live with whatever body I'm given, as long as I'm with you* he conveyed without speaking, and she tucked her head under his chin, listening to his silent assurances.

Moonhawk waited respectfully to make sure they were done communing before he spoke. "You know the consequences," he said. "If you nonetheless decide to enter the physical world, Running Deer will act as your spirit guide as you requested and I'll guide Kalli."

"We'll do what we can to keep you together," Running Deer added. "But be forewarned, I won't override your self-will."

Moonhawk stood abruptly, signaling their departure. "There's no need to remind my brother of that," he answered for him. If impulsivity were to be Elia's downfall, it wouldn't be the first time. "His self-will caused them to separate in their last life."

Running Deer nodded reverently and murmured, "When he was Standing Bear."

Standing Bear…the Earth form that had been closest to Elia's true self, but still hearing the name spoken caused him to grimace. It had been a good life, a good life that ended badly. Running Deer responded to his thoughts, but directed the comment to Moonhawk. "When Standing Bear was killed, they found a way to be together. If necessary they can again."

"Only if Kalli remembers how," Moonhawk countered. "The culture they are being born into barely acknowledges the spirit. Who will teach her?"

"You will," Running Deer replied. "If not face to face like before, then through her dreams. As she walks her path, you'll be whispering to her. You'll be whispering 'Elia'."

Behind the cottage, in their backyard, there was a display of every white flower Kalli had ever laid eyes on. White had always been her favorite color. It was carved so deeply into her character that she carried it with her each time she entered a new life. As a little girl in Italy she chose white frocks with exquisite embroidery, and as an elderly lady on a small farm she made her own white peasant skirts even though they were impractical and criticized by other women. Never did she grow tired of the bouquets of white flowers Elia laid at her feet. They were a symbol of his love for her.

He had created the garden for her, manifested each and every tree and plant that she desired. A circular stone wall enclosed the garden and created a sense of privacy, although no one ever entered it without invitation and would not have even if the stone wall did not exist. The barrier was created more efficiently by their thoughts. It was their own private paradise, their white garden. Inside the stone wall the flowers were always in bloom, the magnolias and the lilies, the hyacinth and the lilacs. They were Kalli's favorite, the lilacs.

Elia carried her with her legs wrapped around his waist and her cheek pressed against his, not because he perceived her as a child or unequal to himself. If anything the opposite was true; he strove to be more like her, to allow love to govern his actions. In Spirit that was an easy task. How difficult could it be to show love to someone as angelic as Kalli or as steadfastly loyal as Moonhawk? But on Earth all souls convene, even those who have not yet evolved enough to understand that Love is the law that governs all that is and all that ever will be. Fools gather with masters and all those, like Elia, who fall somewhere in between. He carried her like a child, safe in his arms, because she longed for the security and because he longed to provide it.

What would she be in their new life? he wondered. Some sort of artist, no doubt. Once discovered, nothing is quite as satisfying or meaningful as self-expression. Kalli had been an artist for dozens of lifetimes. In the American culture he was about to enter Elia could not be a shaman—his calling—but perhaps he could be a doctor.

Elia placed her under her favorite tree, a massive hydrangea taller than any in the physical world, and sat beside her. The decision had been made. Discussing it privately was only a formality. She needed to go and he would never expect her to go alone. Silently he used his hunting knife for the only purpose it served: to cut stalks from a nearby lilac bush.

"You can bring me lilacs in our new life," Kalli said as she took them from his hands. "They'll help me remember our white garden and who we are to each other."

If only her partner thought, knowing full well that shortly after birth, those memories would no longer be accessible. There are always traces that remain—traces that slip out in dreams or a quick flash of déjà vu—but not an entire history. Older souls, however, retain more recollection than others, and Elia was a very old soul.

7

Moonhawk had once said something that often leaked into his human consciousness: *There will be people on your path to encourage you. Stop and give thanks for them. Gratitude is a lifeline to the Great Spirit.* This part he almost always recollected and practiced in his daily living, not because he recalled the actual words but because the truth of them resonated in his very being. It was the second part of Moonhawk's speech that he invariably forgot: *Others will try to discourage you. These are the discontented ones, the souls who have lost their path. They can't help you but they can't harm you either unless you allow it. When you meet these souls, keep walking. Stay on the path.*

"It's never as easy as you make it sound," Elia replied to Kalli's remark, "but I'll follow you. I always do." He held her face in his hands and studied it, her uniquely small but full lips and her large eyes that had always reminded him of those belonging to wood nymphs in fairy tales.

"I won't forget you, Elia," she promised. "You're my heart. I'd know you anywhere."

CHAPTER ONE
Rebirth

It was the year 1977 and according to the plan they had laid out with Moonhawk and Running Deer's assistance, Elia would have been born six months after Kalli, but it didn't happen that way. He was born prematurely when his new mother gave birth only twenty five weeks into the pregnancy. The alcohol she ingested caused him to be born in August instead of November. When Elia drew his first breaths, he found himself confined to a body that weighed a mere two pounds and trembled so much that it felt like it was trying to shake him out of it.

His first emotion as a newborn was fear. What had he done? His eyes were open, but he could barely see. Vision through a physical body never has much acuity compared to that of a liberated spirit, but this was worse than what he recalled. He closed his eyes to rest, but his limbs remained rigid and his breath hiccupped. It was then that he felt the cooling green energy that had healed him countless times before. *Moonhawk*, he screamed inwardly and Moonhawk came into focus, hovering above the incubator. His dark eyes had tears in them. He was crying for his little brother who was caged inside a sick body, but was not sick enough to die and break free.

If newborns could speak with human words, they would have many stories to tell, stories of past lives and lovers, of sisters and brothers who remained in Spirit grieving their departure and of the Spirit World itself that shone with a light brighter than physical humans could conceive of. Elia could still remember all the lifetimes that had come before, the cottage and the white garden extending behind it, his friends—in both human and animal form—that he'd left behind, and Kalli, the way she'd felt in his arms before they parted. But soon it would all begin to fade, the memories would feel like a dream, and he would start to believe that he did not exist at all beyond this frail body.

"Where is she?" he sent out. "Is she safe?"

"She is safe and she is loved," he heard with his inner ear, clairaudiently, like mediums do. It was Running Deer acting as his guide. The emotions swelled in his chest and he wept. His body began to convulse. A female voice startled him; it was a nurse calling for help. She opened the incubator to remove his tiny body, making sure the wires attached to his head, chest and limbs remained attached. She held him close to her breast and he felt her energy. It was love. And then the woman did the most unexpected thing—she started singing softly, a lullaby. And for the first time since he arrived, he felt safe.

"So this is the famous Jeremy, the one you're all in love with?" he heard the pediatrician say soon after he heard his footsteps enter the room.

Jeremy. Was that his new name? He tried to get a good look at the nurse's face, but the picture his eyes created was unfocused and blurry. He couldn't see the doctor either, other than some movement like a shadow when he stepped closer. But he could hear him.

The doctor shone a shockingly bright light into Jeremy's eyes. "Alcohol withdrawal is causing the tremors, but this will help," he said and scratched out an order on Jeremy's chart for I.V. valium.

"It's the rest of his life I'm worried about," the nurse replied. "Does he have fetal alcohol syndrome?"

"Probably. His head size is normal relative to the rest of his body, but he has a heart murmur. We'll have to wait until he's older to test his hearing and vision."

"But you don't think he's mentally retarded?"

With a long exhale the doctor looked Jeremy over. "He might be a slow learner—we'll have to wait and see—but I don't think he'll have trouble functioning. His facial features are perfect."

"He's beautiful," the nurse sighed. "I wish I could keep him."

The doctor laid a hand on her shoulder. Even on Earth, touch is often the best method of healing. "I wish you could too," he said.

Several days passed before Jeremy met his mother. The nurses coddled him, cradled him in a rocking chair one of them had dragged closer to his incubator, and fed him from a bottle. He could see a little bit better now and liked to practice bringing their faces into focus while he took sips and they sang to him. When he'd exited his mother's birth canal she had been screaming and that was what he remembered about her, the abrasive sound of her voice. That's how he knew she hadn't been in to visit him. And that's how he recognized her when she finally did.

Belinda Blake was a tawdry blonde who came across as an old woman in a young woman's skin. She shuffled her feet when she walked as if her torso were too heavy for her legs to carry, even though she wasn't remotely overweight. She bore the thinness of a cancer patient and her eyes that used to be a pretty blue were now a dull grey. But Jeremy couldn't see any of that. He could only feel her energy, as well as the shift in the nurses' energies when she entered the room. To someone as perceptive as Jeremy, women's scorn is easily detected.

The name *Elia* was slipping out of his grasp and with it all that he had known and loved before, including Kalli, although her name was often spoken by the Indian who stood vigil by his incubator. He didn't know anymore that there was a difference between him and the nurses except that the Indian shone with a much brighter light. He could see the auras of the nurses; the glow around them attracted his eyes. When Belinda stood over him for the first time, he noticed that she wasn't surrounded by light like the people who took care of him. As happens when people are sick, her aura was drawn in so tightly to her body that he couldn't see it.

The wisdom of Elia had receded into Jeremy's subconscious mind. He didn't remember the need to be wary of his new mother. Although he was repelled by her scent, he showed no resistance to her holding him. It was the alcohol that soured her breath, but he didn't know that. Jeremy didn't know it was the very same thing that would cause his life to go in a direction other than that which he had so carefully planned, the instrument that would tear him away from his soul mate. He grew to know Belinda and soon Belinda was all he knew. And his Indian friend became less and less visible, until he could no longer see him. Sometime after he'd learned to talk, which for Jeremy happened at the age of four, he told his best friend, Joy, who lived two houses away, about the old Indian who visited him in his dreams.

Joy was the name Mary and Bob Sanders, her parents, gave Kalli because she was a happy baby from the start. She had an older brother, Ethan, an often silent five year old with serious brown eyes like his father, and a two-year old sister, Lily, with buttery white hair and squinty blue eyes that smiled as often as her lips. Lily lavished Joy with affection and although Ethan adored her every bit as much, he was far too reserved, even at his young age, to show it.

Her life from the onset was as different from Jeremy's as summer from winter in the seacoast Massachusetts town of Marshfield where they lived. They both resided in winterized summer cottages that were close enough to the ocean to hear its melodic roar when the windows were open and to smell the salty air. There were only two bedrooms in both the homes, but Joy's father built a wall in the second bedroom so that Ethan could sleep separate from the girls. The second bedroom in Jeremy's house was used by whomever the tenant happened to be at the time, one or another of Belinda's drinking buddies. Jeremy's bed was in the living room. During the day it was used as a sofa. He learned to sleep through blaring music and the obnoxiously loud talk of drunks.

At sunrise he'd hear the sea gulls and reach for his glasses, then scramble to the window so he could watch them soar toward the water. A family of chickadees lived in a shrub outside, and as he listened to their chatter, he often wondered if the mother was scolding her children the way his mother always did. *Don't wake me up, Jeremy. How many times have I told you that? Can't you pour a bowl of cereal by yourself yet?* Before he could talk, Jeremy learned the ground rules of existence with Belinda: walk softly and stay out of her way.

Due to the fact that he was born prematurely, Jeremy was the size of a typical two-year-old when he was four. Sitting cross-legged on the wooden sill in front of the bay window wearing the oversized eyeglasses that he needed to function, he looked like a Lilliputian leapt off the pages of *Gulliver's Travels*. Every morning he waited there for an elderly gentleman, a stroke victim, who walked past his house dragging his partially paralyzed leg behind him. They had met face to face only once.

On that day, Jeremy was next to the road drawing pictures in the sand with a stick when the man approached him. "You're not out here by yourself, are you?" he shouted. (He was partially deaf.) Jeremy could not yet speak so he only raised his eyebrows at the volume of the man's voice before turning his attention back to the drawing. The visual in his mind of the chickadees was so clear that he'd felt sure the bird he drew would look real enough to fly right out of the sand. But it was only a stick figure. As the man's eyes scanned the yard and found no adult lingering nearby his discontented energy invaded the placid blue of Jeremy's aura.

The boy put the stick aside and placed both his tiny hands on the man's ailing leg. Sometimes late at night when his mother's friends were passed out on the floor near his bed, their energy would wake him up and he'd sit next to them with his hands on their heads until the negative energy dissipated. He didn't know he was healing them. To Jeremy, touching a person in pain was as natural as walking by an animal's empty food bowl and knowing it needed to be filled.

"How do you like that?" the old man mused while Jeremy adjusted his glasses on his nose. "My leg feels stronger." Before he continued on his walk, still marveling over the ability to ambulate, he drew a tree branch underneath the stick figure bird Jeremy had created, and the boy smiled his appreciation. "You need to go inside," the old man instructed, "and don't come out unless you're with a grownup."

Jeremy hugged him around his knees before he scurried into the house.

13

From that day forward, he waited on the window sill, and once the old man came into view he tapped on the window to get his attention, but not loudly enough to awaken the sleeping beast that was his mother. The elderly fellow was a predictable creature; he passed by every morning at 7:18. Jeremy didn't know numbers, but he could recognize the symbols that flashed on the digital clock: the one that looked like the cane that the old man used, followed by two sideways eyes, then a stick and a snowman. Every time the old man spotted him in the window he smiled and waved as if greeting a long lost friend, and every time Jeremy's heart soared. He was the only person Jeremy smiled at…except for Joy.

Joy lived within walking distance, even for his small legs. She was his age but much bigger. He'd sit silently and watch her with his startlingly blue eyes while she told him the bedtime story she'd heard the night before, or comb his long brown hair as if he were a doll. She'd take him by the hand and drag him off to wherever she pleased, and he never objected. He was happy just to be in her presence. That good feeling he got in his belly when the old man smiled at him was always there when he was with Joy. When he grew tired of waiting for his mother to wake up he would open the front door and head down the street to her house. Sometimes Belinda noticed and came looking for him, but most of the time she didn't.

CHAPTER TWO

The Dream

Mary Sanders was counting tips on the kitchen table hoping there'd be enough to pay the delinquent electric bill when she heard the familiar sound, *thwk, thwk, thwk,* of Joy sucking her thumb. She was standing in the doorway in her flannel pajamas, her wild yellow curls a nest around her face. It was late—11:35—and Mary was worn out. She'd worked the late shift at the restaurant and Bob had put the kids to bed. In fact, he was still on the floor in the girls' bedroom. He'd fallen asleep while telling them a bedtime story.

"What's the matter, Joy?" Mary inquired.

"I don't—don't know. I'm sad."

"Did you have a bad dream?"

Joy scrambled onto her mom's lap. Mary's hands caressed her hair and their breathing fell into a familiar rhythm. "It was a good dream," she answered, "with flowers…lots of white flowers."

"What about the dream upset you?" her mother asked. Joy's face contorted and she stuck her thumb back in her mouth. "Oh—guess who I saw tonight?" Mary quickly threw out. She was an expert at distraction. With three children under the age of ten she had to be.

It worked. "Who?" Joy asked, her blue eyes round and clear as marbles.

"Henri!" Mary exclaimed and her daughter's face instantly transformed.

"Henri?" her daughter repeated with a perfect French accent and her mother laughed.

The notorious Henri was a French bull dog that belonged to the manager of the restaurant where Mary worked. Bob often brought the children to visit him where he lounged on the back step near the kitchen, and every time he made sure each of them had a small offering: a piece of raw hot dog or a left over sausage. The quirky character was supposed to be a watch-dog but the only person he barked at was Ethan (because he'd once stashed Spam in his coat pocket and the scent remained).

15

"Did you kiss him?" Joy asked.

"Of course!" Mary answered. "Three times, once for each of you."

"And one for Daddy?"

Mary smiled at her clever girl. "Oh yes, that's right and one for Daddy, too. Right on the top of his head, the way he likes it." Joy beamed, apparently having forgotten her dream. "Now let's get you back to bed. Tomorrow I'll tell you more about my visit with Henri."

Joy slid off her mother's lap and held both arms up, silently asking to be carried. Mary lifted her and Joy wrapped her legs around her mother's waist as if she were Kalli with Elia in the white garden. She laid her cheek on Mary's shoulder and stuck her withered thumb back in her mouth. It looked to her mother like it was going to be a smooth transition to sleep. She had already kissed her and was leaving the room when her daughter asked a surprising question.

"Do you know the Indian man?" she asked. "And, and who's Elia, Mama?"

"Who?"

"*Elia*," Joy repeated with attitude.

Mary knew every person in Joy's small world. None of them were Native American, and she'd never even heard the name Elia. "I don't know," she admitted. "Why do you ask?"

"I miss him," Joy said and broke down in tears. Maybe, Mary considered, they were imaginary friends or television characters, but why the strong attachment? Regardless, they were *very* real to Joy. Mary held her while she cried it out until exhaustion overpowered her grief.

Sleep and dreaming must have cleansed Joy of her sadness because the first thing Mary heard from her the next morning was a shriek of delight as Ethan chased her out of his bedroom. Mary grinned—another pillow fight. Joy always attacked her victims while they were asleep. Being the baby, she had to use every advantage she could get.

"Who wants blueberry pancakes?" Mary yelled to diffuse the battle before it became a war. Their house was so small that from the kitchen her voice could reach all the rooms.

"Me, me, me!" Lily answered first and beat Joy in a race to the table.

"They're not quite ready," Mary said. "You'll have to be patient." The girls scowled at each other. Patience was not their strong suit. Their mother gave them grapes to nibble on while they waited.

"Did you know that Jeremy has *never* eaten blueberry pancakes?" Joy was saying to Lily. "And did you know that Jeremy has *never* met Henri?"

"*Never?*" Lily shot back, disbelieving.

"Never ever," Joy responded solemnly and turned her big blue eyes to Mary who was placing the first plate of steaming hot pancakes on the table. "Right, Mama?"

"If you say so, Joy; Jeremy never talks to me."

"Jeremy never talks to anyone," Ethan stated quietly, as he pulled out a chair to sit. Joy narrowed her eyes and tightened her grip on a fistful of grapes. Then Ethan said what she had been waiting for: "I don't think he knows how." He wasn't trying to be mean; he was only making a comment on something everyone in the family had noticed…except Joy. She was adamant that he could talk, even though the rest of them had never heard him utter a word.

"He talks to me!" she screeched and thrust her fist toward Ethan, letting loose at the precise moment so the grapes would pelt him in the face.

"Joy Sanders!" Mary exclaimed. "You pick those up and apologize to your brother," but it was too late. Ethan was already eating the grapes off his plate, his lap and even the floor. He was pouring a glass of milk as if the assault had never taken place when Mary gave up and walked away. They were like David and Goliath, Joy and Ethan, the four-year-old completely capable in her small body of taking on the nine-year-old giant. In fact, the only time Joy was not tough and fiercely independent was when she had to separate from her mother. Then she'd curl up in a heap of sobs.

17

Why do you always get to sit next to Mom? Lily had asked at the dinner table the night before. *Because I'm the baby!* Joy had cried indignantly and wiggled her chair closer to her mother's. It was a statement Ethan and Lily would capitalize on for the rest of their lives. Every time Joy forced her will against them, their comeback was always, *Let her get her way. She's the baby*, which never failed to infuriate her.

Mary was still thinking about Jeremy. He was four years old, too, although the differences between him and Joy were remarkable. To say that Joy could talk would be a vast understatement. She was articulate. Jeremy on the other hand always communicated with hand gestures or a nod or a shake of his tiny head. He was so small that he could squeeze under the fence surrounding their yard, and he could move as quickly as a rabbit—especially if his mother yelled from their house. He must be bright, Mary always thought, to get by as well as he did.

As if her thoughts about Jeremy had spun out the window and carried him back, he knocked on the door. Joy gasped and slid to the door in her feet pajamas—it had to be him because no one else visited first thing in the morning. He was wearing a pair of cutoff denim shorts small enough to fit one of her teddy bears, and nothing else except huge black eye glasses that always looked ready to fall off the tip of his nose. His face and hands were smeared with dirt, and his hair was uncombed. Joy took his hand and yanked him into the house.

"Have you had breakfast yet, Jeremy?" Mary asked. His eyes were on his bare feet as he shook his head. "How would you like some blueberry pancakes?" He jumped up and down to convey his excitement and smiled so wide his teeth showed. "Wash your hands then."

Bob ambled out of the girls' bedroom, stretching his body as he moved, trying to get the feeling of the hard wooden floor out of his back. Once he was asleep, he was like a dead man, virtually impossible to awaken, so Mary always left him wherever he was, be it the couch, his favorite armchair or the floor in the girls' bedroom. He tousled Jeremy's hair when they passed each other, Bob on his way to the kitchen and Jeremy being dragged by Joy into the bathroom.

"I bet Mrs. Sanders has got a nice big plate of pancakes for you," he said and Jeremy turned back to grin at him. Other than Joy, he loved her dad more than any one. Bob always played with him, tossed him in the air and listened to him giggle before he landed safely in his hands. He taught him little things like what his name looked like by writing it on the street with a rock. And every time the Sanders family took a walk to the beach, he'd knock on the door and ask Belinda if Jeremy could come along, and he'd carry him the whole way there on his shoulders. From Bob's 5'10" height, Jeremy imagined that he could see the entire world.

Mary dropped spoonfuls of batter into the pan. "I'll make as many as he can eat," she said. Jeremy was "skin and bones" and every time he joined them for a meal he ate as if it were the first food he'd tasted in weeks. Peanut butter and jelly sandwiches were his favorite food and he could eat three of them in one sitting. Afterward his belly would protrude like the babies on the *Save the Children* television commercials. Mary always made a point of asking him if he'd eaten anything else that day, but he never answered. He'd just shrug his little shoulders and watch her sharply with his distinctive blue eyes that were surrounded by thick black lashes. And she would worry about him even more. That was her role, Bob always said, to be the worrier.

She was watching the pancakes cook but not as closely as she was watching her husband. His limp was getting worse. He had crashed his motorcycle back in high school and a resulting knee injury was serious enough to keep him out of Vietnam—it was 1968 when he graduated—and now the residual pain was always getting in his way. He was a carpenter who had given up on working for contractors who expected at least an eight hour day from a body that wasn't able to do that. Now he had his own small company but the work was inconsistent.

His morning ritual began with a kiss from his wife and a cup of black coffee to accompany his very favorite thing—the first cigarette of the day, the one he thought about when he put the last one out at bedtime. Mary had passed the "no smoking in the house" rule when Ethan was born and it had been in place since. He'd almost made it to the front door, the cigarette dangling unlit from his lips, when he heard a small voice behind him say *Mr. Sanders*. He stopped in his tracks. Jeremy was standing outside the bathroom drying his hands on a towel and smiling at him. The entire family was watching. Even Ethan had stopped stuffing his mouth with food long enough to stare. Still Bob was unsure. "Jeremy?" he asked.

Jeremy approached him. "Pancakes!" he said excitedly.

Laughter flowed out of Bob as easily as breath. He scooped the boy up in his arms and carried him to the kitchen table, Jeremy hugging him like a baby koala. Without a second thought, he stashed the cigarette back into his shirt pocket. It was the first time in his adult life that he'd started the day without one, but Mary's careful eyes noticed that he didn't seem to mind.

While curled up together in bed that night Bob once again brought up the subject that had been plaguing him for over a year, since the first time Jeremy had wandered into their yard. The child was clearly being neglected by his mother. Not only was he always hungry, but he was often so dirty that he smelled bad. They couldn't very well bathe him, but when it was warm enough outside Mary would fill the baby pool with bubble bath and that would suffice. His long hair was always tangled in knots and he was skittish. Bob had it in his mind that they could find a way to gain custody of him.

"Think of what it would do to Joy if Belinda moved away," he said, and Mary agreed it was a good point. Joy and Jeremy shared a bond she had never seen in other children, almost as if they could read each other's minds. That very morning during breakfast Jeremy had put his fork down and turned to Joy. She'd reached across the table for the syrup and squeezed some on his pancakes. Had he somehow silently asked her for it or did she simply know him so well that she understood?

Before Mary rejected his argument based on the fact that they could barely afford to feed the kids they had, he added another point. He'd been offered work by Billy Cosgrove, a local contractor. Billy was a good guy, a classmate at Marshfield High School, and he understood the financial demands of raising children—he had two sons of his own the same ages as Ethan and Joy. But Billy was notorious for working his employees twelve to fourteen hours a day. The last time Bob had worked for him it'd landed him in the orthopedics' office and on narcotic pain medication. That'd started the one and only rough patch in their marriage to date. Lots of times they'd been broke. But never before had they not gotten along.

Mary shot out of the bed. "Don't ask me that again," she snapped as she walked away and her husband knew better than to follow. He could hear her in the kitchen making tea, the kind that helped her sleep, and then the silence that fell as she sat alone drinking it. All the while, he lay awake thinking about the same topic that was causing his wife's insomnia: the little boy next door who was being treated so wrongly. If he thought about it hard enough, he figured, maybe he'd find a way to make it right.

CHAPTER THREE
Butterfly Wings

Jeremy had only been five for two weeks when he and Joy started kindergarten. Although Joy was only three months older, she was clearly the leader. They were standing in front of the Sanders' home with their matching E.T. lunch boxes that Bob had bought them at K Mart, and were holding hands as they waited for the school bus. Mary had noticed that whenever they were within reaching distance of each other they were holding on.

Belinda must have made it a point to get up with Jeremy for his first day of school because his long hair was combed, his face was washed and his shoes were tied. And he was wearing new clothes under his denim jacket. From where Mary was standing she could see Belinda sitting alone on the concrete steps at the front of her house holding a glass of juice, and her heart ached for her. She wasn't the one Jeremy ran to and hugged in anticipation of boarding the school bus. It was Mary who had that privilege, as if he belonged to her.

Of course it angered her to see Jeremy neglected, but she knew better than to condemn Belinda for it. Mary had been around alcoholism enough as a child to easily recognize it and she understood the disease as well as she could for a person who had never suffered from it. What she knew came from watching her father, whom she'd adored as a little girl turn into a raging lunatic under alcohol's reign. The same sweet father who taught her how to fly a kite and swim would strike her mother and smash empty bottles against walls. And the full ones—God forbid anyone touch those. When intoxicated, he shouted vulgarities and drooled at the dinner table. Mary was still in high school when her father killed himself by driving into an oak tree. Although his death came as a shock, it wasn't the monster she grieved. It was her *real* father, the person he was before the demon alcoholism possessed him.

That's who she thought about now as she waved at Belinda, and Belinda lethargically returned the gesture. She also thought of her own husband and the mandate she had passed when she agreed to marry him. He'd been one of the wild boys in high school with a taste for absurd quantities of beer and weed. *I can't raise kids in a house with alcohol or drugs,* she'd told Bob on that day, and to her surprise and delight, he'd agreed. If they were out at a restaurant, he could have his beer, but not at home. Home was the safe zone, and after the childhood she'd experienced, she needed that as much as her kids did.

"Lily, come on!" she yelled because she heard the squeal of the bus brakes two stops away. Lily exited the house with the air of someone who had already been there and done that. She was a second grader now, not a puny kindergartener like Joy and Jeremy. And with Ethan on the middle school bus, she was the big kid. When she reached the street she stepped right in front of them so she'd be first in line.

"No way!" Joy snapped and dragged her out of the way by her new sweater.

Lily's face went red with rage. "Why are you first?" she taunted, "because you're *the baby?*"

Joy let go of Jeremy only long enough to give her sister a sharp shove backward. A moment later they were attached at the hip again and standing first in line as the bus turned the corner onto their road. "Not so rough, Joy," Mary sighed and was given an angelic smile in return.

Joy was a complex kid. The most challenging part of her personality was her keen intelligence. Although Ethan and Lily were bright, intelligence wasn't the mark of their personalities. Ethan was shy, but made friends in spite of it because he was quick to smile. Lily gathered friends like minnows in a net. And they were both easily contented; Ethan could spend an entire day taking apart a clock and putting it back together, and Lily was the picture of happiness whenever she was surrounded by people, which was pretty much all the time.

But Joy was different. She brooded over little things that would not affect other people. Sometimes after a movie Mary would find her crying in her bed over how unfairly one of the characters was treated. All of Mary's arguments that there was no reason to feel sadness for an imaginary character would become powerless when Joy responded with astounding comments such as *but there are people in the world like that, aren't there?* and *mothers really do die sometimes, don't they?*

She had a habit of dragging home injured animals where she'd feed them with a medicine dropper before they invariably died. Bob buried every one of them in their own shoe box in the back yard. But most of Joy's empathy was focused on Jeremy. She was his guardian, his protector and oftentimes his voice...even after it became clear that he could talk.

A few weeks prior, Bob had taken the kids to see the movie *E.T.* And when Eliot had stumbled upon the extraterrestrial, Jeremy had leaned forward to make eye contact with Joy. "No," she'd stated confidently.

Bob, wedged between them, was watching the interaction. "'No' what?" he asked.

"No, that can't happen," Joy whispered. Her dad's weathered face wore a puzzled expression. She exhaled an exasperated sigh. "Jeremy asked if an alien could be in our backyard."

"No, he didn't," her father replied.

"Yes, he did," she argued and Jeremy nodded his head in agreement.

"I didn't hear him say anything," Bob said.

"Well, I did," Joy concluded. That was the moment her father understood that not only did the children communicate wordlessly, but they didn't even realize they were doing it.

Mary waved to the kids who were watching her through the bus window. She saw Jeremy's little hand wave and the excitement in his eyes, and it made her turn her own eyes back to Belinda who was watching from her cottage as the bus pulled away. She wrapped her cardigan snugly around her waist as she walked toward her. She'd made countless efforts to communicate with Jeremy's mother and she prayed every night that she would find help for her alcoholism, but so far to no avail.

"Good morning," she offered. She didn't open the gate to walk inside the yard. There was a distance between the two women that was well served by the fence.

"Mornin'," Belinda replied sluggishly and downed the orange juice.

Now that she was standing closer, Mary could see that her lower lip was swollen and split like someone had hit her. Out of politeness, she shifted her eyes to the front yard. Two trash barrels, a tire, and overgrown tiger lilies. No toys. "Big day, huh?" she threw out.

Belinda shrugged her bird-like shoulders. Her bones were visible through her t-shirt.

"Jeremy looked adorable in his new school clothes."

"He ought to. Spent my last dime on 'em," Belinda remarked. She drew a cigarette from a blue and white Parliament pack and winced as it touched her split lip. "Hope he can keep up."

"I'm sure he will," Mary offered. "He's a smart kid."

Belinda made a scoffing sound and Mary felt like a mama cat with the fur bristled. Admittedly, when she taught Jeremy colors and numbers she'd noticed his struggle with retaining information, but he was insightful in other ways. Once Joy had made a comment about him that Mary thought was apt: *Most of the kids think he's stupid, but he's not. He's a different kind of smart that they don't understand.*

"Want coffee?" Belinda offered.

"Sure," Mary agreed.

She was still stinging from the remark, but she didn't want to miss an opportunity to talk to Jeremy's mother and she'd never been inside his home. Did he have stuffed animals on his bed and art work on his walls like her children did? She opened the gate and followed Belinda inside. It was the same house as hers, built by the same contractor, but Mary had painted the interior in vibrant hues: yellows, reds and iris blues. Belinda's walls were the off-white they had originally been painted, which with time and smoke had turned a jaundiced yellow, and the fireplace in the living room was covered with plastic. At the Sanders' house a fire was almost always burning in the fireplace, and when Jeremy was visiting he was usually sitting right in front of it. *Fire is a sacred thing* he'd said once. When Bob pressed him for an explanation, Jeremy had only muttered, *I don't know why. I just know it is.*

Belinda's entire house could be viewed from the front door. Mary could see her unmade bed and piles of clothes on the floor, but the door to the second bedroom was closed. Strangely, a twin-sized bed was tucked into a corner of the living room. While Belinda mixed hot water with Nescafe, Mary lingered at the mantel where half a dozen framed pictures had been placed.

"Is this Jeremy?" she asked. She was holding a photograph of the tiniest newborn she'd ever seen. It was in somebody's hands and looked to be about the same size as a squirrel.

"He was a premie," Belinda exhaled with the smoke from her cigarette. "Wouldn't know it though, would ya? Except that he still can't see so good. Somethin's wrong with his heart too."

Mary gasped. "He runs all the time with Joy. I—I didn't know."

Belinda waved her hand as if the concern was nothing more than the smoke from her cigarette. "He can do normal kid stuff. It's just—something from being born too soon."

Mary sat at the kitchen table and washed the lump in her throat down with the Nescafe while her eyes absorbed the room: the trash bag overflowing with beer cans and the cheap vodka on the counter next to a carton of orange juice. In a flash of intuition she understood the glass in Belinda's hand while waiting for the bus.

"You got two kids, right?" Belinda asked.

"No, three. Ethan's probably the one you haven't met. He's ten. But I bet you've met Lily."

"She looks a lot like the other one, right, Jeremy's friend?"

"Joy."

"They look like you, same eyes."

Mary agreed. Both Lily and Joy were very close matches to her childhood pictures, back when she used to be a towhead. And Ethan looked exactly like his father.

"Jeremy looks just like his old man," Belinda huffed. "I don't know if that's a good thing."

Jeremy never mentioned his father, except for once when he'd told Mary he'd promised in a letter to buy him some doves. On the landing in the back of the Sanders' home, Joy and Jeremy often sat watching the various birds that gathered in the backyard. While washing dishes, Mary could hear Jeremy's voice identify them: *chickadee, blue jay, mourning dove*. Once, Mary had heard him say that when he was old enough he would fly away like the birds, and her hand had frozen on the silverware. *I don't want you to fly away*, Joy had argued. *Come with me*, he'd replied. Joy's voice had been thick with tears when she'd said, *I can't leave my mom!* Mary had stolen a glance; they'd been holding hands. *I won't go either then*, he'd concluded.

"J's good lookin', but he's not a big worker," Belinda said, breaking through her thoughts.

"Jay is the name of Jeremy's father?" Mary asked.

"The letter J—short for Jeremy," Belinda said as she sucked intently on her cigarette. "He saw him when he was born, but he's been in California since 'cause he can ride year around. Guess he loved his Harley more than me." She cackled and choked on the mucous it called up.

And Jeremy. "I should go," Mary announced. As if on cue, the door to the second bedroom opened revealing a man in ratty sweatpants, his shirtless belly sagging over the waistband. Stubble littered his bloated face and his fingers were tugging at his greasy hair. His energy had a darkness that made Mary think not *evil*...but *sick*.

"My brother, Tommy," Belinda offered casually.

27

It was then that it dawned on Mary; the bed in the living room was Jeremy's. He didn't have a bedroom or toys or anything to suggest that it was his home. The lump in her throat was growing again, and this time she was sure no amount of coffee could wash it down.

"Can I take Jeremy today when he gets off the bus?" she asked, her brain in overdrive trying to concoct a reason. But she needn't have worried. Belinda wasn't looking for one.

"Knock yourself out," she said.

Mary arrived back home with the images of Jeremy's home life haunting her. When Bob called from a pay phone to see how the morning had gone, she could hear him exhaling smoke as he listened to her story. "We could call a lawyer," he suggested. "Or just spend as much time with him as we can. He knows we love him. That's what matters."

Bob, with his simple wisdom, filled Mary with hope. She hung up the phone and readied a picnic for the kids to share in their favorite place, under the weeping willow tree in the back yard. She made peanut butter and jelly sandwiches (they were still Jeremy's favorite), brownies and lemonade.

Preparing the food reminded her of when she was nineteen and first married to Bob. They'd found the picnic basket at a local flea market together with a metal fold-up bench that served as their kitchen table. Every night before Bob returned home, worn and dusty from building the extravagant houses on the waterfront, Mary adorned it with a table cloth and flowers from the garden. Over Spaghettios or Kraft macaroni and cheese, they'd laugh about the outlandish demands of the rich people who would be living in the homes Bob was building.

The ability to cook came with time, like everything else. Ethan was their first miracle. Mary hadn't realized until he was born how completely she could trust Bob, but she'd known it ever since. When she became pregnant again, she suggested Bob choose a name. Mary had named Ethan, after her father. Bob surprised her and chose *Tiger Lily* after the Indian princess in *Peter Pan*, his favorite childhood story. She finally convinced him that Lily was enough. And Joy was Joy from the start because she seemed so happy to have been born.

When the picnic basket was packed, she carried it onto the front steps along with a library book, *The Water is Wide* by Pat Conroy, to wait for the bus, determined to be for Jeremy everything that his mother was not.

They pulled all the money out of their Christmas savings account to pay for the lawyer, F. Samuelson Wright, whom Mary chose from the yellow pages because his name sounded lawyerly. It turned out his name was Frank. He made Bob and Mary wait in his lobby for half an hour with no explanation or apology before he called them into his office and informed them that they had no right to be seeking custody of Jeremy, regardless of his living situation, because they were not relatives.

"I would suggest you call the Department of Social Services," he advised.

Mary and Bob had talked about this possibility. If they called D.S.S., Jeremy might be placed in a foster home, but how could they be sure they'd be chosen as his foster parents? What if their phone call became the reason for the separation?

"We're not doing that," Bob stated calmly and took Mary's hand in his. "If we call D.S.S. they'll take him away. We're the only family he's got."

Frank shrugged his shoulders that were squeezed inside a shirt two sizes too small, which Mary thought might explain his odd pattern of breathing that bore a remarkable resemblance to that of Henri the French bulldog. "We can't all change the world," he said.

"Maybe not all of us," Bob replied.

Life went on as always, except that Jeremy was more tightly woven into the fabric of it. Mary asked Belinda if she could get him off the bus every day after school so that he and Joy could work on their letters together. Belinda agreed, but only after she made Mary promise she wouldn't back out of the agreement because she was planning to get a part time job. On her way home from the hair salon where she'd secured work as a receptionist, Belinda often stopped at the corner bar (Bob would see her car on his way home) and call to say that she had to work late. Could Jeremy stay longer? *Of course*, Mary always said and breathed a sigh of relief. Usually, by the time Belinda arrived home, Jeremy would be dressed in pajamas that Ethan had outgrown. Every night Bob would walk him home or carry him if he was asleep.

Almost three years went by in that fashion, with Jeremy as much a part of the Sanders family as the rest of them. He participated in every birthday and every other family celebration. When Ethan was accepted to the vocational program at the high school and Bob brought home pizza to celebrate, Jeremy was there. When Bob scored a big construction job and Mary prepared a feast, Jeremy was there. And when Mary had the privilege of babysitting Henri because his owner was on vacation, Jeremy was there (and was the one the little dog followed for the entire weekend).

Then, when they least expected it, the dynamic changed. Belinda got fired from her job which triggered a downward spiral in her life. With time on her hands, she started drinking more, and with her deterioration there was a visible change in Jeremy. At times he was so withdrawn that he barely spoke. Joy reverted to treating him as she had when they were much younger. Every day she'd brush the tangles out of his hair, wash his face and behind his ears, and afterward kiss his cheeks. On days that he was particularly distant, she'd tuck him in her bed and read him a book. She used her natural affinity for drawing to coax him into conversation. *What should I draw?* she'd ask and wouldn't start until he'd mutter *bunny, cocker spaniel, tulip* or whatever else flashed through his mind. Sometimes she'd make him a cartoon flip book to carry home with him so he could watch the rabbit or the squirrel hop, run or gather nuts.

There was nothing Jeremy loved more than being doted on by Joy. If he joined the Sanders family for a movie, he'd always share a chair with her and eat popcorn out of the same bowl. Mary noticed that they still communicated silently as often as they did with words. Jeremy occasionally did the same with Bob, but to a lesser degree. Every weekend night that he'd visit their house his mother would issue an order of what time he was to return home. And when that time would draw near, he'd turn his eyes to Bob to indicate it was time to walk him home. But once he was inside with the front door closed, it was anyone's guess what was going on behind it.

One Saturday evening in the spring, his mother told him he could stay until 7:30. At 7:25 when Bob and Joy walked Jeremy home they arrived to find a party going on at the house.

"How'd you like to sleep at our house tonight?" Bob asked casually.

"Can he, Daddy?" Joy exclaimed and clapped her hands together excitedly.

"No," Jeremy quickly interjected. "She'll be mad if I ask."

"Okay, then I'll ask," Bob said. "Walk home with Joy and wait for me in our yard."

Jeremy hesitated, but didn't object. Bob watched as Joy took his hand and led him home before he made his way past the crowd on the front lawn. The smell of weed clung to the cool night air and to the grass beneath his feet. Through the open front door, Bob caught a glimpse of three women huddled at the kitchen table—one with an exposed swastika tattooed on her breast—snorting lines of white powder. Belinda wasn't one of them. Regardless, Bob decided to call the police if she insisted he leave Jeremy there. He could not with good conscience leave him in that house.

The guy who stepped in between Bob and the open door looked like a sausage, squeezed into a black t-shirt and leather biker vest. "What do you want?" he demanded.

"Belinda around?" Bob asked.

The bathroom door opened and he had his answer. Belinda stumbled out of it with a beer in her hand, her eyes already on him. It seemed to take her a minute to figure out who he was, though.

"Ohhhh," she finally said. "Bob. It's Bob, right?"

For everything that he had been to her son, still Belinda could only barely remember his name. "I got your kid, remember?" he said roughly. "Jeremy."

"So, where is he?" Belinda slurred.

"He's spending the night at our house."

"Is that right?" With her tight skirt sliding up her ass and heels so high she could barely walk, Belinda closer resembled a prostitute than the mother of an eight-year-old boy.

"Just thought I'd let you know," Bob grumbled, "In case you were wondering where he was."

"Who said?" she snarled. "Who said you could keep him?"

He was walking away when Belinda grabbed his shoulder. Bob pushed her hand off. "You ever heard of the Department of Social Services?" he asked. Her mouth snapped shut.

With that he walked away, fuming but coaching himself not to reveal that to the kids. Joy and Jeremy were sitting on the fence in front of the house as he approached. The sky was darkening so he could only see their silhouettes at first, and he was wondering if they'd heard the argument.

"What happened?" Joy shouted and jumped off the fence.

A nervous laugh escaped him. It served his purpose. "We're having a sleepover," he said.

Jeremy's eyebrows shot up. "Really?" he spewed.

"Really," Bob assured him. The kids shrieked with delight and ran toward the house. "Hold up, Jeremy," he added as an afterthought, and both kids turned back. "Go on inside," he said to Joy.

Jeremy sat on the front steps. "You're mad," he said softly when Bob sat beside him.

"No. Well, not at you. But I need you to do something for me." The boy met his eyes. "From here on out, if something's wrong at home you need to tell me so I can fix it." Jeremy nodded and stood up. "One more thing—don't think for a second that I see you different than Ethan and the girls."

"I know," he said.

"Okay, good. Go find Joy then," Bob concluded and tousled the boy's hair before he scampered off.

After the screen door shut, Bob waited for Mary to show up. He knew it would take all of ten seconds for her to figure out that something had gone awry.

She stepped out the front door to find her husband with his forehead resting on the heel of his hand. Mary lifted his face and kissed him. "Tell me about it tomorrow," she suggested. "Tonight I want to enjoy it."

Her comment instantly lightened the mood. Bob followed her inside where Ethan was watching television in the living room. Lily and Joy were building Jeremy a "nest" out of blankets on their bedroom floor.

"He can't sleep with the girls," he stated when he saw them.

"They're only eight," Mary countered.

"Sweetheart," Bob started then lowered his voice so the kids couldn't hear. "I'm not worried about it, but if D.S.S gets involved, it could hurt us."

Mary strode assertively into the room. "Jeremy can sleep with Ethan tonight," she announced. "Why don't you build a nest on his floor?"

Joy was about to put up a fight, but decided against it. "His floor's bigger, anyway," she noted. There was only a single bed in Ethan's room, whereas the girls shared a queen-sized mattress. The kids moved the blankets into Ethan's room and later, after watching *Charlie and the Chocolate Factory*, the girls tucked Jeremy into the nest and Joy gave him her favorite teddy bear.

Ethan was almost fourteen, and although other kids his age might have objected to sharing a bedroom with an eight-year-old, he didn't mind. He liked Jeremy. Besides, he was used to close quarters. The five of them had been sharing eight hundred feet of living space for his entire life. What was one more? He wasn't even that surprised when he woke up the next morning and discovered Joy curled up asleep in the nest of blankets with Jeremy. He stepped over them en route to the kitchen, where he mentioned it casually while he poured a glass of orange juice. Mary's head snapped toward Bob who was reading the newspaper in his favorite arm chair.

33

"They're only eight, remember?" he remarked.

But curiosity had them. They tiptoed to Ethan's room and peeked in. The kids were holding onto to each other like two little monkeys, their foreheads pressed together and the tips of their noses touching. Mary took Bob's arm and pulled him away so she could share her thoughts without waking them.

"When you were in middle school, did your class make those pictures out of ink…?"she asked.

"By folding the paper in half, you mean?"

Mary nodded. "You'd make whatever design you wanted on one half of the paper then fold it and smudge the ink so there would be two?"

A small laugh escaped Bob. "I know where you're going with this. The two sides would look like one big picture, but it was really a mirror image."

"Right," Mary agreed. "That's what Joy and Jeremy look like to me, the way they're holding on to each other. They're almost identical."

Bob thought about it for a moment. "Like a butterfly," he suggested.

"What do you mean?" his wife asked.

"Two wings on the same butterfly."

CHAPTER FOUR

Eagle Feathers

Jeremy was already looking out the window—at two small finches that were eating seeds off the ground—when the motorcycle pulled up. The man was wearing leather chaps even though it was August, and a helmet with the letter "J" on it, which was how Jeremy identified him as his father. He'd never seen him before.

He took a step backward and tripped on a pair of high-heeled shoes his mother had left there when she arrived home at 2:00 a.m. and fell onto his rear end. Curling his legs beneath him he sat cross-legged on the floor with his head in his hands and began to rock. What could his father want? Lately his mother had been absent more often and he'd been left to fend for himself. He didn't mind, though. It was better than when she was home and behaving unpredictably. But maybe his father had come to take him away.

The motorcycle engine was loud enough to wake the dead, and it did. Belinda staggered out of the bedroom. Jeremy heard the sound of a man's voice behind her. "What are you stupid?" his mom yelled and pushed the half-naked guy out the back door a split second before J walked in the front one.

Jeremy didn't look up when he heard the sound of boot heels on the scratched wooden floor. He didn't even steal a glimpse when his father came within a couple feet of him and stooped down, his breath deep and raspy near his ear like a beast in a nightmare. He recognized the energy as discontented and angry—was he mad at *him*? He was failing English and Math. Maybe his mom ratted him out and now he was *gonna get it* like she always threatened. Instinct told him to hide, so he drew his legs under his chin and wrapped his arms around them, like a turtle withdrawing into its shell.

"What're you doin' here?" Belinda asked as she tied the belt on her bathrobe. The sound of his mother's voice was foreign to Jeremy. Never before had he heard that kind of fear in it.

"What's wrong with him?" J asked and squeezed a finger under the dirty red bandana on his head to scratch an itch. His hair was long and brown, like Jeremy's, but starting to gray. Although he was ten or twenty pounds overweight, he had a strong body with sculpted biceps that showed through his t-shirt. And his face, covered with whiskers, was still a handsome one with good features, especially the eyes that, like Jeremy's, were astoundingly blue.

"Nuthin'," Belinda responded. "You scared him."

"Looks more like I scared you," he scoffed.

Belinda filled the teapot with water and turned on the burner. J placed a hand on Jeremy's back and Jeremy stopped breathing. He was trying to picture himself somewhere else: at the ocean, sitting next to Joy with his feet in the water. He could get there for a quick flash, but then the weight of the unfamiliar hand and the smell of tobacco and whiskey on his father's breath brought him back.

"No foolin', J, why're you here?" Belinda asked again.

J stood up...finally, and Jeremy slowly lifted his head. His father was staring at him, taking him in the way Jeremy might take in a hawk, with great awe. "It's the kid's birthday, ain't it?" he threw out and Belinda looked taken aback. She'd forgotten. Jeremy had already figured as much. Four days before, while he'd eaten his grilled cheese sandwich, his mom had talked on and on about what a great day it would be when he turned nine. They'd get up early and go out for breakfast, walk to the beach and cook out at night, and Joy could come along even though she'd never been invited before. But that was four days ago, and at nine years old Jeremy knew that the whole world could change in four days. There was no point in counting on anything.

J snorted at Belinda's reaction. "Get up, kid," he ordered. Jeremy scrambled to his feet and adjusted his glasses on his nose, then turned his vibrantly blue eyes to the same blue eyes of his father. He was still frightened, but instinct told him not to show it.

"Looks decent size," J pointed out.

"He is. He's on the chart now," said Jeremy's mother.

"What's that mean *on the chart*?"

"At the doctor's office they have a chart that shows how big your kid is next to other kids. Up 'til last visit he was too small to even be on the chart. But now they say he's almost average."

"He'll be more than that. He'll be a big man like his dad, won't you Jeremy?" Jeremy nodded solemnly. J must have liked the response because he grabbed him and gave him a fierce hug, the first one ever. Jeremy wanted to like it. He wanted to hug him back, but he couldn't. His body stayed stiff in his father's arms. "After I eat we'll head out," J said with a wink and dropped Jeremy on his feet.

"Head out where?" Belinda asked.

Jeremy watched his father saunter into the kitchen like he was *King of the Goddamn world* like his mother always said, and rifle through cabinets until he found what he was looking for.

"Make mine Irish," he said and handed Belinda a bottle of Jack Daniels.

"He's never been on a bike," she said quietly.

"Well, it's 'bout time then," he chuckled. "What? I got him a helmet."

Belinda did what she always did with J—let him run her down like he was paving a driveway. Even if the thought occurred to her, and it didn't, she never would have dared to object to her son riding on a motorcycle with someone who'd been drinking whiskey in his coffee.

"When you turn twelve, I'll get you a dirt bike," J proclaimed. Jeremy's eyes widened, not out of excitement as his father presumed, but from terror. He'd only recently let Joy's dad teach him how to ride a bicycle. "Where's Tommy?" J suddenly asked.

"He moved out three months ago," Belinda answered.

"So why's my kid crashed in the living room?"

"Tommy never came for his stuff. What am I s'posed to do, move it myself?"

"I got it," J, the *King of the Goddamn world,* said.

After breakfast he loaded Tommy's possessions into the back of Belinda's old Jeep Cherokee and then lifted Jeremy onto the back of his Harley. Belinda followed them to Tommy's new apartment and they dumped all his stuff on the front lawn before they went on their way looking for a birthday present. By the time they returned home, they had a large cage, a bag of feed (*make it last* his mother warned) and half a dozen mourning doves.

So on his ninth birthday, Jeremy got three things he never expected: a father (whom he never saw again), a bedroom, and a cage full of doves. Later, after J tore out of the driveway and his mother left on a date with the half-naked guy from the morning, he got what he did expect: homemade pizza and yellow cake with chocolate frosting at the Sanders' house. He even got a birthday song, a bird encyclopedia and a walk to the beach. It was exactly what he wanted.

From that date onward Jeremy had a place to go even when his mother wouldn't let him visit the Sanders. He'd go into the back yard to be with his mourning doves who took to him as quickly as he took to them. They'd make sweet melodic sounds with their throats whenever he stroked them. Sometimes he'd open his hands to let them fly free and he'd imagine that he was the bird, flying up and over his house and disappearing over the horizon. The birds had more in common with Jeremy than he understood. They always came back. No matter how far they flew, they always came back to him, even though they knew it would mean being caged.

He developed a ritual that he carried out before school. At 7:10 he'd choose a dove from the pen and prop it on his shoulder, then set forth on an expedition around the neighborhood—down Fairview Lane to Sea Street, across it and down one of the roads that ran perpendicular to the ocean. From there he followed the sea wall to the fourth parallel road that led back to Sea Street and Fairview Lane. Every day at 7:18, he'd stop in front of the same house, a weather-washed ranch with sea grass growing around the door and sand dunes in the front yard. With the bird perched on his shoulder like a young falconer, he'd pause and gave silent thanks for the person who had lived there until he died. It was the old man's house he somehow knew, the one who'd been burdened by his own disability but still cared enough to make Jeremy feel welcome in the strange world he'd entered.

An old man with no family of his own had been the source of badly needed encouragement. Jeremy thought of him as a grandfather, even though he'd actually spoken to him only once. For him the word "family" had a different connotation than it did for most people. It was defined by action, not blood lines. The old man was family because he was kind to him. J was his father, but Mr. Sanders was his *dad* because he was the one who watched out for him and kept him safe. Ethan and Lily were his brother and sister because they defended him against all others, even though the kids on the bus made fun of him for claiming it to be true. And Joy was so intricately entwined with him that he understood her to be something much more than any of those relationships: his soul mate, though he didn't use that term because he'd never heard it.

On stormy days when he couldn't venture outside, he'd read his bird encyclopedia. Before long he had read it so many times he'd nearly memorized it. In school he had much greater difficulty with books designed for children his age. His teachers ordered testing, which revealed that his IQ was significantly below average. This caused him to be placed in special classes, but nonetheless he often missed recess because he couldn't keep up with assignments. Conversely, Joy's standardized tests indicated she was reading at a high school level. In fourth grade they were placed in different classrooms to meet their individual needs, so the only time they could spend time together at school was during recess and lunch.

As a child Joy never believed that Jeremy was less intelligent than her, even though she helped him with his homework. There were aspects of life he understood that were unfathomable to her. For instance, he always knew when animals were scared and when they were sick; when an electrical storm was brewing, he'd tell her it was time to run home even before her mother's voice called from the front steps; and sometimes during a conversation, he'd whisper the words the other person was thinking before they were expressed. And every time he'd walk under a streetlight at night, it would blink. He'd even predicted events before they occurred. *The pretty teacher on T.V.* who was to ride the space shuttle *might not come back. Henri* (the French bull dog) *has a sickness in his stomach and won't live much longer.* And *someday you'll have a new best friend.* To the last prediction he'd added *but you'll still be mine.*

There are many words in the English language to describe a person like Jeremy: empath, intuitive, sensitive, clairvoyant, psychic. Not one of them could he have written with his own hand. If you asked, he'd say it was no magic trick at all, and that he knew things because he was good at listening. He was right in a sense. He was clairaudient—he could hear the voices of those in the Spirit World—but he didn't know that word either.

"When you're an artist, you'll need to see the person's light," he told Joy once, because he'd retained the ability to see and read auras. "If you want to paint the outside you should know what the person is like on the inside…that's what the light tells you."

"When I'm an artist, what will you be?" she asked.

"If I could pick, I'd be a doctor," he replied.

"My mom says we can be anything we want," Joy reminded him.

"My mom says being a doctor is too hard for someone like me."

Joy pondered his words. She wasn't sure, but she suspected his mother's comment was related to his difficulty reading. "Maybe you can be a veterinarian," she suggested and he nodded pensively.

Because he was separated from Joy, for the first time in his life Jeremy was more miserable in school than he was at home. And Joy had new friends, a group of three girls who were in her homeroom and played with her at recess. On the days Jeremy was allowed to go outside, she always chose him over the girls and they'd push each other on the swings or hang upside down on the monkey bars. But when he was kept inside, he knew she was playing with them and that awareness caused a new feeling to be born inside of him, a suspicion that in some shadowy, undefined way he was replaceable. At lunch the girls were always at their table, giggling about things he didn't understand. But once, when one of them—Kaitlyn—called him a "retard", Joy knocked her out of her chair right there in the cafeteria with everyone watching.

A year or two clipped by, and despite the separation at school, at home they remained inseparable. Belinda found another job answering phones, and while she was working Jeremy could do as he pleased. The kids loved to walk on the sea wall and leap off it into the soft sand. Joy always took off down the beach and yelled for Jeremy to catch her. A few years prior he couldn't have, but now he was as tall as Joy and as fast as the wind. He liked to imagine that he was a Native American boy racing against horses like he'd read about in a library book. He'd quickly catch up and she'd shriek with laughter as he caught her around the waist.

Then he'd hold her down and say *do you give?* even though every time she'd shake her head stubbornly and refuse to say it. Afterward they'd sit on the shore line and hold hands while the waves washed over their bare feet. In the kitchen of the Sanders' house, lined up with the rest of the family portraits Joy had drawn, there was a pencil sketch of Jeremy smiling serenely at the water's edge. If he could've frozen time into one moment, that's the one he would have chosen. It would have been the moment Joy would have

41

chosen, as well. Whenever she held his sandy hands in hers, she felt safe and happy. It was a moment she would call on for the rest of her life whenever she needed to feel like Jeremy was by her side and holding her hand even when he no longer was.

There was no reason to think that a day would come when Jeremy would not be in her life, but it was heading their way, building like a thunderstorm when it rolls over an open plain. Although they lived on the same street in the very same kind of house, their realities could not have been more different. Jeremy's home life was rapidly deteriorating. Belinda had lost control, and she was hurting Jeremy in ways that until recently not even Joy had suspected.

Before she witnessed the abuse with her own eyes, she'd twice noticed bruises on Jeremy that he'd admitted his mother caused. Both times he made her link pinkies and swear she wouldn't tell anyone. The first discovery was a large bruise on his belly that was already turning yellow when she saw it— Belinda had kicked him in a drunken fit. The second one was smaller, on his back, but it was as purple as a ripe plum. She'd discovered both injuries when he'd taken his shirt off at the beach, so Joy was sure there had been others. On cold days she'd wonder what might be hidden underneath his clothes.

"You can't say it to anyone," he'd remind her. "They'll take me away if they find out."

"Who will?" Joy always asked, and Jeremy would say that he didn't know who, he just knew that someone would come because his mother and even Uncle Tom had told him so. The thought was more menacing than anything Joy could have conjured with her vivid imagination. Still, it was difficult to believe that Jeremy could be taken away from her family; in her mind he was a part of it, a puzzle piece as necessary to the whole as Ethan, Lily and herself.

"Let's not talk about it," he'd suggest and they'd go back to whatever they were playing.

On that day—the day that changed everything—it was September and school had already started. They were eleven now and Joy was in the sixth grade, but Jeremy had been kept back and was repeating fifth grade. Finally the blackberries in the woods behind his house were ripe and they were on the path, pushing branches out of their way en route to claiming them.

"What're we gonna put 'em in?" Jeremy tossed out. "We forgot cups."

Joy stopped and Jeremy walked smack into her. She fell forward and scratched her leg on a wild rose bush that was spilling its branches onto the path. It wasn't the first time she'd been clawed by it. The lovely pink blossoms always made her forget there were thorns on the stems.

He sat beside her on the path. "Your knee all right?" he asked and placed his palm on the scratch, something he always did when she was hurt.

Joy's white teeth stood out as much as her long sun-bleached hair against her tanned skin as her lips curled into a grin. "I know what to put 'em in," she said instead of answering him. Jeremy didn't object when she snatched the Red Sox cap from his head, the one that Bob had given him for his birthday, but he was hoping he'd get it back. "I've got another idea!" she suddenly threw out. "We can be blood brothers! Use a thorn from the wild roses to poke your finger."

"How come?" Jeremy asked with his eyebrows tugged tightly together.

"So we can be like a brother and sister."

"Aren't we already?"

"Well, this way my blood would be in your veins and yours would be in mine."

"Okay," he agreed, "but I know something better."

"You're just scared to poke yourself," Joy accused.

"Not if you do it. But when we get to my house I'll show you the other thing."

Joy wasn't scared to poke him with a thorn. But she *was* scared to go inside his house, where the evil Belinda lived. Jeremy offered her his hand and closed his eyes. Joy stabbed his thumb with a thorn. His bright blue eyes

43

shot open and stared at the red liquid bubbling up like water from a spring. When his eyes met hers he smiled so big that it made her want to kiss him, so she did, quickly on his lips. He laid his thumb against her knee and rubbed it gently to mingle their blood, then kissed her back, longer and deeper than she had kissed him. She felt his warm breath in her mouth and it made the heat rise in her neck and her cheeks.

"Let's go," he said and stood up. But she was still looking at him and thinking about what they had done, mixed their blood together and kissed the way she'd seen her dad kiss her mom. Jeremy reached for her hand because she was trailing behind. Thousands of times she had held his hand, so why did it feel different this time? It made her tummy flip.

"Whatsa matter?" he asked more than once as they filled his baseball hat with the berries and ate some straight off the bushes. "Nothing," she answered because she didn't know.

By the time they got back to his house their mouths and hands were stained magenta from the blackberry juice. Jeremy stopped at the bird cage and dropped in a handful of berries before they entered the house, then held his index finger to his lips as they crept past Belinda's bedroom and into his. Once Joy was seated on his bed he broke out the bird encyclopedia.

"See here? Eagles have twin feathers. They need them to be the same so they can fly straight," Jeremy explained. "The boy Indian keeps one feather and the girl Indian keeps the other one. Listen to what it says." He slid his glasses on before he read out loud. *"Offering one of the twin feathers is like saying I cannot fly without you. As long as you keep this feather, wherever I am, I'll be with you. Even if my body is far away, my spirit will be near.* See, it's like blood brothers, only better."

"Let me see that," Joy ordered. What did it mean, *I can't fly without you?* It only took her clever mind seconds to determine that the reference to "flying" was a metaphor. The book was talking about two people's inability to live fully without each other. The words made her think about the kiss again and the funny feeling in her stomach. "It says the feathers make them inseparable."

Jeremy asked, "What's that mean?"

"They can't be separated, no matter what. But we don't have any eagle feathers."

"I got lots of doves," he replied, "I bet they have twin feathers, too."

He led her back outside where he spent several minutes looking through the wire walls of the cage, trying to find a bird with two matching feathers. The night before Joy had dreamed about the doves. She'd been crying because they were flying into the night and she knew they weren't coming back.

"Why don't you use two birds?" she suggested. "Take one feather from each."

He gave her an incredulous look. "The book said the same bird. They have to be twins."

The book had also said *eagle* feathers, not *dove* feathers, Joy thought but she didn't voice it. She didn't want to say something to make him not want to do it. Or what if he decided to give the feather to Amanda instead of her? She was one of Joy's friends who was usually mean to Jeremy, but she was pretty and once Joy had arrived at the playground and found her pushing him on the swing.

"Just do it," she snapped and he gently prodded a feather from the dove.

"Take it easy," he whispered and kissed the bird's head. "One more and I'll let you go free." He plucked one and then kept his promise. He opened his hands and the bird flew from them over the roof and out of sight. "If we were Indians, we'd wear them in our hair," he said, more to himself than to Joy. Then he muttered a word, the same word he'd said to her other times when they'd played Indians. She didn't know how to spell it, but it sounded like *Segonaway*. He'd told her once that it was her Indian name and that he knew it because he dreamed of her that way sometimes.

With blackberry stains on his little boy mouth, Jeremy held both feathers over his head ritualistically, as if he were a shaman. "So we can be…what's the word?"

"Inseparable," Joy offered.

"Inseparable," he repeated and smiled big, like he did before when she kissed him, but this time she didn't. She was waiting for him to do it. Instead he handed her one of the feathers. Had she known it would be her last childhood day spent with him, she would have kissed him—a thousand times—but she didn't know. She thought it was a day just like every other day.

"Come on, we need to find a safe place to keep 'em," he advised.

Against Joy's better judgment she followed him back into the house. He headed straight for the kitchen trash can and retrieved an empty carton of Belinda's Parliament cigarettes. "This'll do," he remarked and brushed coffee grounds off of it. Then he swathed Joy's feather in paper towels like a newborn in a blanket before placing it in the carton. Just then a loud noise came from Belinda's bedroom. Jeremy jumped and sputtered, "You have to go now!"

"Why're you making noise so early in the morning?" Belinda bellowed.

"It's not that early, Ma."

It was the wrong thing to say. Belinda pushed the bedroom door open with a crash and stormed toward them. *A troll*, Joy thought. *She's just like the troll in the Billy Goats Gruff story. Don't wake it up or it will attack you.* Her heart was pounding but seemingly in the wrong place—her throat instead of her chest.

"What do *you* want?" Belinda demanded of her, but she was struck dumb.

"She doesn't want anything," Jeremy replied and stepped in between Joy and his mother.

Belinda's bloodshot eyes fell on the Parliament carton in his hand. "What's that you've got—my cigarettes? That's what you brats are doin' out here, stealing my cigarettes?"

46

"No, Ma. We weren't doing that. It's empty—"

Belinda backhanded his face with a loud *smack*. The impact was so strong it knocked him off his feet and the Parliament carton out of his hand. His glasses flew off, so he didn't see it when she came after him again, this time grabbing his long hair and yanking him off the floor.

What Joy noticed before the frozen feeling in her limbs melted away was how quiet Jeremy was when he was attacked. Not a sound escaped him. Everything her parents had taught her about behaving respectfully toward adults went out of her mind when she heard the sound of Jeremy's body being thrown against the refrigerator. She pounced on Belinda's back and with all ten fingers yanked on her hair as hard as she imagined Belinda had pulled Jeremy's when she lifted him off the floor by it. When someone was fighting back, Belinda wasn't so tough after all. She melted into a pile of sobs on the floor like the wicked witch in the *Wizard of Oz*.

"I hate you!" Joy screamed at her, and kicked her hard before she backed away, hoping she had left a bruise as purple as the one on Jeremy's back. "I'm telling everyone about you," she hissed.

The sound of crying almost drowned out her threat. It took a minute to comprehend that it wasn't Belinda's sobs, but Jeremy's. Through everything she'd witnessed in his life, she had never seen him cry. It never occurred to her that her own words had provoked it.

"Don't do that," he begged. "Please don't. Take the box and go."

Joy snatched the Parliament box off the floor and walked out. Once she felt sunlight hit her face and heard the storm door slam behind her, she started to run and didn't stop until she was safe inside her own home. And she did everything that she had promised Jeremy she wouldn't do. She told her parents how his mother had been hitting him, and about the bruises. She told them how she'd seen Belinda hit him so hard that his feet came off the floor, and how she'd picked him up by his hair. And Mary and Bob did something they had promised each other they wouldn't do. They called the Department of Social Services.

CHAPTER FIVE
Throwing Rocks at the Sky

Joy wasn't there when the D.S.S workers came to remove Jeremy from his home at 7:35 on Monday—just as he was arriving home from his morning walk, but she sensed something was wrong when he wasn't waiting at the bus stop. Even when the bus finally rolled around the corner he still wasn't there. Never had he missed school without calling first to tell her.

"I'm sick!" she spurted at the bus driver when he opened the accordion-like door, and darted home. She used her key to get back in the house and ran for the bathroom. Mary had recently resumed her waitressing job, now that Joy was old enough to get herself dressed and onto the bus. When Joy reached the toilet she started retching out the cornflakes and milk she'd eaten for breakfast and couldn't seem to stop. Then the tears started, and she couldn't stop them either. "I need my, my m-mom," she said out loud though there was no one there to hear it.

Mary had been worried when she left for work and saw a strange car parked in front of Jeremy's house. Now her boss was screaming to her from the kitchen that she had a phone call from "home". She glanced at her watch—no one should have been at home. "Hello?" she breathed into the receiver.

"Ma-ma," Joy sobbed and fear rose like water over a dam in Mary's body. Joy hadn't called her *Mama* in several years. She was *Mom* now. "The bad people took him."

"What, Joy? Who are you talking about?"

"Just like he said. They came and t-took him and I can't, I can't, I can't do this."

"Do what, Joy?" Mary asked, but Joy didn't answer. She'd hung up the phone. Mary yelled to the cook that she had to leave. On second thought, she dialed Bob's work pager and hit 911, their code for emergencies, before she bolted out the door.

Mary arrived home to find Joy sitting in the middle of the living room floor rocking and humming the way she'd seen Jeremy do when he was upset, and she was clutching the cigarette carton she'd carried home with her from Jeremy's house. She didn't look up when Mary knelt beside her. "Joy," she crooned. Mary noticed the vomit in her hair and added, "Are you sick?" Her daughter only rocked harder. Then Mary noticed her jeans—she'd wet her pants.

"They t-t-took him," Joy whimpered. A hiccupped sob escaped as she lifted her face. "He said they would. He s-said it. But how can they t-t-take someone who doesn't belong to them?"

"Come here," Mary coaxed and dragged her limp body onto her lap. "Daddy's coming. We'll find out where Jeremy is."

"It's too late!" Joy cried. "He's gone…because…because I told."

"No, Joy. You did the right thing. You protected him so no one could hurt him."

"He's hurt now!" Joy screamed and pushed her mother's arms off. Mary started to follow her into her bedroom, but right then saw Bob's truck pull into the driveway.

"What happened?" he asked as he burst into the house.

"I don't know. I think it was the D.S.S. workers that came for Jeremy."

"They took him?" he shouted. "What the fuck is wrong with those people?"

"Bob!" Mary scolded and pointed to Joy's bedroom.

"She knows?" He exhaled loudly. "Now what?"

"First you need to see Joy. There's something…wrong…."

"What do you mean 'wrong'?" He took long strides toward her room.

"Wait," Mary pleaded, but it was too late to warn him. His eyes were on his little girl whose pants were soaked with urine and she was humming as she caressed her face with a feather. Bob made eye contact with his wife and threw his arms out—*what the hell?*

"First this," she directed. "Then we call D.S.S."

50

When they entered the bedroom Joy was swaddling the feather. Mary found clean clothes in the closet and approached her with them, but Joy didn't acknowledge her intention. She was preoccupied with folding the paper towel like she was making origami art.

"Let's unsnap your jeans, Joy," Mary suggested, "so we can put clean ones on." Joy still didn't acknowledge her so Mary lifted her under her armpits to put her feet on the floor. Mary and Bob exchanged a glance. This wasn't the same kid who had insisted on privacy the night before when she changed into her pajamas. Mary was sliding the clean sweatpants over her feet when Joy began to mutter.

"I can't, I can't without him, I can't, M-Mama…"

Bob took a deep breath before he asked gently, "Can't what, Joy?" It was taking everything he had in him to keep himself from crying like a baby.

"Fly," she replied and stared at him, her big blue eyes spilling tears.

"Okay, listen," Bob said and held her tiny waist with his strong, callused hands. "You've got to be strong right now. I'll call and find out where Jeremy is. We'll do everything we can."

But it wasn't about strength and it wasn't about phone calls. Joy knew that the separation could not be fixed. Her *soul* knew it. "No, Daddy," she cried. "He's far away. I can feel it."

Once they had tucked her into bed they found out that she was right. Bob made the call to Judy McGuire, the D.S.S worker he'd called the day before, the woman who'd promised nothing would be done without notifying him first. Bob had made it clear that they wanted Jeremy to live with them if he was taken from his mother. "We love this kid like our own," he'd told her.

"Mr. Sanders," Judy breathed with a little too much compassion, "I was just about to call you."

"Were you now?" Bob snapped. "Yesterday you said you'd call *before* he was removed!"

"I know. I'm sorry—"

"We trusted you, and now my kid's having some kind of breakdown because you didn't bother to pick up the God damned phone."

"Mr. Sanders, please, if you'd just listen—his mother has a criminal record. Two D.U.I. convictions in the past three years and one possession charge that's still pending."

"Possession," Bob repeated. "What's that mean?"

"She was arrested for possession of narcotics in her home. Somehow the fact that she had a child living with her slipped under the radar."

Bob snorted. *Fucking Belinda.* Three times she'd been arrested and while she'd been getting finger-printed, Jeremy had been alone in that house and he'd never once mentioned it. "Where is he?"

The social worker noticeably hesitated. "He's on his way to western Massachusetts, close to the Vermont border. He'll be staying with an aunt."

"Who the hell is she, Belinda's sister?" erupted out of Bob.

"She's the father's sister. We talked to him. That's where he wanted Jeremy to go."

"Well, who'd know better than the father who abandoned him?" Bob said caustically.

"It's only temporary—she doesn't want to keep him. His father's signing away his rights, too."

Pressure was building behind Bob's eyes. It took a moment to realize that it was emotion, seeking release. *How could anyone not want Jeremy?* "I want him," he said. He swallowed hard to choke back tears. "So what did Jeremy say about all this?"

"He hasn't said anything," the social worker replied. "Not a word. Even children with abusive parents sometimes shut down when they're separated from them."

"It's because you took him away from Joy. Let her talk to him. He won't talk to anyone else."

"That would be inappropriate," Judy quietly stated.

"Inappropriate?!" he shouted.

Mary jumped to her feet and hand motioned him to calm down.

It distracted Bob enough to allow Judy to jump in. "I'll give you one piece of advice, Mr. Sanders," she spoke so loudly into the phone that Mary could hear her. "If you have any intention of seeking foster care of this child, get a grip on your temper or it *will not happen*."

Bob bit his bottom lip so hard it bled. God fucking damn it, how was he supposed to stay calm when someone had ripped out his little girl's heart? He couldn't, but he could fake it. "I'm telling you right now we want Jeremy," he said with as much calmness as he could muster.

"There's paperwork—"

"I'm on my way." He hung up and noticed Joy watching from her bedroom doorway.

"He needs to be near the ocean," she said softly. "Is he near the ocean, Daddy?"

Bob felt so bad about the truth that he considered lying. But that would only make things worse. "No, Joy, he's not. He's staying with his aunt on the other side of the state. I'm going to change this—if there's any way I can— I'm going to change this."

But he couldn't, at least not right away. He learned at the D.S.S. office that there were plenty of hoops left to jump through before they even stood a chance of becoming Jeremy's foster parents. The rest of the day was spent gathering required documents and trying to get Joy grounded. That night when they tucked her into bed she insisted on sleeping with the Parliament carton, and when they finally walked away, she was caressing her face with the feather.

"It's been the longest day of my life," Bob grumbled as he tugged his t-shirt over his head. He couldn't stop thinking about the time Jeremy had shown up at the house with a split lip. He was only seven or eight years old and said he'd fallen from a tree. *What tree?* Joy had asked, and narrowed her eyes when he'd only shrugged his little shoulders. Was it happening even then?

"Like being in labor," Mary noted. It was 11:10 p.m. and finally all the kids were sleeping. It had taken them two hours of storytelling and lullaby singing just to get Joy to close her eyes. Ethan and Lily had taken turns with the stories, too. Lily was in eighth grade and had recently been chosen as a cheerleader, so all her stories revolved around the other cheerleaders and the cute football players they got to ride with on the bus to games. Ethan knew better than to talk to Joy about cars, his biggest interest. Instead he made up silly stories about Henri the French bulldog who he had *swear to God* seen shopping at the grocery store or taking a walk on the beach with a Siamese cat. He even dragged his sleeping bag into the girls' room and camped out on the floor in case Joy woke up and needed someone.

They were nearly asleep when they heard Joy's voice from the bedroom doorway. "Daddy?"

"What's the matter, Joy?" her mother asked.

"I'm worried about Jeremy's birds."

Bob let out a sigh and rubbed his face with his hands before he turned the switch on the table lamp. It had just occurred to him that she'd spoken in a complete sentence without stuttering for the first time that day. "Why are you worried about the birds?" he asked.

"They don't have food. Jeremy sets them free at night so they can find some."

"He sets them free and they come back?"

"Because it's where they belong. He says they're like people; they go where they're loved."

"Joy," Mary said softly, "we'll talk about it in the morning. Right now you need to sleep."

"But what if they die?" Joy cried. "What, what, what if..." She took a breath. "What if Jeremy comes home and they're d-d-dead?"

The threat of that happening was more than Bob could risk. He'd already been second-guessing every move he'd made to protect Jeremy. "Go get your shoes," he instructed.

"What?" Mary reeled. "You're not going over there!"

"Yeah, I am," he stated as he slid his jeans back on and spotted a pair of sneakers in the closet. "If I get arrested, I get arrested."

"Oh my God, Bob, you're not thinking—"

He spun to face her. "I can't fight over this! If anything else happens to hurt that kid…"

Joy returned, wearing a jacket and boots. He perused her face. She trusted him. And he couldn't afford to break it. Some aspects of parenting baffled Bob, like discipline for bad behavior and homework guidelines, but other parts came so naturally to him that he never had to question his role. Protection, that was his specialty; his job was to protect all four of the children in his life.

He coached Joy the whole way there on being as quiet as possible and not turning the flashlight on unless it was absolutely necessary. They were on the path that led to the small stretch of woods behind Jeremy's house, the same path that led to the blackberry bushes. Joy knew it well. She'd walked it with Jeremy hundreds of times. His house looked deserted and the night was dark, so dark that Bob couldn't see his feet. "You know where they are?"

"I know where they are and I don't need a light," Joy replied and handed him the flashlight.

Bob's heart was pounding in his chest as she walked authoritatively away. His daughter was completely out of view in the backyard of a child abuser whom she herself had blown the whistle on. Fear got the best of him and he turned on the flashlight. It caught the top of Joy's head as she crept toward the cage, her yellow curls gleaming like moonlight on water. "Turn it off!" she hissed, and he did, feeling like *he* was the eleven year old and *she* was the adult.

It was more drive than lack of fear that was allowing her to put one foot in front of the other. She had to make sure Jeremy's birds were safe. It was exactly like fighting Belinda. She'd had no choice. She *had* to protect Jeremy. Her loyalty ran deeper than her fear.

There, she felt it, a wall made out of chicken wire. No sounds at all were coming from the cage. Had Jeremy freed them before he was taken away? No. Her hands found the latch and it was closed. Because Belinda had refused to spend money on the birds, Jeremy used a stick instead of a metal combination lock. Joy felt the rough bark with her fingers before she pulled it out and heard the cage door creak as it opened.

"Please don't be dead," she murmured as she cautiously slid a hand into the cage. The tips of her fingers made contact with the warm, soft body of one of the mourning doves. She stroked it gently like Jeremy had taught her and it made a sound in its throat. *I won't hurt you*, she thought. Jeremy always said that they knew what he was thinking. The dove climbed onto her hand, and she drew a breath. At least one was alive. Two more birds stepped onto her arm. She slowly removed it from the cage and inserted her other arm in its place. Within seconds, the last three birds had climbed on. When she realized all six of the birds were safe, she exhaled her breath, and a cry of relief escaped with it.

Bob heard it and turned the flashlight on. What he caught in the dim glow was a vision that would stay forever etched in his memory. His brave little girl was standing next to the cage with her head back looking up at the sky; her arms were outstretched with the birds perched upon them. He watched in awe as one by one they left her arms and took flight into the night.

While they waited for the department's decision, they stayed in touch with the social worker, Judy McGuire, who kept them abreast of Jeremy's progress—or lack thereof. On the first day he'd uttered one sentence, but it had been misinterpreted: *Call my dad, he'll come get me*. It was Bob he was crying out for, not his biological father like the social worker presumed, so it was never reported to the Sanders. After that one attempt he didn't communicate with anyone, even with hand gestures. There was talk of having him tested for autism and placed in a school for special needs. He was losing weight because he didn't eat unless he was forced to.

It seemed like months had gone by, but in reality it had only been weeks when Judy called and told Bob that a review of Jeremy's medical records led his new physician to a diagnosis of fetal alcohol syndrome. His regular pediatrician had not picked up on it because there was no record of him being seen at that office until just before kindergarten began, and by then he was talking, even to strangers. And Jeremy didn't have any of the facial features of a child with fetal alcohol syndrome, a thin upper lip or smooth skin between his mouth and nose as opposed to the groove that most people have. His face was flawless. He was a perfectly beautiful boy with injuries below his surface caused by his mother's alcoholism that were not visible to the human eye. The damage had been done, Judy said, but it did help to identify the problem so that he could be adequately assisted with schoolwork.

Joy wasn't faring much better. She had been evaluated by her pediatrician who recommended counseling. After a few days she returned to school, but isolated from her former friends, sitting by herself at recess and at lunch. Her teachers were baffled by the changes in her. Bob and Mary met with the teachers on Joy's sixth grade team and each had accounts of Joy's behavior to share with them. Prior to the change, they explained, she had been the class storyteller. The kids were focusing on writing fiction and Joy's stories were so good that she was often asked to read them out loud to the class. But now she rarely finished her assignments, and her characters were no longer strong and full of life. The stories were dark, ominous tales about witches and monsters invading people's homes and stealing the children.

No one described her as the vibrant force she used to be. Even the counselor was at a loss. Joy threw a fit every time she mentioned Jeremy's name. After four or five sessions, it was fruitless to drag her there. Like Jeremy, she was turning inward and didn't want any company on that journey.

She refused to join her family, whether they were watching a movie, throwing a football in the yard or walking to the beach, because to her it felt

57

like disloyalty. Why pretend that her family was whole when it wasn't? Sometimes she'd venture onto the back landing where she used to sit with Jeremy to watch for birds and stare at their willow tree, but she never went near it. Once, a year or so before, she'd smuggled a screwdriver from her father's toolbox in order to carve their names into the bark, but Jeremy had stopped her. *If you cut the tree, it might die* he'd stated quietly and that'd changed her mind because she couldn't bear the thought of her backyard without the tree. Now the tree was there, but Jeremy was gone.

The only time any of them heard her say his name out loud was heartbreaking. Every night before she climbed into bed, she'd kneel beside it and repeat the same prayer she'd recited since she was a toddler. *Dear God, please bless my mom, my dad, Ethan, Lily and Jeremy.* Her father had his own prayers, not spoken out loud, only thoughts of *Please God, let him be safe.* And maybe any day now, he hoped, they'd get the call that would let them know everything was going to be all right.

The call never came. It was an over-cast Tuesday afternoon in February when they received an official letter denying their claim for foster care of Jeremy Blake. According to the letter, they had been seriously considered, but ruled out because of their geographical proximity to Jeremy's mother. A separate letter from Judy McGuire was attached, asking them to refrain from contacting Jeremy as it could impede his progress and result in emotional trauma. Bob read both letters out loud to his son who was the only one home at the time. Ethan wiped his tears on the sleeve of his flannel shirt as he followed his dad outside onto the front steps and stood beside him, his hands jammed into the pockets of his baggy jeans.

It was cold out—they could see their breath, and neither of them had thought to bring a coat. The world looked like they felt; the sky was gray and the ground soggy from melted snow. Bob lit a cigarette and then used it to catch both the letters on fire. As he turned the blaze methodically in his hand, together they watched the painful words turn black and disappear.

"That second letter from the social worker—it never happened. Got it?" Bob instructed because he knew it would be more than his wife could bear.

Ethan nodded solemnly and watched his father until had no choice but to drop the burning papers or be scorched. Still, it wasn't enough. Bob snatched a nearby stone off the spongy earth and hurled it upward. His old pitching arm still had its strength—their eyes lost sight of the stone as it whirled higher and higher into the grayness until finally they heard it hit the fence in someone's back yard. Bob stood there, looking helpless, until Ethan began gathering more stones into a pile.

He handed one to his dad, then threw his own with all his might, aiming at nothing but the depressing winter sky as if he were intending to break through the clouds to Heaven. He was Captain Ahab in that moment, one seemingly inconsequential human being challenging God himself, and God would take the hit, even though it wasn't his fault. Ethan was only doing what everyone else on the planet did when things went desperately wrong. He was trying to find some way to channel his anger, some person or entity to blame because his family had been hurt, his baby sister so deeply wounded that she was barely recognizable. There was no one else to scream at, no one to call out and demand they make things right.

After several throws, Ethan turned his attention to the streetlight closest to their house. The first stone skimmed across the wooden pole it was attached to. Bob grinned with one side of his mouth and took his turn. If Mary were at home, he knew, they never could have gotten away with this behavior. But it was okay, he decided. It was just a God damned light, nothing of any real value.

He could hear Ethan heaving behind him, his anger venting by way of his breath. His hands were on his knees. Bob wound up and took a shot. It was a miss, but close. It took them six or seven tries apiece before Ethan's stone slammed into the dome and countless pieces of shattered glass fell like rain from the heavens. He allowed himself a brief moment of triumph before he turned his brown eyes to those of his father.

59

"I'm sorry, Dad," he muttered and Bob embraced him right there on the front lawn. It had nothing to do with the street-light, but with what they had lost, and with what Ethan understood that loss had meant to his father. "I'll get the broom," he added when he backed away.

"I got it, Ethan," Bob reassured him and turned his attention to cleaning up the mess.

CHAPTER SIX

In a Garden White

She was walking on Fairview Lane toward Jeremy's house. The mourning doves were on the roof watching her and she smiled up at them and waved as if they were human friends. Just as she reached the front steps and lifted her hand to knock, the door opened. The man who had opened it smiled at her and crouched down so they were seeing each other eye to eye. There were feathers in his hair and she reached for them. It was someone she loved...Jeremy, but not Jeremy at all. He was a grown man with hair lighter in color than Jeremy's and he was strong—his bare arms and chest were muscular. But the eyes were similar, bright blue eyes that loved her.

She kissed his smiling lips the way she had done when they were picking blackberries and his arms encircled her, lifting her off the ground. He stepped into the house with her safe in his arms, but then it wasn't the house at all. It was a garden, a beautiful garden contained inside a circular stone wall. And all the flowers were white.

It felt like she was part of the garden, and the garden was part of her. She let herself merge with it, still aware of the strong arms holding her, and felt herself stretching her neck toward the glorious light like one of the flowers. It was feeding her, making her grow. The soft texture of the petals, the sweet aroma of the nectar and the music—yes, it was music they were making—all of it was speaking to her, and still she felt the strong arms and the neck that she clung to. It was all so very familiar. "I am Elia," the man said softly near her ear. And she woke up.

"Elia," Joy said out loud, and Mary, standing at the end of the bed, gasped. It was early morning and she'd been making breakfast before she'd heard her youngest daughter mumbling in her sleep. "What's the matter?" Joy asked when she saw her mother with her hand over her mouth.

"Oh...nothing," Mary stammered. "I heard you—did you have a bad dream?"

"No. It was a good dream," Joy yawned and sat up.

61

The words *a good dream, with white flowers* went through Mary's mind. Lily was asleep beside her, her pajama top tugged up so her belly was showing. Joy blew a raspberry on it and Lily was shoving her off as Mary left to flip the French toast before it burned.

Ethan was at the kitchen table drinking coffee and reading an Auto Week magazine. He was sixteen and in the voc-tech program at the high school. His school day started earlier than the girls'.

"Is Joy all right?" he asked his mom as she re-entered the room.

"She's fine. It was just a dream, and she's playing with Lily now," Mary reassured him and kissed the top of his head. Even though he showered frequently and thoroughly scrubbed his hands, he always had black under his fingernails and smelled like a car engine.

Ethan's serious eyes scanned his mother's face. Joy hadn't played with anyone since Jeremy's departure. He could count the times she'd smiled on one hand. He heard her laughing with Lily and broke into an unbridled grin. "Some dream, I guess."

"Yeah, some dream," Mary agreed. She was still thinking about the name Joy had uttered.

After Lily followed the smell of maple syrup to the kitchen table, Joy reached under her pillow for the feather. Every night she slept with it. It made her feel closer to Jeremy. Maybe it was the reason she'd seen him in her dream. He was okay; she knew that now, and even though he lived far away, he'd found a way to visit her. The magical mourning dove feather had kept them inseparable.

Joy bounced out of bed and carefully folded the paper towel around the feather as she'd done every morning since Jeremy'd been taken from her and tucked it into the cigarette carton before turning her attention to the magic markers. What color should she choose? Blue was Jeremy's favorite color and the color of his eyes…and Elia's, the man in her dream who wasn't really Jeremy, but somehow was.

She popped the top off the marker and with her best handwriting wrote in the white margin of the Parliament box: *I dreamed of you last night*. She took a moment to assess her work then added a second line: *in a garden white*.

"Hey kid," she heard Ethan say from the doorway. She ran and leaped into his arms.

"Guess what? I'm happy!" she announced then pressed her cheek against his. He hugged her closer and rubbed her back with his big hands. *A gentle giant* their mom always said.

"Want to do something after school?" he asked as he placed her back on the floor. They made their way together to the kitchen with Ethan's arm around her shoulders.

"Like Monopoly?" Joy asked as she took her place at the table beside him.

"Sure. If it gets warm enough, we can walk to the beach."

Mary turned from the stove to see Joy's reaction. Walking to the beach was something she had always done with Jeremy. Joy's eyes shifted to the portrait on the wall, the one she had drawn of him sitting in the sand with his feet in the water. "Okay," she agreed.

And so began Joy's ascent from grief. The spring was breaking through the hard winter and she was re-entering her life, without Jeremy. After all, Joy was nothing if not a survivor. There had been times that she'd been strong enough to carry them both, but she'd never realized how many times he had carried her. Without Jeremy she felt lost and alone. To live a normal life, she would have to make new friends in school and start spending time with them at home, as well. That place in her life had always been reserved, and it would have continued that way forever if she could have had it her way. But she couldn't, so she did what all surviving creatures do: she adapted.

Lily took her under her wing and taught her how to be more like a "girl", something she would later regret. Lily was naturally buoyant and cheerful. Joy was not; she was far too analytical for that, but she had something Lily didn't develop until much later in life, a sense of confidence that was rare in someone her age. For her twelfth birthday, Lily accompanied Joy to the mall to have her hair cut in layers like the cheerleaders, and on her advice Mary and Bob gave Joy birthday money to buy clothes like other girls. She retired her mud-stained Converse sneakers that used to be Ethan's, her torn jeans and baseball caps. The result was more than Lily had bargained for. When Joy walked through the food court at the mall, it wasn't the sixth grade boys who were throwing their attention at her; it was the eighth graders, Lily's classmates, who unabashedly stared. For Joy, it was the day she started seeing herself differently.

That summer she spent with her new friends, Amanda (who she never quite forgave for her attention to Jeremy), Hannah and Kaitlyn. They lived in a nearby neighborhood, in homes that peered out over the ocean. On her way there, she'd walk past Jeremy's house and try not to look at it because Belinda's car was in the driveway like nothing had happened. But the mourning doves weren't on the roof like they used to be. Once, en route to Amanda's house, something significant occurred—she saw Belinda watching her through the bay window. Joy bolted to Sea Street and was sobbing on the side of the road when she went numb. She'd been born with the gift of empathy, but even God-given abilities can be lost or altered. A singer's vocal cords can become diseased, an artist's hands paralyzed. For Joy it was trauma that desensitized her feelings. It was a defense mechanism, that unknown to her was created by her own mind to prevent future injury.

She never told anyone what happened to her after glimpsing Belinda in the window, that on that day she had closed like a flower does at night…and never opened again. Instead she made a conscious decision to go it alone and to proceed as if there had never been a Jeremy. The mourning dove feather became a bird feather, instead of a magical gift from her best friend. She tucked it into the cigarette box and stashed it under her bed. Her open longing for Jeremy was present only in her dreams, which he visited regularly. In the white garden she walked with him night after night, and promptly forgot every morning.

64

When the fall came around, and a whole year had gone by, her grades were back to normal. By all outward accounts, Joy appeared to have recovered from the trauma. In eighth grade she was elected student council president, and was informed that she would be placed in all honors level classes for ninth grade. All her academic ducks were firmly in a row. But there was still a piece missing that only those closest to her recognized. The way she viewed it was that a sliver of her personality—the part that had laughed without effort and loved without question—had died, and could never be resurrected. But there were other parts that could, and would, survive.

After a while her family didn't talk about Jeremy as much as they used to, except for her mom, who was like a parent who had inexplicably lost a child to cancer or a car accident. She couldn't bear the empty space, so she mentioned his name just to acknowledge his existence. Sometimes when she was alone in the house Joy looked at the portrait she had drawn of him and thought about how he might have changed. He was almost fourteen now, wherever he was, and must have grown tall. She wondered if he still wore his hair long and if his shoulders were broadening like the boys in school. But she never let her mind imagine who he might be spending time with. That piece was still too painful to contemplate.

Sometimes when Mary couldn't sleep, she'd tell Bob how much she believed that Jeremy should have been their son and that somehow it had all been a big mistake. It was like a scar she couldn't get rid of no matter how much she picked at it. Every time Bob would give her the same response. "Some day when they're all grown up he'll come back for Joy, they'll be married and you'll have your son."

When the words left his lips for the first time he believed them with everything he was, that Joy and Jeremy were destined to be together. He hadn't read about soul mates in some New Age book like Mary had. Books knocked him out like a drug, but his gut spoke to him about things of that nature, just like it'd told him that Mary was his partner the first time he'd kissed her at the drive-in theater in Wellfleet (even though she was a straight A student and not fond of his bad boy lifestyle). By the time Joy started high school and he'd recited the same words to his wife a hundred times, he didn't know any more if he spoke them because they were true or because they were a tale he could spin to help his wife get a good night's sleep.

But his gut was pretty close to right. It didn't happen with the swiftness and ease that Bob predicted, but it did happen…in a way that very few people who have walked on this earth have consciously experienced. Their story was the stuff of dreams, of fairytales, of love triumphing against all odds.

CHAPTER SEVEN
A Big Glitch in Bob's Plan

Ty Connors had gone to school with Joy since kindergarten, but he didn't catch her attention until freshman year of high school. He wasn't one of the football players that Joy and her friends flirted with, the guys who emitted testosterone like aftershave cologne, pulling the girls in like flies to a web. In her eyes, Ty was a reformed geek. Then, during freshman year, he was elected class president and that made her take a second look. They had classes together because they were both bright overachievers, but it took until half way through sophomore year to convince her to date him. Once he had her attention, however, he had it. Joy was fiercely loyal.

When Ty extended his metaphorical hand to her, Joy took it and finally felt safe. What she had longed for over the years was a sense of security in another human being's presence, like she'd felt with Jeremy. When they were children, Mary used to say that she and Jeremy were like Siamese twins separated at birth. And although her relationship with Ty didn't come close to re-creating that bond, with Ty she found something else, an intellectual synergy that she'd never experienced.

Like her other friends, Ty lived within walking distance from her home, although they never met that way. He was a year older than her because his parents waited an extra year to start him in kindergarten, so he could drive. The day he received his license, he returned home to find a glacier blue BMW waiting for him in the driveway. It wasn't that big of a surprise. Ty expected good things to fall into his lap and they always did, right on schedule. His father was a renowned cardiac surgeon in Boston and his mother was a stay-at-home mom. They lived in one of the big oceanfront homes that Bob had helped build when he was nineteen and newly married. From Ty's bedroom Joy could see the stretch of beach where she used to play with Jeremy.

The first time she looked out that window, she decided that one day she too would live in a house like that. For as long as she could remember, she had wanted to be a portrait painter with her own studio. But once she was introduced to Ty's lifestyle, her vision of the future began to shift. Her mind sculpted a different outcome: college and a career where she could make enough money to buy expensive clothes, drive a car of her choosing, and live in a big house. Joy didn't think of herself as a snob, though many of her classmates did. In her mind, her new perspective was a result of having come to understand the world and her family's place in it.

Ty had plenty of reasons to be a snob, but he wasn't one. The infamy of being a middle school geek had left a residual insecurity in him that wasn't obvious by his exterior. Ethan and his friends held a high place in his regard. They knew stuff that he would never know, like how to fix cars, ride dirt bikes and drink as much beer as they wanted without vomiting. He didn't like it that he was polished, that he knew how to valet park a car and how to choose the right champagne for New Year's Eve, but couldn't start a bonfire at the beach. Ty felt less masculine because his fingers were long and refined, *those of a surgeon* his father always said, and not callused like the guys in the technical programs at school. He could not have built a house if his life depended on it, although he very likely could have drawn up the plans.

Like Joy, he was born with a sharp mind that could analyze anything, a mathematical formula, an essay on quantum physics or the workings of human anatomy. He acquired foreign languages easily and played piano with a startling fluidity. It was gross motor skills that he was lacking. Ty was always coaching himself *walk with more aggression, use your hands and upper body when you speak, and above all, don't cross your legs when you sit down*. He had the straightest posture of anyone Joy knew, which she found attractive even though it caused her brother to refer to him as the "guy with the railway tie up his ass".

She didn't see Ty the way he saw himself or the way Ethan saw him. To her he was the brightest boy in school, and she found his refinements alluring. She liked it when he took her out to nice restaurants, opened doors for her, and invited her for lobster dinners at his house. His mother looked like she'd just walked out of a magazine even when she was cooking, and his father was eternally dignified sitting by the fireplace reading the New York Times or discussing the most recent novel he'd devoured.

Ty was an only child. He was raised by two well-educated and sophisticated people who doted on him as the center of their universe. The person he grew to become was predictable, as predictable as the only son of an abusive alcoholic reaching maturity with a lack of trust and self-esteem but an excellent understanding of the complexities of human nature.

Joy threw herself into Ty's world and convinced herself that she was part of it. She already looked the part and was intelligent enough to become the part with more education. Wasn't that enough? For Ty it was more than enough. Having Joy by his side boosted his confidence. He perceived that he had found in his girlfriend what he had been deficient in before, a higher opinion of himself. Ty understood that to keep her in his life he would have to bring her deeper into his world, so he lavished her with luxuries uncommon to teenage girls. He had roses delivered routinely, took her to plays and the most expensive restaurants in Boston. In sum, he spent money on her as if it were not a precious commodity like it was in her home. After all, it wasn't that hard to part from cash that had only flowed from his parents' bank account into his own. But to Joy all these gestures were symbols of his love for her. Like Ty, she felt lucky to have the relationship, and also like Ty, she was determined not to lose it…even if she wasn't *all that* attracted to him.

Ty was classically handsome. With his hair cut short and not a whisker showing on his square jaw, he looked like a doctor long before he was one, which had been his goal since third grade. His big rebellion in life was choosing to be an emergency room physician instead of a surgeon like his father. Joy listened with little patience to his complaints about his parents' inability to understand that he wanted to be his own person. Her mother's words often came to mind: *poor little rich boy*. Ty had no idea who he was or what he really wanted. His longings were like those of a toddler, confined to what was already in front of him—his car, an education, the girl of his dreams.

Sometime after their first anniversary together during their junior year, Ty finally got around to approaching the topic of sex. Joy's friends had lots of advice, but Amanda was the expert because she'd done it with just about everyone. "You ought to be doing it by now," she said over a square slice of cafeteria pizza and Joy sighed. She knew. So that night when his parents went out to dinner she let him feel her breasts like he'd done before, but this time she told him to lie on his back, and promptly climbed on top of him. If Ty was not already a slave to Joy, he was from that moment on.

Sex added an element of intrigue to their relationship, but it didn't feel the way she'd expected it to. It didn't have much in common with love, and although her lack of emotional response made her question their relationship, she would never breathe it out loud, not to him, her friends or her family. She needed them to think she was one hundred percent with Ty, because she knew—even then—that the slightest crack in that carefully constructed wall could cause the whole thing to crumble.

She was walking back from Kaitlyn's house one day after working on a paper for her Advanced Placement English class. It was late September and she was a senior in high school, seventeen years old. Her assignment was to analyze a poem by EE Cummings, *Anyone Lived in a Pretty How Town*, a difficult piece even for an AP student. Intellectually she didn't understand all of it, but emotionally she did. She felt the characters' loneliness and sense of isolation. She *remembered* it. Her arms were still covered in the goose bumps the poem had given birth to as she walked home, and she used her hands to rub them away. At that moment she heard someone call her name and looked over. It was Belinda on her front stoop holding a bag of groceries.

"Please, stop," she pleaded when Joy hastened her step.

Joy's feet stopped moving. She didn't know why, but they did. "What do you want?" she demanded as she turned to face her nemesis.

It was the first time she'd looked her straight in the face since that awful day. She'd seen it in nightmares, but never up close in real life. Her feet felt cemented to the pavement, her body a boulder that she could not budge. Belinda put the grocery bag down on the front steps and walked closer. Joy couldn't believe it—it looked like she was crying. She came all the way out to the edge of the road. Still Joy didn't move. It occurred to her that if a car came down the road it would have to run her down because her survival instincts seemed to have fled. Belinda was a little bit older, she noticed, but somehow she looked better. Her face was thinner, not bloated anymore, and her hair was a natural color, a medium brown closer to Jeremy's.

Belinda said, "I'm sorry," and tears burst out of Joy like a river broken through a dam. "It might not mean much to you and I can't say I blame you, but I stopped drinking about a year ago. I need to set things right with lots of people. You're at the top of the list."

"You mean behind Jeremy?" Joy snapped.

Belinda tried to speak but her voice caught in her throat. Joy couldn't help noticing that she seemed like a different person. Even her clothes, a long-sleeved t-shirt and navy corduroys looked like something her own mother would wear. There was nothing flashy about her anymore, nothing slutty. "I guess you know better than anyone how badly Jeremy was hurt by my behavior," she mustered.

"Your behavior?" Joy challenged. "You mean your fists?"

Belinda cringed and her eyes filled with tears again. "That too."

It was the eleven-year-old inside of Joy rising to the surface. She sniffed back tears and realized it was the first time in six years that she'd actually cried. Jeremy appeared in her mind's eye curled up on the floor, his face a blazing red from being struck. He had sunk like a shadow into the floor when Belinda hit him, like she had beaten his very existence out of him. To

Joy she had. She'd beaten Jeremy right out of her life. And there was still a gaping hole.

"Do you ever talk to him?" his mother ventured.

Joy stared at her blankly. No. Every bit of him had been gone since that heinous day, his voice, his words, his very presence in her life.

"I was just wondering how he was," Belinda mumbled. "If you do, please tell him I said—"

"I don't. I don't even know where he is," Joy hissed and turned away.

"He's in a foster home," Belinda said to her back, "I think this time in Westborough."

Westborough, Joy processed as she hastened home. *Nowhere near the freaking ocean.*

CHAPTER EIGHT
Déjà Vu

She should have known before she arrived at school that day what was about to happen. If she had remembered her dream long enough to analyze it, she might have figured it out. Premonitory dreams were nothing new to Joy. They'd occurred before many significant events in her life. When she got out of bed and trudged to the bathroom, the image in her dream of the mourning doves returning to the roof of Belinda's house was still spinning around in her brain. But by the time she had assessed her complexion in the mirror and brushed her teeth, the thought had vanished as if she'd spit it out with the toothpaste.

She was wearing her new white cashmere sweater when Ty picked her up for school that morning. It was March and although spring was officially set to arrive any day, it never came on time in Massachusetts. So far, the birds were the only ones celebrating the end of winter. Joy grumbled the whole way to the car because her new Steve Madden chunky heels were getting wet. In her tightly gripped fingers was the latest copy of PROM Magazine. She was carrying it not for something to read but as a *what the fuck Ty?* to nudge him along. They'd been dating for two years so obviously they were going to the prom together, but still was it too much to expect him to ask her? The fact that he hadn't made her think her illustrious boyfriend had not one single romantic thought in his highly charged brain.

Ty was dressed in a sweater with khakis. *Thank God*, Joy thought. The day before, he'd worn jeans with a hooded sweatshirt and a "wife beater" tank underneath, trying too hard to be like Ethan. He'd looked ridiculous and numerous classmates had taken pleasure in pointing it out. Joy took her place in the passenger seat of his BMW and routinely brushed her lips across his cheek. At seventeen it was an odd awareness to see herself and Ty as an old married couple, but there it was every morning.

73

"Another magazine?" Ty asked as he carefully shifted the BMW into reverse.

Joy's eyes flitted across his face and landed in an icy stare. How could he be so brilliant and so stupid at the same time? In Ty's defense, Joy did spend a lot of time reading fashion magazines. That was because she was planning to study fashion design after high school. That way she could use her artistic talents and still make money. Her guidance counselor had said so.

Ty's highly charged brain wasn't even thinking about the prom. The only topic that took up space in his mind was the college applications he had long ago mailed out. He knew that come September he'd be pre-med somewhere. The question was *where*. He could see the Holy Cross campus in his mind's eye as he cautiously pulled out of Fairview Lane and onto Sea Street. His inner eye meandered over the campus' green lawns and the brick buildings with white pillars as he passed two teenage boys on the sidewalk that caught his girlfriend's attention. They were *bad boys*, not guys she'd hang with. Nonetheless, Joy couldn't resist the temptation to check them out.

She tried to recall their names as she watched them in the BMW's rearview mirror, passing a blunt and laughing about something. She'd known them when they were in grammar school, back before kids got separated by their intellectual abilities. One of them—Jeff she thought his name was—had those metal things in his ear lobes with the skin stretched around them like a rock star. His black hair was long and wild and his eyes were always sleepy-looking, *probably because he was stoned* she now realized, but *God damn* he was cute. She glanced at Ty and wondered what other girls thought when they looked at him. He was one of the best looking guys in school, but no one would think he was sexy and wild like Jeff.

That's probably a good thing she told herself and opened the magazine to the page with the dress on it that she was hoping to buy. Sexy and wild wouldn't help her keep her place in the top 2% of her class. Sexy and wild wouldn't get her into the college of her choice in New York City. And sexy and wild would never make a half million dollars a year. But still...

She sighed as the BMW pulled up in front of the school. Ty always dropped her off next to the
curb before he parked the car so she wouldn't ruin her shoes. He's considerate like that, she reminded herself before she carefully emerged from the car like a queen stepping out of a carriage. Sexy and wild would have made her walk through the snow.

Amanda, Hannah and Kaitlyn were in front of her locker, Dunkin Donuts coffee cups in hand and gossiping already. "Who are you talking about today?" Joy inquired as she entered the inner circle and shed the winter coat—finally she could show off the cashmere sweater.

Kaitlyn quickly filled her in. "There's a new guy."

"No, no, no," Amanda corrected. "That does not do him justice. There's a hot new guy," she clarified. "I mean *smoking fucking hot*."

Joy threw her long blonde hair gracefully off her face with her free hand. The other hand was applying lip gloss in the makeup mirror glued onto the door of her locker. "Who is he?" she asked, but before the girls could answer, she saw his reflection in the mirror. He was right across the hall, at his locker. No wonder the girls were talking so loudly, she realized. They were trying to get his attention. The guy was tall and had long brown hair tucked behind his ear on one side and he was wearing a black motorcycle jacket with faded jeans that were just low enough in the back to show the shape of his ass. "Holy shit!" burst out of her.

"I told you," Amanda hissed. "He's mine. I'm claiming him."

For the first time ever (Amanda was always claiming someone), Joy almost argued against her. Then she remembered that she had Ty and no right to claim anyone else. She took two textbooks out of her locker and meant to shut it decisively, but she was a little too decisive and slammed it loudly enough to get the guy's attention. Joy could feel his eyes on her as she walked away from the group, but purposefully didn't return his gaze.

"Joy," she heard from behind her. It was a man's voice and it seemed like it belonged to the guy she'd been watching in the mirror, but how would he know her name? "Joy!" he said again and she stopped walking. She turned slowly and it *was* him standing there in front of her, the cute guy in the motorcycle jacket. He was smiling at her affectionately like she knew him, but she didn't. And then she noticed his eyes, his surprisingly blue eyes with the black eyelashes. She dropped her books and bolted for the bathroom. She was eleven again and running home from Belinda's house, Jeremy still curled up on the floor with his bruises.

For once in her high school life, Joy, the queen of appearances and composure, lost control. She was sobbing before she reached the ladies room door, and she entered with such force that she startled a couple of stoner girls trying to squeeze in a quick high before the late bell.

"Are you all right?" one of them asked as they pushed open the stall door and peered out. "Oh my God, are you with him?" the other one sputtered.

Joy spun and saw him standing in the doorway, holding the books she had dropped. It *was* Jeremy, but he was practically a grown man, tall and developed through his chest and shoulders. His face was angular, and his lips looked more mature. The only thing that remained of the little boy who used to somehow belong to her was his eyes, his shockingly blue eyes.

The stoner girls left and Jeremy sauntered in as if there was no reason for him not to. They were alone. Still Joy couldn't stop crying. Seeing him was a shock too immense for her mind to absorb.

"You okay?" he asked gently and stepped closer.

"No, I'm not okay!" she shouted. "What the fuck?"

His feet stopped moving. For some reason she felt overwhelmingly angry. How dare he show up here now? After all those times she'd day dreamed about it, he had arrived after she'd given up hope. And she had made a new life. The little girl he used to love was dead. She couldn't survive without him, and so she had died and been reborn as someone else.

"Mr. Blake," a man's voice said. It was Mr. Williams, the principal, standing in the doorway. "I realize you're new here, but surely you can read." He pointed to the word LADIES on the door.

Jeremy's head fell back on his shoulders "I just wanted to talk to her," he replied.

Mr. Williams looked back and forth between the two of them, at Jeremy's pained expression and Joy's tear stained face. "Did he hurt you, Joy?" he asked.

Joy snorted condescendingly. It was a ridiculous question. Jeremy had hurt her deeper than that moronic principal could ever begin to comprehend, but not in the way his sick mind was conjecturing. He had given her everything she ever needed and then without warning taken it all away. He had left her alone to fend for herself. And what that process had turned her into was someone even she didn't like very much. "No," she snapped and snatched the books from Jeremy's hands. "We used to be friends. A long time ago, we were friends."

The late bell pierced the eerie silence that followed her statement, and Joy walked out as fast as her legs would carry her without actually running. *English test, English test* her brain began to spit out. It should have repeated *defense mechanism* because that's what it was. Jeremy's appearance like a ghost of someone long dead had transported her back to a place where her new psyche was unable to survive. *English test,* her mind chanted, *the prom, graduation. Design school, design school, design school.*

"Controlled" and "calculated" were the key words to her new existence. Her life was controlled and calculated right down to the very details, her Steve Madden shoes and cashmere sweater, the PROM magazine, the perfect boyfriend who was smart and reliable and going places. Every inch was thoroughly planned so no one could pull the rug out from under her feet ever again.

"I'm sorry I'm late," she sputtered at Ms. Slavick, the English teacher who was passing out the blue composition books when she burst through the door, and promptly claimed her seat in the front row. The teacher let it pass with nothing more than an understanding smile. After all, this was Joy Sanders, not some burnout kid that perpetually wandered in after the bell.

The first part of the test was good therapy. It took all her concentration, focusing on Hamlet and his annoying indecision. Joy had no tolerance for people who got hung up between their minds and their emotions. For six and a half years she'd relied strictly on her mind. If Prince Hamlet had lived that way, he could have killed Claudius from the start and saved everyone the misery.

The second essay, on *Wuthering Heights,* was not as simple. Intuitively she understood the bond between Heathcliff and Cathy, but finding words to describe it seemed impossible. Physical attraction was a massive understatement. Intellectual synergy? Not at all. *Whatever our souls are made of, his and mine are the same,* she wrote, quoting Cathy Earnshaw, and looked up just in time to see Jeremy pass outside the door.

Had he followed her? When they were little, he used to follow her everywhere, at the beach, down the paths behind his house, even into their favorite tree in her back yard that she never looked at anymore because it reminded her too much of him. Once, in kindergarten, she'd climbed all the way to the top, and still he'd followed her. "Aren't you afraid you might fall and die?" she had asked him.

"I'm not afraid to die," he'd stated. "It's prob'ly just like being born." The comment was so astounding that she'd prodded him to explain, and he'd told her about a dream. The two of them were holding hands and had purposefully fallen into a pool of water. When they came out on the other side, they were in a different world. "I think that's being born," he'd said.

The bell rang, and sure enough, Jeremy was leaning against the wall outside her classroom. She didn't feel as angry now that she'd been thinking about them together as children. Never had she loved anyone the way she loved Jeremy. She had tried to, but it wasn't the same, not even with her family. With him, she had been instantly understood and that was what made it different. And she had always understood him. As a child she hadn't known how rare that was. She had taken him for granted. In Joy's little girl consciousness he had always been there and always would be.

"Hey," he said softly when she looked over at him and allowed her eyes to linger on the beautiful little boy face that had changed into the handsome but still vulnerable face of a man.

"Where are your glasses?" she asked. His eyes were as blue as a Caribbean sea, and had the power to cause several girls walking past them to miss a step.

"I got contacts," he explained. "Like…years ago. Want to take a walk?"

"I have Physics in eight minutes, but you can walk me there."

He laughed and she saw his familiar teeth and his eyes that could never stop smiling when he was happy. "I was thinking more like a walk on the beach," he explained.

"Oh." She was completely taken aback. Her schedule was strictly regimented. It never would have occurred to her to miss class.

"But that's okay," he said with a shrug before he playfully asked, "should I carry your books?"

"I think I can handle it," she responded with a laugh and finally allowed herself to look straight at him and smile. *My God, those eyes*; they made her heart feel like it was caving in. She thought of the last day they were together, how he had kissed her on the path behind his house, and the feelings it had evoked. *What would it be like now?* She pushed the thought away and started walking. People were staring at them—Joy Sanders walking to class with the new hot junior boy. Nothing their little minds cooked up could have been as complicated as the truth.

"Are you back…on Fairview Lane?"

He licked his lips, faltering too over touching down on the subject of his abusive mother. "Yeah, my mother finally got sober."

"I know. She told me." It was then that Joy realized she should have put the puzzle piece in place on that day. Belinda was sober; she should have known she'd want her son back.

Her disclosure made Jeremy's step fall behind and he had to take a couple of quick strides to regain his place next to Joy in the stream of pedestrian traffic. "You talk to her?" he asked.

"No, only once last fall. She wanted to apologize."

"Joy." Jeremy took her arm and pulled her out of the crowd of students moving like a herd of animals. They were pressed against a stretch of lockers. "I'm sorry, too."

She turned her eyes away. A red hot fireplace poker had somehow been launched through her chest. Everything the boy said was laced with pain. "It wasn't your fault," she conceded.

"You're mad that I left. That's why…"

"Yes, I guess I am mad. Where have you been all this time?"

He sighed. "Everywhere, fucking everywhere."

The "f" bomb startled her. It was something a teenage boy would say, but in Joy's mind, even though she was looking right at him, he was eleven. He was still her Jeremy, the little boy her entire family adored. "My parents…"

He nodded gently, understanding without her saying it. "Judy told me."

"Who's Judy?"

"Judy McGuire, my social worker. She said your parents tried to get custody of me."

Such an old deep wound. If Joy could've thought of a way to circumvent it, she would've, but every path led to the same place. "They're still not over it. I'm still not over it," she admitted.

The late bell rang and Joy's posture shot to attention. "I have to go."

"Wait for me after school?" Jeremy suggested.

Joy dropped her gaze to her fingers gripping so tightly to her Physics book that the knuckles were white. How could reality have shifted so drastically from the time she'd stepped out of Ty's BMW? "I can't," she muttered and instantly felt guilty. But she would have felt just as guilty if she'd agreed to meet him. It was the birth of a new dilemma: Ty versus Jeremy; she couldn't be loyal to them both.

She started walking again and Jeremy followed. "Why not?" he asked and placed his hand on the small of her back. It sent a vibration up her spine and down into her groin. She'd been naked with Ty, had let his hands explore her body however he pleased, but never once had he drawn from her sensations like that of Jeremy's hand pressing firmly on her back. The next four words that came from her mouth were the hardest she'd ever breathed, but decency and a sense of loyalty made her release them. "I have a boyfriend."

Jeremy pulled his hand off her back as if it were burning hot. "Later then," he mumbled and walked away after offering her only the tightest, most polite of smiles.

As if it hadn't already been the most confusing day of her life. Now she was alone, watching his back as he moved farther and farther away and trying to resist the urge to chase after him. She hadn't hugged him or said *I'm glad you're back. I missed you.* And she was crying again. She strode hastily toward her classroom, using her cashmere sweater as a Kleenex.

The rest of the day she waited to be ambushed, *hoped* to be, but Jeremy didn't come looking for her again. She saw him once off in the distance, standing near the buses as she waited for Ty after school. He was surrounded by a group of girls who were trying to drag him off to the parking lot. Even though she was about a hundred feet away, he felt her gaze and looked over at her. She turned away. Seeing him be chased by all those girls was making her nauseous. The BMW pulled up and Joy got in it without a word, still feeling Jeremy's eyes on her.

That night she didn't return home until she was sure he would have come and gone. The warm tangible energy and her mother's voice singing while she washed the dishes confirmed the fact that he'd visited. Joy bypassed her family and went straight to her room. Lying on her bed she could finally be alone with her emotions. A storm had been born inside her that she couldn't control. Who was this guy who'd followed her into the bathroom and then confidently waited outside her class room? And the way his hand had felt on her back…and worse, the way she'd felt when he moved it, like it didn't belong there anymore. From that second on she hated Ty. She loved him but she hated him, too. Until that day his presence had given her a sense of stability. What had once felt like an anchor now felt like a prison door.

The sound of Ethan and Lily playfully arguing over something infiltrated her bedroom. Joy strained to listen. "He's three years younger than you. You're rocking the cradle."

"It's *robbing* the cradle, not *rocking* the cradle," Lily shot back. "And he's only two years younger. Remember he got kept back?"

Joy shot up into a sitting position. They were talking about Jeremy.

"He's practically your brother," Ethan argued.

"Joy used to sleep with him!" Lily taunted, "Why can't I?" She was playing, and Ethan chuckled, but it threw Joy into a frenzy. She sprang from the bed and opened the door so abruptly she nearly tore it off the hinges. Her siblings burst out laughing.

"It's not funny!" Joy turned to her mother. "Why do you let them talk about Jeremy like that?"

Bob caught Mary's eye and raised an eyebrow before he lifted the paper in front of his face.

Joy slammed the door shut before her mother could reply and crawled into her bed, even though she wasn't remotely tired. Thoughts of Jeremy hung over her like storm clouds. She'd seen a motorcycle in front of his house when Ty had dropped her off. Was it his?

She couldn't knock on his door without risking a confrontation with Belinda, but she was tempted to throw pebbles at his bedroom window like boys do in movies. Her mind was flooded with questions: Before Westborough, where did he live? Did he stay long with that aunt in western Massachusetts? Had he seen his father or even moved to California to live with him? Was he the one who'd taught him how to ride a motorcycle? Was he scared to move back here? Did he have a new best friend?

Her eyes filled with tears and for once she didn't try to stop them. Even an hour later when Lily came in and crawled into her own single bed, Joy was still crying. "I wasn't really going to sleep with him," Lily whispered. "I just think he's cute."

"I know," Joy admitted.

Lily had always respected her place with Jeremy. Even when they were little kids, she had never tried to step in between them even though she was always so fascinated by him. She used to collect little things for him, like blue pieces of sea glass at the beach and stones that were rubbed smooth as marbles by the waves. Lily was considerate like that. She always noticed what made him smile: chocolate ice cream with extra jimmies at Dairy Queen and M&Ms without the peanuts, red leaves from the maple trees in autumn, and green frogs, slick as water.

Once Lily's breath was deep with slumber, Joy tugged a sweatshirt on and slid her feet into socks and sneakers before she quietly opened the bedroom door. There was no sign of life. She knew Ethan was asleep because she could hear him snoring. Sometimes her mother had trouble sleeping and sat up drinking herbal tea. She wasn't at the table, though. On second thought, maybe tonight for the first time in six and a half years, there was nothing to keep her awake.

As soon as she crept out of her room, she was startled by a noise in the living room. Then she noticed the sleeping figure of her father in his favorite armchair. Mary had covered him with a blanket and he was knocked out for the night, but every once in a while his pattern of breathing was disturbed by a sharp inhale, and that was what Joy had heard. Bob always left his work boots by the front door. Joy noticed his black knit hat tossed on top of the boots and reached for it. It smelled like her dad, like cigarette smoke and coffee and wood chips. She slid it on, not caring how she looked because no one was going to see her anyway, and then slipped out the front door, being careful to unlock it on her way out.

The night air was crisp and refreshing for the first few minutes as she walked across the grass, silently in her sneakers, but soon it seemed to nip at her skin and she was glad she had taken the hat. The moon was shaped like a scythe above her tiny house, hanging in the sky like an ornament on a Christmas tree. There was enough light to see what she needed to see—the weeping willow tree with its droopy branches that seemed to be mourning in the winter air, crying for the birds who had flown south and the children who had outgrown climbing it.

But one more time, she told herself. One more time she would venture into its branches and remember who she'd been when it'd cradled Jeremy and her in its arms, the little girl who'd spent countless hours there talking about things adults never imagine children understand: life, freedom, the universe…even love. To have one best friend that you know will always be there is the greatest love of childhood. Adult romantic love cannot outshine its purity, especially when it is shared by two children whose lives have become inexplicably but undeniably entangled.

She reached for the lowest branch and hoisted herself onto it, imagining that Jeremy—the eleven-year-old—was higher in the tree waiting for her. With every step higher, his face became clearer in her mind's eye. She sat on their favorite branch and hugged the tree's trunk to her chest. With her eyes closed, she felt the bark on her skin and inhaled the familiar fragrance, so similar to the smell her father carried on his clothes, and for a moment she was a child again. The world had not shifted beneath her feet; she had not changed; Jeremy had never left.

"When I was eleven," she said out loud, "I was…" She had to breathe in the cold night air a few times before the list started to make itself. "I was smart, brave, happy." She opened her eyes that were as clear and blue as the sea glass she used to collect with Jeremy and looked toward his house. His roof could be seen from the tree, but not the windows. No sign of life was visible. "I was a good friend. I was not beautiful. I was…loved."

When she was a little girl, there was never a doubt in her mind that every member of her family and especially Jeremy loved her. But she was different now…polished from head to toe, sophisticated and attractive. Males of all ages fought for her attention. She was one of the brightest kids in school with a promising future. But she was not happy. Her family still loved her—she knew that—but she wasn't sure they liked her. And Ty? Well, Ty adored her for what she was now: polished, sophisticated, educated and beautiful. But the brave and happy part that no longer seemed to exist? Ty had never even known that Joy, the one Jeremy had loved.

The night slipped away as Joy lingered in the tree trying to trace the path that led from the old Joy to the new Joy. When the sky started to lighten, her eyes turned toward the beach. She couldn't stay long enough to see the sun rise the way she wanted to without risking running into her father on the way back inside the house. But she did spend a few more minutes remembering the walks on the beach, the gathering of sea glass and precious stones, the feeling of flinging herself off the sea wall and landing in the soft sand, and running toward the water with Jeremy so close behind that she could hear his breath before his arms caught her around the waist. And she promised herself she wouldn't bury those memories any more like a dead child forever closed in a vault. She would take them out often and admire them, and she would treasure them like the sea glass and stones they used to carry in their pockets.

CHAPTER NINE

The Color White

It was April and the lilacs were blooming in the front yard next to the door. At the Sanders' house the lilacs were purple, planted by Mary when Ethan was a toddler, and so big now that Bob had to cut them back every year or they'd scratch people coming and going. Between Jeremy's house and the Shanahan's house next door there was a white lilac bush near the street that they used to cut stalks from and bring to Mary when they were little. Joy had always loved the white ones the most. It was in bloom, she noticed, when she passed by it with Ty that morning en route to school. And the motorcycle was in the driveway, waiting for Jeremy to ride it…late again.

At least a dozen times she'd seen him on it, and could tell from her bedroom when he left and returned by the roar of its engine. Two weeks had passed since his arrival and still Joy hadn't talked to him. When she passed him in the halls he was invariably wearing a band shirt, usually Led Zeppelin, and was always with that cute boy, Jeff, the one she'd seen smoking the blunt on his way to school. He'd nod his head at her, but nothing more. He never visited the Sanders' house when she was home. According to her mother, Jeremy was avoiding her because his feelings were hurt. Still, it irked her to hear her family talk about his visits.

She heard the knock on the door after dinner as she lay on her bed writing an AP essay, but she figured it was one of Ethan's friends. They were always stopping by with their cars so Ethan could check something out under the hood. While Lily scrambled to be around them, Joy did her best to ignore them. She figured that it was Eddie because he spent more time at the Sanders' house than all the rest of them combined. He was a mechanic, too, so Joy couldn't figure out why he always needed Ethan's opinion. He was always staring at her freakishly like he was a hawk and she was small prey that he couldn't wait to gobble up.

His full name was Eddie McCormack and he was probably Ethan's best friend, though Joy had never heard him say so, maybe because boys don't label their friends the way girls do. He was average height and weight, average everything Joy thought, but even she would have admitted that there was something striking about his looks. His jet black hair was long for someone in a trade, and his eyes were almost as black. Lily had been in love with him since she was twelve. Every August Ethan took her to the Marshfield Fair and she got to ride with Eddie on the Ferris wheel. And that was the highlight of the summer for Lily, sitting next to "Black Oil Eddie" as Joy called him behind his back. To his face she didn't call him anything at all. She acted like he didn't exist.

It wasn't Eddie at the door this time. It was Jeremy, looking for her, but she didn't know that when she heard Lily call her name and stepped out into the living room area. Her entire family was staring at her like a whole flock of Eddies. "What?" she asked with attitude.

Her dad was sitting in his favorite chair with his boots off and his hair sticking out in all directions like it always was after a hard day's work. He jerked his head toward the open door and Jeremy standing there out of her view until she turned. He was wearing the leather jacket and his hair was mussed, but in his arms was a huge bouquet of white lilacs. The contrast was so bewitching that it caused her to gasp even though her first thought was that he was bringing the flowers to her mother. That alone was enough to make her eyes water—he'd remembered. But then he stepped forward and silently offered them to her.

"They're for me?" she asked and he nodded slightly. "I love white lilacs," she stammered.

"I know," Jeremy softly replied, and her throat tightened so much she couldn't speak. "Can we go outside for a minute?"

She swallowed and found her voice. "Yes, of course."

Jeremy held the door open and Joy walked out before him. Her first instinct was to sit down on the front steps until it occurred to her that her family might hear their conversation. She could hear *them*, the clink of dishes against each other as her mother washed them, and her father coughing like a mad man. He'd be heading outside with a cigarette hanging from his lips any minute now. When they reached the street, her hand brushed against Jeremy's and it made her realize how natural it used to be to take his hand in hers, and how she couldn't do that now.

The early evening air was cool and fragrant with the aroma of lilacs. Her eyes scanned the neighborhood. In six years not much had changed. Her dad had painted the house, but it was still white with dark green shutters like it always was. The wooden post and rail fence still surrounded her yard, the same one Jeremy used to scurry beneath when he was three years old and smaller than the neighborhood dogs that used to do the same thing.

"I was wondering if you'd go to prom with me," he suddenly blurted.

"Oh." It was the last thing she'd expected him to say. The prom this year—*stupidly* she had thought until this very moment—was being shared by the senior and junior classes because of the expense of the hall. "I really wish I could, Jeremy, but you know Ty…my boyfriend…"

"He already asked you?"

Joy could barely contain the urge to laugh. A few days prior she'd showed Ty the picture of the sleek white Armani gown that she was hoping to buy. His eyes had glanced away from the anatomy textbook he was reading to the magazine, but he hadn't said *we're going together, right*? So she'd said it and now regretted it. She looked down at her Mary Janes and tried to figure out how to answer Jeremy. His feet were clad in Doc Marten boots and he was shuffling them, making a scratchy sound against the sand. The last time they'd stood together on Fairview Lane their feet had been the same size and they'd been able to wear each other's sneakers.

"No," she admitted. "Ty never bothered to ask me. He just assumed I'd go with him." She looked up at Jeremy's face. He was biting his bottom lip and his eyes were taking her in.

"He assumed you'd be his prom date?" he asked and it sounded so ridiculous when spoken out loud that she didn't have it in her to answer him. He watched her, waiting for her to do so, but it wasn't awkward. He was the only person she knew who didn't require her to speak. "That's too bad," he said, then smiled sweetly before he walked away. The expression on his face stayed with her after he left. She couldn't decide if it was disappointment or sympathy.

Of all the questions she still harbored about his life, there was one thing she was burning to say. "Jeremy," she called after him. He turned back to face her but his feet were still moving backward toward his driveway. "I set them free...your birds."

He looked like she'd pierced him with an arrow. His feet stopped and he gazed at the sky, the clouds, the trees; anything and everything but her. "I know," he replied. "I knew you would."

Someday looking back at the Monday before the prom Joy would suspect it was the Universe—or at least Moonhawk and Running Deer—conspiring to bring her back to Jeremy. But on that day, it seemed like nothing more than complications. It began when Ty's mother voiced her disapproval of the white Armani gown Joy had bought after visiting practically every dress shop and department store in Massachusetts in search of it. "It's inappropriate," she said. "You're not getting married."

Joy looked to Ty for support, but he averted her eyes without challenging his mother even though he had driven her to buy the dress. Ty's father turned the page in his novel with barely a sigh. And an idea was born in Joy's clever brain: Ty's mother was the CEO of the Connors family. She used her Ivy League business degree to manage the men in her own home. The resentment grew quickly and wildly. She snatched the gown from Mrs. Connors' hands and heard her haughty gasp as she stormed out the front door. For the first time since they'd started dating, she walked home from Ty's house. She couldn't bear to sit with him in the small space of his car, even if it was only a three-minute ride. He was being weak and his weakness would suffocate her.

By the time she crossed Sea Street and was only a few houses away from her own, she was starting to rethink what had happened. Would Ty's mother hate her now? She looked down at the white silk gown slipping like sand through her fingers and felt tears stinging her eyes.

"Whatcha got?" she heard a male voice say and turned in its direction. It was Jeremy sitting on the roof of his house holding a mourning dove. Another bird was on his lap as if waiting its turn to be coddled. They loved him, like the other ones had. The realization made her smile. There was something almost mystical about Jeremy and his birds.

"The dress I was supposed to wear to the prom," she answered.

His blue eyes did their intuitive dance across her face before he placed both birds' feet securely on the roof, then he slid down it onto the grass. "Let's see it," he directed, and she held it up against her. For a full minute he did nothing but absorb her with his eyes. Her hair was a mess and her makeup was running; nonetheless it was the most beautiful she had felt in her entire life. "It's perfect," he proclaimed. "What's wrong with it?"

"It's…white," Joy said and burst out laughing. It sounded ridiculous. *So what if it was white? That was what made it so beautiful.*

"You look good in white," he offered and broke into a grin.

"Ty's mother said it looks like a wedding dress." She faltered when Jeremy's smile disappeared. "It's a long story, but I have to return it. I bought it in Hyannis. That means I have to drive all the way to the Cape *and* find another dress by Friday. It just…sucks."

"Let's take a road trip." Jeremy gestured toward his bike.

"On your motorcycle?" Joy gasped.

"Yeah, on my motorcycle," he laughed. "Wait here." He walked inside his house and returned with a second helmet and a heavy jean jacket lined in sheepskin. She held her arms out and he slid the coat on, then attached the strap on her helmet before they mounted the bike.

"I know you're scared," Jeremy noted, "but I promise you'll be safe."

She wrapped her arms around him. Jeremy always kept his promises.

He turned the key and she felt the vibration from the motor move through his body and into hers. The highway was the scariest part, seeing the pavement race past underneath them, but after a while she grew so used to the feeling of him in her arms that she wished Hyannis was another hour away and began to let her imagination fly free. Maybe she should forget about the stupid prom dress and drive with him all the way to Provincetown. They could climb the sand dunes and visit the art studios. Once, when they were children, her parents had taken them there and her dad had tried to explain why the men were kissing and the women were holding hands. The idea of a gay community hadn't caused a blink from Joy and Jeremy, who had always been teased by the kids on the bus for their hugging and hand-holding because they *weren't* the same gender.

Her hands were cold from the wind so she slid them under Jeremy's jacket onto his warm belly without thinking twice about it. If her mind had made the decision instead of her heart, she never would have climbed onto the motorcycle and she would have missed out on the feeling like her spirit was racing outside her body, flying like the seagulls over her head. She was smiling, not at anyone, just at the blue sky and the clouds and the sunlight. The world was so beautiful when whipping through it as fast as the wind. It was almost like jumping off the sea wall into the sand. The blur of colors racing by was like a piece of art she wished she could paint. Maybe, she considered, it was what Jackson Pollock had in mind.

When they reached the Sagamore Bridge she gave him a quick squeeze to convey her excitement. He slowed the motorcycle down so she could get a good look at the canal underneath them speckled with the white sails of boats and washed in golden light that made the small waves look like shimmering fish washed up on a sunny beach. The feeling in her chest was indescribable, a joyfulness that had eluded her for so long she had forgotten how it felt.

Once they reached Carolyn's dress shop in the Hyannis Mall, Joy started tearing through the selection on the rack. "How 'bout this one?" Jeremy asked and held up a gown similar in its simplicity and sleekness to the Armani she had just returned, but with a plunging backside.

Joy stepped closer. It was stunning, but she was unsure about how the color would look against her skin. The fabric was somewhere between blue and gray, a more muted sophisticated color than a typical prom dress. She tried it on and it fit her body perfectly, even better than the white one had. It accentuated her long, slender and completely exposed back.

"That's the one," Jeremy surmised when she stepped out of the dressing room.

It didn't miss her attention that Jeremy had chosen her prom dress. As she slid out of it in the dressing room, she thought about how he had brought her white lilacs when he'd asked her to be his date. Her heart throbbed to think of it—it was such a romantic thing to do, and in all honesty, she'd rather go with him than Ty, but she couldn't justify it. Jeremy was fun and sweet and made her feel like the most precious creature on the planet, but Ty was smart and sophisticated, and more importantly he'd been her boyfriend for two years.

"What do you think of the color?" she asked as they stepped back into the bright sunlight.

"It looks like the sky in the morning on the way to school, like blue with sunshine in it."

The poetry of his comment took her aback. She couldn't even remember what the sky looked like in the morning. And it was a whole lot more whimsical than what Ty would later say when she asked him what he thought about it: that it was the same color as a worm he'd dissected in Biology.

She wondered what color Jeremy's date would wear. He hadn't mentioned who he was going with but Joy had seen him at school talking to someone she'd christened *the druggie girl* because she was always wearing t-shirts with pot leaves and drug paraphernalia. Every time she walked past them in the hallway, the girl would grab onto his arm like she was taking possession of him, and Joy would have to battle her own emotions to keep her face from reddening.

"Can I take you somewhere else?" he asked as they climbed back on the bike and Joy agreed without bothering to ask about the destination. It made no difference to her. Her heart was racing again in her chest, but not because she was scared. This time it was pure adrenalin.

Once they'd crossed the Sagamore Bridge again, Jeremy pulled the motorcycle off the highway onto Route 3A and checked street signs until he found the right one. Soon Joy could see the ocean in the distance. It looked green from where they were—a translucent celadon with areas of indigo scattered throughout. Seagulls were flying in that direction and Jeremy seemed to be following them.

The tires kicked up pea stone as he steered the bike into a small parking lot with no cars parked in it and no signs identifying the beach. They walked wordlessly toward the water and reached a wide stone path that led to the beach. It was a fairly steep slope downward, and from where they were standing the ocean laid out in front of them looked like a photograph. Not another human being was in sight, as if the entire seascape belonged to them alone. Joy turned her eyes to Jeremy's to communicate her awe. He smiled and zipped her coat up under her chin.

At the bottom of the stone path was a set of wooden stairs that led to the beach with wild rose bushes growing on either side of it. They weren't yet in bloom but Joy stopped to regard them, remembering the ones that grew near the path behind Jeremy's house.

"Still like them?" Jeremy asked and she nodded.

He reached for her hand before they descended the steep steps. At the bottom they tossed their shoes and took off running toward the water. Joy was laughing not because anything was funny but because it felt good to be playing again, like recess after a long cold winter in a classroom.

Joy threw her arms out and felt the wind's resistance and the sun warming her face. Her long hair was whipping away from her head, tangling like seaweed in the ocean. She was flying, like when she was on the motorcycle, her feet moving faster than she had imagined they could. Beads of sand sprayed out from her Achilles and landed, untraceable behind her.

She closed her eyes and dreamed that she was a sea bird taking flight. If she were a Tibetan Buddhist, she'd pray to be reincarnated as one of the white birds with the black beaks that walked so deftly on the sand and took to the air as if they had small engines whirring inside them. That way she could always keep the beach within her sight, the sand that was as soft as her new silk dress on her bare feet and the water with its constantly changing depths and colors. She heard a splash and opened her eyes to see Jeremy with his feet in the ocean, the bottoms of his faded Levis soaking wet. He was smiling at her and his pretty blue eyes were squinty in the late day light. She ran toward him then abruptly shot off in the opposite direction.

"Catch me!" she dared and shrieked with laughter when he began the chase. She felt the familiar sensation of being pursued, of hearing the dull thump of his bare feet in the wet sand and then his breath when he was too close for her to stand any chance of escaping. It didn't take him long this time to grab onto her waist and pull her down onto the sand that wasn't as warm as it looked. And they lay side by side for only a few minutes with their feet barely in the frigid water before their toes started to hurt from the cold and they decided to head back home.

Fifteen minutes later they were driving north on the highway, Joy wrapped around Jeremy with her hands tucked snugly under his jacket, and feeling more at peace than she could remember being in her entire life. She wasn't thinking about the prom dress tucked inside his leather coat, the item that only a few hours prior had seemed like the most important thing in her world. Instead she was remembering how they had played together on the beach and only spoken a handful words the entire time, and how they could have gotten by with none.

CHAPTER TEN

Smells like Teen Spirit

The prom was held at The Sand Castle which had been around since the 1940s and was once a grand ballroom where wild parties had been held by the rich. Inside it was perfunctorily elegant. The round tables were draped with white linens and topped with crystal vases stuffed with pink peonies. But what made the Sand Castle *the* place to have a party was the huge porch-like dance floor that looked out over the ocean. Four sets of French doors led from the ballroom to the open-air veranda where the teens could dance under the stars.

While the guys clamored around outside drinking, Joy and her friends, the "in" crowd, claimed the best table, the one closest to the set of French doors next to the parking lot so they could access the stairs to the beach or the limo if they needed to refill their drinks.

"Hey, there's Jeremy's date," Amanda mentioned and Joy snapped her head around to look.

"Did you see him?" Joy asked.

"No, just the druggie girl. She looks pretty good tonight." Joy's eyes scanned the room. "Over there with the stoners. I don't see Jeremy, though."

"I heard he took you to get your dress," Kaitlyn snickered and looked away so Joy wouldn't catch the devious glint in her eye. It didn't work. Even if Joy hadn't noticed she was far too perceptive to miss the malice in her tone. With her naturally flushed cheeks and honey-colored hair, Kaitlyn looked far more innocent than she was. In groups of girls there's usually one that it is not wise to turn your back on. In Joy's group, Kaitlyn was that girl.

"Where'd you hear that?" Joy asked.

"From me," Hannah admitted. "I didn't know it was a secret."

"I don't think he's here," Amanda interjected and adjusted the bodice of her royal blue dress that her breasts were falling out of. "He's not with the stoners, and where else would he be?"

"That's kind of sweet," Hannah remarked. Joy met her eyes and shook her head slightly. She picked up the cue and stopped talking, but Amanda missed it.

"I think so, too," she said. "Since he couldn't go with you, he didn't go with anyone."

Kaitlyn gasped dramatically. "Jeremy asked you to be his prom date?" she shrieked. "What was he thinking?"

Joy pushed her chair away from the table. "Maybe that we've been friends since the day we were born," she hissed and stormed off, but the conversation continued behind her back.

"Yeah, but still…" she heard Kaitlyn say as she paraded toward the veranda.

Joy had never talked to a stoner, but she was about to. She'd had just about enough of the prep girls, her regular crowd that dated the jocks and the student council guys. By far the nicest of all her friends was Hannah. With her waist-length chestnut hair and flawless ivory skin, she was as pretty as she was nice. Amanda was kind of a slut, but funny as hell, and Kaitlyn was usually okay, but when it came right down to it, she couldn't be trusted. Joy knew she'd sleep with Ty in a heartbeat if she had the chance. But what about the girls who hung out with Jeremy? Did they bicker and bitch, too, or were they nicer to each other? If Jeremy was there somewhere, she was going to find him and meet the girl he came with.

She walked out the French doors on the far left, onto the opposite side of the veranda from where the "in" crowd was hanging out and recognized a couple of boys. One of them was that cute Jeff with gauges in his ear lobes that she often caught sight of with Jeremy. "Hi," she offered as she passed him, and surprisingly he called her by name. They hadn't exchanged a word since middle school. She stopped and turned back. "It's Jeff, right?"

Jeff nodded bashfully. He'd lost the tie already and his shirt was unbuttoned. He seemed unconventional and sweet. "Hey Joy," he called out after she walked away. "Want to dance later?"

"Sure," she replied and smiled at him. Maybe it was the schnapps she'd been drinking in the limo, but tonight she felt up for anything, even a stoner boy with gauges in his ears.

The "druggie girl" was leaning against the railing wearing a black gown with a side slit, and her hair was off her face in a French twist; in contrast to the elegant appearance, she was puffing on a Marlboro. The girl's eyes slid across Joy's face. "Are you Jeremy's date?" Joy asked her.

She dropped the cigarette and stepped on it with her stiletto. "You're the one he asked."

"I'm here with Ty Connors," Joy stammered. "I thought Jeremy might have asked you."

"I asked him. He said 'no' 'cause he wanted to go with you."

"Oh." Joy had been thinking bad things about this girl, *saying* bad things about her, based on…nothing really, just a misperception on her part. "I'm Joy," she offered and held her hand out. "Jeremy and I grew up together."

"Lucky you," the girl grumbled but took her hand anyway. "I'm Tracy. This is Nate." The oversized guy standing on the other side of her shook Joy's hand then pulled a pint of Jack Daniels from his jacket pocket and handed it to her.

Before that night she'd never drunk anything alcoholic. Belinda's antics had done more than the DARE program to keep her sober. The Jack Daniels nearly came back out as quickly as it went in, but *God the dress*, she couldn't spill it on the dress. Tracy and Nate laughed at her pained expression.

"You're funny, Joy," Nate boomed with his deep voice, and it struck Joy that she couldn't remember the last time someone had said that about her. She was beginning to feel really good. The muscles in her face were so relaxed she couldn't help but smile.

She took another haul and this time the taste didn't shock her so much. "I kind of like it," she said delicately as if she were tasting fine wine, and they thought that was funny too, so she pulled a pint of peppermint schnapps out of her silk clutch and shared it with them.

"You're not as much of a snob as I thought you were," Tracy announced sedately.

"Uh…thanks?" Joy replied.

"That's not playing nice, Tracy," Nate scolded.

"It's true," Tracy argued. "I never got it why Jeremy bothered, but…maybe I was wrong."

"I didn't like you either," Joy confessed and Nate took exaggerated steps backward like he was trying to escape. "But you have been really nice."

"Why'd you turn him down?" Tracy asked.

Nate was still trying to make it into a joke, bearing his "claws" and teeth.

"I have a boyfriend. What was I supposed to say, 'hey my old friend came back to town unexpectedly and I really love him and want to go to the prom with him so too bad for you?"

"Do you?" Tracy asked. "Really love him?"

Joy felt like every person on the veranda was waiting with bated breath for her answer, but they weren't. Only Tracy and Nate were. "That's a complicated question," she finally said.

"Or a complicated answer," Tracy countered.

Nate was at the breaking point. "Okay, that's it. We're all doin' shots and changing the subject. Let's talk about Joy's friends. Who's available?" Joy lifted a perfect eyebrow. "We aren't going out," he added. "Tracy's my best friend. So, the chica in the red dress?"

"That's Hannah," Joy told him. "She's a sweetheart, but she won't go out with you, not because she's a snob, but because she's in love with Vinnie, the guy with the plastic gun."

Vinnie Perrone, one of Ty's friends and a soon to be film major, had become so enraptured with *Pulp Fiction* that he'd foregone renting a tux and instead purchased a black suit and skinny black tie. He was even donning Ray-Ban Wayfarers and toting a plastic machine gun.

"*The guy with the plastic gun*," Nate chuckled, his eyes still on Hannah. "He's the shit that guy, even if he did steal my girl."

99

"He hangs on the boulevard once in awhile," Tracy explained. Driftway Boulevard was the stoner hangout.

"Vinnie Perrone?"

"A/K/A Vinnie Vega," Nate quipped. "A/K/A Ganja."

"Ganja? Get out!" Joy exclaimed. That would be hot news among the preps. Ty would have a heart attack over it. *Marijuana is an illegal substance,* he always said. Gag, gag, gag. It was like pulling a string on a Dr. Connors puppet, exactly to the word what the great surgeon would say. "Hey, can I hang out with you guys for a while?" she asked. There seemed to be more freedom on this end of the veranda. It was easier to breathe.

"Stay as long as you want," Tracy offered. "No hard feelings, I swear."

"I'll tell you a secret," Joy whispered. It was the booze talking. "If you asked my friends if you could hang with them, they'd say no." Her eyes turned to her impeccably painted toenails.

"That's sad," Nate said. "I mean for you guys." Joy looked up; she'd never thought of it that way. "You guys think the 'in crowd' is so badass, but the 'out crowd' has way more fun 'cause we don't give a fuck who hangs with us. You want to come out? Cool, we'll see you on the boulevard. Don't want to? That's cool too." Joy nodded her tipsy head. She got it.

After almost an hour Ty found her. It was the best time she'd had in high school she told Tracy and Nate as he dragged her away. She might even consider becoming a stoner herself.

"See you on the boulevard!" Tracy yelled behind her with a laugh. Joy answered with an exuberant wave and nearly fell out of her high heels.

The disc jockey had been playing mellow seventies and eighties songs while everyone devoured their dinners. Joy was one of the few still eating her stuffed chicken breast when the DJ very obviously shifted gears. He dimmed the lights and let loose a ten second intro of *Smells like Teen Spirit* then stopped it and growled into the microphone, "This one's for Kurt."

In the long pause before the Nirvana song blasted out of the speakers, the room grew silent as they all paid homage the only way they knew how to the passing of Kurt Kobain. Joy looked over at her new friends. They reacted differently than the prep kids to the DJ's words.

"To Kurt!" Jeff bellowed as Nate lifted the Jack Daniels bottle respectfully.

The DJ hit "play"and kids from both sides of the veranda started dancing and singing along. The scene was as foreign to Joy as watching indigenous tribes dance around a fire on the education channel. She had never really connected to rock or grunge music, but maybe because with Ty she'd always listened to whatever was on the pop stations. Watching her classmates convulse on the veranda, she noticed their emotional connection to the music. Kurt Cobain's vulnerable voice sang out and she saw Jeff head bang his long glossy hair off his face. Nate played along with an invisible pair of drumsticks. It wasn't only the guys—Tracy was moving her head to the rhythm of the song. And Joy wanted to be part of it.

"Let's dance," she implored of Ty.

"To this?" he sputtered and shook his head. *Poor Ty*, she thought; Even when he was intoxicated, which he was, he couldn't loosen up enough to dance in front of people.

"She's drunk," Kaitlyn said down her nose.

"You're right, I am," Joy admitted. "But I'm not drinking anymore tonight. See you guys. I'm peacing out," she added, a phrase she'd heard Nate use, and headed straight for Jeff.

"Like this," he suggested with an adorable grin and used his hands to turn her so that her back was to him before he wrapped his arms around her waist. She let her head fall back on his shoulder and he swayed with her in his arms, moving so her hips were in motion with his. The DJ was crooning along with the vocalist of the new song that was playing.

"There's something I want you to teach me!" Joy shouted over the music.

Jeff spun her so she was facing him. "Wait, I think I slipped into fantasy," he spewed. "What'd you just say?" He was grinning like an imp and his dark brown eyes were laughing. "Seriously, I had that exact fantasy once, but then in third grade, you stopped talking to me."

He was funny and brighter than she'd expected. For once, she laughed without restraint. It sounded different, light and free, like it had a will of its own…and it felt amazing.

"Let's see," Jeff continued, "what could the illustrious Joy Sanders want to learn from me, how to smoke from a bong? Ride a dirt bike? I'm pretty good at that, actually. Play bongos? I'm not so good at that. But wait—" He gazed out over the ocean. "Is there skinny dipping involved?"

"No!" Joy protested, but she laughed again. "I want you to teach me how to head bang."

Jeff groaned and threw his head back dramatically. "You had my hopes up," he complained. "Well, you better take those pins out of your hair or you'll blind someone, besides it'll be so much more fun." So she did, and soon Joy was head banging with the stoners to Alice in Chains, the Stone Temple Pilots, Pearl Jam and other bands she couldn't remember the names of the next day.

"Is that guy saying what I think he is?" Joy shouted over the sexually rhythmic music.

"*That guy*?" Nate taunted. "Dude, that's Trent Reznor. You don't know the Nine Inch Nails? They're *the shit*."

"I'll make you a tape, tomorrow," Jeff promised. "Seriously, your life is about to change."

It was right about then that Ty showed up, grinning with the pale-faced simplicity that only a drunk can bear. Joy recognized it at once. "Oh no. Are you all right?" she asked. Ty nodded somnolently. "Did you throw up yet?" she added and everyone laughed like she'd meant it as a joke even though she was completely serious.

"Nope," Ty answered simply and smiled at everyone, one person at a time.

"Joy can teach you to head bang!" Nate shouted and Vinnie shot off the plastic gun.

"Yeahhhh!" Ty howled like a caveman.

It was the most undignified sound Joy had ever heard come from him. "That's really not a good idea," she argued. Ty's jacket was already strewn over the railing and for some unknown reason he was taking off his shoes and socks. Then Jeff was pouring Jack Daniels down his throat. As far as she could tell that was what led to the puking scene that occurred ten minutes later while they were slow dancing to the prettiest song she'd ever heard; it was "Creep" by Radiohead Jeff told her, which was good to know, but for the rest of her life every time she heard it she thought of Ty barfing down the front of her prom dress.

After that things got a little chaotic. She went down to the water with Jeff to wash the vomit off her dress and didn't come back for a while (because they decided the best way to get the puke out was to dive into the ocean). And while Ty waited for Joy to come back with Jeff, Kaitlyn told him everything she knew about Jeremy asking Joy to the prom and driving her to Hyannis on his motorcycle to get her dress. And it was this information in Ty's drunken brain that caused them to argue the whole way back to Joy's house in the limousine where she scrambled out of the car and slammed the door not once, but three times just to make sure he got the message.

CHAPTER ELEVEN
Butterfly Wings, Part Two

Jeremy was on the roof of his house when he saw the white limousine cruise by and heard the door slam three times. He artfully descended and made his way silently toward the Sanders' house. The limousine was gone already, but Joy was standing on the side of the road with her face in her hands.

"Joy," he said and closed the gap between them. "Are you okay?"

"N-n-no," hiccupped out of her.

"What's wrong?" he whispered and brushed her hair off her face. It was wet. And then he noticed her dress was soaked, too. "What happened?"

"Everything, everything happened tonight. Ty got drunk and th-threw up on me and then he was mad because I went swimming with Jeff Cosgrove even though he was with my friend Kaitlyn, and then I said I wanted to go home and Johnny—Kaitlyn's date— came looking for her after he'd been off with Melissa freaking King all night and yelled at Ty for having his arm around K-Kaitlyn and I told Johnny about the puking thing and Kaitlyn said it was all my fault because I was hanging out with the s-s-stoners so I called her a bitch and then she said—she said she never fucking liked me anyway. And then we all had to ride h-home together."

Jeremy was completely silent for about five seconds…then burst out laughing. "I'm sorry," he managed to get out, but then the laughter overcame him again and he bent over. "I'm not laughing at you. It's just funny what you said. I thought something bad happened."

"Something bad did happen—Ty *threw up* on me," Joy whined. "Do I smell like puke?"

"No, but you look like you're freezing. You better get inside."

"I don't want to. I thought I'd be out for the whole night and it's not even midnight."

Jeremy took off his flannel shirt that he was wearing like a jacket over a long-sleeved thermal and a Radiohead t-shirt, and slipped it on her arms. "You know that band?" she asked.

"Radiohead? Yeah, I know that band," he laughed.

"Let's go sit in our tree," she suggested. He lifted an apprehensive eyebrow. "I haven't had anything to drink in a while. Really, I'm not drunk."

He held his hand out and she took it. She couldn't stop thinking all the way to the back yard about how holding Jeremy's hand made her feel like everything was right in the universe. They were standing right under their willow tree, but Jeremy hadn't let go of her, and he was watching her face. He knew intuitively that she was about to say something.

"When I was little…and even now, when you hold my hand, it makes me feel safe."

He grinned and said an astounding thing: "Two can be like one holding hands."

Joy stared at him, thinking about it for so long that he said, "What?" before she pulled him closer and kissed him. And then his soft mouth was kissing her back and she couldn't stop. His hands were under the flannel shirt on her bare back, pulling her against him, and hers reached for his neck and brought him down onto the grass. Within seconds they'd lost all control. There were no thoughts of Ty, or anything else in Joy's brain, telling her to stop or even slow down. There was only the pure energy of the moment they were in, the strongest desire she had ever known to merge with another human being in every conceivable way.

It all mixed together so perfectly that nothing seemed separate, the cool grass underneath them; the smell of his hair as she pressed her lips against his neck; his warm belly when she tugged his shirt over his head; his breath in her ear as his hands undressed her; and the hard smooth metal of his belt buckle as her fingers struggled with it. It all felt like one taste, one sound, one movement, like an infant being rocked on an ocean wave.

She kissed his mouth, wanting to make the moment last as long as possible, then laid back and watched his face, that to her would always look like the little boy she'd loved more than anyone, while his eyes took her in. How much of her could he see in the moonlight? She was lying naked in the darkness like a mermaid washed up on the shore. She met his eyes and silently gave him permission to touch her. It was a slow and tender mission for someone who had never used his hands to explore a woman's body. When his breathing quickened, she pulled him on top of her, and she couldn't help noticing that everything was perfect, right down to the width of his hips, as if their bodies had been made for each other.

That night in her back yard, making love over and over again, it never occurred to Joy that someone could stumble upon them. They were under their tree, a sacred space. She could see its limbs bent toward them as she peered over Jeremy's shoulder, their two bodies moving together like one. The entire night seemed to belong to them alone. No one else had a right to be there.

When the air became too cold, she slid Jeremy's flannel shirt back on and handed him his jeans. They formulated a plan to walk to the beach and watch the sun rise from the sea wall once the sky started to brighten, but that was still a few hours away, so they rolled his thermal shirt and band t-shirt into a pillow and curled up together on it to talk. Joy had planned to ask him a million questions about the past six and a half years, but she ended up entertaining him with stories about the prom. "So maybe we can get stoned together sometime," she suggested.

"I don't get stoned anymore," he informed her. "I haven't smoked weed in probably two years. It makes me too paranoid."

"You're a stoner who doesn't get stoned?"

"Who said I'm a stoner?"

"No one. I guess I just thought you were. Why do you hang out with them then?"

"'Cause they're the nicest kids. I've been in so many schools…" He used his fingers to count. "Seven, I think. In every school they're the nicest ones."

It was a shocking statement to Joy, but it shouldn't have been. She'd just spent the evening with a group of kids exactly like that who had welcomed her into their midst as if she were a lifelong friend even though she hadn't bothered to acknowledge their presence in years.

"Jeff's probably the happiest person I've ever met," she said.

"I doubt that."

Joy looked over at him. "Why do you say that?"

"We all go through crap as kids that make us weird in some way when we're older."

"What happened to Jeff?" she ventured.

"His mom died and his dad's never really around. I think that's why he drinks so much. He's lonely. I'm not drinking right now—you should prob'ly know that—'cause it makes me crazy. I think I'm like Belinda."

"No you're not," Joy argued. She felt offended by the comment, like someone had slapped her, or worse slapped *him*. "You're nothing like her." He didn't answer, only rolled onto his back and gazed at the stars. "Do you always call her Belinda?" she asked.

"Someone beats the crap out of you enough it gets hard to call her *Mom*."

Joy nestled her face against his chest. "How'd you get to be so brave?" she asked. His laughter was warm and unexpected in the darkness.

"What makes you think I'm brave?" he challenged.

"You ride a motorcycle." That prompted more laughter. "You hang out with the wild kids, and you live with Belinda."

His laughter abruptly stopped. "How else was I supposed to come back?" he challenged.

She wiggled onto her elbows so she was looking down at him and kissed his lips, and he settled back into his bed on the grassy earth. They were better at touching than talking, she realized. They always had been. "I only meant you don't seem afraid anymore."

107

Jeremy sighed. "The worst thing that could happen already happened. My mind can't make up anything worse than when…when I was eleven, so nothing else is really a threat."

"Oh," is all she said, but she understood. Jeremy's removal was an atrocity that would remain unrivaled in her life too, she told herself, because at seventeen she couldn't imagine anything worse. She laid her head down on his chest again and closed her eyes. After a while the sound of his breath became indistinguishable from the breeze that was blowing the grass. His arms were holding her and she felt safe and warm, even though it was dark and cold all around her. They were like a nucleus floating together in a small sea. That was the last nearly coherent thought she had before sleep overtook her. "Do you love me Jeremy?" she mumbled, not even knowing if he was still awake. She was drifting somewhere between the two dimensions.

"I've never loved anyone else," he replied and she carried his words with her into a dream.

They were wrapped around each other like vines on a tree when Bob found them at eight o'clock the next morning. He had no reason to think anything was amiss because Joy had told him and Mary that after the prom all the kids were planning to make a bonfire on the beach near Ty's house and sleep there. He was smoking on the front steps when he saw Belinda walking briskly in his direction.

"Is he here?" she called out frantically before she even reached the walkway.

"Jeremy? No."

"I don't know where he is," came out of her in a cry.

In all the years Bob had known Belinda he'd never seen such an expression of anguish on her face. He was about to tell her that he'd go looking for him in his truck when he noticed Joy's sandals strewn on the grass, the same ones he'd given her money to buy for the prom. It only terrified him for about three seconds before he had a thought, a memory really—the weeping willow tree. That had always been Joy and Jeremy's hideout.

"Wait here," he said and took off for the back yard. And there they were, holding onto each other with their foreheads and noses touching just like when they were kids, except this time they were barely dressed. Joy's prom dress was flung on the ground, she was apparently wearing Jeremy's shirt, and her bare legs were entwined with his that were clad in faded jeans. Bob had to admit that there was something striking about the way they were wrapped around each other, but there was no denying what they'd been doing. Jeremy's arms were still inside her shirt.

"Wake up!" he barked. All four blue eyes shot open like they were one person, not two.

Joy gasped and pulled her shirt closed before she sprung into a sitting position. "Daddy!" she exclaimed. "What are you doing?"

"Um, *what*?" Bob snapped. "What am *I* doing?"

Jeremy was sitting up, too, dragging fingers through his long hair like he was trying to figure out what to say. He was shirtless and Bob noticed for the first time how strong he looked, like a grown man. He turned his eyes to Bob's face, ready to be reprimanded.

"Go *home*!" Bob ordered.

Jeremy didn't move without looking to Joy first, and that was when Bob knew that nothing had changed between them. She met his eyes and they communicated God only knows what in the secret language that only they understood. He nodded slightly before he stood up and walked toward the front of the house where his mother was waiting. When Jeremy passed by her dad, Joy realized that Jeremy was now the taller of the two.

"Get inside and put some clothes on," Bob directed. After Joy left he stood alone under the weeping willow tree for a couple of minutes trying to figure out what to do next. Should they discipline her? And what would Belinda say? He reached for Joy's prom dress on the ground. It was damp and made him wonder what she'd been up to the night before.

Bob had expected Joy and Jeremy to navigate toward each other. That seemed as certain as every other law of nature. What he hadn't expected was to find them half naked in the back yard the morning after the prom. Lily, yes. But Joy? Not in a million years. On reflection, it seemed ridiculous to discipline her. She was following a force, like Jeremy was, the same force that had been obvious to everyone who'd seen them together since the time they were toddlers. He shook his head playfully at the complexities of love as he rounded the corner toward the front yard and heard the phone ringing inside the house. Who would be calling at eight o'clock on a Saturday morning? Someone else looking for their kid he figured, and he was right.

It was Mrs. Connors. When Bob entered the house, Joy was on the phone explaining that Ty had dropped her off before midnight and she had not spoken to him since. From what Bob could gather, during the phone conversation Ty walked in the door, still wearing his tuxedo but smelling like vomit. His mother's first reaction was to blame Joy, but Joy deftly reminded her that she was *at home* and had been *in bed* when the phone rang. Therefore, she had no reason to know anything about her son's miscreant behavior. With that, she self-righteously hung up the phone and turned to see her entire family watching. All the commotion had managed to awaken Lily and even the slumbering grizzly bear, Ethan.

"Is Ty okay?" Mary asked.

"He's fine," Joy said dismissively and tried to run her fingers through her hair. But it was all stuck together from the hairspray and salt water and God knows what else.

"What happened to your hair?" Lily ventured in a small wounded voice.

Joy groaned. She had always thought hangovers were a myth, but as it turned out they weren't. Her head was pounding, her stomach was queasy, and her mouth was so dehydrated that her tongue felt hard…like a parrot's. "Oh, long story," she said.

"What were you doing in the back yard?" Mary asked innocently. "And dressed like that?"

Joy tugged on the flannel shirt, trying to cover her rear end. "Just...talking to Jeremy."

Bob held up the grass-stained dress and she gasped. Lily and Ethan burst out laughing.

"Oh Joy," she heard her mom say behind her as she paraded toward the bathroom. There was one other thing wrong with her body that she'd just realized. Her bladder was fuller than it had ever been in her entire life. When was the last time she'd peed? *Oh my God.* It made her blush to remember. It was on the beach with Jeff the stoner kid, her new best friend, after they'd swum in the ocean in their prom clothes. Alcohol was so much more dangerous and so much more interesting than she'd thought it would be. It was like some huge hand had reached down and given her world a good shaking, and everything had fallen into a new place. Jeff, Tracy and Nate were *in*, but Kaitlyn was *out*; Vinnie was a prep by day, but stoner by night; Ty was a drunken moron, and Jeremy wasn't a stoner after all, but most importantly, he was...her lover. *Her lover.*

She turned the shower on as hot as her skin could tolerate it and stepped into the flow. The steaming water felt heavenly, like it was stripping her body of all the impurities—the alcohol and the smoke, the vomit and the sticky salt water and whatever she had slept on in the back yard. She opened her mouth and filled it with water, letting it soften her tongue before she swallowed it into her poor dehydrated body. What was she going to say to her parents? What was she going to say to Ty? And where the hell had Ty been until eight o'clock in the morning? Had he been with Kaitlyn? And did she even care?

She forced her brain to stop thinking about it while she scrubbed her body with soap. Jeremy. That was the one thing she couldn't stop thinking about. The way his mouth had felt when he'd kissed her and his body moving on top of hers. Good thing she'd been faithfully taking birth control pills. They hadn't used anything else, but Jeremy had never been with anyone before, so there was no other risk. *Riding bareback;* that's what Amanda called it and Joy had thought it was slutty, until now.

After she was dried off, she buried her face in Jeremy's shirt so she could smell his skin, but she couldn't wear it. She was about to catch a truck load of shit from Ethan and Lily, and they didn't need any more ammunition. Joy was a little worried about what her mom and dad were going to say, too. What exactly was parental protocol regarding sleeping in the back yard with the boy next door?

She slid on her mom's bathrobe and opened the door with the assuredness of someone in the right, even though she knew she was in the wrong. The silence was ridiculous. They'd obviously been talking about her. Lily held the newspaper in front of her face. *As if.* Joy'd never seen the girl read a newspaper in her entire life. She was pouring coffee when Lily exploded with laughter. Ethan couldn't control it anymore either and laughed so hard he sprayed his coffee onto the kitchen table.

"Daddy, you *didn't,*" Joy whined. She'd been holding out hope that he'd spared them the details.

"Oh no you don't, Joy. You're not blaming me for this one. You're the one who did it."

"Right there on the lawn," her sister giggled. Joy glared at her as she took a seat. "I wasn't criticizing you," Lily added. "I think it's ballsy. I've never done it. Have you, Ethan?"

He gulped his coffee. "What, got laid in the back yard? Nope, not once."

Joy threw her hands out—*what the hell?*—and turned to her mom. Bob was rubbing his temples with his fingers, waiting for the whole escapade to end.

"I would appreciate it," Mary commented, "if you would all watch your language."

Ethan and Lily exchanged a confused glance. "You said 'laid'," Lily suggested.

"Is that a swear? I didn't think it was," Ethan asserted.

"So how was the prom?" Lily ventured.

"And how in God's name did you end up with Jeremy instead of Ty?" Bob asked.

Joy stomped into her bedroom. She could still hear Lily and Ethan's hysterics in the kitchen while she dressed. Her plan was to go to Hannah's house to find out what had happened at the bonfire, but she lay down on the bed for a minute and the next thing she knew Lily was waking her.

CHAPTER TWELVE
The Stoner Boy

According to the clock on her table it was 12:07....of the same day, even though it felt like she'd been unconscious for a week. And her head was still pounding.

Jeff was in the kitchen waiting for her, drinking coffee with her dad. He was wearing a hooded sweatshirt unzipped over a white beater but unlike on Ty it looked perfect on him. "You never told me you were friends with Jeffrey Cosgrove," Bob scolded once she'd thrown on clothes and joined them. Joy stared blankly. "He's Billy Cosgrove's son. We graduated from high school together."

She nodded, understanding now. Billy Cosgrove owned the construction company that her mom didn't like her dad to work for because the hours were too long.

"I made you that tape," Jeff interjected. "Want to hang out?"

Joy turned her eyes to her dad. "Be back in time for dinner," he said coolly.

As soon as they were climbing into Jeff's Nova with the torn upholstery, he said, "Jeremy didn't call because he thinks your parents are mad. He said to tell you 'midnight'."

She closed the door behind her and breathed in a thick dose of pine air freshener that didn't quite cover up the smell of weed. "He said what, 'midnight'? Was he being metaphorical?"

"I have no idea what that means," Jeff admitted, "but I don't think so." He slid a cassette into the tape player and smiled at her as the Radiohead song started playing.

"Aw, thanks Jeff," she crooned. His thoughtfulness brought to mind Jeremy's comment the night before about the nicest kids in school. "Where are we going?"

114

"To get you stoned," he playfully replied. Joy laughed then noticed his mischievous grin. "Seeing how Jeremy's dry and I'm his closest friend—I mean, except you—I figure I get the honor."

"*You get the honor*? That sounds disgusting."

"Stop being such a prep. There's a worse way of putting it."

She lifted a skeptical eyebrow.

"Pop your cherry." He pulled a fat joint out of his Winston pack and lit it. "So can I?"

"My life is spinning out of control," she complained but took it from his hand anyway.

Jeff turned up the volume on the stereo. Scott Weiland was singing about promises being broken as the Nova made its way past the early beach goers and Joy held the smoke in her lungs.

"Remember when we were kids what it was like here?" Jeff remarked. "So much quieter."

The melancholy lyrics were making Joy pensive. "Do you remember me when I was little?"

"Sure. You used to get on the bus with Jeremy."

"You're probably one of the kids who used to laugh at us for holding hands."

"Yeah, probably," Jeff admitted. "But who's laughing now, right?"

"What do you mean?"

"You guys are so lucky you've got each other."

"Don't you have a girlfriend?" Joy asked. He had gorgeous brown eyes that turned down at the corners. He smiled easily and his hair was long and free like he didn't care what anyone thought. *Sexy and wild*, Joy thought and grinned to recall how she'd watched him from a distance.

"Not at the moment," he answered. "Wish I did, though."

They'd smoked two bones by the time they parked the car in front of the sea wall at Brant Rock and Joy was feeling nice and relaxed, but she hadn't figured out that she was stoned.

"Let's sit on the sea wall," Jeff suggested and they stepped out of the car into the sunlit day.

"I'm sorry I peed in front of you last night," Joy offered and he laughed.

She was so captivated by the way the sun was hitting the waves that she wasn't paying attention to where she was walking. Jeff convinced her to sit down, and when she did she was looking at her feet dangling twelve feet above the sharp rocks, admiring her sandals, and Jeff was smiling really big and saying something about his car and how much he loved it.

"What year was it born?" she asked and couldn't figure out why he was looking at her funny.

He burst out laughing. "It wasn't born," he answered once he regained control.

"What wasn't?" she asked and that set him off again. He was rocking dangerously on the sea wall like he was about to fall off. She kept thinking about Humpty Dumpty, but couldn't think of his name. "You're just like that egg!" she accused.

"That *what*?" he reeled.

"Wasn't it an egg?" She tapped her forehead, trying to think of something fragile.

"I don't know what the fuck you're talkin' about. It wasn't born 'cause it didn't come out of another car." He thought about it too much and second-guessed himself. "I mean, right?"

Nothing he said made sense. Joy tugged on the roots of her hair, her eyebrows pinched seriously together. "I can't...understand you," she finally squeezed out and Jeff erupted with laughter. "And I really, really want Kraft macaroni and cheese, don't you?"

Jeff groaned with pleasure. "Oh my f***ing God, yes, and Bugles with cream cheese."

They both laid down on the sea wall with the tops of their heads touching and watched the clouds and seagulls overhead before Joy finally asked, "What's a Bugle?"

"Like a wicked good like chip thing. I'll get us some."

"Popcorn with melted nacho cheese," she tossed out.

"But how would you eat it?"

"With a spoon."

That made Jeff laugh some more and Joy worried that he'd wriggle right off the wall. "Peanut butter and jelly sandwiches with potato chips," he suggested.

"Egg salad," Joy countered.

"Girl, you're stoned. No way would you want egg salad if you weren't stoned."

"I'm definitely stoned," she admitted. "You did it, Jeff. You popped my cherry."

"Yeah," he breathed out with satisfaction. "Now let's go eat."

At Jeff's house he prepared them a feast out of macaroni and cheese, Bugles with cream cheese, a bag of Chips Ahoy cookies and slush made in the blender with frozen lemonade and a whole can of vodka. "You're a bad influence on me," Joy complained, but her new friend didn't reply. He was too busy massaging his brain freeze because he'd downed half a glass in a swallow. She scooped cream cheese with a Bugle and tossed it in her mouth.

"Ho-ly shit," she crooned. "This is the best thing I've ever tasted!"

"Told you," Jeff groaned.

Slouched against the back of the couch, Joy examined a cookie. "I haven't eaten one of these in years," she confided. "Know why? 'Cause I wanted my prom dress to look good." She defiantly shoved a whole cookie in her mouth so the rounded ridge showed on her cheek. "You should see it now!" The cookie blasted out of her mouth along with the words and landed on the rug.

"Covered in puke!" Jeff laughed.

"And grass stains," she added hysterically. The air got caught in her nose and she snorted.

"You just snorted like a frickin' guy. You're not as sweet and pure as you pretend."

"Yes, I am," she argued and sat up straight as if her posture could vouch for her character.

"Give me those cookies," Jeff ordered. He dug his hand in the bag, but he didn't take his eyes off her. "Okay then, sweet and pure, how'd you get the grass stains on your dress?"

She opened her mouth wide in shock, but nothing came out.

"Yeah, I figured," he concluded. "So, how're you breakin' it to Ty?"

"I thought I'd get Hannah's advice. Want to take me there?"

"To Hannah's house? I'd carry you on my back if I had to." Joy narrowed her eyes. "What, you're jealous? You're the most beautiful girl I know, but you're already taken, aren't you?"

She met his eyes seriously for the first time that day. "Yeah, I guess I am. Let's drink another slush then go to Hannah's," she suggested. She was not only cured from her hangover, but feeling completely chilled out. The world seemed to move slower on slush time.

Jeff was still looking at her seriously. "It kills me to think about it," he finally said. "All that time I thought you were a good girl, but really you were a bad girl waiting to happen."

�֍✾�֍✾✾✾✾

It was late, almost midnight, when Joy first heard a small sound in the distance of her consciousness as she teetered on the brink of sleep. All day she'd been re-examining the events of the prom and what occurred after it. She couldn't find peace. Ty never called. They weren't officially broken up and she wasn't officially with Jeremy. Only Jeff and Hannah knew the whole truth. There it was again, a tapping sound. She sat up in bed. "Lily! What's that noise?"

Her sister sat up and pulled the curtain back. "It's Jeremy," she stated simply. Joy gasped. Having sex in the back yard, getting stoned on the sea wall and boys coming to the window at midnight were all well beyond the parameters of her straight-laced student council life. "Maybe you should try to be quiet," Lily added, "and I'll let him in."

118

"You'll *what*?"

"Shhhh!" She lifted the window and hand motioned him inside. He landed first on Lily's bed before his bare feet hit the floor soundlessly. Lily reached for her watch on the night stand "It's set for four thirty," she whispered, "so Jeremy can leave before dad gets up for work, and if you guys have sex in here while I'm awake to hear it, I'll scream. Okay?"

Jeremy was fighting a grin as he took the watch from her hand. Joy moved over to make room for him in her bed. She felt his body in her arms and finally found the peace she had been trying all day to find. His feet were cold against her warm skin. "Why didn't you wear shoes?" she asked.

"I never use shoes unless I have to. I like to feel the earth with my feet, like an Indian."

The comment made her smile. She gave his mouth a tender kiss. When they were little they used to talk about living like Indians all the time. Where had that idea originated? Then the recollection hit her…the dreams. They used to have the same dreams, about two Native American men who were their friends. "Do you remember the Indians…?"

"Sure. I still see them sometimes. Don't you?"

"No," Joy answered. She didn't say so, but she felt a bit betrayed by the information.

"I can't always remember what they say when I wake up like I used to."

"Do you remember their names?"

"The old one," he said thoughtfully, "with the long white hair—his name is Running Deer."

Running Deer. The words felt mystical on Joy's tongue. Before they were separated, the world had been a magical place where love always prevailed and their Indian friends advised them through dreams. They'd assumed everyone lived like that until they'd brought it up over hot dogs and potato chips one day at lunch. Joy's parents had quietly dismissed the notion that strangers can communicate in dreams, but Ethan and Lily had been brutal; they'd called them *the mental cases* for months.

"When I was gone, did you dream about the garden?" he ventured.

His words made her gasp again. *The white garden*. "What is that place?"

Jeremy shrugged lightheartedly. "Heaven, I think."

It was too much to consider. "So, are you in trouble?" she asked to change the subject.

"Not with Belinda, but maybe with your dad. I'll talk to him tomorrow."

"Where's Belinda think you are now?"

"Here. She said if I pulled that crap again to at least have the decency to leave a note, so I did."

"What'd you write?"

His eyes moved over the ceiling where a few plastic stars remained from the time they studied the solar system when they were nine. "If you're looking for me I'm in Joy's bed."

"Shut up! You didn't write that."

"Somethin' like that," he said playfully and smiled sweetly before he kissed her. She tried to kiss him silently so Lily wouldn't hear them, but they were quiet for too long.

"When you stop talking, I know what you're doing," Lily snapped.

"Use my headphones," Joy suggested. "They're on the table." Lily shot into a sitting position. She looked like a rag doll under a Christmas tree with her wild blonde curls falling down over her night-gown and her clear round eyes glaring at them.

"All riiiiight," she fussed, then put them on, and within only a few minutes had dropped off the face of the Earth. They could hear her rhythmic inhalations and knew they were alone.

"So, am I your girlfriend now?" Joy asked.

"I always thought you were," he replied. "It doesn't matter what word we use. It's just a word. I know who you are to me."

She unbuttoned his shirt and ran her hands over his chest and belly, wishing she could live her whole life like the moment she was in, when every atom circling inside her felt like it was tingling with an electric force. "We can make love," she whispered, "but we have to be quiet."

"We don't have to."

"I know." She unzipped his jeans anyway.

If the rules of their relationship were written down somewhere on stone tablets like the Ten Commandments, she'd never have to read the words to understand them. Not having sex wouldn't make a difference. Even if they had never kissed, they would have stayed who they were to each other. She couldn't have described what those roles were. She only knew that they were permanent and immutable. "Jeremy, are you mad that I didn't wait for you?"

"What, you mean 'cause you had sex with Ty?" he exhaled and buried his face in her long hair. "Not really. It wouldn't be right to judge you for something you didn't understand." He lifted his head off the pillow, and in the dim light from the street she could see the blueness of his eyes. "But if you did it now, it would be different. Not so much mad. I'd be…"

"Hurt?"

Jeremy thought about it. "I don't think hurt is a big enough word," he said.

She felt a million miles behind him, like he had a perfect understanding of the universe and their place in it. She was sensing a difference in their paths since they'd parted. Jeremy's spirit had continued to grow. He'd stayed open to his teachers and they'd led him through the pain of separation and taught him to have faith in what would always be, even when he didn't realize it. They'd spoken to him like all guides and spirit teachers, through his dreams and his intuition. And he'd learned to trust them.

Joy, on the other hand, had turned her pain inward, and it had brewed inside her like a poison until it turned into something hard, the wall of a maze that she couldn't find her way out of. Jeremy would lead her out if she'd let him, but for her that would mean embracing a humility that was completely foreign to her. She wasn't used to being led.

She leaned into him so that their foreheads and noses were touching, two puzzle pieces snapped into place. The sound of his breath was familiar and comforting as his hands brushed across her nipples, reading her like Braille. He tugged the panties off her hips and the vibration of his lips tickled hers when he asked her, "What do I do?"

She took a moment to appreciate the beautiful, sweet boy who cared enough to ask a question that made perfect sense but very rarely came from the lips of men. Then she held his hand and showed him. That night she fell asleep in his arms again, but this time Lily's watch alarm awakened them in time for Jeremy to scramble out the window before either Bob or Belinda discovered he had been there. And Lily proved to be a trustworthy ally. She didn't tell Ethan or anyone else about Jeremy sneaking in through the window, not even after it became something of a ritual.

CHAPTER THIRTEEN
Family Portrait

While Joy and Jeremy were rediscovering each other, two rooms away Bob was coming clean with his wife. Jeremy had been helping him out with work projects on a part-time basis, which Mary knew about, and that arrangement had been working out well for both of them. On the practical side, it gave him an extra pair of hands and a strong young body to carry materials, and it put some money in Jeremy's pocket. But beyond that, they enjoyed spending time together. Even as grown men they were like father and son.

What Mary hadn't known before this moment was that the two of them had hatched a plan for Jeremy to work for Bob full time. Jeremy was failing too many subjects to begin the next year as a senior; therefore, he'd have to repeat junior year, which he didn't want to do. Dropping out of school was Jeremy's idea, not Bob's, but Bob had gone along with it.

"Are you crazy?" were the first words out of his wife's mouth. She reached over to the nightstand to turn the light on, and there was Bob in the soft glow, rubbing the throbbing veins on his temples. "You didn't encourage him, did you?" she demanded, "and why is he failing? He's always been so bright." It was a stretch and she knew it. They'd been informed long ago that Jeremy's IQ was significantly less than average.

"He's always been street smart," Bob countered. "That's not the same thing as book smart, and he's been moved around so much it's a wonder he stayed in school this long. You remember what the social worker said?" It was a stupid question, Bob realized but it didn't register until the words had exited his mouth. He could get away with saying every pornographic word his brain could conjure, but he could not say the following loathsome three words without a serious reprimand from his wife: fetal alcohol syndrome.

Mary snapped her head toward him. "Don't you say those words in this house Bob Sanders!"

If he didn't cut this off quickly, she'd go on a tangent about how the doctors had no idea what they were talking about and soon it would be his fault for believing it. But in the privacy of his own brain he couldn't help thinking that a diagnosis of fetal alcohol syndrome wasn't all that unreasonable. "Mary, stop," he pleaded. "I was only trying to make a point that it might be harder for Jeremy to learn than it is for other kids."

"I know that," she admitted. "I just…can't believe it."

"You're overreacting. The kid's good with his hands. I'll teach him to be a carpenter." Mary still looked like she wanted to cry. "Sweetheart," Bob urged, "Have a little faith in me, would you?"

"I always have. And we've always gotten by, but it hasn't always been easy." She paused to word it right. "It's not the life I imagined for Jeremy."

"Or for Joy?"

Mary nodded solemnly, then turned the lamp off before she curled up in her husband's arms. His breathing was raspy in the darkness. The cigarettes were getting the best of his body, but he wouldn't give them up, no matter how much his family chided him about it.

She whispered, "Don't be mad that I said that."

"I'm not mad," he answered, but she couldn't tell for sure by the tone of his voice. In the silence that followed, she thought about how excited he'd probably been over the prospect of bringing Jeremy into his business. They'd both had concerns about his ability to maintain the business alone due to his bad knee. Some days it was a struggle for him to walk.

"It never made a difference to me what you did for work. But with Joy…"

"Her expectations are higher," Bob said, finishing her sentence. "But she loves him too much to walk away. She's always loved him."

Mary agreed with his statement, but she wasn't convinced that his prediction was accurate. She kept thinking about a comment Joy had made about Ty going to Holy Cross, and how he was going to be a doctor. She'd seemed so impressed by it. And Jeremy's IQ was probably only half of Ty's—how could he possibly compete?

"She doesn't know yet, does she, that he's leaving school?" she asked.

Bob chuckled. "Nope," he confessed, "and I won't be the one to tell her."

Joy awakened with a resolve to officially end things with Ty. What she'd learned on her visit to Hannah with Jeff was that after they'd dropped her at home the night of the prom, the group had gone to the beach by Ty's house, and Vinnie had managed to get a fire going. According to Hannah, Kaitlyn had been "all over" Ty until he threw up on himself and passed out in the sand. The kids had then dragged him closer to the fire, and he hadn't moved until the morning when he came to and walked home to find his mother on the phone with Joy. Hannah's words made Joy feel sick. Then Jeff said something worse: "At the Sand Castle when we were coming back from the water, I saw them pull away from each other."

Had Ty been kissing her? trickled through Joy's mind as she lay in bed analyzing it. It was Sunday and her mom and dad were working in the yard. Through her bedroom window, Joy could see her dad digging holes and her mom plopping plants in them, so she knew Jeremy had the day off. She found Lily in the kitchen making pancakes and curled up in her favorite chair at the table while she waited for them to be ready. Sunlight was spilling through the lace curtains making snowflake-like designs on the table. It made Joy realize how glad she was that winter was finally over.

All the portraits she'd drawn as a child were still on the wall next to the windows. She craned her neck so she could look at the drawing of Jeremy. In her mind's eye she carried a perfect visual of him in his cutoff shorts toting a bright blue pail filled with sea shells.

"I like Mom's," Lily said. "You made her look like the Virgin Mary."

"Oh, you mean because of the halo?" Joy asked and looked over at the coarsely drawn portrait of her mother with the golden circle around her head. "I did that because Jeremy told me Mom has a yellow light around her." She shrugged. "And Dad has a green one."

"Jeremy can see auras?" Lily gasped. "I never knew that, but on second thought I'm not all that surprised. What are you guys doing today?"

"Well, first I have to go see Ty."

Lily spun to face her. The plastic spoon in her hand splattered pancake batter on the wooden floor. "Joy!" she hissed. "You slept with Jeremy and Ty doesn't know you're broken up?"

"Are you seeing anyone, Lily?" Joy asked innocently.

Her sister laughed and loaded a pan full of pancakes onto a plate. "I know you're just changing the subject, but I'd *like* to be seeing Eddie McCormack."

"Who's that?" Joy asked and dove into the plate of perfectly golden brown pancakes.

"You know Eddie—Ethan's friend."

"Oh. Black Oil Eddie."

"You shouldn't call him that, Joy. It's mean."

"It is?" She'd never thought of it that way. She'd never really taken any of Ethan's friends seriously. To her they were like a gang of cartoon characters, in existence for the sole purpose of amusing her overly analytical brain and sharp tongue. "So what's the problem?"

"Ethan. Eddie thinks he'll kick his ass if he touches me."

"Why do you think Ethan never dates? All my friends think he's cute."

"You might want to tell him," Lily pointed out, "especially if Hannah's one of them. He's got a huge crush on her, but don't tell him I said so."

When they were done eating, Joy got dressed and began the trek to Ty's house. Jeremy was perched on his roof and saw her coming. He jumped off the edge, met her in the street and kissed her. Her nerves were frazzled, but the feeling she got with Jeremy was a perfect reminder of why she was visiting her soon-to-be ex. Ty she admired, Ty she respected, but Ty had never made her heart feel like the wings of a humming bird just by touching his lips to hers.

"I'm going to tell Ty," she disclosed.

I know he said without having to vocalize it. *I'll wait for you.*

Along the ridge of the roof lined up like soldiers were all six mourning doves, watching them with their flickering black eyes. It was a beneficent image, reminiscent of childhood, and it suddenly reminded Joy of the dream she'd had that they'd returned. In an instant she understood that they were a symbol of Jeremy coming back to her. Someone out there in the universe had tried to let her know that a second chance was coming her way…and she'd nearly missed it. She cradled his face in her hands. Too many days she'd told herself she would never see that face again, and too many others she'd convinced herself that whatever attachment ran between them like an umbilical cord had been severed. They were venomous tales she'd fed on, only to spare herself from future disappointment, but the poison had sunk its teeth into her. It'd made her stop believing in magic and happy endings.

"I love you Jeremy Blake," she told him right in the middle Fairview Lane. Then she kissed him and allowed herself to feel the love that was breathing again inside her and the appreciation for whomever or whatever magic had brought him back.

A storm was brewing in her belly as she walked away. Something painfully mundane and something fantastical were happening at once; she was breaking up and falling in love all in one swift movement, like the thrashing of a sword. What was making her sick to her stomach and weak in her legs, saying goodbye to Ty or opening herself up to Jeremy, to Love? It felt like stepping forward on a downward plunging escalator and hoping it would continue to move steadily and not thrust her off. *Vulnerable,* that was the word—not since she'd been eleven years old had Joy felt so vulnerable.

The wind was blowing hard closer to the ocean, chilling her bare arms and whipping her hair into her eyes. At Ty's house, his BMW was parked in the usual place, assuring her that he was inside. To her relief it was Ty, not his mother, who answered the door, but within three seconds of perusing his face she knew he had done something wrong. Guilt was written all over it. She had done something wrong too, she reminded herself, and looked down at her feet still standing on the brick steps.

Ty stepped outside and led the way to two Adirondack chairs painted periwinkle and placed tastefully on the lawn. With her vision focused on the crab apple tree blossoming nearby, she sensed his energy. He was nervous, more so than she'd ever known him to be. She had a talent for feeling people's emotions, and Ty, she knew, was in pain. *You're breaking up with him to be with Jeremy, not because of some foolishness with Kaitlyn*, she told herself. Make the cut clean, then get up and walk away.

But she couldn't do it. The wound caused by their betrayal was throbbing inside her. Joy's blue eyes could be as soft and beneficent as pool water or as sharp and dangerous as cut sapphires. She turned them, as weapons, onto Ty. What would be the best opening line? There were so many ways to twist that knife. But not saying anything at all seemed to be working just as well. He crouched under her glare. Her eyes cut him a few more times before she parted her lips—the very same lips that minutes before had been kissing someone else. "It's over," she tossed out lightly as if it were nothing to her.

He looked up, his eyes moving rapidly; he was analyzing. "What did she say?" he asked.

"Who?" Joy asked innocently.

"Kaitlyn," he spit out, like the word itself was vulgar to him.

"She hasn't called. She won't because she knows I know. Stupid girl—now we all hate her, apparently even you." Her face was red, which was more than she wanted Ty to see. She stood up to leave.

"Joy," he pleaded, following her like a puppy. "I don't care about her. I don't even remember it."

"But I won't forget it," she countered.

When she got back to Fairview Lane, Jeremy was sitting on his front lawn with a mourning dove on his lap waiting its turns to be coddled, like the lucky one in his hands. She sat next to him without comment and he handed it to her. "I forgot how soft they are," she noted.

"Try this, sweetheart," Jeremy suggested and stroked the bird's throat with the tip of his finger. The word *sweetheart* didn't escape her notice. It sounded grown up and made her grin a little bit. She might have outright smiled if she'd realized that he'd subconsciously picked it up from her father.

After a while they walked back to Joy's house holding hands like they used to when they were children and Jeremy offered to take over the planting so that Bob and Mary could have a break. The older couple sat on the front steps with their iced tea and watched him teach their daughter how to separate petunias without damaging the roots. "Where'd you learn this?" Joy asked.

"From one of my foster mothers," he revealed as he took the tiny plant from her hand. "But I didn't live there long enough for her to teach me much." He used his free hand to prepare the hole with peat moss. "She had too many foster kids."

As a result he'd been moved on again Joy realized. *Seven schools* he had said. It was something she couldn't imagine. She carefully tore a plant away from the others, this time without Jeremy's help. He smiled at her when he looked up and she handed it to him. After they'd finished, Bob suggested they go out for ice cream and the whole family piled into his truck.

It was a revelation to Joy, how much she enjoyed being with her family. Throughout high school she had ignored them for the most part, but now it was like someone had opened the blinds and what had once been murky and dark was now as clear as a sunny day. To Joy, Jeremy had always been the center of the Sanders family. Now that he was back, she could resume her place beside him. She snuggled under his arm with Ethan on her other side and his big hand on her knee. Her heart felt as eager as when she'd been eight years old and on her way to visit Henri the French bulldog. "Remember Henri?" she asked and everyone whined about how much they missed him. He'd died of stomach cancer when they were still children. "I want a dog like that someday," she told Jeremy.

"Okay," he softly agreed and kissed her forehead.

When her dad looked away from the road to meet her mother's eye, she knew what they were thinking…and she didn't mind because she'd never been so sure of anything: that this was her family riding together to Dairy Queen. Her mom and dad, Lily, Ethan and Jeremy. That was the family portrait. It was a quiet, familiar knowledge, the way truth usually is. It sneaks up and taps you on the shoulder and lets you know that even though you've been looking everywhere else for it, maybe even for eons, it was right beside you the whole time. She rested her cheek on Jeremy's chest and he held her with both his strong arms. Ethan didn't budge. His hand stayed comfortably on her knee. He might be worried about Eddie hurting Lily, but she knew he wasn't thinking that about Jeremy.

At Dairy Queen, Jeremy still wanted chocolate with extra jimmies and Joy still wanted vanilla dipped in cherry. As kids, Jeremy's cone had always taken on a new allure once she saw it in his hand, and she'd fuss about how she'd made a mistake until he offered her his. This time he didn't wait for her to complain. He held it out without comment and she bit the peak of it before eating her own.

"Why should she get both?" Lily threw out for nostalgia's sake.

"Because she's the *baby*," Ethan said with a wink and everyone laughed, even Joy.

They stayed with the family all evening, through a cookout and a Monopoly game that ended when Bob fell asleep in his chair. By then it was good and dark, so Joy and Jeremy ducked outside for a walk to the beach, borrowing a blanket from Ethan's car en route.

"Let's go skinny-dipping," Jeremy suggested. They were wrapped in the blanket like two expectant butterflies in a cocoon.

"It's too cold," Joy argued and snuggled her face against him.

"I'll hold you. Come on, I've never gone."

Joy laughed. "And you want to start in the ocean? It's freezing, and there are sharks."

"You can't have it both ways. If it's cold, there won't be sharks."

130

"I'll skinny-dip with you in a lake, not the ocean," she countered.

"You're finished with finals on Wednesday, right?"

"Mm hm," she replied. "Why, you want to go then?"

"No, I was thinking we could double date." She propped her head on her hand so she could watch his expression. "Jeff and Hannah," he revealed before she had to ask.

Joy snorted and lay back down beside him. "I thought you were serious."

"I am serious. She called him this morning and said she broke up with Vinnie 'cause he's going to college in California and he knew it all along but never told her."

"Oh my God, Hannah broke up with Vinnie? That's huge! I bet he's going to UCLA. I saw him with that catalog last fall and he totally lied about it."

"But the good part," Jeremy pointed out, "is Jeff. He's out of his mind with excitement. We'll have to feed him Valium or something."

"Oh, that's so nice!" Joy shrieked. "That makes me feel good. Doesn't it make you feel good?" She kissed him and rolled him on top of her. His long hair was falling down around his face. She tucked it behind his ears so she could see him better.

"That makes me feel good," he answered with a grin and kissed her back. And in that moment Joy had an epiphany: that she was finally, completely and blissfully happy…and that she hadn't been anything close to that for six and a half years.

CHAPTER FOURTEEN
The 'Out' Crowd

The three days leading to the Wednesday night double date went by in a blur. On Monday, Jeremy drove Joy to school on his motorcycle and shocked the senior class by walking her to finals with his arm around her shoulders. They'd showed up early to clear out Joy's locker so she didn't risk running into Kaitlyn, whom she had no intention of ever speaking to again.

Tuesday was the hardest day because that was when the Physics exam was scheduled and she had always sat next to Ty. Apparently he'd gotten word of her new relationship because she could feel the bolts of lightning radiating from his eyes the moment she stepped into the classroom. During the final exam she stole a glimpse of him. His face was freckled with whiskers, and his hair wasn't gelled either. The miserable guy scribbling answers on the exam didn't look remotely like Ty.

When she left class, Jeremy was waiting. As they walked away holding hands a voice behind them hissed the word "sped", which was followed by a burst of laughter. It didn't occur to Joy that Ty and his friends were laughing at Jeremy because he needed special help with academics. The insult was not missed by Jeremy, however. Even though he didn't acknowledge it, he stored it away with every other taunt that had ever been thrown at him: *retard*, *moron*, *dimwit*, *idiot* and his least favorite *stupid fuck*.

On Wednesday after school, Jeff showed up at Joy's house stoned out of his mind and she had to take him inside and feed him coffee. He wasn't prepared to date a girl like Hannah, he confessed, and he looked so pathetic when he said it that Joy felt sorry for him.

"I can help you pick out clothes," she offered. "Would that make you feel better?"

His eyes performed a surprised perusal of his torn jeans and flannel shirt, but then he looked up and nodded. "I guess you know how I should look for a smart prep girl."

132

"Not all prep girls are smart." Joy countered. She was trying to think of a way to say that Hannah wasn't particularly bright without sounding mean when she heard the roar of Jeremy's motorcycle and ran to the window.

"Hey Joy?" Jeff said, but her eyes remained on Jeremy, who had taken his helmet off and was combing his hair with his fingers. "You guys got a good thing. Don't fuck it up, okay?" She looked over with a quick smile, thinking he was playing, but his expression was completely serious.

"Okay," she agreed then met Jeremy at the door and threw her arms around his neck.

They dragged Jeff off to his house where Jeremy made food while Joy helped him get ready. She quickly made the selections from his closet. A white collared shirt with blue pin stripes and baggy jeans with Doc Marten boots would be somewhat dressy but with edge, perfect for a first date.

"Do you have any gel?" she asked.

"I'm not gelling my hair like the preps," Jeff snorted.

"Not like the preps. You know those things in your ears?"

"The gauges?"

"Yeah. They're sexy as Hell. Use the gel to push your hair off your face so they show."

He looked at her with new respect. "My brother might have some."

"You have a brother?" Joy asked through the bathroom door. Jeff was crouched down looking through the drawers.

"Yeah, Chris. He's twenty-four. He knows Ethan."

"No kidding," she commented. "Do you know Ethan?"

"Sure. He's my mechanic."

Once again she felt like she'd been living in a bubble and she had the strongest urge to pop it. "Wait," she chirped. He'd poured too much gel into his palm. She stooped down next to him and rubbed some from his hand onto hers, then worked it through his hair.

"Dude, you're seriously hot," Joy announced authoritatively, and Jeff broke into an unbridled grin.

"Would you go out with me," he asked, "I mean…you know…if you didn't have Jeremy?"

"In a heartbeat," she said.

They galloped down the stairs and found Jeremy making nachos in the kitchen. "You know what would be great with those? Vodka slushes," Joy suggested and Jeff reached for the blender that was sitting right there on the counter like it was waiting for him.

"I'm not drinking," Jeremy stated quietly.

"Why not?" Joy asked.

"'Cause when he drinks he's a psychotic mother fucker, that's why," Jeff said and was about to add commentary when the telephone rang. That spun him into a panic over the thought that it might be Hannah. "Pick it up," he pleaded, but Joy wasn't paying attention. She was watching Jeremy. Emotion was flashing in his eyes, though exactly which one she wasn't sure.

"I told you already," he snapped. Okay, so it was anger. But what was he so mad about?

"Joy, please answer the God damn phone!" Jeff shouted.

She picked it up and it *was* Hannah. Joy told her to come over, which introduced a whole new level of hysteria into Jeff's psyche. He started racing like a madman to make the slush so he could suck one down before she arrived. Jeremy calmly reached into a cabinet, pulled out a bottle of Wild Turkey and handed it to his friend. It seemed like a routine to Joy's eyes, as if they'd done the same thing countless times. Maybe, she considered, it was no coincidence that Jeremy knew exactly where that bottle was.

As soon as Jeff was done slugging down the Wild Turkey, she ordered, "Now go brush your teeth!" and he took off.

The doorbell rang and Jeff's feet pounded back down the wooden stairs. Joy joined him in greeting Hannah and left Jeremy in the kitchen, the energy thick and foreign between them. Jeff was adorably shy with Hannah and she couldn't keep her eyes off him, so Joy figured things were off to a good start. When they got to the kitchen, the food was already laid out.

"Got another one of those?" Joy asked and gestured toward the Coke in Jeremy's hand.

When he bent down to get one out of the refrigerator, she crouched next to him and whispered, "I'm sorry. I really don't get it, but I didn't mean to make you angry."

"If you saw me drunk you'd get it," he said and cocked his head to the side before he kissed her. The kiss made her so lightheaded that she had to hold onto his arms as they stood up. he pushed the door closed with his foot, his arms grasping her tightly around her waist, and pulled her against him. He could hug her like no one else, with his whole body, not just his arms.

Sometimes, when she was so close to him that she could feel his chest moving with each breath, it felt like they were floating, and she understood the expression *walking on air*. Maybe it was caused by the amount of oxygen storming her brain from her heart beating like a maniac. It took them a minute to realize that their friends were watching them. "Sorry," Jeremy mumbled.

"Don't be sorry," Jeff said.

Hannah spoke up next. "I remember one time in junior high you came to my house crying because you missed him. I didn't really get it like I do now. I mean, even then you loved him, right?"

Joy met Jeremy's eyes and let them linger there. "Right," she agreed.

"I can't remember not loving Joy," Jeremy said. "I think I always have."

In 1995, Joy's birthday—May 19th—fell on a Friday, which was perfect for a birthday party bonfire at the beach. School was already out for seniors, but Jeremy still had a month left. Her part time job serving coffee at Mary-Lou's News wasn't starting until Memorial Day, so she could sleep in. Later, she planned to sun bathe at the beach with Lily so she'd look fabulous for her party. When her eyes opened, the first thing they saw was a huge bouquet of white lilacs on the floor beside her, the stems tied together with a pretty blue bow. She yelped and woke up her sister.

"What's with all the white?" Lily asked with a scruffy voice. "You guys getting married?"

"It's my favorite color. Jeremy always remembers. Come on, let's get breakfast. Mom's making French toast—I can smell the cinnamon."

Mary was as thrilled as Joy to see the flowers. She didn't even ask how they came to be in her bedroom. "I'm so glad you're finally together," she said and gave Joy a big hug. "I haven't seen you this happy since you were a little girl."

"My stomach's doing wheelies," Joy admitted.

Mary laughed. "The last time I heard that word, the two of you were practicing them on your bike." Joy beamed, remembering. They'd once been able to fit on the banana seat together.

"It's not fair," Lily whined from behind her, "I want to be in love, too."

"Let's have tea and talk about it," Mary suggested, like she always did. In the Sanders home a cup of hot tea could fix just about anything, maybe even Lily's pouty expression.

"I know!" Joy suddenly exclaimed. "Let's invite Eddie to the bonfire!"

"We can't do that," Lily protested as she filled the teapot with water.

"Sure we can," Joy insisted. "On our way to the beach, we'll stop at the garage and tell Ethan he's invited, and we'll ask Eddie too. I'll say it's my birthday and he has to come."

"He'll come because of you," her big sister fussed. "He's always liked you more than me."

"What if you bring French toast to the garage?" Mary interjected. "It's true what they say about the way to a man's heart."

"Like Jeremy and yellow cake with chocolate frosting," Joy pointed out.

Ethan and Eddie, like most men being swept up in a carefully conceived plan, had no idea what hit them. The girls delivered the food and the guys accepted it, along with the invitation, without thinking twice. That evening, once they were dressed for the party, the girls chatted excitedly while they made the salad and frosted the cake for Joy's birthday dinner.

As soon as Ethan returned from work, bearing a bouquet of flowers for his baby sister in his greasy hands, they pounced on him to find out if Eddie would be attending the party.

"That's what he said," he answered, and kissed Joy's cheek. "Who else is going?"

"Out of my friends, I think Hannah's the only one you know. Oh and Jeff Cosgrove. Why?"

He shrugged his shoulders and reached for the refrigerator door to grab a cold Budweiser.

As soon as he was out of the room, Joy whispered, "She's dating Jeff, anyway."

"She is?" Lily whimpered. "Jeff was my backup plan if Eddie doesn't work out."

"You don't need a backup plan," Joy replied, then nearly leaped out of her skin with excitement because a knock signaled Jeremy's arrival. She trotted happily to the door. If she felt like cantering like a race-horse, well, so be it. It was nothing Jeremy hadn't seen before.

"Did you bring me a present?" she immediately asked him.

"Joy!" her mother scolded from the kitchen.

Jeremy laughed good-naturedly and hugged her so tightly he picked her feet up off the floor. "Of course I brought you a present." The top of a box wrapped in silver paper was poking out the top of his shirt pocket. "But you can't open it yet," he added and held his hand over it.

Is it time yet? she asked a dozen times throughout the evening. They were at the beach, sitting on a piece of driftwood near the bonfire, when he finally told her it was time to open it. They didn't have to walk far to be alone. Sitting on the cool sand, Jeremy slid the box into her hand.

Joy caressed the shiny silver wrapping paper with her fingertips. "This is the best birthday I've ever had," she said softly. "Thanks for coming back."

He was silent at first. Her comment was deeper than what he'd expected. "I'll always come back, Joy," he said, "No matter where I am."

Inside the box was a silver bracelet with five charms on it already: a dove, a feather, a starfish, a tree and a motorcycle, each one symbolic of a key moment in their relationship. "I drove all over Massachusetts to find those," he told her as she examined them by the flame from his lighter. "The tree's not right though. I couldn't find a weeping willow."

"It's perfect," she said. "Do you remember what you said that day...about the feathers?"

"That they made us inseparable." A small laugh escaped him. "But we already were."

"Do you still have yours?" she asked.

"Sure. When I went into foster care the only thing I had was that feather and the bird encyclopedia—oh, and the stuffed bear you gave me. I still have him too." He laughed again. "He's a little beat up, though. You might not recognize him."

His comments cast a noticeable shadow on her face, but nothing compared to what was happening on her interior. Inside it was downpouring. The emotional trauma she'd suffered as a child had never really been dealt with. Had Jeremy known the extent of it, he would have backtracked, but he didn't. Joy had buried it so deeply that even she didn't know.

"Someday you'll need to forgive Belinda," he continued. Joy met his eyes, and to Jeremy she looked eleven years old again, small and inconsequential against his adult mother, but defiant and stronger than he had realized. "She's been trying real hard to make it up to me."

"You can forgive her," she softly voiced.

"I already have." She looked back at the party like she was yearning to be a part of it. "Joy," he said, "when you don't forgive someone it doesn't hurt that person. It hurts you."

Her breath escaped in a sob, startling him. He embraced her and something wasn't right—her body felt limp in his arms. She was reacting the same way she had when he'd been taken away, but Jeremy had no way of knowing that. Since his return, he'd noticed the change in her; the lack of empathy that used to be a hallmark of her personality. Still, he didn't understand the extent of the damage. He pulled her onto his lap and clasped the bracelet on her wrist. Distraction had always worked well when she was upset. "Want to go back to the party?" he asked softly.

She smiled unexpectedly and scrambled to her feet, but he was worried about the shift in her personality and how easily it was brought on. When they arrived back at the fire, he sat beside her, even though she was busy showing off her new bracelet to Lily, Hannah and Tracy who had recently arrived with Nate. He didn't wander off to talk to the guys, like he usually did at parties. He kept one hand touching her, as if guarding against whatever darkness might be lurking nearby.

Tracy took a seat on Jeremy's other side. "You're still not drinking?" she asked. He shook his head. "Nate brought a bottle of J.D. for Joy's birthday."

With his history, he had no right to tell anyone not to drink, but after what he'd just witnessed, giving his girlfriend Jack Daniels seemed like a bad idea. He was starting to feel trapped beneath alcohol's reign. Someone was always drinking too much of it: Belinda, his father, himself, Jeff, and now Joy. She was so pure in his eyes; it was like pouring sewer water in her mouth.

But it was too late to object. Nate was approaching with the bottle, and as soon as Joy caught sight of him, she jumped excitedly to her feet. To her, Nate was a great big teddy bear, a funny and sweet, completely harmless tough boy. He had grown a goatee since the prom and she was teasing him about it, stroking it with her fingers and calling him a *playa*.

When Jeff and Hannah wandered over from the other side of the fire where they'd been talking to Ethan and Eddie, Jeff sparked a few bones and got them circulating. Hannah handed one to Jeremy; he passed it on to Tracy, bypassing himself and Joy. From across the fire, Ethan gave him a nod of appreciation. He didn't like drugs of any sort, particularly near his baby sister.

Joy didn't mind. Her eyes were on Jeremy's face. In the firelight it was breathtakingly beautiful—and hauntingly familiar—the way the light danced over his lashes and full bottom lip, casting shadows on his cheeks and jaw. "Don't move," she instructed. "I want to draw you in the firelight." She had the strangest feeling she'd done it before.

Jeff walked her back to the house where she rifled through her old drawer of art supplies for pencils and a sketchpad. When they returned, he sat beside her and watched. "I'm a little nervous," she admitted. "I haven't drawn a portrait since I was like…eleven."

"Why not?" he asked.

She licked her lips. "Jeremy left." Jeff stroked her back in support.

Jeremy was shy about the attention, but he allowed it because he understood on an intuitive level that art was the way Joy's soul expressed itself in the physical world. The fact that she had stopped drawing portraits when he was taken away was a clear indication of her detachment from life.

"That girl's amazing," Jeff said as he watched his friend's face appear like magic on the paper.

"I know," Jeremy replied. Those were the two words that knocked any lingering hope out of Tracy's mind of ever being with him. The bracelet teeming with symbolism of their intertwining lives had not convinced her that he belonged to Joy, but those two words did; she finally let go of him. And Eddie McCormack, who had for years been struggling to get Joy's attention, took one look at the portrait she'd drawn of her boyfriend and threw in the towel, as well. It wasn't a defeat on either front, but rather a surrender that allowed them both to move closer to their intended partners.

CHAPTER FIFTEEN
The Summer of '95

It was a Thursday night in July when Jeremy cashed in on the skinny-dipping date. They were with Jeff and Hannah, per usual. A gallon of lemonade with vodka mixed into it was their jug for the night, although Jeremy still wasn't drinking. So far he hadn't said much to Joy about her new habits or about his old ones. Truth, he knew, had a way of revealing itself.

His head was out the window of Jeff's Nova so he could gaze at the canopy of trees above them on the narrow road that led to the pond in Hanson, a nearby town. Sometimes when they visited the pond he walked the long stretch to the parking lot underneath the trees that made a tunnel out of their branches while the Nova trudged beside him. As Joy liked to point out, Jeremy worshipped nature the way some people worship God. *They're the same thing*, he replied every time she did.

After a messy chug on the bottle, Hannah dragged her forearm across her mouth and announced, "I'm not skinny dipping 'cause I don't want to strip in front of you guys."

"Hannah," Joy exhaled impatiently, "you don't have to 'strip' in front of anyone."

"Why not?"

"Yeah, why not?" Jeff asked with an impish grin.

"Because you can take your bathing suit off after you get in the water."

"You just took all the fun out of it," Jeff complained and winked at Joy in the rear view mirror.

When they arrived at the empty parking lot where they usually parked, they re-evaluated. A dirt road led from the parking lot to the beach. It was wide enough for a car, but generally used as a foot-path. Now it was cordoned off with a rope. According to a sign, the beach closed at eight p.m. and was followed by the words *Police Take Notice*.

"If the cops come they'll see our car and bust us," Jeff observed.

"So we don't park here," Jeremy countered and jumped out of the car to unhook the rope. "They won't even know we're there unless they hear us from the parking lot."

Jeff drove onto the path, stopping after Jeremy reattached the hook to let him in the car. At the beach they finished off the plastic jug and left what remained of the vodka on the floor under a towel. Three docks were lined up in the pond for swimming races. Jeff stepped onto the middle one with the girls, lighting up, but Jeremy trailed behind to test the water with his feet.

"Like Heaven, huh bro?" Jeff observed when Jeremy caught up to the group. Out of politeness, he offered him the joint and lifted an eyebrow when his friend took it from his hand.

"It is Heaven," Jeremy replied as he lay down on the dock to take it all in— the panoramic night sky, the tepid water that his feet were dipping into, and the frogs singing to them. Joy curled up with her head in the crook of his arm and he held the joint to her lips while she inhaled. When he brought it to his own mouth for the second time, Jeff chided him to pass it over.

"Light another one. We're smoking this one," he answered. Then he took a deep inhale, rolled on top of Joy and exhaled the smoke into her mouth.

"It's always sex with you two, isn't it?" Jeff teased, but he sparked another one anyway.

They didn't answer him. They barely knew he was present. Jeremy's face was still lingering inches above Joy's. "Do it again," she said. This time when he blew the smoke into her lungs, he didn't pull his mouth away. He kissed her until she exhaled it back into his mouth. "More," she insisted and they continued the game until they'd smoked the whole thing.

"I'm gonna be freakin' blazed," he laughed and flopped onto his back.

"I already am," Hannah slurred. She lost her balance as she got to her feet, so her boyfriend had to hold onto her while she slipped out of her t-shirt. Then she did a hand-spring off the end of the dock into the water, and they forgot all about being quiet so the cops wouldn't hear.

"I want to do it!" Joy exclaimed and stripped down to her bikini, but every time she put her hands on the dock she chickened out. Finally, Jeremy held her torso and flipped her so that she landed feet first in the pond. When she came up for air, she was ecstatic, whooping and hollering about her new trick. The guys followed her into the water with cannonballs, and within seconds Jeff's shorts shot into the air and landed with a wet plop on the dock. Everyone else quickly shed their suits, except for Jeremy. "This was your idea, remember?" Joy teased.

Paranoia had set in. His bloodshot eyes were focused on the other couple.

"They can't see you, Jeremy. You can't see me, right?" Joy wisely pointed out.

"Well, no, but I can feel you."

"Then don't get close to them. If you get too close to Hannah, I'll have to kill her anyway."

He blew his breath out noisily, but nonetheless took his shorts off. He folded them neatly and placed them on the dock. "It's not the best night to be jealous," he noted.

Joy ignored the comment and swam away from him. "Try to catch me!" she called.

"You know I can't catch you in the water."

"That's why I said *try* to catch me." She took off and he trailed behind her in the deep water for a good ten minutes before he gave up. When he swam closer to Jeff and Hannah, he was careful to leave a safe distance between them.

"What's Joy doing?" Jeff asked.

"Waiting for me to catch her, but I can't."

"I bet I can," Jeff bragged.

"Doubt it. She's like seal." Jeff took off in Joy's direction anyway and she squealed with excitement as soon as she saw him. "Don't swim too close," Jeremy warned Hannah, "or Joy'll rip your head off."

"My naked boyfriend is chasing her!" Hannah began, then lowered her voice. "She's ridiculously jealous—once in school she punched Amanda for saying something about your ass."

Jeremy chuckled. "But seriously, move over there," he advised, and Hannah swam behind the dock. Only her head and arms showed over the top. "You should have heard what Amanda said *to* me," he confided. "That girl's nasty. But don't tell Joy. It'll start a big fight. Hey, check it out; she lost him." Jeff was floating on his back, contentedly gazing up at the night sky.

Off at a distance but sensing a conspiracy Joy shouted, "What are you two talking about?"

Jeremy winked at Hannah. "I was just telling her that if she swims too close you'll grab her hair like an alligator and drag her to the bottom of the pond."

"Get away from him Hannah!" Joy threatened before she gasped. "Wait, what did you say?"

"Oh shit," Jeremy muttered under his breath, then "nothing, sweetheart."

"You said *alligator*."

"Did I?" he replied, then softer to Hannah, "She has an irrational fear of alligators. I think it's a past life thing."

"A past what?" Hannah spewed.

"Jeremy, I'm scared!" Joy whined.

"I'm on my way, see?" he said as he swam to her, breast-stroking so his head was above the water. "There are no alligators in Massachusetts, Joy. It's too cold."

"There could be. Someone could have put one in here and it would live until winter!"

"Now who'd want to do that?"

"A b-bad person."

The stutter was alarming. "I'm right here," he repeated, and she threw her arms around his neck. "Shhh. It's okay." He'd have to talk her down quickly before she drowned them both.

"It might be right under, under, underneath us," she cried into his neck.

"There's nothing under us. Listen to me. If anything touches you, I'll drag *it* to the bottom of the pond." He stroked her back and she softened in his arms. "You're safe, see?"

"What's going on?" Hannah yelled over.

"Nothing," Jeremy reassured her. It would have taken days to explain the intricacies of Joy's brain that he had always been able to read like a road map. Just then his peripheral vision caught the headlights of a car pulling down the road to the beach. "Joy, listen," he coached, "get to the dock as quick as you can and get your clothes on. Hannah! Get dressed!"

Joy took off like an alligator really was chasing her and Hannah snatched her suit off the dock.

"Jeff!" the girls shouted repeatedly, but he was still floating fifty feet away, oblivious.

"What's up?" he yelled when he finally heard them, but then he saw the headlights.

"Cops," Jeremy advised and both girls nearly had a mental breakdown. Before they'd heard the word they had assumed it was another carload of kids and the biggest threat was being caught naked. "Throw me my shorts, Joy," Jeremy instructed from the water once he was close enough. It took a minute to get them on. They were army fatigues cut off at the knees, and were hard to pull on because they were wet.

Jeff was swimming toward the dock when he stopped and yelled, "Jeremy, the bag!" Joy saw the bag of weed first and stuffed it in her cutoffs. But just as Jeremy tossed the shorts to Jeff, who was still in the water, one of the officers caught the hand motion in his flashlight. Suddenly an obnoxiously loud voice was shouting, "Get your hands over your head!" Jeremy complied and exchanged a glance with Joy. "You in the water! Drop what you're holding and put your hands where I can see them…on the dock!"

"But—" Jeff started.

"Now!"

Jeff dropped the shorts. He placed his hands on the dock, then laid his forehead down on it too, letting out a groan as the wet shorts began to sink.

"Get up here where we can see you."

"Are you freaking kidding?" Jeff challenged.

"Does it look like we're kidding?" the loud cop clamored.

Jeff lifted himself onto the dock. In the illumination from the flashlights he was completely naked and so high that his eyes were like slits, his long hair dripping water onto his shoulders.

"Oh my God," Hannah mumbled into her fist and Joy busted out in a fit of nervous giggles.

"Where are your shorts?" one of the officers asked.

"Far as I can tell, they're at the bottom of the pond. You told me to drop 'em."

With his response, they all burst out laughing, even the cops. "Do us all a favor and go find them. Your buddy can help." Once they were diving for the shorts, the girls were told they could wait in the car, but then as they walked away the loud cop asked, "Which one of those two is Jeffrey Cosgrove?" They'd already run his license plate number.

"The naked one," Hannah answered innocently and both police officers chuckled.

"Any relation to Billy Cosgrove?" The girls nodded fervently. "His son?" They nodded some more. "His father was a wild man, too. We went to high school together."

Joy spotted an opportunity. "You might know my dad then, Bob Sanders?"

"You mean you're Bobby and Mary's kid? And you're, what, dating Billy Cosgrove's son?"

"No, no, no," Joy corrected. "My boyfriend's the one *with* the shorts."

The officers got a good laugh out of that one. "Miss Sanders—" The girls were already walking away toward the car. "Your boyfriend can drive. He doesn't look as stoned as the rest of you." Of course he was every bit as stoned, but he wasn't drunk.

After ten minutes of diving to the bottom of the lake and feeling around in the mud and muck, the guys gave up on recovering Jeff's shorts. They climbed onto the dock and Jeff tied his t-shirt around his waist. The police officers walked them to the car and did a quick perusal inside it with a flashlight, but thanks to the girls, the vodka bottle was safely stashed under the seat.

"Mr. Cosgrove? Tell your dad Rich Leo said hello."

"Rich Leo?" he repeated with a crooked grin.

"Now get in the back seat with your girlfriend. Your buddy's driving." Jeff opened the car door. "Oh and from now on," Rich Leo added, "keep your stoned naked ass out of Hanson."

"Right," Jeff said seriously and crawled into the car before they all burst out laughing.

And that became the line of the summer. Every time they had the most remote opportunity, they teased Jeff about his *stoned naked ass*. Even years later, when the group had disbanded and life had become much more complicated than it was during the summer of 1995, they each in their own ways would think back on that night and laugh, or in Jeff's case, at least grin a little bit.

On Jeremy's eighteenth birthday in August, he took the day off from work so he could spend it with Joy. The plan was to have his favorite breakfast, blueberry pancakes with powdered sugar, at a restaurant in Brant Rock, and then venture down to the beach in Plymouth with the cliffs. All was going according to schedule until their flirtatious waitress asked for a ride on his motorcycle and Joy stormed out of the restaurant before they had a chance to eat. What Jeremy didn't always understand was that her fits of jealousy were deeply rooted in fear. Every person they met held the threat of snatching him away.

He didn't say anything once he caught up outside the restaurant, only mounted his bike and waited for her to do the same before he headed to Plymouth. Joy had her bathing suit on under her clothes and quickly stripped down to it, but Jeremy was stuck with his jeans. He rolled them up to his knees and took his shirt off before they ambled down to the tidal pools to investigate. The water was warm on their feet, and clear, making it easy to find hermit crabs, and even a few star-fish. Black-headed birds raced past them on skinny legs. (They were called laughing gulls, Jeremy said).

Whenever she was with him at the beach, Joy had noticed, the sea birds came closer, like they were drawn to him. At home it was the chickadees who hopped brazenly near. Even when he took a step toward them on his silent feet they didn't fly away.

"I'm hungry," she fussed. Jeremy was squatting down next to a tidal pool.

"Next time we go to breakfast, we ought to eat," he teased.

"I hate that girl," she fussed. "I'm never eating there again."

Jeremy watched a crab walk into his hand like an old friend. "Me neither," he agreed with a mischievous grin. "Want to hold him?"

"Will he bite me?"

Jeremy shook his head and deposited the crab into her hands. Joy gasped when she felt the feet scurrying across her palm. He smiled at her reaction before his eyes scanned the steep cliffs that lined the beach and then the water itself, rolling in as melodically as musical notes.

"This would be a good place to die," he mused.

"I hate when you say things like that," she countered.

"Why? It's not like dying is the worst thing that can happen."

"Most people think it is," she argued.

"Most people are wrong. Besides, it won't happen today."

"How do you know?"

"'Cause I haven't had my birthday cake yet." He smiled and he was the little boy Jeremy again, playing in the sand and eagerly awaiting the yellow cake with chocolate frosting.

His comment reminded her of his birthday present that she'd slipped into the pocket of his leather jacket. "Wait here," she directed and ran to where they had dropped their stuff. When she returned, she handed him the small box that contained a stone arrow head strung on a leather cord.

"You used to like them, remember?"

"I still like them," he said softly and tenderly kissed her lips.

"So put it on," Joy urged impatiently.

He brought the box closer to his face to study the deep grooves on the stone. The arrowhead was black and had three tiny stones tied onto the neck, a rough piece of turquoise and two jade spheres. "Will you hold it in your hands for a few minutes?" he asked.

"Why?"

"We leave traces of energy on everything we touch. I want yours all over that stone."

She lifted the arrowhead from the box and held it between her hands, like they were in prayer, enchanted by his words. She had no idea how he knew the things he did, but there was no doubt in her mind that he was right. He smiled his satisfaction before he turned his attention to the hermit crab who had found its way to a group of three others. When he was done playing with them, he turned back to her and she slid the cord over his head.

"Want to go eat?" he asked and she took his outstretched hand. The necklace looked good on him, like it belonged there. It reminded her of the dream stories he used to tell her about when they were children. They were different than the ones about the two Native American men they both dreamed about, Running Deer and the other younger man whose name she couldn't recall. He said they were dreams about the two of them together in a past life.

"Jeremy, do you remember the dreams you used to tell me about?" He stopped walking and waited for more information. "You said you dreamed about us when we were Indians." He grinned and started walking again. "What did you say my name was?"

"It sounded like *Segonaway*."

She nodded at the familiar word. "Do you remember what it meant?"

"I think they said *Sleeping Star* because you didn't talk until you were older—like me this time. Then later you became a storyteller."

She was taken aback by the detail of his response, and also the fact that if she'd lived before she might not have been the intellectual she was in this life. "It's not about the mind," he said as if she'd expressed it out loud. "The mind is temporary. It's the soul that survives. Our soul is perfect. Once we pass out of our bodies, we're perfect again—that's what Running Deer said."

"What else?" she prodded. "What were we like when we were Indians?"

"You know that place between awake and asleep? Sometimes when I'm in that place, I see us near a river, looking for rocks as little kids. But once I saw us in the river when we were older and we were making love. We weren't married yet and we weren't supposed to, but we did."

"But how do you know all that?" she asked. "If you're only seeing it?"

They were dressing now to get back on the bike. Jeremy fell onto the sand to tie his boots. "It's like someone's telling me the story while I'm seeing it—like I'm watching a movie but there aren't words. There's just a knowing. It's different than when Running Deer talks to me—then I hear—in my head I hear words." He laughed. "That sounds crazy."

"I don't think you're crazy. But do you think it's real, Jeremy? I mean, really?"

"I know it's real," he said quietly.

He'd left his shirt open and her eyes were focused on the arrowhead on his chest. It looked like it belonged there. She couldn't fully accept that she'd been Native American in a past life, but she was completely convinced that he had. "What was your name?" she asked.

"Stands like a Bear," he answered, then made a small hand gesture to clarify. "Standing Bear."

150

When they arrived back home for Jeremy's birthday feast with fists full of wild roses they'd found on the beach path, Mary gave them the corn to shuck. They were on the landing where they used to watch for birds, with corn silk on their legs, when Ethan approached and told them that he was moving out of the family home and into an apartment with Eddie McCormack.

"Is this good or bad?" Joy asked Lily on the sly as soon as she got a chance.

Lily sighed, "I don't know yet." Eddie had called the house a few times and asked for Lily instead of Ethan, but she hadn't been forthcoming with details. She'd been smiling a lot, though, Joy had noticed, as if she'd had plastic surgery to hold her lips in place. "But the good news for you is that I'm moving out of the honeymoon suite into Ethan's room."

"That is good news," Joy happily agreed and rushed over to whisper it to Jeremy.

The rest of the evening was a hit, especially Mary's cake. Joy could still taste the chocolate frosting on Jeremy's lips when she kissed him good night in the front yard. Everything seemed to be exactly as it should be in the universe.

Then, the next day after work, he dropped the bomb about leaving school. He hadn't showered yet and there was sawdust in his hair that was pulled into a ponytail for work. He and Bob were working with another small construction crew, building a new house in the Rexham Beach area of Marshfield. Joy and Jeremy were sitting on the front steps and he was inexplicably smoking a cigarette, which made the wall between them seem even higher, like he'd been harboring two secrets instead of one.

"How long have you known this?" she asked.

"I found out in May that I wasn't passing."

"How could you be so irresponsible?" she flung out recklessly. He turned his head to look at her and his tongue moved methodically over his bottom lip, but he didn't say anything. "Do you have any idea how stupid you're being? Now you're never going to get a good job."

He stood up and backed away from her energy. "I have a good job," he stated calmly.

She snorted disgust out her nostrils. "Is that all you're ever going to do, build houses?"

Bob was right inside the screen door reading the newspaper in his favorite chair, within earshot, though it hadn't occurred to Joy. Jeremy stepped closer and bent down so his face was close to hers. "Don't you have any respect for your dad, for everything he does for you?" he demanded.

"Is that why you're doing this, because you think you have to be like him?"

Jeremy took her hand and dragged her closer to the street so her father wouldn't hear anymore of her angry comments before he shouted, "I'd be proud of that!"

She sighed. "Don't you understand that you can do anything with your life?"

"Like what, Joy?" He threw his arms out.

"We used to talk about you going to veterinary school, remember?" she suggested as he fumbled another cigarette into his mouth.

"We used to talk about me being a doctor, too, but how the fuck is that gonna happen when I can't make it through high school?"

"You could if you wanted." To Joy, Jeremy was a modern day sage. How hard could it be to graduate from high school when you knew secrets of the universe?

But her words hit Jeremy like bullets in his chest. He wasn't good enough. "Ask me to move to the other side of the world, I'll go," he said angrily. "Ask me to build you a house as big as Ty Connors', I'll do it. But what's the point in asking me to do something I can't?"

"You just think you can't."

"Don't you think I'd be a doctor if I could? I failed Biology twice, Joy, *twice*. And the third time I got a D but only 'cause the guy was nice. I didn't know what the fuck he was talkin' 'bout." *I'm not like Ty*, he thought, but didn't express it. *I don't have his brain.*

Mary pulled the old Chevy into the driveway and stepped out of it in her waitress uniform. Both sets of youthful blue eyes took her in as she greeted them, but what those eyes saw was something vastly different from each other. To Jeremy, Mary was someone who loved her kids (and he included himself in that group) so fiercely that she returned to the same tiresome job day after day, and then came home to take care of them. But to Joy she was a woman who'd reached middle age with no education, no career and a life that was financially insecure. Life could be more than that, she was so sure, more than just a struggle to make ends meet.

"Sorry you're disappointed," Jeremy said once Mary was inside the house. The cigarette fell from his lips and he took a few strides down Fairview Lane toward his house before he turned back and added, "But I can't change this, Joy, not even for you."

CHAPTER SIXTEEN
Billy Jack and the Sea Wall

Joy never followed up on the design school in New York. The idea of living five hours away from Ty for the next four years hadn't made her blink an eyelash, but to be that far away from Jeremy was unfathomable. Therefore, she took art and business classes at the closest state college and kept her part time job selling coffee at Marylou's News.

For the first year and a half, life didn't change much. Jeremy continued to work for Bob and spend most of his free time at the Sanders' house. Then, through a work contact, he stumbled upon a year-round rental in the Rexham Beach neighborhood in Marshfield. It was a small two bedroom ranch, and on New Year's Day, 1997 he moved into it with Jeff. Initially, it was a vast improvement in Jeremy and Joy's lifestyle. She spent more nights at his house than her own so they could curl up in their own bed knowing they had the whole night together without Jeremy needing to scramble out the window. For four months it was paradise....

Then Jeremy picked up a drink. And all bets were off.

It was only a matter of time, given the lifestyle he was surrounded by. Not only did his roommate drink daily, but they had parties at their house several times a week. Joy had not been able to wrap her imagination around Jeremy's need for abstention from alcohol until the Saturday night in May when he gave in to her request to join the group in shots of tequila.

The first thing she noticed was how talkative he became after only a few shots. He was usually thoughtful in his speech, but now all kinds of asinine comments were pouring out of his mouth. The two couples were congregated on the small deck behind the house after a cookout, Joy on Jeremy's lap, when he did something that struck her as grossly uncharacteristic—he swallowed the worm at the bottom of the tequila bottle.

"Oh man, I've fucking missed this part of you!" Jeff exclaimed excitedly. All the while Joy was thinking *I don't even know this part of you*.

And she didn't. There were many things in Jeremy's past that he'd not told her about. He'd started drinking when he was thirteen and had been arrested three times for alcohol-related incidents before finding his way back to Marshfield. In addition to the foster homes, twice he'd spent time in a juvenile detention center, but not even Jeff knew about that.

"I hear the buzz you get from those worms is like trippin'," Jeff threw out.

"It's been frigging years since I've tripped on acid."

"You've done acid?" Joy gasped.

"A long time ago," Jeremy said simply. "Got a butt, Jeff?"

Jeff tossed him his Winstons and Joy got off his lap because she was afraid he'd catch her hair on fire. The combination of Jeremy + alcohol was giving birth to an unsettled feeling in her gut, but she figured it could be fixed by not inviting him to join in the next time they drank. Unfortunately, her scenario was the equivalent to closing a barn door after the horses have run out of it.

A few shots later he was climbing onto the deck railing and walking across it like an acrobat at the circus. The visual was one Joy would forever hold in her memory. He was barefoot and wearing the suede fringe coat she had given him for Christmas with no shirt under it, and his arms were out for balance, so the coat was open, revealing the arrowhead on his bare chest. The most defiant look was in his eyes and around his lips that were pursed on a cigarette. That was the most shocking part to Joy—even more so than the behavior that was scaring her—the defiance that seemed to have replaced the innocence his mouth usually revealed.

"You're doped, man," Jeff pointed out. "You could fall."

"Please get down," Joy urged.

"It's only ten feet high," Jeremy replied with a laugh, and continued across the two by fours surrounding the deck with his strange ambulation that resembled a rain dance.

"Maybe twelve, Billy Jack," Jeff stated. "And the ground's still frozen."

Jeremy became as still as a statue. "I love that movie!" he suddenly exclaimed. "Let's go get it." A war cry howled from his lungs as he leaped from the railing. Joy and Hannah both gasped, but he landed safely on his bare feet.

"Hide his keys," Jeff instructed. Joy stared at him, silently asking *are you serious*? "Do it!" he snapped and took off after Jeremy who was headed toward the driveway.

She bolted into the kitchen and opened the junk drawer where he usually tossed his keys. There they were, exactly where she expected them to be. She heard the guys' voices coming closer, grabbed the keys and ran to Jeremy's bedroom. The idea of him driving his motorcycle while drunk was so un-Jeremy-like. He was ridiculously cautious, almost anal, when it came to his bike. But this new Jeremy, the one she'd just met, seemed unpredictable and dangerous. She heard the kitchen door squeak as it opened and threw the keys under the bed.

"What the fuck, bro? Let me drive," she heard Jeff say.

Jeremy's hand was rifling through the junk. "What'd you do with them?" he asked. Joy entered the kitchen to intervene. As soon as he saw her face he knew she'd taken them. "Hand 'em over," he ordered and stepped aggressively toward her.

"Don't touch me, Jeremy," she warned and held her hand up, ready to push him. He stopped walking, and looked at her like she'd slapped him.

"It's all right, man," Jeff coaxed. "Come on, let's go get that movie."

Jeremy stood motionless, his brow wrinkled in thought. His eyes were boring through Joy and she was staring back at him, trying to figure out who the hell he was. "I would never hurt you," he said. She stepped toward him and slid her hands around his neck. Still, he didn't budge.

"I know," she assured him and touched his mouth with hers. She had to push her tongue in between his stubborn lips to get him to kiss her back. His response was animalistic. He roughly unbuttoned her blouse, and his mouth followed his fingers down her neck to breasts.

"Wait, wait—I'm still here," Jeff pleaded but neither one of them acknowledged him. Joy pushed Jeremy's fringe coat off his shoulders onto the floor. Her hands were on his ass already pulling him against her when Jeff retreated.

"Un-fucking-believable!" he lamented when he plopped down in the lounge chair outside next to his girlfriend.

"What?" Hannah asked, twirling a long, glossy strand of hair around her finger.

"They're frigging screwing again."

"They are? What happened to Billy Jones?"

"Who?"

"*Billy Jones*—the movie Jeremy wanted to see."

"Just…hand me the tequila," he said gruffly and downed the last of it. "It's *Billy Jack* and I don't think he cares about it anymore."

They stayed outside until they figured the coast was clear to re-enter the house. Jeff cautiously opened the door, half-expecting to find the couple naked on the kitchen floor. Jeremy came out of the bedroom first. "Where's the tequila?" was the first thing he asked. "Didya' get the movie?" was the second.

"I'll drive to Blockbuster," Joy offered as she embraced him from behind.

But Jeremy's mind was on the tequila. He pushed her arms off to go in search of it, and grumbled when he saw the empty bottle in the trash. He found a full one in the pantry and took a slug, his fingers clutching the neck. Joy didn't want the bottle in the car but she didn't say so. He'd already promised not to drive his motorcycle after he'd been drinking and that was enough of a victory for one evening. Jeremy, she knew, always stood by his promises.

He was loud and obnoxious again by the time they made it to Blockbuster, so Joy suggested he and Jeff wait in the car. When the girls returned with the movie, the guys insisted they go to the beach instead, and they'd been doing some serious work on the tequila bottle.

"Just drive home, Joy. We can walk to Rexham Beach," Jeff suggested.

"No, Brant Rock!" Jeremy insisted and Joy acquiesced.

Numerous cars were parked along the concrete sea wall; the passengers watching the dark water wash onto the sand. It was a perfect summer night to be in Brant Rock, Massachusetts. The air was balmy and sticky with salt, and clouds were swimming past a nearly full moon. The girls sat on the warm car hood and the guys wandered down the concrete sea wall, laughing, practicing Billy Jack kicks and passing the bottle back and forth. From a car radio, Led Zeppelin's *Goin' to California* was blaring and the girls could hear Jeremy and Jeff singing along in the distance. Everything felt safe and familiar.

Then a sound changed the course of the night. It was the voice of someone shouting—Jeff, Joy thought— and when the girls looked over, only one silhouette was visible on the wall. If the guys had been down at the other end of the beach where the sea wall was shorter and an easy leap from it to the sand, it would have made sense. But they weren't. And below the twelve-foot wall were piles of sharp rocks, not sand.

"Jeremy!" Joy shrieked and took off running. Soon she could see Jeff darting toward her.

"He's in the rocks!" he shouted and bolted down the steps that led to the beach. She was right on his heels with Hannah close behind. Curious onlookers were exiting their cars. "Call an ambulance!" Jeff screamed at them. "Don't touch him," he said to Joy, but it was too late. She was on top of him trying to speak, but couldn't get her voice to work. Jeremy was unconscious, dead she thought. His head was cut open and his face was splattered with blood.

"Don't touch his head, Joy," Jeff said as calmly as he could manage—his breath was coming in heaves. She dropped her face to his chest and wailed.

A moment later, someone was shining a flashlight on Jeremy and they could see that his neck was twisted to one side in an odd position and that there was blood dripping from his skull. All around him was broken glass from the tequila bottle, and one of his hands was still grasping its neck. Jeff loosened his grip on it, revealing deep wounds on Jeremy's palm. He was barefoot, so his feet were cut up from the rocks, too. The fringe coat had protected his torso, externally at least.

"Honey," the man with the flashlight said, "back away from him. His neck might be broken."

"No!" Joy screamed but not at the man. It was directed at Jeremy. "You can't do this—you can't leave without me! Jeremy don't...please don't, please don't leave without me!"

The paramedics were already heading down the steps with the board when he regained consciousness. Joy's head was on his chest, her whole body convulsing in sobs. In the strangeness of the moment it occurred to her that the motion of her body shaking him might have brought him back from death, but to Jeff and Hannah who had been watching the scene with horror, he had come back for one simple reason—because Joy had insisted on it.

While the paramedics moved him onto the board, Jeff embraced Joy and stroked her back to calm her down. She was distressed but also in pain—her head felt like *she'd* fallen off the wall.

By the time they caught up with him at the emergency room, a spinal cord injury had been ruled out, and a doctor was stitching the numerous lacerations. Jeremy had also fractured his skull and three ribs, broken an ankle and sustained a concussion. But the bottom line was that nothing had happened to his body that wasn't going to heal in time—which was remarkable for someone who'd been drunk enough to think it was a good idea to walk along the edge of a sea wall twelve feet above jagged rocks as if it were a tightrope. For when it was all said and done, that's what they discovered he'd been doing. About a third of his head was shaved so the doctor could stitch it, and that was his biggest grievance. They were feeding him Demerol through an intravenous line to keep the headache and other bodily pains at bay.

"I'll look like a punk," he complained when his fingers grazed the shaven part of his head.

"With those eyes?" a young nurse said, and Joy's fingernails protracted like cat claws.

"You could have lost a whole lot more than your hair," Belinda scolded. "Am I staying here tonight or are you?" she asked a little while later, after everyone else had gone home.

"I am," Joy answered without looking at her.

It was the first time they'd been in the same room since the day Joy had witnessed the physical abuse, and she still had no intention of acknowledging the woman. Belinda kissed Jeremy's forehead and turned to leave. There was a moment where she hesitated as if she considered saying something, but then she kept walking. Joy laid her head on the mattress. The pain was intense. She was feeling Jeremy's head trauma, though she didn't know it.

"Come here, sweetheart," he said and she nestled her face against his belly. He laid his hands on her head and she felt warm energy permeate her scalp. Finally, the pain began to subside. She closed her eyes, not realizing that her boyfriend was healing her, and fell asleep.

CHAPTER SEVENTEEN

Hitting Bottom

If Belinda had spoken the words out loud that she had been thinking when she walked out of the hospital room, Joy would have heard *make sure he gets sober or you're in for one hell of a ride*. Although they were words of wisdom learned through her own history and heartache, Joy never would have taken the advice, not from Belinda. She thought she knew Jeremy better than his mother did, and although for the most part she was right, when it came to his alcoholism—for that's what it was—she was dead wrong.

The alteration in Jeremy once alcohol re-entered his life was immediate and far-reaching. When sober, he had little to say, but he wasn't quiet in the thoughtful, introspective way that he used to be. His energy was often discontented and angry. And when he was drinking, he was wildly unpredictable. He was a risk-taker and a fighter who would take on anyone just to get the anger out. As his alcoholism progressed, Joy did what most people do with the alcoholics in their lives that they don't recognize as sick— she made excuses for him and she tried to negotiate. But alcoholism is a disease; a person might as well attempt reasoning with cancer cells.

During daylight hours, Jeremy would accompany her to the sand dunes at Rexham Beach so she could draw the sea gulls or the wild grasses. Sometimes she'd make him lie still while the ocean breezes blew his hair so she could try to capture the way it fell on his neck and shoulders. Like when they were children, he gladly went anywhere she dragged him. But once the sun set and Jeff returned from work, the dynamic shifted with the alcohol intake. Joy started spending more nights at home on Fairview Lane than with Jeremy, because he was too difficult to be around when he was drunk, and at night he was always drunk.

One thing happened in May of 1998 that held the potential to change their entire future: Hannah missed her period. On the way back from CVS where they went to buy a pregnancy test, she told Joy that her parents would never accept her boyfriend into their family.

"Why not?" Joy asked. "Jeff is the nicest guy I know, except Jeremy."

"And your brother," Hannah replied, looking out the window, not at Joy.

"Well, yeah." That was a given. Ethan was always coming to their rescue in one way or another, fixing their cars or slipping Joy money, but still, why the comparison?

"My parents talk about Ethan all the time because he works on their car. They say he's so responsible and polite," Hannah continued. "And they don't like Jeff. They think his hair's too long and he drinks too much."

"Yeah, blah, blah, blah, Ethan's the greatest. My parents say that all the time too. But you love Jeff, don't you?" Joy challenged.

"You know I do. They don't want me to date him, though, never mind have a baby with him. If Jeff wants to get married they won't let me."

"They won't *let you*? Hannah, it's not their decision."

Hannah shrugged dejectedly. "Do you think you'll marry Jeremy someday?"

"Of course," Joy replied, "I could never marry anyone else."

Hannah took the pregnancy test at the Rexham house while the guys were still at work and as she predicted, the little blue plus sign appeared like magic on the stick. Jeff wasn't upset like she'd thought he'd be—like she was. To him, having a baby meant having a family again. He'd been fourteen when his mother died from cancer, and shortly thereafter, his dad had started disappearing with his new girlfriend. Chris, his older brother, had been off at college by then, so Jeff had basically been on his own until Jeremy'd wandered into his life…and became his family.

That night at bedtime, after they'd begun to digest the news, Jeremy said something to Joy that surprised her: "I think we ought to lay off partying for a while." His breath was labored, and his voice trembling. She sat next to him on the bed and stroked his back. "I'm not sure I can do this," he admitted, "but I want to try."

162

It was the perfect opportunity to talk about his alcoholism but Joy missed it because she didn't understand the rarity of his disclosure or what was driving it.

"That could be us," he sighed. "It could be us having a baby."

"Is that what you're worried about? I'm really careful about taking the pills."

"I'm not worried about having a baby, Joy. I'm worried about being a father."

"Isn't it the same thing? Besides, you'll make a great father."

"No, I won't. Not like this," he murmured.

Once in bed he told her that he'd like to find his own father, to discover what he was like and why he'd left. Joy interpreted it as a passing comment, the kind of thought that drifts through the mind before sleep, not one so deeply embedded that it might prompt him to take action.

For four weeks, the two couples stopped drinking, though the guys smoked their share of weed. The girls didn't mind that. It didn't incite the behaviors that brought on arguments with them or fist fights with other guys, like alcohol did. For weeks they were happy, all four of them living together in the Rexham house and excitedly anticipating the baby's arrival.

Then it changed. They were at Brant Rock Beach when Jeff noticed a trickle of blood moving down Hannah's thigh. It was that one moment, Jeff later said—that thin line of blood—that changed all their lives forever. Hannah miscarried, and within days had moved out of his house and ended the relationship. And Jeff—who had not the slightest idea how to cope—didn't. He started binge drinking, and Jeremy supported him by drinking alongside him.

Joy tried unsuccessfully to convince Jeff to accept the breakup and move on with his life. "It's not your fault," she told him. "This isn't about you. It's about Hannah's parents."

"It's about me not being good enough," he said with his head hanging heavily.

She had to resist the urge to slap him. How could he think that about himself? "Listen to me," she scolded and noticed that she sounded exactly like her mother, "Hannah is the problem here, Hannah bowing to her parents instead of following her heart. That's the problem, Jeff, not you."

"You think she still loves me? So you think she'll come back?"

"Jeff," she began, then sighed. This wouldn't be easy for her to say or for him to hear. "I know she loves you, but I also know she won't be back."

"How could you know?"

"Because I know Hannah. Whoever she dates next will be someone her parents approve of."

When Joy finally talked to her after leaving numerous unreturned messages, Hannah indicated that she'd been spending time with Amanda and Kaitlyn. To Joy it was a three-foot dagger through her back. She surrendered the friendship, but Jeff still held out hope. There was zero chance of reconciliation, and his failure to grasp that reality led to an even greater disaster.

It was in June of 1998 when Hannah miscarried and the group splintered. On August 15th of the same summer Jeremy turned twenty-one. He and Jeff were picking up a keg of beer for his birthday party when they ran into Amanda. Jeff told her to invite Hannah to the party. Hannah declined; nonetheless, Amanda showed up with Kaitlyn and Vinnie Perrone. The party was going full throttle when they arrived, the boom of electric bass exploding from a stereo on the deck and making the small house shake.

"Ganja!" Nate yelled as they entered the yard, and that was the call that captured Joy's attention.

"What the hell are you doing here?" she demanded. She hadn't spoken a word to Kaitlyn since the infamous junior/senior prom.

Jeff quickly intervened. "It's all right, Joy. I invited them."

Joy spun to look him in the eye. "You what?" The crowd on the deck grew silent. The *bom-sh, bom-sh, bom-sh* of the bass played as background music through the speakers.

"We ran into Amanda when we picked up the keg, and we told her to ask Hannah."

"Oh Jeff," Joy sighed with pity in her voice.

"Do you want us to leave?" Amanda asked. Joy was already shaking her head *no* when Vinnie opened his notoriously big mouth.

"Still the bitch, huh Joy?" he taunted, which was all it took to call Jeremy out of the kitchen where he'd been talking about dirt bikes with Ethan and Eddie.

"What'd you just say?" he asked as he pushed open the screen door, Ethan on his heels.

"Whoa, whoa, Vinnie, watch your mouth," Jeff coached, trying to diffuse the tension.

Vinnie's eyes shifted to Jeremy and Ethan, but it wasn't enough to send a message to his brain to stop spitting out stupidities. "Ah, so you're still screwing the Cherokee," he muttered.

"The *what*?" Joy screamed, outraged.

She'd never heard the nickname the prep guys had given Jeremy, largely, she figured out later, because of the fringe jacket she'd given him and he insisted on wearing every single day, even in hot weather. She noticed Vinnie's horror-stricken expression and turned in time to see her boyfriend pounce off the deck rail. Within seconds, the situation went from tense to explosive. Jeremy landed on top of him, and started pounding him with both fists. Luckily for both of them, Ethan was there and pulled him off. Vinnie got in one good punch, enough to later blacken Jeremy's eye.

Once the police arrived, Jeremy might have escaped arrest if he'd kept his mouth shut, but he didn't because he was wasted. Even though Vinnie was the one covered in blood, Jeremy insisted that the police should be arresting him. In the end, they were both arrested for assault and battery, and Jeremy got slapped with the extra charge of resisting arrest.

"Stay here, Joy," Ethan ordered and followed the cruiser to the police station.

She plopped down on the deck steps. Most of the kids had scrambled when the cops arrived with flashing lights, but Amanda and Kaitlyn were lingering awkwardly. The bass from the stereo was still thumping and making the deck vibrate. Jeff slapped the power button. In the silence the energy between Joy and her former friends grew even more uncomfortable.

"So how's my ex-best friend Hannah?" Joy tossed out angrily.

"Not that great, actually," Kaitlyn ventured.

"Is she okay?" Jeff asked.

"Who cares, Jeff?" Joy interrupted before they could answer. "She fucked you over, remember? She fucked us all over."

Jeff was standing behind her and kissed the top of her head. "Yeah, I remember," he said sedately. "Come on inside, girls. Let's put this high school crap behind us."

Amanda and Kaitlyn exchanged a furtive glance, waiting for Joy to object, but she didn't, so they followed Jeff inside the house and sat silently at the kitchen table while he dug out a gallon of vodka and 7-Up and handed them each a glass.

"Let's toast Jeremy's birthday," Amanda suggested.

Jeff's eyes met Joy's. "To Billy Jack," he said and held his glass up. They all tapped their glasses and took a drink, even though the other girls weren't in on the private joke.

"Just so you know," Kaitlyn suddenly said, "nothing happened between me and Ty."

The silence that followed was so uncomfortable that Jeff muttered, "Yeah, I shoulda left the stereo on," and Amanda released a nervous giggle.

"I didn't even like him. I just thought…"

"Thought what?" Joy challenged.

"That you didn't love him."

"I did," Joy quickly replied. Jeff cocked his head to the side in response to her comment, and she continued, "Obviously, not the way I love Jeremy. But I did love him."

"You're where you should be," Jeff offered. "Nothing else matters."

Joy nodded her agreement. For several hours afterward, the vodka flowed and old friendships were rekindled, although Joy was beginning to worry that Amanda and Kaitlyn were a little *too* friendly with Jeff. They were making risqué comments about his body that was in great shape from building houses with his father, and were lifting his shirt to check out his abs.

"You guys shouldn't be doing that," Joy scolded. "Remember, he's Hannah's ex?"

Right about then the door swung open and Ethan walked in with Jeremy in tow. His eyes coldly appraised the scene at the table, the half empty gallon of vodka, and the tanked group that was gathered around it. He shook his head disapprovingly.

Jeremy's eye was bluish-black and swollen half-shut. "I'll get your money, Ethan," he stated quietly and headed toward the bedroom.

"Wait," Ethan's deep voice boomed and Jeremy stopped in his tracks. "I don't want your money, Jeremy. I'm not pissed off about the God damned bail money."

"What *are* you pissed about?" Jeff asked, but he was buzzed and there was laughter in his voice.

Ethan's eyes laid him out. "Stay out of this Jeff. This is the last time I bail you out of jail, Jeremy, you got that?" Jeremy nodded slowly. "You'll have to deal with Dad tomorrow."

"No," Joy intervened, "Daddy won't find out."

"Bullshit he won't," Ethan snapped. "I'm telling him first thing in the morning. What the hell happened to you, Joy? Your boyfriend gets arrested and you don't have any more sense than to sit here and get trashed? You used to be smarter than that." He pointed at Jeremy. "Get your shit together," he admonished and exited the house.

"Dude's a buzz kill," Jeff joked.

"Shut up, Jeff," Jeremy said. "He's right."

"No, he's not," Jeff argued.

"Yeah, he is, man. He's right about everything." Jeremy walked to his bedroom and Joy followed him. "I don't want to talk about it," he said before she asked. "Let's just call it a day, all right?" The springs from the old mattress creaked as he plopped down on it.

"But it's your birthday."

He made a scoffing sound with his head resting in his hands. "Yeah, it's my twenty-first birthday and I've already managed to fuck up my entire life."

"That's ridiculous," Joy argued. "You got into one fight."

"Tonight. How many fights have I been in this summer, five…six? I'm all done, Joy."

"What do you mean you're done?" she asked and sat next to him on the bed.

"I don't know what I mean. I just know I can't live like this anymore."

Joy kissed his mouth but he barely kissed her back because he was annoyed that she didn't seem to be listening or trying to understand, which was verified by her next comment. "Come have a drink with us. You'll feel better."

He lifted his eyes and looked straight into hers like he was trying to catch a glimpse of whatever was inside her brain. "If I have a drink, it won't be one drink. Do you get that yet?" He held his other hand out and it was trembling because he'd gone too long without one.

"You're just upset about Vinnie. It wasn't your fault; it was his."

"It was mine. It was my fault, Joy. I lost control…again. I'm so tired of this. I'm so tired of trying to control something I can't control. Can't you understand that?"

She didn't understand, nor did she pretend to, so he let out a frustrated sigh and let her lead him to the kitchen where she immediately joined back into the groups' antics. They were doing shots of Sambuca, and Amanda was dangerously close to Jeff with her hand on his thigh. No one liked the fact that Jeremy refused to do shots, particularly given the fact that it was his birthday they were supposedly celebrating. At his urging, Joy finally relented and went to bed with him.

"He only would have had to ask me once," Kaitlyn said as they walked away.

Jeremy half expected Joy to knock her out of her chair like she did in fourth grade, but she was too drunk to catch Kaitlyn's meaning. She fell onto the squeaky bed and whined about the ceiling fan making her dizzy. He had to explain that it wasn't turned on. It was the Sambuca in her bloodstream that was making it rotate.

Jeremy pulled her onto his chest. Her breathing was falling into rhythm with his until a loud thump next door in Jeff's bedroom startled her. "Shh," Jeremy crooned. "Go to sleep."

A burst of female laughter made Joy snap into a sitting position. "They're in his bed."

"Good for him." He meant it as a dismissive statement, but Joy didn't take it that way.

"What do you mean by that?" she demanded.

"Oh man, are you serious? 'Cause I'm not gonna frigging fight over this. The guy's lonely. Big God damned fucking deal—he's got a girl in his bed."

"He's got two girls in his bed, and Amanda's a wicked slut. She'll do anything."

"Yeah, I remember." Joy's eyes narrowed and her body took the posture of a rattlesnake ready to strike. Jeremy sat up beside her so he was looking straight into her bloodshot eyes. "I've never touched anyone else and you know that. What more do you want?"

"Did she try something with you?" Joy asked.

He let out an exasperated sigh. "Okay, listen. In high school, okay? When you were with Ty. I told her to fuck off. I don't like the girl and I never have."

Despite his reassurances Joy reached over the headboard and pounded on the wall between their bedroom and Jeff's. "Amanda!" she screamed.

"What's the matter, Joy?" Jeff shouted through the wall.

Jeremy had a moment of lucid thought. "Lock the door!" he yelled. "Hurry before Joy beats the crap out of her." She took off in the direction of Jeff's bedroom, but he beat her to the door and locked it.

"Why're you mad?" Amanda asked meekly through the door.

"Did you try to sleep with Jeremy?"

"No!" she exclaimed, but then added, "oh wait, do you mean in high school?"

After about ten minutes Joy's hysterics gave way to silence, so Jeremy got out of bed to make sure she wasn't passed out on the floor. He found her on the couch under a blanket. "Why're you out here?" he asked.

"I don't want to sleep with you," Joy replied. He pivoted and headed to his bedroom. "Things have got to change!" she shouted at his back.

"Yeah, no shit," Jeremy answered and kept walking.

CHAPTER EIGHTEEN
Goin' to California

The change was quicker and more drastic than Joy had imagined. Notice of it came in the form of a letter that was left on the front steps of the family home on Fairview Lane. It wouldn't have come to that if she had talked things through the morning after the argument, or if she had taken Jeremy's phone calls over the following two days, but she hadn't done either of those things.

It was just after 2:00 a.m. on Tuesday when she awakened with a premonitory feeling and a memory or dream—she wasn't sure which—of the roar of his motorcycle engine. She sat up and looked out the window, but no one was there. It was in that moment of quiet solitude that she had an overwhelming urge to talk to him. She missed him, all the way to her bones. If she could stay awake, she could apologize when he arrived for work in another three hours. Joy imagined him in bed beside her, the way the muscles of his chest fit her hands so perfectly, and the soft hair on his belly. She didn't realize she'd fallen asleep until she became aware of a presence in her room and opened her eyes. The sun was up and her father was standing over her.

"You need to get out of bed, Joy," he announced and sighed wearily. "We need to talk."

The sick feeling she always got from drinking too much, the nausea and the crawly sensation below the surface of her skin, set in immediately even though she hadn't drunk since Jeremy's birthday. It was the bad news in her father's voice that was making her ill.

"Something happened to Jeremy?" erupted out of her.

Bob hesitated, and in that prolonged moment, Joy was sure he had driven his motorcycle into a tree. "He's not hurt," he replied. "But he's not here either. He left you a letter."

"What do you mean he's not here? Where else could he be?" came out in a nervous shriek, because even though she was challenging him, her intuition recognized his words as truth.

"On his way to Venice, California," Bob breathed out heavily, and walked out of the bedroom to join Mary, who was drinking tea at the kitchen table and fighting back tears.

"You let him go?" Joy screamed as she stormed after him. "Why would you do that?"

"Your dad didn't let him do anything," Mary said diplomatically. She held Joy's arms to stabilize her, but she pushed her off. "Joy, calm down. We didn't know. He left us a note, too."

"What the hell happened between you two?" her father demanded.

"Bob, no!" Mary scolded. "Don't do that. This is hard enough."

Joy's eyes fell on the envelope with her name scribbled on it. She snatched it off the table and ran with it into her room. Her hands were shaking so much she had trouble opening it, and ripped not only the envelope but the letter too and had to hold the two pieces together to read it.

Joy,

Im on my way to Venice, California to work at a bike shop Jeffs dad hooked me up with. I gotta stop drinking. I cant do it here and I want to find my father. When we got split up sumthin got broken in you and I can't fix that. Maybe only you can. We should be apart til we work shit out but if you need me sooner call me back. You know Ill come.

I love you, J–

172

Joy grabbed her keys and took off out the door before her parents could stop her. There was an overwhelming sense of anguish, of desperation and fury, wrapped inside her skin like a package ready to explode. They hadn't spoken since his birthday because she was still angry and had refused his calls, but how in a mere two days could he have come to such a foolish conclusion? The mere thought of him three thousand miles away heaved acid out of her stomach that she had to vomit onto the driveway before she sped away. Tears were blurring her vision by the time she reached his house. The empty spot where his motorcycle was usually parked caused an electric impulse to radiate from her chest through her arms. "Oh my God," she stammered.

The door to the kitchen was unlocked like always and Joy walked in without knocking. She passed the bedrooms—both beds were empty, but then she heard someone moving in the bathroom. "Jeremy!" she cried and banged on the locked door with her fist. It opened and Jeff was standing there with his toothbrush in hand wearing only a pair of worn Levis. The sympathy in his eyes made a sob escape her throat. She tried to walk away, but he caught her by the hips.

"Take it easy," he was saying when she turned and struck him so hard across the face that the toothbrush flew out of his hand.

"How could you do this?" she screamed at him. "How could you help him leave and not tell me?" He was trying to explain, but she couldn't hear anything over the sounds of her own hysterics. "You were my friend, Jeff! You were my friend, too!"

"I'm still your friend," he said and tried again to take hold of Joy, her handprint on his face.

She pulled herself free from his hands. Someone was calling her name. For a split second she thought it was Jeremy, but when she spun around it was only her father. He pushed the screen door open and stepped into the kitchen. "Your mother's driving your car home. You come with me." She walked aggressively past him into Jeremy's room and flung open the closet doors. All his clothes were gone. A moment later, she was somehow on her knees, her head spinning like she was on the Tilt-a-Whirl at the Marshfield Fair.

"I can't, I can't, I can't do this," she was sobbing.

"I'm so sorry, Joy," Jeff offered. "I tried to talk him out of it. I didn't want him to go either. He said he had to get his shit together and he couldn't do it here."

Joy slowly moved herself into an upright position by holding onto the closet door. "So is that why you hooked him up with a job in California, Jeff, because you wanted him to stay? I don't trust you anymore. You're a fucking liar and you're not my friend!"

"Yeah, I am," he said to her back as she walked away. "If you need me, I'll be here."

"I won't need you because you're not my friend!" she screamed before she walked out the door. For Joy, it would go down in history as the most emotionally traumatic day of her life—to date—but she never stopped to think what that day had been like for Jeff. It was the final blow to the family he had created out of his girlfriend and two best friends.

Joy was hyperventilating by the time she got home and had to breathe into a brown paper bag to restore her respirations to normal. Once her parents were satisfied that she was safe to be left alone, she closed her bedroom door and crawled into bed. The reality of what had transpired was cutting at her insides like a blade. On their last night together she hadn't made love to him or even slept in the same bed with him. As far as she could remember, their last kiss was before they rejoined the group; he was upset and didn't kiss her back. She'd awakened alone on the roach-burned couch that smelled like nachos from the time Jeff had passed out while eating them.

She could still see the image of Jeremy in his bed that morning with only the sheet covering him. He'd been facing the door so she'd been able to see his face. His mouth, deeply colored with the warmth of sleep, had made him look younger than he was. The black eye was more prominent, though, than it had been the night before. Even his notoriously thick lashes couldn't hide it. She had stopped in the doorway to admire him. Why hadn't she gone in?

Because she was too pissed off and resentful, that was why. She wasn't mad that he'd beaten up Vinnie, even though his getting arrested for it had ruined the party. That was Vinnie's fault. But when Jeremy had returned from the police station, she had expected him to jump back into the party, but he'd been disinterested, stand-offish, and that had annoyed her. And the admission that Amanda had propositioned him in high school had been the final blow. He'd held back that information for years—had basically lied about it. What else hadn't he told her? All this analyzing was only refueling her anger, and with every passing minute, he was driving farther away. To Joy it seemed that he had opted out of her life. He'd hopped on his motorcycle and driven away without even a goodbye.

Although he was correct in thinking he needed geographical distance from Joy, Jeff and their lifestyle together to get sober and have any chance of staying that way, Jeremy's presumption that Joy would use the time comparably to work on her own issues was outright miscalculated.

The day he arrived in Venice, he called the house as Mary was putting dinner on the table. It was 3:10 p.m. in California; 6:10 p.m. on the east coast. Bob answered it and Joy knew the instant she saw the tension melt from his face that it was Jeremy on the line.

"I'm not talking to him," she hissed. "Tell him I said to go fuck himself."

"Joy!" Mary scolded as her daughter stormed off to her room and slammed the door.

Ethan had stopped by for dinner, and was gobbling down a biscuit. "He's in good company," he joked. "She said the same thing to me yesterday."

"This isn't funny, Ethan," his mother said sternly. "Talk to him. Tell him to come home."

"Why would I do that? He's got a drinking problem and he's been trying to tell us that, but no one wanted to hear it. That's why he left."

175

Bob covered the mouthpiece of the phone. "Joy?" he mouthed. Mary shook her head.

Ethan took the phone from his dad. "Is he okay?" Mary whispered.

"He's fine," Bob said.

"Bro-ther," Ethan said into the receiver. A grin spread across his face when he heard Jeremy's voice.

"Does he have a place to stay?" Mary asked. Bob nodded his head but held his hand up. He was trying to listen in on the conversation.

"Yeah, he told me that," Ethan said into the phone. "Well, how long will you be gone?" His eyes flitted over to his mother's. She hand gestured *say it.* "Don't get too settled in out there, all right? 'Cause Joy's having a frickin' meltdown. She says she hates you, but don't feel too bad—she hates me too. Somehow it's all my fault you left." He stopped talking momentarily to hear Jeremy's response. "Dude, I don't know, 'cause I told you to get your shit together I guess."

"Ask him if he needs money," Bob interrupted.

"Dad wants to know if you need money," Ethan reported then shook his head at Bob when he heard Jeremy's answer. "Yeah, all right bro, you too. Yep, later." He placed the receiver on its cradle.

"Well, what did he say?" Mary asked.

"His dirt bike's at the garage. He said Eddie can use it while he's gone."

"What else?" she pushed.

"Mom, he's not coming home anytime soon." Ethan saw his mother's anxious expression and added, "Jeremy can take care of himself. He's not a little kid like you seem to think."

Mary's eyes grew wide and she picked her plate up from the table. "You didn't eat your dinner," Bob pointed out. She ignored him and scraped the food into the trash. Ethan opened his lips to speak again, but Bob silenced him with a hand gesture. "We all want him home, Mary," he said, "but we'll have to wait for him to get whatever this is out of his system. And Joy's going to have to learn to deal with it."

After two to three telephone calls per day for weeks that Joy refused to respond to, it became clear to the family that she was not learning to deal with it. Nor would she read the letters he sent. They went promptly in the trash. She wouldn't admit it, but she did read the postcards when no one was around. The pictures on them taunted her: long haired boys on surfboards riding waves, or palm trees lined up along streets that looked as foreign to her as a different country. How could Jeremy be living there, in a place not even familiar to her? It was worse than when he was a foster child living in a strange town, because then he hadn't had a choice. But this time he had chosen to leave her. It was a concept too painful to be negated by the *I love you more than anything* messages he wrote on the cards. She'd trace his messy handwriting with her index finger until tears blurred the ink, and then drop them in the trash barrel.

He had betrayed her. No matter what he wrote on the cards, he had betrayed her with his actions, and she couldn't find it in her heart to forgive him. Months went by and no contact was made between them. She was trying to force his hand, which was a foolish position, given the fact that he had indicated he would return at her request.

By the time December rolled around and they'd suffered through three snowstorms already in Massachusetts while Jeremy still basked in the golden state, Joy had convinced herself that he would return for Christmas. Then, one particularly icy Wednesday after Joy slid the whole way home from school in her car, Bob entered toting a package from Jeremy. Inside it were Christmas presents for each member of the family. "He's not coming home," Joy stated, more to herself than to her parents, before she burst into tears and fled to her bedroom.

Mary followed her. "Joy, he wants you to go to California for Christmas. He's been talking about it for months. Didn't he write to you about it?"

"I—I didn't read the letters," she stammered.

Mary was surprisingly angered by the statement. "Listen to me," she said coolly, "because this might be the most important thing anyone ever says to you." Joy crossed her eyebrows; her bottom lip extended into a pout. She was five again and in trouble. "You're making the biggest mistake of your life punishing Jeremy like this. Maybe he was wrong to leave, but that boy loves you and you love him. You're a fool if you let this relationship end because you got your feelings hurt. Now, if you're as smart as I think you are, you'll pick up the phone and talk to your boyfriend. Tell him you still love him because I'm not sure he knows. He hasn't heard it in four months."

When Mary left Joy alone with her heartache, there was a moment when she actually considered taking her mother's advice. Years later, she would look back more than once and wonder why the hell she hadn't.

She didn't open the present Jeremy sent her, but Lily did it for her. It was a tiny silver palm tree for her charm bracelet, symbolic of his hope that she would accept his invitation to spend her Christmas break with him in California. Lily showed it to her, but she didn't let her hold it. She didn't trust her not to flush it down the toilet or throw it out in the snow. The day Jeremy had left, Joy had torn the bracelet off her arm and flung it across the kitchen. Mary took possession of the charm and put it away in her jewelry box where the bracelet was already safely stashed.

As it tends to happen, one mistake led to another. Joy didn't call Jeremy, nor did she talk to him when he called on Christmas day. But she did get on the phone the next day when Ty Connors called. He was home on winter break and had heard about Jeremy moving out to California. And in her anger and obstinacy and loneliness, she made the biggest mistake yet—she agreed to have lunch with him. That small act, that one *yes* became something she could never undo because word of Joy's life traveled to Jeremy through Jeff as easily as events in Jeremy's life traveled to her through her family. Joy's intent was not to date Ty, but that was how it was interpreted by Vinnie, who told Amanda, who told Jeff. Jeremy had been planning to return home in time for Joy's college graduation in May until he heard she was dating Ty. Even though it wasn't true, by the fall it technically was.

When Ty started medical school at the University of Massachusetts School of Medicine in Worcester in the fall of 1999, he and Joy saw each other on weekends that he was home, but they weren't a couple. Joy was still holding out for Jeremy and she told Ty that. He wasn't discouraged by her honesty. He didn't perceive Jeremy as a real threat to his long-term goal, which was to marry her. Ty saw Joy as a perfect partner. She was intelligent and well-read, curious and articulate. It never occurred to him that Jeremy might be better suited for her. Ty assumed Joy and Jeremy's relationship was built on physical attraction, and he believed Jeremy was the one who knew only part of Joy's personality: the reckless teenage side that was seeking expression by dating one of the school's infamous bad boys. Ty's plan was controlled and calculated, the way Joy's life had been before Jeremy re-entered it.

Joy saw the time she spent with Ty differently than he saw it. Since she'd lost Hannah and Jeff, he was her only friend. Her family was furious that she was seeing Ty and that she had stone-walled Jeremy—especially Ethan. He couldn't forgive the disloyalty. To Joy, the fact that Ty brought her flowers or took her out to dinner didn't mean that he had taken Jeremy's place. She had no desire to have a physical relationship with him. It was Jeremy that she loved, Jeremy that her body still longed for, Jeremy that she dreamed of at night. One day he would return; it was only a matter of when.

Contrary to Joy's belief, Jeremy had no intention of returning to Massachusetts. He thought she was dating Ty to hurt him, which of course *was* part of her motivation. It was another desperate attempt on her part to force his hand, but it only caused him to dig his heels in more. What it came down to was Joy's will versus Jeremy's. She was biding her time waiting for his return, but she refused to call him and ask him to do so. And Jeremy would not return until she called to say that she had broken it off with Ty and wanted him back. They might as well have been ten years old and wrestling on the beach, each one too obstinate to give in to the other.

In the beginning, he'd moved into a spare room in his newly divorced boss's house. But after about a year, he felt secure enough about his job to take on a small studio apartment. Most evenings Jeremy spent at AA meetings, which were free to attend, aside from the couple of bucks he threw in the pot to help pay for the hall. He learned from his AA sponsor that most alcoholics have a reservoir of anger that needs to be dealt with in a healthy manner. He started lifting free weights and bought a bicycle that he liked to ride to Venice Beach. That was one of his favorite places to spend time, even though it couldn't have been more different than the beach he'd grown up on in Marshfield, or the beach in Plymouth with the cliffs. Venice Beach was more about the human beings than the natural grandeur; the energy they created when all their quirky differences came together in the same place. There was a sense of camaraderie that always made him feel like he wasn't so alone.

On weekends, he'd take day trips in search of his father. He called Belinda regularly to check in and ask for ideas, but she was as bewildered about the whereabouts of Jeremy Blake Senior as he was. The truth was, though Jeremy never discovered it, his father didn't stay in any place for long because he was hiding from the long arm of the Massachusetts Department of Revenue that was tracking him down for failure to pay child support.

He used to have a friend in Mendocino, Belinda told him—Mike Garret— and Jeremy wrote down the address. The next time he had enough money saved to pay for a hotel, he took off before sunrise on a Saturday. It was dark by the time he pulled into Mendocino Village, and as it turned out, Mike Garret's house was in Fort Bragg twenty minutes away. Jeremy was sure he'd found the right place when he pulled into the driveway of the cottage that was tucked neatly into some redwood trees and saw a 1999 Harley Davidson Fat Boy parked there. A middle-aged woman was in a rocking chair on the front porch. She offered up a warm smile as he removed his helmet and dragged his fingers through his long hair.

"Mike Garret live here?" Jeremy asked, still straddling his bike.

"He's right inside," the woman responded. "Are you a friend of his?"

"We've never met, but I guess he knows my father and…well, I've been looking for him."

"Why don't you come in the house," she offered while her eyes took him in. She was a pretty lady. Something about her wavy blonde hair and easy smile gave Jeremy the impression that she resembled the way Joy might look some day when she was approaching fifty.

"Thank you," he said. He approached and held his hand out. "I'm Jeremy."

The woman nodded with a satisfied grin. "Blake, right?"

"Right. You know him, my father?"

"I knew him. It's been six years since he last stopped by. You're his spitting image, except you're even better looking," she laughed. "He'd be mad as a bull if he heard me say that."

When they stepped inside the house, Jeremy's eyes scanned the place, expecting to see signs of dysfunction. What he remembered of his father—from that one visit on his ninth birthday—was the whisky on his breath and his mother pouring the Jack Daniels in his coffee. He knew first-hand what kind of home environment results from that kind of drinking. And if Mike Garret was a friend of his father's, well, he suspected he was in the same class. But he was wrong about that and there were signs of it from the moment he stepped over the threshold. There was nothing lavish in the way the place was decorated, but it had a warm energy that reminded him of the Sanders' house. It was clean; there was a colorful braided rug in the middle of the living room floor, and vases filled with flowers on the tables. This was the man's home, not his crash pad.

The woman's name was Sarah Wilson, and she and Mike had been living together for twenty years. Jeremy watched Mike's face when Sarah introduced him. There was a mixture of emotions displayed on it, but surprise didn't seem to be one of them. Mike was quiet by nature. He was a good listener, a lot like Jeremy in fact, introspective and thoughtful until he had a bellyful of alcohol. Mike had been sober for almost ten years, he told Jeremy, and was pleased to find out that Jeremy was sober, too.

"Forgive me," he said quietly, "But your dad isn't someone I can spend time with anymore."

Jeremy nodded. He knew the concept well from his time in AA. His sponsor had said it this way: *You don't go to a barber shop unless you want a haircut. So why hang out at bars or with drunks unless you plan to drink?*

"When's the last time you saw him?" Mike asked.

"The day I turned nine."

Sarah handed him a cup of coffee in the awkward silence that followed his statement. "That's a shame," she offered, "a real shame that he missed so much."

"I had someone…" Jeremy started, but wasn't sure how to finish. "I mean, he was like a father to me. He still is."

"Oh that's right, your mother got married," Sarah remarked, and Jeremy noticed it when Mike caught her eye and gave his head the slightest shake.

"No," Jeremy replied. "She didn't. It was someone else, a neighbor."

"In New Jersey?" Sarah asked and Mike nearly dropped his coffee. Jeremy still wasn't catching on. He only knew that Mike was uncomfortable, not why he was uncomfortable.

"No, in Marshfield, Massachusetts," Jeremy said simply. "That's where I grew up."

He caught the confused look on Sarah's face and the pained expression on Mike's and suddenly he understood. He wasn't the only kid that J had walked out on. Somewhere in the state of New Jersey he had a half-brother, close to his age. He was wondering if he'd made the rounds through foster homes too, when Mike interrupted his thoughts. "Why is it you want to find him?" he asked.

Jeremy couldn't help but conclude that it was a very good question. Maybe it was time to give up the search…but one more inquiry. "When he stopped by here six years ago, where was he headed?"

Mike glanced at Sarah before he answered, "Laconia, New Hampshire. Bike week."

Jeremy set the cup down and stood up. His journey was over. Now he knew that his father, whom he'd traveled three thousand miles and spent weekends scouring California to find, had been in the next state over when he was a teenager and he hadn't even bothered to stop by. "Thanks for your time," he said sincerely and offered his hand to Mike.

"I'm sorry kid," Mike offered. "But you know what alcoholics are like."

"Yeah, I do," he agreed and offered his hand to Sarah. She hugged him instead.

When he left their house he found a motel on the Pacific Coast Highway that he could afford. In the lobby they had postcards of the Mendocino Coast. As his eyes surveyed the beautiful scenery that he'd be able to see the next morning, he thought about Joy and wished that she could see it too. Jeremy knew that Joy was slow to forgive, but he was sure she would in time. He believed that they had been paired together in this lifetime as they had in many others, and no one in Heaven or on Earth could have convinced him otherwise.

In his hotel room, he ate the salad and whole grain bagel he'd bought at a super market and stared at the postcard he'd chosen, trying to figure out what to say. He didn't know how to write an eloquent sentence like Joy did. Everything she wrote sounded like poetry. When he'd finished eating and had still not written a word, he put the postcard aside and shifted into a comfortable position to meditate.

Someone at AA had mentioned from the podium that meditation was a good way to relieve stress and become more focused. And what he had noticed, other than the fact that he wasn't feeling as much anger, was that he was beginning to hear Running Deer's voice speak to him again, mostly in his pre-dream states. It had been a number of years since he'd been able to hear clairaudiently while fully awake. When he'd started drinking again he'd unknowingly cut off his ability, but it was coming back. Sometimes during meditation if he was successful in quieting his thoughts, he could pick up a few words. Once he'd heard Running Deer clear as day inform him that he was serving as his spirit guide. *I've known you since I was a child,* Jeremy had responded, and it'd felt like Running Deer laughed. "Much longer than that," Jeremy'd heard him say.

After a few minutes of focusing only on his breath he began to see the familiar white lights with his third eye. It was Running Deer, affirming his presence. Occasionally he'd see the old man's wrinkled brown face and his long white hair like he was sitting right across from him. Sometimes his hair was in braids, but other times it was loose. Always he was smiling, pleased by Jeremy's ability to see him. This time it didn't happen. His breath was coming so slowly that he was afraid he'd fall asleep, and he wanted to write the postcard first. He didn't feel right going to bed in Fort Bragg, California without first writing to Joy and telling her that's where he was.

He grasped the pen and tried to use his very best handwriting when he wrote *I wish you were here.* The sentence reminded him of the Pink Floyd song even though that wasn't what he had in mind when he wrote it. On a whim he drew a fishbowl with two little fish swimming around in it. His eyes appraised it. It wasn't a work of art, but hopefully she'd follow his train of thought. He put the pen to the paper again and signed it *I love you. J-*

It was the last postcard he sent.

CHAPTER NINETEEN

A Controlled and Calculated Life

Joy soon discovered one of the truths of adulthood: the older we get, the faster time moves, and it becomes a vicious circle. A new year begins and quickly draws to an end. Birthdays clip by like illustrations in the flipbooks she used to make for Jeremy when they were children.

"Lily, wake up," she hissed. It was 1:55 a.m., May 12, 2001, one week before her 24th birthday and the morning of her wedding day. Lily had spent the night in her old room so she would be there to help her get ready in the morning. Joy got out of bed and shook her shoulders. Her big sister was sleeping like she always used to when they shared a room, on her belly with her wild curls covering her face.

"Now I remember why I moved out," Lily groaned.

"Come on, Lily. I need to ask you something."

"Hurry up and do it before I wake up."

"Do you think I'm doing the right thing?" Joy asked.

Lily pushed onto her elbows. "What?" she mumbled. "What did you just say?"

Joy pouted. "I can't sleep—I'm scared."

An exasperated sigh escaped Lily. "I shouldn't ask because I'll end up regretting it, but what exactly are you scared about?"

"Promise you won't tell Mom?"

"Say it, Joy."

Joy took a breath and it discernibly trembled when she released it. "What if I'm marrying the wrong person?"

Lily didn't even try to hold back. "I'm going to slap you!" she threatened. "Did I not say this to you months ago, before I got stuck planning the shower with Ty's obnoxious mother?"

For nine months Joy had been engaged to Ty, and for nine months she had pushed Jeremy from her mind every time something associated with him sought entrance, which was quite often. Her family hadn't celebrated their engagement. No one knew what to say when Ty accompanied her home after dinner that night to make the announcement. Her parents had congratulated them, of course, but Joy could read the disappointment in her mother's watery eyes and her father's stunned expression. *Can't we have a cup of tea and talk about it?* Joy had suggested after Ty went home, but her mother (for the first time ever) declined the invitation.

"I know, I know," Joy mustered. "But what do I do?"

"Pick up the phone and call Jeremy. Let's go. His number's by the phone." Lily sat up and threw her legs over the side of the bed.

"I can't do that. I haven't talked to him in almost three years. How can I call him in the middle of the night, only hours before I marry someone else?"

"First of all, he's in California, so it's only eleven o'clock there. He might not even be in bed yet. And second of all, if you still love Jeremy, you *cannot* marry Ty. Do you?"

"Lily, don't be ridiculous. You know I love Jeremy."

Lily unleashed a growl loud enough to wake the house. "Then why'd you get engaged to Ty?"

"I don't know," Joy admitted. "It's complicated."

"How complicated can it be? I've been waiting years to marry Eddie and I still have to wait for his grandmother to die. If he asked it would be *yes, absolutely yes*, not complicated at all."

"Ty will make a good husband," Joy argued weakly.

"Well yeah. He's a great guy. Too bad he's not the one you're in love with."

"Don't say that—you're making me feel sick. There has to be more to marriage than that. I mean, there is, right? Besides, I don't even know if Jeremy loves me anymore."

Lily stared at her blankly. "Every time I think it's the stupidest thing you've ever said, you say something even stupider. It's Jeremy—he'll love you forever. How can you not know that? *I know that* and I'm not even in your skin."

Joy fell back onto the bed, her head pressing comfortably into the pillow, but there was no chance she'd fall asleep, not that night.

"Hannah said this to me yesterday," Lily whispered after she crawled back under the covers. One snowy Sunday the prior winter, Ethan had surprised the whole family by showing up for dinner with Hannah. He'd finally gathered the nerve to ask her out. Now they were in a serious relationship, and since she'd mended her friendship with Joy, they were to be partnered together at the wedding.

"What'd she say?" Joy sniffed.

"That you told her once you could never marry anyone but Jeremy."

"Hannah has no right to criticize me. She did the same thing."

"She wasn't criticizing you—she was stating a fact," Lily hotly replied, "but if you ever say that to Ethan, I swear to God Joy, I really will slap you." She rolled over and went back to sleep after that, but her words had penetrated Joy's conscience.

Thoughts from the past began to flood her mind: the way the Rexham house used to smell like a campfire, and how she still associated that smell with home, and how there was a heavy blue blanket they used to store in a closet during the summer, then drag out on the first fall day...and curling up in that blanket with Jeremy on winter nights. In her mind's eye she could see him slipping back into bed with her in the morning after he'd crept out to make a pot of coffee. How silently his bare feet had walked on those floors...*like an Indian* he'd always said. She'd never known when he was moving around the house, only when he returned, his skin chilled from the brisk winter air. She'd snuggle against him to warm his body that was as familiar to her as her own.

After a while, she got out of bed and stepped out the front door to sit on the steps. The aroma from the lilacs blooming brought tears to her eyes. She could never smell them without thinking of him. Ty never understood the way Jeremy did that she'd rather have fresh cut lilacs from the yard than dozens of roses from a florist. *Jeremy. Please come home.* Even if he could hear her, he wouldn't return. She knew him too well to expect that. By now he'd assume she was sleeping with Ty. So far she hadn't been able to be that intimate with Ty and he had played along like she was a born again virgin waiting for her wedding day. But as of tomorrow she would be his wife, sleeping with him every night. The thought of what that would do to Jeremy wrenched a sob from her throat. *Hurt isn't a big enough word*, he'd said.

What was she thinking, agreeing to marry Ty? *Wait*, she quickly reminded herself, *stop thinking with your heart.* Every time she made decisions with her heart it led her directly to Jeremy. But her brain, she believed, was so much wiser. And her brain had led her to Ty.

Her mind started to make the familiar list, all the reasons why Ty would make a good husband. He was reliable, predictable even; he was loyal, hardworking and intelligent; he adored her and would provide a good life— a house of her choosing near her mother. But most importantly, he would never, no matter how angry or confused he became, hop on a motorcycle and drive away from her. As his wife, she would never want for anything…except Jeremy. Marrying Ty would sever the cord that still pulsated between them.

Analyzing it wasn't making her feel better. She stood up and gazed at the sky as her feet moved toward the street. There were no stars and only the dim glow of a barely visible moon. Clouds were hanging overhead, covering up everything bright and beautiful. She felt like one of those rain clouds, full of tears instead of raindrops. Crouched on the edge of the road, her fingers played with the sand like when she was a child. She tried several rocks before she found one able to write on pavement and used it to scratch out *for the last time—I love you Jeremy Blake.*

Three thousand miles away, he was sitting on the end of the pier at Venice Beach, clutching the arrowhead that Joy had given him for his eighteenth birthday in his fisted hand. He'd ventured there with the intent of tossing it into the ocean, of withdrawing from it all the power it held over him. But even with the points of the triangle cutting into his skin from holding it so tightly, it was far too precious to lose. He shoved it into the pocket of his board shorts and stood up, feeling aimless. Where to go now? His direction in life had always been the same, like a compass forever pointed toward a life with Joy. Even when they were living apart, he understood its purpose was to strengthen them so they could have a better life together.

He allowed his feet to wander off the pier and down the boardwalk, past the little shops and kiosks, then onto the main roads. His brain was barely conscious of where he was until his eyes fell on a sign in front of a tattoo studio, and a new thought was born.

Joy never did fall asleep that night. She was still lying awake in her little twin bed that she used to share with Jeremy when the birds started singing outside her window and the sun eked through the blinds. She tiptoed out of the room. No one in the house was awake yet. She could hear her dad snoring as she turned the front door-knob and stepped outside. It was a beautiful day, a bride's dream come true. But she was sick inside and unsure about her decision. She walked out to the street, worried that everyone—Ty, his family, and her family—would see what she'd written on the pavement out of desperation. But it was gone. Overnight the clouds had let go of their hold on the rain and washed it all away.

As if it never existed.

When Ty graduated from medical school two years later, his parents' gift to him was a down- payment on an oversized colonial-style home in a new upscale neighborhood in Marshfield that was only a five minute drive from Bob and Mary's house. Fortunately, Joy could still join her mother for tea in the mornings and even occasionally before bed, as had been her habit when she still lived at home. Ty had landed a residency in the emergency room of a hospital the next town over, which was only a fifteen-minute drive from their new home on Dragonfly Lane. Everything was falling into place exactly the way Ty had imagined since he was a boy. But everyone's life is full of surprises, even people like Ty, who plan their future down to the details.

The Sunday they moved in, Bob helped Ty carry an antique desk into the new house. "I want to hear your opinion," Ty said as they made their way across the lawn. "You're in the business."

"I build houses. I don't sell 'em," Bob rebutted.

"We dropped almost a million dollars on a house. So is it worth it?"

"What you really want to know is if it'll be enough to make Joy happy…"

Bob placed his end of the desk on the ground and bent over with his hands on his knees. He was struggling to catch his breath, something his son-in-law found concerning for a fifty-something year old guy who'd been working with his body his entire life.

"Are you all right?" he asked. Bob waved the concern away with his hand as if it were a mosquito and picked up his end of the desk again.

Inside the house, Joy was slicing cheese to serve on the new platter her parents had given them as a house-warming gift and Mary and Lily were sipping tea at the kitchen island. When the guys entered with the desk, Bob immediately went into a coughing fit and ducked into the small downstairs bathroom. They could hear him hacking out mucous from the kitchen.

"What's wrong with Daddy?" Joy asked.

"It's the smoking," her mother answered.

As Bob exited the bathroom, Ty walked into it. The trio of women was conspicuously quiet as Bob approached them. "What're you saying about me?" he asked.

"We're worried about your cough," his wife informed him.

"I have a chest cold," he explained as he took it from her hand.

Joy was turning back to slicing the cheese—she'd swallowed his explanation—when Ty somberly entered the room. His demeanor caught her attention. Ty always looked uncomfortable in his own skin, but never more so than that particular moment. In the silence of the room, the whoosh of air exiting his body could be heard by everyone.

"How long have you been coughing up blood, Bob?" he demanded. "I saw it in the toilet."

Joy's hand froze on the knife. For a brief moment, her father looked like he was going to deny it, but then he turned his eyes away from Ty's and she knew it was true.

"How long?" Ty repeated.

"I don't know exactly," Bob admitted, "Awhile though."

Mary's face turned sunburn red, like she'd been the one having the coughing fit. "No more cigarettes," she said firmly, as if abstention could make the whole problem go away.

"You need to have tests run," Ty advised. "I'll arrange it in the morning."

And so it was that Ty was the person who set the cycle in motion, although it was another doctor who made the actual diagnosis, the surgeon who performed the biopsy of the mass on Bob's lung. It was one of those unexpected events on the well-planned course of Ty Connors' life that his first official duty as a physician was to inform his wife that her father was suffering from small cell lung cancer that he could not possibly survive.

Without treatment, Bob's oncologist advised he would likely not live more than six months. However, with a combination of radiation and chemotherapy, she believed it possible that his life could be extended by three or four times that. For the entire family, the shocking reality of the diagnosis had a feeling equivalent to awakening in the middle of the night and gasping for breath, or being chased by a beast rapidly gaining ground. But there was no waking up from this nightmare and no escaping this monster's grasp.

Life shrank—each day became the focus, not a month or a year. The kids returned, with or without their spouses, to the family home most days after work so they could be together for dinner. Day-to-day routine became a lesson in perspective. Preparing Bob's coffee became a privilege, washing his dishes no longer a chore. Every birthday was precious, every holiday cherished.

For Ty, it was the first time he felt accepted by the Sanders family. Ethan finally acknowledged him as his brother-in-law, a huge stride forward for the two men who had never been friends, and in Ty's estimation, never would be. They were too different, and Ethan's allegiance to Jeremy too strong for a close bond to exist between them. Ethan had married Hannah about a year after Ty and Joy got married. The two couples tried several times to double date, but the women invariably spent the evening trying to keep a conversation going. It was an odd mix: Ethan with his permanently blackened fingernails and Ty with his perfectly white long fingers that he used to fix people instead of cars. They were outward signs of their inner differences.

Although Ty still longed for and tried a little too hard to obtain Ethan's acceptance, he never voiced it, and Ethan, not having been born with the gift of perceptivity, didn't intuit it. After a long day of work, he had no desire to dress up and patronize a restaurant where he barely recognized the items on the menu. If he planned the evening, he would have bought four tickets to the Bruins game and stopped at Halftime Pizza across the street beforehand to grab a slice or two. Ty, on the other hand, barely knew the difference between the Bruins and the Red Sox. For that reason, Ethan never talked to him about sports and instead would ask him questions like, "how many people did you sew up today?" or "any car accidents?" and Ty would laugh good-humoredly.

It was Bob's illness that changed the dynamic. Much like Joy's first affiliation with him in high school, Ty became the stabilizing force in the family. He was turned to for guidance on medical decision-making, but he was also included in other family discussions that he had previously been excluded from. In short, he became a full-fledged member of the Sanders family.

CHAPTER TWENTY

Dr. Jekyll

On August 13, 2005, at the age of thirty, Lily finally married the love of her life, Eddie McCormack, six months to the day after his Irish Catholic grandmother passed away and carried with her to the Spirit Realm all objections she had to him marrying a non-Catholic. The reception was held on a perfect New England summer night at the Sand Castle, the same place Joy's prom had been held ten years prior.

Joy was sitting at the head table between Lily and Troy, Eddie's brother and best man, and sipping a martini when someone entering through the French doors caught her attention. He was tall with broad shoulders and was wearing a nicely tailored jacket but no tie with a crisp white dress shirt. And, whoever he was—one of Eddie's friends, Joy presumed— he had a great haircut, recently trimmed but still long enough to look a bit messy. From where she was sitting with the bright lights on her, she could barely make out his profile in the dimmer light by the doors, but then as if he'd heard her thoughts, he turned and looked directly at her.

And she dropped her martini glass.

It was Jeremy, seven years older than he had been the last time she'd had the privilege of looking at him. She couldn't take her eyes off him, not even when Troy placed a napkin on her lap to prevent the gin and vermouth from seeping into her dress. He was a gorgeous grown up man now and he was in the same room with her—she didn't know whether to cry or scream or throw her arms around him. He was walking straight toward her, too. Then Ethan caught sight of him and intervened. Joy's eyes filled with tears as she watched the two of them embrace.

Without stopping to think about the impropriety of it, she swung her arm backward and hit Lily in the stomach. "You said he wasn't coming!" she bellowed.

"Oh my God," Lily finally mustered, "you knocked the breath out of me."

"I can't believe you did this to me," Joy sputtered.

"I can't believe you hit me! For God's sake, what are you talking about?"

"Jeremy!"

Lily gasped. "Is that him with Ethan? He cut his hair!" She narrowed her eyes and let her breath out slowly. "You two," she hissed, "are ridiculous" before she sped away to welcome him. Joy wanted to follow her but couldn't convince her feet to carry her. It was torture keeping her distance while the rest of her family encircle him. The most painful part was seeing her father struggle to his feet so he could get his arms around him. The cancer was eating away at him and every day depleted more of his energy. Bob needed a cane to walk and to move into a standing position. Joy saw Jeremy's face when he took him in—the expression around his mouth like he was trying not to cry—and bolted for the Ladies' Room.

She had dealt with her father's illness a day at a time, as it unfolded. But for Jeremy the picture revealed to his eyes must have been shocking. He stayed in touch with her parents. She didn't know the degree of it, but her mother would occasionally drop a remark about him. "Jeremy bought his own motorcycle shop" or "Jeremy likes to surf now"—random comments that would create painful images in Joy's mind that haunted her.

Her life with Ty was predictable and steady. There were no surprises, good or bad. Their bank account was fat enough to remove any financial worries and to meet Joy's day-to-day whims. She had tried various jobs that she never stayed at for long, but Ty made enough money that she didn't need to work. He was an all-around good guy who worked hard, didn't spend time at bars, strip clubs or the race track. And he was respectful of her family. There was not one single thing about him that she could complain about. So why the hell wasn't she happy?

There were only two legitimate issues in their marriage and the first arose so seldom that it was hardly a problem. Ty got lit every time he drank, and by the end of the night, he'd have to be carried home because he was passed out cold. In fact, when Jeremy arrived at Lily's wedding, Ty was unconscious on a couch in the bride's dressing room. Ethan had carried him there at Bob's command. And it wouldn't be long, Joy knew, before her dad instructed Ethan to cart him home. The second issue was much deeper, and could not be fixed by her family's intervention: Ty had been pushing for children from the moment they got married, four years earlier. And Joy had no reason not to get pregnant, other than it didn't feel right. But she couldn't tell Ty that so she just kept saying she wasn't ready and hoping her feelings would change.

In the ornate Ladies' Room mirror, Joy assessed her reflection. The pale yellow strapless that Lily had chosen was lovely for a bridesmaid's dress. It looked fabulous on Joy's long slender figure. Her hair was cut above her shoulders and swept off her face, like Catherine Deneuve in a Chanel commercial. At a glance, she appeared composed, but her hands were shaking. She took a breath and reached for the door, determined to greet Jeremy amiably without looking like she belonged on a psychiatric ward.

As she re-entered the hall, she stole a glance at her parents' table where she knew Jeremy would be sitting. He was talking excitedly to her mom, but his bright blue eyes shot over to hers when he felt her glance. She saw his lips move as he excused himself, and her feet froze. He took confident strides toward her, and once he reached her held her hands and gently kissed her cheek.

"I didn't know you were coming," she stammered.

His hands squeezed hers. "You look beautiful," he offered.

"Thanks," she mustered. The waiters and waitresses were clearing the tables and Lily was trying to get her attention—it was time to cut the cake. "Did you eat?" she asked.

"Lily asked the waitress to bring me something vegetarian. I think she…wants you."

"Maybe we can talk later?" Joy suggested.

"Sure," he agreed and took a couple of steps backward before he turned and walked away.

Joy watched the shape of his body as he glided across the floor. It was nearly impossible to make her own body move in the opposite direction. Once she did, she still couldn't keep her eyes from venturing over to him. She'd finished her wedding cake and was eating Troy's when she noticed Jeremy pointing at his cake, offering it to her. She smiled but politely declined. Three slices of cake and twice as many martinis might be going overboard. Still, she was flattered that he remembered how much she loved it. His offering reminded her of how effortlessly they'd always been able to communicate, and after that numerous glances were exchanged.

"Stop being such a whore!" Lily hissed in her ear.

"What are you talking about?" Joy asked, wide-eyed.

"Oh please. I remember when he used to crawl through our window. I wasn't always asleep."

Joy's jaw dropped, but she couldn't think of a good retort. "So?" she finally said.

"So you two can't keep your hands off each other. You've never been able to. And tonight you can't keep your eyes off each other. So what do you think will happen next?"

"Um, Ty will come out of his coma and Jeremy will fly back to L.A.?"

"That's *tomorrow*," Lily said confidently. "I'm talking about *tonight*."

Lily got up to dance with Ethan. Joy had promised her dad a dance, but she couldn't imagine how he would be able to stand through an entire song. Tonight would probably be the last opportunity she'd ever have to dance with him. The thought made her throat cramp, and her martini glass was annoyingly empty. She stared into the glass, waiting for the emotion to pass.

"What's wrong?" she heard and looked up.

Jeremy had slid soundlessly into Lily's chair. He had a quiet quality to his personality that she'd always found appealing—except when he was drunk. *Dr. Jekyll versus Mr. Hyde* he'd said to her once. It used to feel good to be in the silence with him. When they'd been a couple they sometimes stayed in bed together for hours and not said a word.

"My dad," she revealed and her eyes flickered for a moment until they met his. There was so much that could have been said, but none of it was necessary. He understood. "I told him I'd dance with him tonight, but I'm scared he won't be able to. He's weaker than he lets on."

"Last time I talked to him on the phone, he told me he was still working."

"When was that?"

Jeremy slouched in his chair. "Sunday. Good thing your mom straightened me out."

"He wants you to think of him the way he used to be—" She couldn't finish her thought without bawling her eyes out. He reached for her hand.

"What if I cut in?" he suggested.

She nodded. "He probably wants us to dance."

"He does. He mentioned it already."

"That's a little pathetic, my dad having to line up my dance partners."

"Only because your date just left over your brother's shoulder."

It didn't miss Joy's attention that he called Ty her date and not her husband. "He's not mean to me or anything, Jeremy. Don't get the wrong impression."

"Sweetheart," he said softly, "if there's one thing I know about you, it's that you know how to defend yourself. If there's any fighting going on, my money's on you." Then he stood up abruptly and walked away without giving her any indication if he was kidding or not.

She drank another martini at the bar with Troy before she ventured over to dance with her dad. Once he was standing independently, Joy placed her hands on his shoulders and watched him anxiously. "I'm fine, Joy," he told her impatiently. That was the word he always used, *fine*, to describe his physical condition, regardless of how he was feeling. She faked a smile.

"Do you know why we named you Joy?" he asked her, once they were moving a little bit.

"Not really. Mom said you both picked it."

"When your mother first held you in her arms, you were the picture of happiness. You looked like you knew exactly what you wanted and were so sure you were going to have it."

"Why are you telling me this?" she asked. Her father had always been able to see through her, and she was feeling too fragile to have her unhappiness psychoanalyzed.

"I guess I've become philosophical at this stage of my life. It seems to me now that your name is a gift. It's a reminder of the way you came into this world and the way we'd like you to always be." She turned her still youthful eyes away from his seemingly ancient ones and looked over his shoulder at Jeremy. "Someone is waiting to dance with you," he said.

Bob gestured to him, and within a few seconds Jeremy was at her side. Joy took his hand as naturally as if they were five years old and walking home from the beach. She had a dim recollection of her mother saying *always hold hands when you cross Sea Street*. They'd held on to each other and had had trouble letting go ever since. He led her to the veranda so they could dance under the stars. It was with familiarity that his hands slid around her waist.

"We were lucky to grow up around here," he stated as his eyes scanned the beach.

"Mm hm," she agreed.

"I have a lot of…gratitude…for your parents, what they did for me. I can't imagine what would have happened to me without them."

"You're still close, closer than I realized," Joy admitted.

"We talk every weekend. Once I came home for Christmas. You were in Europe, though."

She could have screamed when he said that. No one in her family had ever mentioned his visit and it was two years prior that Ty had taken her to Paris for the holidays. Not one word, not one God damned word, not even from Lily. "My family hates me," she finally said. "They probably wish I was the one who moved to California."

"That's not true. They love you as much as they always did. They just don't always understand you." She was mad now, furious. She moved her face away so it wasn't touching his. They didn't seem to have any trouble understanding *him*. He was the one who'd mounted his motorcycle and taken off, deserted all of them—not only her—but they still loved him every bit as much as they had when he'd been a little boy. She was the one they couldn't forgive. He took her face in his hands as gently as if he were cradling one of his mourning doves.

"I can't look at you right now," she said and jerked it away.

"Why not?"

"Because it hurts too much," she admitted and laid her head on his shoulder. She felt his hands return to her waist and pull her closer. From her peripheral vision she saw her parents watching them from their table. And Ethan was standing with them, nursing his Budweiser, which was a clear indication to her that Ty was back at home.

"It's been a long time since we danced ," Jeremy commented casually.

"Or anything else," she snapped. She couldn't force the anger back down anymore. It was like an uncompromising Jack-in-the box with an agenda of its own.

He took a step back like she'd slapped him before he found his voice again. "Since we're being honest, I was really thinking that it's been a long time since I've been able to kiss you. That last time, I didn't know it was going to be the last time."

"Neither did I, Jeremy. I didn't know you were about to *take off*." He let go of her and she sputtered, "I'm sorry I said that." How could she withstand the blow if he turned his back and walked away again? "Just so you know, I never kiss Ty like I kissed you."

His eyes took her in for a long moment before he whispered in her ear like it was a secret, "I never imagined you did." It wasn't at all what she had expected him to say. "Joy," he sighed. "When you married him, it didn't change *us*. It only changed the rules."

It undid her in some way, like she was unraveling from the inside out. She pushed her face into his neck. It wasn't humanly possible to stop the tears this time. They spilled onto his skin and into his hair. "I'm so sorry," she finally said out loud. Thousands of times she'd thought the words, had gone to sleep at night sending them out into the universe wishing that somehow they could reach him, but never had she said them directly to him.

"Listen," he prompted and wiped her tears off her cheeks with his hands. The song had changed. *Love is all around you. Love is knockin' outside your door* was playing through the speakers.

She wiped her nose on her hand. "I remember—it's that song we liked."

He offered up his sleeve as a handkerchief. She rubbed her nose on it as if she were a child. "Hey, remember that night in Hanson with Jeff and Hannah?" he asked to distract her.

"Yeah," came out as half sob, half laugh. "The summer of '95. The year Jeff popped my cherry and all hell broke loose."

Jeremy threw his head back with a groan. "Don't say that," he pleaded and dropped his forehead deftly onto hers. "I still can't stand the sound of it." Joy wrapped her arms tighter around his neck. "Hannah looks happy with Ethan," he said, "and of course Ethan's the happiest man on the planet."

"You talk to him, too?" Joy asked. She didn't want to reveal that she barely did. They saw each other often at their parents' house, but there was a wall between them now.

"A couple of times a week," Jeremy offered. "He's still like a brother to me—Jeff, too."

"Really, Jeff? How's his stoned naked ass?"

Jeremy laughed. "Not stoned, actually. We're both sober. I haven't had a drink since the last night I saw you, on my twenty-first birthday. But before I forget to tell you, Jeff said to tell you he misses the old Joy and he wants you to stop by. He moved back into the family house after his dad died. He owns that construction company now."

Love is gonna find a way a way back to you the vocalist sang and Jeremy smiled. "It's a good sign, that song playing tonight. Don't you think?" She nodded half-heartedly, still thinking about the comments he'd made. *The old Joy.* The words felt like they were made of broken glass. And the remark about him being sober bothered her, too. She had never thought of Jeremy as an alcoholic, not even at the end when things were out of control. When he left for California, she'd thought he'd used it as an excuse to run away.

"Want to take a walk?" he asked and offered his hand. They were at the top of the stairs when Mary called to them from the French doors.

"Let them be." It was Bob's strained voice trying to shout.

"You can't change what is, Bob," Mary snapped. She was insinuating Joy's marriage to Ty, but Bob's simple wisdom flipped it upside down.

"That's right, Mary," he agreed, "That's exactly right."

Jeremy looked to Joy before proceeding. They were still clasping each other's hands.

"We're taking a walk," she announced. They could hear her parents arguing behind them as she led Jeremy down the wooden stairs, her mother's comment on Joy's disregard for her marriage and her father's observation that she'd been miserable the entire four years.

"Is that true?" Jeremy ventured as they stepped into the sand.

"I've always been miserable without you," she replied.

"Then why do you keep doing it?" he asked, but Joy had already kicked off her high heels and was running recklessly toward the ocean. Jeff's words had stirred something in her. She'd missed him, too, and she'd missed Jeremy, so much more than she'd allowed herself to feel. She was tired of being grown up and well behaved. She couldn't even remember the last time she'd had fun. It was during a different lifetime, before Jeremy left for California.

"Don't you dare!" he yelled and heard her laugh as he tossed his shoes and chased her. She was heading straight for the water that looked as cold as it was. "What're you doin'? Your dress'll get wet."

"I want to go swimming!" She hopped over the shoreline like it was a jump rope. "Like I'm seventeen again and swimming in my prom dress. Only this time I want to do it with you."

"Well, I'd just like to point out that you've been drinking and I haven't, so what sounds reasonable to you might not to me…"

"You're a big baby!" she accused.

"Well, how cold is it exactly?" Jeremy asked cautiously.

She shrugged. "I can't feel my feet anymore."

"Ah shit," he groaned. "How am I going to talk you out of this? Wait—I know—the water here is cold and there are sharks in it."

"You can't have it both ways," she giggled and Jeremy burst out laughing.

"God damn, the girl's smart. You know, Joy, it doesn't really matter if you're seventeen or you're twenty-eight."

"You're just trying to change the subject. What do you mean by that?"

"You're as beautiful tonight as you were then. Come to think of it, you were pretty cute when you were three and I imagine I'll still think so when you're eighty."

"Eighty? Eighty!" The shocked expression on her face made him laugh.

"Sweetheart, you look like you're three years old right now."

"How am I supposed to live without you until I'm eighty?" she screamed.

He was taken aback by the comment and stepped into the water to appease her. "Holy shit, it's cold," he complained. She scornfully watched him approach, then suddenly her mood shifted. "You can't catch me!" she taunted like she really was three, "not in the water!"

Jeremy's head fell back on his shoulders as she dived into the ocean. Now there was no way to escape submerging in the frigid water.
"One...two...three," he counted loudly and she shrieked with excitement. Watching him with her wet hair clinging to her neck and her face streaked with makeup there was a playful smirk on her lips that gave her the look of a demon child just tossed out of Hell.

Jeremy shouted, "Ready or not here I come!"

CHAPTER TWENTY ONE
Promises Made

Jeremy's playful call echoed over the isolated beach, and Joy's parents heard it from the veranda. Bob's eyes crinkled up and a hoarse laugh left his lips, but Mary remained as silent as a stone. "It would be just as impossible to keep me away from you," he offered and reached for her hand. Joy's resounding laughter rolled over the water as Jeremy caught hold of her and pulled her into his arms. "Can't you hear how happy she is?"

"She had her chance. She should let him go so he can love someone else."

"Mary," Bob chided. His voice was disbelieving, scolding even. He leaned forward in his chair and grimaced as he moved his back. "If the boy wanted to fall in love with someone else, he would have fallen in love with someone else. But he hasn't done that, has he?"

"Because he thinks he has a chance with her," Mary argued.

"He does," Bob said softly, but he didn't dare look at his wife when he said it.

Ethan wandered out onto the veranda with Hannah before she could respond. They picked up the solemn energy and exchanged a glance. "Are you all right, Dad?" Ethan asked.

Bob offered his customary response: "I'm fine. Come sit with us."

"Sure, Dad," he replied. "But we won't stay long. Hannah's worried about the baby."

The "baby" was three-year-old Robbie, named after Bob, and the new center of the Sanders' universe. Hannah's hand was on her pregnant belly, the new baby due to arrive in December. Her brunette hair was shorter, but she was every bit as stunning with the moonlight glowing off it as she had been on the same veranda ten years prior when she was the prom date of Vinnie "Ganja" Perrone. She wasn't bubbly and idealistic like she was on that spring night, though. They were all sensing Bob's impending departure from the family. It made them silent and reverent.

"I want you to promise me you'll watch out for your sisters," Bob said gruffly. "Especially Joy. I know it's not always easy, but be patient. Help her find her way back."

In the semi-darkness of the veranda the two men facing each other could have been the same person gazing at each other from different points along the same life path, youth gazing at age or health at illness. Even the curves of their backs, shoulders and heads matched, like mirror images, but Bob's profile was more diminutive now. The cancer was shrinking him.

"I'll take care of her, Dad, I promise," Ethan agreed. "I'll do anything you ask me to."

"I know that, Ethan. That's why I asked, because I know I can trust you. Help me up, would you? My legs have run out of strength."

Ethan jumped to his feet to help his father. "We're leaving?" Mary asked. She blew her nose on a Kleenex and wiped away the tears brought on by Bob's words. "What about Joy?" Ethan crouched down beside his dad and Bob rested his slight weight on the younger man's strong shoulders.

"Jesus Christ," he moaned. The cancer had metastasized to the bone. The doctors hadn't figured it out yet, but he knew. The unbearable pain was sufficient notice. "She's with Jeremy. I trust him the same way I trust Ethan. Anyone want to challenge me on that?"

"No, Dad," Ethan reassured him and kept his arm around his waist to help him to the car.

Mary handed Bob his cane then walked to the railing, giving the guys a chance to walk ahead. In the distance she could make out the figures of Jeremy and Joy leaving the water. He was carrying her. Hannah followed her gaze, and for a couple of minutes they watched Jeremy trudge through the waves with Joy clinging to him like a child, her legs wrapped around his waist.

"She never should have let him go," Hannah said softly.

"She's as stubborn as her father," Mary stated flatly. "You know that old saying about biting off your nose to spite your face? That's Joy."

"I'm cold," she complained as soon as Jeremy set her down on the sand. He pulled her close, his hands moving in circles on her back. "Unzip my dress," she said. She couldn't see his expression; her face was resting on his chest, but she felt his hands stop moving.

"Joy—" He quickly kissed the top of her head. "Let's go back inside." He backed away from her like he was going to stand up, but he didn't.

"You should have been with me at the prom and gone swimming with me," she said. "So many nights we should have been together, like when Ethan and Hannah got married."

He stood up abruptly. "I have a jacket inside. I can get it for you."

"Why won't you listen?" she demanded. "I'm trying to tell you something important."

He bit his lip but only for a split second. "Tell me what, Joy, how you hurt me? Don't you think I wanted to be there? Ethan asked me to be his best man. You must have known that."

Joy stared at him in stunned silence. He'd never raised his voice at her before and he was moving wildly in front of her eyes now, practically gnashing his teeth. "They're my family, too. Don't you think I want to be here for your dad? And what about the prom? How do you think I felt when you went with Ty instead of me, and then spent the whole time with my best friend?"

If he'd gone with Tracy that would have caught her attention, but he hadn't. He'd stayed home alone. Sometimes Joy wondered if Tracy, who had married Nate and bought a house with him near Rexham Beach, still carried feelings for Jeremy. They bumped into each other once in a while at the super-market and there was always that unspoken common thread. Every time they made eye contact she could practically hear the words *what were you thinking*? racing from Tracy's brain.

"I don't love Ty the way I love you," she admitted. "I never have."

205

"Then why'd you marry him?" he shouted, his voice reverberating off the water.

Her gaze was on her hands folded delicately on her lap. "It's a big decision, marrying someone. There are a lot of things to think about."

"Like what? Like what, Joy?" he demanded. Suddenly it didn't seem so dark outside, like everything was being thrown into the light, the little circle made out of the two of them, all their promises and secrets, the disloyalties. "What counts more than love?"

"I didn't say it counted more…"

"Yes, you did!" he exclaimed. "You did say it when you started dating him again and you said it when you stood up in that church and became his wife." Jeremy spit the last word out of his mouth like it was poison. Tears were stinging his eyes. He rubbed at them impatiently with the heels of his hands. He turned away, but she was at his feet and hugged his legs.

"Please, don't do this," she pleaded.

Jeremy fell to his knees beside her and held her face that was damp and cool from swimming. "You were my wife," he said softly. "What right—" He threw his head back, silently coaching himself to breathe. "What right did Ty Connors have?"

She clung to his neck. "I know. I'm sorry. I told you I'm sorry. I know it's my fault."

His eyes met hers. "Then change it," he challenged.

She let out a cry. "How can I change it? It's too late. But I'll always be yours on the inside."

He brought her hands to his chest. "This—this is the part that can't be changed. You're my wife, Joy, and you always have been. You can tell everyone else that you're married to him because it says so on a piece of paper, but you can't say it to me 'cause it's a lie…and we both know it."

Every word felt as slick as a knife because every one was true. And a new thought was penetrating: was she being unfaithful to Ty with Jeremy…or was it the other way around?

"What if I stood up in some church and said I was married to another woman?" he tossed out.

"I'd hunt her down and kill her," she said menacingly.

Jeremy laughed. "Yeah, you would. But what I meant is you wouldn't believe I could love anyone like you. No one could take your place."

"No one can take your place either," she agreed with her lips an inch away from his and then finally they touched. It was so easy, climbing back into his embrace and feeling his soft warm mouth kissing hers again. She turned her back, inviting him to unzip her dress and this time he did. She wiggled like a fish on the shore to shed it as quickly as possible so she could feel him inside her. He peeled off the wet shirt and she couldn't take her eyes off his chest, more muscular than it used to be. She wondered if he noticed the changes in her body, the roundness in her belly, and her breasts not sitting up as high as they used to.

"I want to show you something," he said and turned his back. She moved closer and drew her breath in. It was their tree, the weeping willow, covering his entire back. The trunk moved sinuously up his spine and the branches hung gracefully over his shoulder blades and middle torso. And there were mourning doves in the branches, looking out like they always used to from the ridge of his roof. "That's my wedding ring," he said as he faced her.

A sob escaped with her breath. Her eyes felt cavernous as they gazed back at him, like she was dead and looking at him from the grave. How disposable the symbol she carried seemed compared to his. A gold band with diamonds embedded in it, worth thousands of dollars meant nothing compared to the ink he'd had needled into his skin, a picture that represented not only their adult love but their childhood friendship, their trust and their loyalty—everything they had ever been to each other. She'd clung to those diamonds as tightly as Jeremy had clung to her. Still, she'd been the one to doubt.

"Why are you crying?" he asked.

"I always think you forget me when you go away."

Kneeling in the sand with his weight on his haunches, he pulled her on top of him so she was straddling him. She gasped when he entered her then rested her face on his shoulder while he lifted her up and down, and she felt as weightless as the moon hanging in the sky above them. There was no need for her to do anything, only hold onto him and let him love her. And all was as it should be in the universe. She closed her eyes and wished that when she opened them she would be seventeen again, making love to Jeremy on their beach when they were first discovering each other's adult bodies.

"I love you Jeremy Blake," she said in his ear. "I have always loved you and I will always love you."

"How could you think I'd forget you?" came out of him in almost a cry.

They made love until they couldn't anymore. It seemed like everything important had already been said. Joy knew there were things she'd need to think about, but she wasn't ready to make a decision. It felt like the entire world would gasp with horror if she divorced Ty to be with Jeremy. But Jeremy, usually the silent one, still had something to say.

"When I left for California, I thought it would help our relationship, not end it. I've always known we were together, and I thought you knew it, too. It surprises me every time you think different."

"You shouldn't have left," she murmured.

"I know that now," he said and kissed her head. "And I'm sorry, Joy. Forgive me for it."

This new body of his was familiar to her eyes and hands already. She stroked his belly. "You went off and made a life without me. I couldn't accept that—I still can't. So I decided to make my own life without you. If you hadn't left, I never would have married him."

"Did you not read the part of the letter that said I'd come back if you asked me to?"

"I read it," she said fiercely. "I memorized that letter. I could recite it even now. But what it came down to was that you left me and I never dreamed you would do that."

"You wouldn't get on the phone. You wouldn't return my calls."

"Here's a thought, Jeremy: you could have got on your motorcycle and driven back."

"For what, so I could get here and find you with Ty?"

"Stupid me, I thought you would. See, that's the one thing about Ty—he's predictable." She laughed at herself for making the comment. The character trait that had drawn her into the relationship with him was the one that now repelled her the most.

"You were with him—you must have known Jeff told me."

"Of course I knew. But for everything Ty's given me, I've never been happy with him. Jeff must have told you that too. He tries really hard, and everyone says what a bitch I am because it never works. But you—all you have to do is walk into the room and I'm ecstatic. I'm glad he was passed out tonight and didn't have to see my face when you walked in."

"He has no idea how you feel?"

"Ty knows exactly how I feel. Only he pretends it isn't true. I told him that I was in love with you. He called it a crush. He said all girls have crushes on dangerous boys, but they always outgrow them. His mother must have told him that."

"I'm a dangerous boy?" Jeremy joked.

"For me you're as dangerous as they get."

He sighed. "So, what do we do now?"

"You've got to drive me home."

"What do you mean home?"

"I mean my house on Dragonfly Lane where I live with Ty. I don't have a choice, Jeremy."

"Sweetheart, you always have a choice. If you forget that, we don't stand a chance."

She looked away from him, out over where the ocean was licking at the shore, although it was barely visible from where they were settled. The tide had moved out and left them alone. "I don't want to spend my life without you, but I don't know what to do. I made a mistake and I don't know how to fix it."

"Come here," he said and she laid her head down on his warm belly. His hands stroked her hair and she felt like she was home. He sighed again, a long, discouraged one that seemed painful to let go of. "I've been waiting for you pretty much all my life. I'll keep waiting. Do what you need to do and when you call me back, I'll come. No matter where I am or what I'm doing, I'll come back."

"Promise, Jeremy?" she asked and met his gaze.

"Promise, Joy," he said.

The next day Jeremy was invited to a cookout at Ethan and Hannah's house. Joy and Ty were the only family members who didn't attend, because Ty was too hung-over Joy reported, but no one was surprised by her cancellation. Word of her frolic with Jeremy the night before had spread like a virus through the family, though no one knew the extent of it.

"Do you know who this is?" Hannah asked Robbie when Jeremy entered the raised ranch that was their home and was embraced by Lily and Mary at the foot of the stairs. His eyes darted past them looking for Joy even though she had told him the night before she wouldn't be there.

"Uncle Jeremy?" the three-year-old asked.

Jeremy crouched next to Robbie, being careful not to move too quickly. He still remembered what it felt like to be smaller than everyone else. He smiled warmly and offered his hand. Robbie raised his eyebrows comically; never before had an adult made such a gesture.

"You look a lot like your dad and your granddad," Jeremy told him and tousled his hair.

Robbie patted his head in return. "You're blue," he stated authoritatively.

It took Jeremy a moment to catch on. To anyone else it would have seemed nonsensical, but he understood it meant that the boy could see auras. "You're right, I am," he agreed.

At the top of the stairs Bob was sitting with Ethan and Eddie. "We were just talking about you," he said as Jeremy joined the circle. His words were strained—he was having trouble breathing. There was an oxygen tank at home, but he refused to cart it along when they left the house. Jeremy had to turn his eyes away from Bob's to hide the fact that he had a pretty good guess what they were talking about, and looked up just in time to catch a can of Budweiser tossed to him by Eddie.

"You don't do that to an alcoholic," Ethan scolded and snatched it out of his hand.

"Hey—I'm sorry," Eddie stammered. "I forgot."

Jeremy ran his fingers uncomfortably through his short hair. "It's all right, man. I'm good."

"How long's it been now?" Bob asked and handed him a Coke instead.

Jeremy shrugged his shoulders noncommittally. "Awhile," he muttered. The next day—his birthday— would mark seven years. "How you doin' today?"

"Great," Bob responded. "I've decided I want to stick around to see Lily's kids."

"Sounds good to me," Jeremy agreed.

"Hell, maybe even yours." There was no possible response to that comment so Jeremy pretended it wasn't directed at him and tapped the Coke can before he took a swig. As if the awkward silence weren't enough, Bob added, "I think it's time you move back."

Jeremy bit his lip. What could he say? *Everything in my future depends on your daughter?*

Mary slid her arms around his shoulders. "We all love you so much, and we miss you."

"I miss you too," he admitted. Life was lonely in California. He had friends, guys he'd ride or surf with, but no family. Jeff flew out during the winters when construction was slow, and that was the best time of year. He'd tried dating. Women seemed to show up wherever he was, at the beach, at his shop, even at the grocery store, but his heart was never in it.

"Let's toss a ball around," Ethan suggested. "You come too, Robbie."

The little boy leaped into Jeremy's arms. The feeling was more than Jeremy could have imagined. He had to blink tears back as he moved into a standing position. *The happiest man on the planet* he'd called Ethan. Now he actually understood that statement. He would be, too, if he had his life. Ethan walked out the back door and he followed with Robbie clinging to him like a baby chimpanzee. Jeremy's heart thumped in his chest when he saw the steep stairs leading to the back yard. He took one arm off of Robbie so he could hold onto the wooden railing and noticed the satisfied grin that swept Ethan's face.

He handed Robbie the football as soon as his feet were on the ground and the boy beamed to be in possession of it. "Let's see what you can do," Ethan challenged, like he was talking to a teenager, and Robbie thrust the ball with all his might. It spun wildly upward and came down on his head before it landed on the grass. "Now run it over," his father coached. He scrambled over to it, his legs as wobbly as the ball had been a minute prior and picked it up. When he reached his dad, Ethan scooped up both the boy and the ball in one clean sweep.

"How'd things go with Joy last night?" he asked Jeremy after they'd played for awhile.

Jeremy drew in his breath and crouched down to gently toss the football to Robbie who was eagerly anticipating it, his arms outstretched far too wide, as if the ball were four feet around. "We finally talked," he answered and stroked his chin with the stubble growing on it. "We've made so many mistakes. There's a lot to clean up, ya know?"

Ethan sighed. "Yeah, I know. I swear that girl hasn't smiled in seven years, since the day you sat your ass on your bike and rode out of here."

Robbie rolled the football in the direction of his dad. It bogged down halfway there. "Mommy says ass is a bad word," he mumbled.

"That's right, it is a bad word. I'm sorry I said it," Ethan quickly corrected.

"I know you think I should move back," Jeremy stated. "And I know your dad thinks that, but I can't yet. I wish I could, but I can't. I told Joy—"

Ethan held his hand up to cut him off. "Hey buddy," he said to his son, "go play in the sandbox. I'll be right over." Robbie jetted over to the green plastic frog and lifted the lid apprehensively as if he had no idea what might be hidden underneath. Jeremy couldn't resist smiling at the excitement on the little boy's face when he discovered his trucks and shovels. "Told Joy what?" Ethan asked.

"I'll come back when she asks me to—when she's ready," Jeremy replied.

"When *she's* ready? What about Dad? He needs you here now. And what about you? What Joy's doing isn't fair…to any of us, or to Ty."

"To Ty? What the fuck, Ethan? You have no idea how hard this is."

Ethan snorted. "What, you think I don't know that my wife would be married to your buddy Jeff Cosgrove right now if her parents hadn't stepped in? You think that's easy to live with?"

"I don't know what you're talking about—"

"Well, maybe you ought to. 'Cause see, I might not know what it's like to be you, but I sure as hell know what it feels like to be the other guy."

Jeremy turned angrily and walked away. It had never occurred to him that Ethan—or any of the Sanders—might side with Ty. He was halfway up the stairs when Ethan called after him.

"You're not leaving, are you?"

"No," he answered without looking back. "Your mom made a cake for my birthday. And I want to spend time with your dad."

He cantered to the top of the stairs after that, but he heard Ethan's words behind him when he said, "It'll be the last time, you know."

CHAPTER TWENTY TWO

A Parting of Ways

His cheeks and nose had the familiar sun-kissed sting of having spent the day on his board as he headed back toward Venice with his buddy Ryan in Ryan's old Chevy van that worked perfectly for dragging their surfboards to whatever beach they felt like checking out. Today it was Cardiff in San Diego. The rest of his body wasn't sunburned like his face, because the California air and water was cool enough by November to merit him wearing his wetsuit. Ryan had a Corona between his legs, but that had never posed a problem to Jeremy. Most of his surfing and riding buddies drank. They didn't even know he was in AA. That was an entirely different group of friends—the ones who told him to stay away from guys like Ryan.

Jeremy had programmed different ringtones into his cell phone for every important person in his life. For Joy, he had the Tesla song that they danced to at Lily's wedding, but he hadn't heard that ringtone yet. For Ethan it was *Over the Hills and Far Away*, for no other reason than that it was Led Zeppelin, his favorite band. When it went off in the van it didn't occur to him that Ethan was calling with bad news, but it did the moment he heard his voice.

Bob had passed away less than half an hour before. *When I was still riding waves*, Jeremy thought. He saw himself on the surfboard instead of by the bedside like the rest of the kids, and his body folded underneath him so his head was suddenly between his knees. Grief and guilt were competing for dominance. What right did he have to be three thousand miles away and playing at the beach while the person he owed more to than anyone was dying in his bed? The truth was, though Jeremy couldn't see it through his grief, the only time he ever felt weightless was on his board or his bike. Every other moment of his life he felt cemented to the Earth, like the sky was coming down on his shoulders.

"Tell me what happened," he said into the phone.

Most of it Jeremy already knew, from Mary whom he'd been calling every two or three days for updates. Bob had been bedridden for over a month with hospice coming in to help take care of him. But the rest of the story had Ty's name mixed into it…like he was part of the family.

"Dude," he heard Ryan say and glanced over. "What the fuck?" Jeremy was lying on his knees, squeezing his calf with his one free hand and crying.

"Pull over!" he told him. "I'll call you right back," he said to Ethan.

The van pulled off the road and Jeremy vomited out the open door. He stepped outside and tried to find a place to be alone, an impossible feat—cars were flying past him on the San Diego Freeway. His head was swimming with every wrong turn he'd made. He shouldn't have left Massachusetts, chasing the ghost of a father who never cared about him and leaving behind his real dad, the one who would have done anything for him.

And Joy…he'd given her all that space and time thinking they would have a future that wasn't tainted by his alcoholism and the emotional injuries she'd suffered as a child. But his absence had only deepened them. He'd given up his place beside her, and Ty had taken it. His stomach convulsed and he threw up again. Jeremy stripped off his t-shirt and wiped his eyes and face with it. His hands were shaking so much they were barely functional, like when he was drinking. Then he had the most asinine thought his brain had spit out in years: *a couple beers would fix that*.

"Toss me one," he directed as soon as he got in the van. Ryan happily complied. It was a language he spoke fluently, a reality in startling contrast to his trembling, sweating friend who'd been vomiting on the side of the road. After he'd downed the beer, Jeremy offered an explanation. "The guy who basically raised me, Bob—I told you about him—he died." A sob escaped with the last word. "Let's get out of here. Stop at the next packie."

"Next what?" Ryan asked.

"Liquor store." Jeremy handed him a fifty-dollar bill before he picked up his cell phone. "Buy whatever you want. I'll drink whatever you're drinking." It could have been turpentine and he would have swallowed it.

215

The alcohol was already working, subtly kicking in so that his nerve endings were no longer screaming and he could breathe a little easier, when he speed-dialed the phone. "I'm sorry bro—sorry I hung up like that," he offered as soon as he heard Ethan's voice.

"Man, I wish you were here," Ethan said. "You have no idea how much this sucks. There's a snowstorm, and we're all waiting here for the guys from the funeral home."

"Is your mom all right?" Jeremy managed.

"She won't leave him. He's gone, you know? But she won't leave the bedroom."

"You mean your dad's body is still at the house?"

"Yeah, I told you. The funeral guys aren't here yet."

"Fuck," Jeremy breathed. The bright California sunshine was permeating the windshield. The reality of the moment he was in could not have been any more different than theirs. His chest tightened. "Where's Joy?"

"In her old bedroom, I think. She's not in the living room with the rest of us."

"Put her on the phone, Ethan," Jeremy demanded.

He heard the sound of her sobbing before he heard her voice on the receiver. "Jer-Jeremy?"

"It's me, Joy," he reassured her. "You okay sweetheart?"

"N-no. Daddy, Daddy died."

"I know. I know, sweetheart. Where are you, in your bedroom?"

"In our bed."

Our bed. The words soothed him as nothing had since the last time they were together. "Can you stay on the phone for a minute? I'll tell you a story." He caught Ryan's glance in his direction and scrambled into the back of the van. "Are you under the covers?" he whispered.

"Yes, but I'm in my clothes. We stayed up all night with Daddy."

"That's okay." He didn't want her to leave her room and see her father being taken from the house in a body bag. "Stay there in your room, okay?"

"I miss you," she suddenly cried. "I wish you were with me."

"Me, too, Joy. I'll be there as soon as I can."

"I want you to come through my window. I wish we never grew up."

The van stopped abruptly and Jeremy fell sideways. The door slammed shut as Ryan left to buy some alcohol and Jeremy opened the slider so he could step outside. "Hang on," he said to Joy and shouted, "Ryan, buy me a pack of butts."

"Who's Ryan?" Joy asked.

"Just a guy I surf with." Jeremy stepped onto the side rail of the van so he could see the surfboards on the roof. He reached for the red and white striped McTavish fireball with the black flame licks on the solid red side and stroked it. The rhythmic motion was calming.

"I hate that," she said.

"What?"

"That you have a life without me."

He looked up at the blue California sky that Joy couldn't see and wished he could explain to her that it meant nothing to him. "I hate that you have a life without me, too," he finally said.

"What's the story you were going to tell me?"

"Oh. I wanted to remind you about something Running Deer used to say. Remember he told us there's no such thing as death? When we die, our spirit wiggles out of our body and is free again like before we came here."

There was a silence as Joy thought about what he'd said. She not only remembered him saying it but *why* he said it: because a classmate had been hit by a car while riding her bike down Sea Street, and she and Jeremy had gone to bed crying. "That's how Daddy is now?"

"He might be in the house watching over you. Running Deer said sometimes people do that."

"I remember. Do you still talk to the Indians?"

"I talk to Running Deer. I've been meditating and it helps me hear him. He's my spirit guide. I think the younger Indian might be your spirit guide."

She was quiet, trying to digest the information. "When you talk to him again," she finally said, "ask him why they stopped talking to me, if they're mad at me because we're not together."

Jeremy's fingers rubbed the furrows on his brow. The depth of Joy's issues sometimes scared him. Ryan was approaching and tossed him a pack of Marlboros. He peeked inside the brown bag: a quart of Bacardi Rum, a 2 liter bottle of Coke, plastic cups and a six pack of Corona; that ought to get them home. Jeremy moved two fingers in a circle—*mix 'em up*, and fumbled a cigarette between his lips.

"We'll talk about it when I get home, all right Joy?" he said into the phone. Ryan was still watching him and the lack of privacy made him uncomfortable.

"Jeremy," she said cautiously, "while you're home, if I'm not the way you want me to be, try to understand why and remember that you're the only one I really love."

She wasn't leaving Ty any time soon. If she was, she wouldn't have given him that kind of heads up. "You're the only one I love too," he murmured and had to fight back tears when the words left his mouth. He was in the van and had swallowed a whole cup of rum & Coke before he let his head fall back on the seat and the tears escape from his eyes.

Jeff dropped him off at the Sanders' house and Robbie answered the door when he knocked, which was a good beginning. In contrast to everyone else, he was full of energy and giggles. He jumped into Jeremy's arms and let him hug him until Mary approached. She looked ten years older and completely alone. The other women waited their turns to welcome him, first Lily, then Hannah, and finally Joy. It was unlike Joy to be last at anything, but it only took him a minute to figure out why. She didn't want anyone to rush her or to listen in on the things she whispered in his ear. And when she let go of her embrace, she laced her fingers through his and led him to the couch where she was sitting so he would stay beside her.

"I put these aside to show you," she said and handed him a stack of pictures.

The room was silent as he flipped through the photos, every one bringing him back to the childhood that'd been snatched away: at the beach, coated in sand, he smiled at Joy while she looked at the camera…on the fence in front of the house next to Ethan, his feet dangled in the air while Ethan's touched the ground…with Joy and Lily in the baby pool, Bob spraying them with a water gun…propped on Bob's shoulders like the tiniest king of the world, holding on with both hands to his smiling jaw. Jeremy closed his eyes.

"I'll make you copies," Joy offered and stroked his back. He turned his head to meet her eyes and she laid her head on his shoulder, something that obviously made her mother uncomfortable.

"Can I make you something to eat?" she asked Jeremy.

"No, thanks. I had lunch with Jeff when he picked me up at the airport."

"I'll make you coffee," Joy volunteered.

"How are things in California?" Hannah asked. She was sprawled in Bob's favorite chair, her pregnant belly so big it was now possible to believe there was a human being inside it.

He tried his best to pull out a smile. "The same I guess. Business is steady. I work a lot."

"Do you still think about moving back?" Lily asked.

"All the time. When's the baby coming, Hannah?"

"Ten days. We were hoping Bob would…well…"

Jeremy's thick lashes covered his eyes as they looked down at his hands on his lap. It was hard to imagine Bob wouldn't be there to meet his new grandchild. "A girl this time?" he asked.

"We didn't find out," she replied with a smile, "but I think it's a girl. Do you think so?"

He hesitated, wondering why he thought it, but he did. He *knew* it. "Yeah," he said then turned his eyes to Lily. She grinned, but didn't give it up yet. "You, too?"

"Joy told you!" Lily exclaimed. Her little sister made a scoffing noise from the kitchen.

"She didn't tell me," Jeremy said. "But I just had this feeling there are two girls coming."

"I'm having a girl!" Lily shrieked and leaped from her chair. She had to call Eddie to tell him the news. The entire family trusted Jeremy's intuition.

"Do you still like cream and sugar?" Joy called out.

"Black," he answered and called her *sweetheart* before he thought twice about it. "Can I help with anything?" he asked Mary, trying to draw attention away from the oversight.

She sighed. "After we're done with pictures, we'll work on the eulogy. You could help with that." He grew instantly self-conscious. Mary noticed and added, "Joy's writing it. What we need help with is collecting memories—little things about Bob that show who he was."

Like teaching someone else's kid how to throw a football and ride a bike, Jeremy thought. *Buying an awkward fifth grader clothes for picture day even though he was broke and had to use a credit card, or teaching a high school dropout how to make a living.*

Joy brought him his coffee and sat so close beside him that their hips touched. Robbie scrambled over to them and deposited a book onto Jeremy's legs, *The Mouse and the Motorcycle*.

"You like motorcycles?" Jeremy asked and lifted Robbie onto his lap.

"I like the mouse," Robbie answered seriously.

Jeremy laughed. "I like that mouse, too. His name is Ralph, isn't it?"

The boy nodded and opened the book to the middle of the story. "You read," he commanded.

"Tell you the truth, buddy, I'm not so good at reading."

Robbie's big brown eyes evaluated his face. "The pictures are better," he said.

"Bob used to read you that book," Mary noted and Jeremy nodded. He remembered.

The rest of the afternoon was pieced together like an old familiar quilt, a story about this, a memory about that, a book or song for Robbie, snacks made by Mary and just being together in the same space that Bob used to occupy, but no longer did as the sky darkened and night slipped in. The wake was planned for the next day, and Mary informed Jeremy that Bob had requested he stand in the receiving line. One last time he'd made sure Jeremy was treated like part of the family.

Jeff drove him to the funeral home and agreed to stay the whole time, even though it was difficult for him to be in the same room with Hannah and Ethan together as husband and wife. "Get it over with," he advised as soon as they arrived and saw Ty sitting in a metal fold up chair next to Joy. Jeremy was surprised when he saw Ty, how distinguished he looked. There was gray in his hair, he still had that straight posture that served him as a grown man much better than as a teenager, and he had laugh wrinkles around his eyes that softened his appearance.

Jeremy left Jeff in the hallway next to a table that held the guest book and photographs of Bob. He approached Mary first and hugged her while she cried on his shoulder. Ty was the only one he didn't embrace. It was difficult enough to offer him his hand, but he did. "It's nice to see you, Jeremy," Ty said like he meant it. Jeremy hadn't expected him to be nice. For Christ's sake, he'd made love to his wife only three months before. Of course Ty didn't know that, but still.

He barely pecked Joy's cheek afterward, and then approached the closed coffin. Jeremy knew that Bob wasn't in that wooden box any more than he was. If he had to venture a guess, it would be that Bob was sitting right next to Mary, like always. In fact, if Jeremy had believed he really was gone and couldn't see his actions, he might not have stood in the receiving line because he'd never felt as uncomfortable in his entire life. But he knew better. Bob had asked him to and he could either go along with it or hear about it when they met face to face again.

Jeremy was kneeling in front of the casket when he felt Joy take his hand. She wanted to be beside him when they said their goodbyes. In their world, that made perfect sense, but he couldn't help thinking that in Ty's world it must have hurt like hell. He glanced over his shoulder and saw him watching, and the thing was, he recognized the expression in his eyes. He'd seen it every day in his own mirror. It was pain eating him from the inside out because he believed the woman he loved didn't love him back. It brought to mind Ethan's words *I know what it's like to be the other guy.* Jeremy tried to imagine how he would feel if he saw Jeff holding Hannah's hand right in front of Ethan. *He'd be fucking rip shit.* That was the moment he made the decision to head back to California and stay there. Unless Joy ended it with Ty, he couldn't come back. He silently asked Bob's forgiveness for giving up before he let go of her hand.

The next day, after the funeral, he said his goodbyes to everyone at the Sanders house—even Joy—but she followed him out the front door into the snow-packed driveway even though she wasn't wearing a coat. "Where are you going?" she demanded.

"I told you inside, I'm going home."

"This is home!" she shouted.

He led her to Jeff's Mustang parked in the street, the same vehicle he'd driven her home in from Lily's wedding. The temperature was below freezing and the wind was whipping. They climbed into the car and Jeremy automatically looked at the house to see if anyone was watching. Within a minute or two the windows were fogged up from their warm breath, giving them a wall of privacy. But Jeremy had grown uncomfortable being alone with Joy. As much as it hurt him being away from her, he didn't want to hurt someone else by being with her. He didn't have it in him to be cruel.

"All I ever wanted in my entire life was to be with you—" he started.

"I know," she interrupted.

"No, you don't know. For as far back as I can remember it was all I needed." She parted her lips to speak, but he stopped her. "I'm never going to say this again so you need to hear me out."

Her breathing became irregular like she was about to cry, which made it difficult for him to continue, but he had to. If he didn't say it now, he'd never say it. "I'm not coming back here."

"What?" she gasped. "But you promised! You said you'd come when I ask you to."

"If you ask me because you've ended it with Ty, I'll be on the next flight. But otherwise, I'm not going to be your lover. You chose him, Joy. I don't know why you did, but you did."

"You're the one who said we'd always have each other!" she threw out desperately. "You said you can't break something that's unbreakable."

"I'll never stop loving you," he said. "I couldn't even if I wanted to, but I've got to hold on to some self-respect, and there's got to be respect for other people. I don't hate Ty. I feel sorry for the guy, because even though you're married to him you'll never really be his." She didn't deny it, which only drew a long sigh from him. "Or mine," he added.

"How can you say that? I've always been yours. Everyone knows it…"

"Even Ty," Jeremy breathed out slowly. "But that doesn't give me the satisfaction I thought it would. You need to go inside and be with your family. And I need to get out of the way."

"How can you do this to me after Daddy just died? You know how much I need you."

"Sweetheart," he said softly. "Try to understand that when you lost your dad I lost my dad, too. You've got your family and you've got Ty. What the hell do I have?"

She scrambled out of the Mustang and slammed the door without a goodbye. He used the sleeve of his pea coat to clear the fog off the window so he could watch her storm into the house. It was the last time his blue eyes took her in.

CHAPTER TWENTY THREE

One Step Forward, Ten Steps Back

Alcoholism is a poisonous snake coiled inside the belly waiting to be awakened. It only takes ounces, not gallons, to bring it to full consciousness. With every drink ingested, the battle becomes less and less even-handed. The serpent grows in strength; the person shrinks and weakens. Jeremy didn't drink at all during the three days he spent in Marshfield, but that didn't matter. The demon had been born inside of him. On the sunny San Diego Freeway coming home from surfing at Cardiff, his old enemy, alcoholism, had staged its return.

Jeff bid him farewell in the security line and went on his way without Jeremy mentioning to him that he had picked up a drink. Usually he flew out to Los Angeles in January, but this year he promised to arrive in time for Christmas, not because he suspected that Jeremy'd started drinking, but because he didn't want his friend to be alone after Bob's death and his new separation from Joy. In the car heading north to the airport, Jeremy had stated that he felt like an orphan. It was an odd comment, Jeff thought, for someone who'd basically been one all his life.

Jeremy didn't have to deliberate what to do with the down time. A glass of Jack Daniels at the airport bar had his name on it. It was gone before he remembered to take his pea coat off. Underneath, he was still wearing the clothes he'd worn to Bob's funeral, a black V-neck sweater that stretched nicely across his chest with gray dress slacks. The bartender, wearing a short skirt and tall boots, refilled his glass and tried to catch his eye. He had the strongest urge to call Joy's phone even though he never did that. Jeremy reached into the coat pocket for his cell phone and hit the button for his contact list. An alert came up warning him that the battery was low.

"Would you like a menu?" the bartender asked him.

"No thanks," he replied without looking at her. "Is there a men's room near here?" She pointed a finger outside the bar area into the main corridor of the airline.

He left his coat and his phone at the bar while he used the urinal, not worrying that someone would steal them. The bartender had her eye on him. He knew the look, the quick flirtatious smile, followed by a slow visual appraisal of every inch of his body. It wasn't likely she'd allow someone to walk off with his stuff. She was grinning at him appreciatively when he returned to his barstool.

"Nice ring tone," she teased. "Very romantic."

"Romantic?" he shot back. *Fuck.* He reached for the cell phone. *1 missed call.* He pushed the button to see who'd called; it squealed and then died. "No, no," he pleaded and banged it against the bar.

"That's not going to help. Where's your charger? You can plug it in here if you want."

He pushed the power button. The alert message came up again indicating the battery was dangerously low then the phone died again. "It's in my suitcase. Can you believe this?"

The bartender shrugged her shoulders. "Was it important?"

He shut his eyes to think about it, feeling drained from his confrontation with Joy. What if it'd been her? It would be unlike her to call after everything he'd said. Joy had a personality trait that usually prevented her from being the one to set things right. It was the same stubborn quality that kept her from saying *I give* when they were kids wrestling on the beach. Come to think of it, it had always been hard for him to say it, too.

His heart plummeted into his stomach. *It was probably Ethan who called*, he suddenly realized. The Zeppelin song was romantic. His eyes shot open and caught the bartender's attention. She leaned against the bar so her cleavage was showing. "Listen," Jeremy said conspiratorially and she moved closer. "This is important—what was the ringtone?"

"Um, a pretty song with a guy singing."

"Was it Led Zeppelin?" She shook her head. "You're sure?" he pressed. Hope was rising inside him—should he let it float there and enjoy it, ride the high, or squash it now and get it over with?

"I'm sure. Wait a minute." She was trying to sing the song inside her head while she wiped down the bar. She started humming and his heart skipped. It sounded like the Tesla song. Finally she began to utter words. *So you think that it's over, that your love has finally reached the end. Anytime you call, night or day, I'll be right there for you if you need a friend…"* She was still struggling to figure out the rest of the song, but she didn't need to.

"Love is all around you. Love is knockin' outside your door," Jeremy said out loud.

She pointed at him dramatically. "That's it," she agreed. "What's it called?"

"*Love Song*," he sighed and dropped his head into his hands again, this time out of pure relief. All the hairs were standing up on his arms. "Can I ask you one more favor?"

She eyed him like she wanted to eat him for dinner. "You can pretty much name it," she admitted.

"It's…nothing like that. Sorry, I only wanted to know if I could use your cell phone for a minute. I wouldn't ask if it wasn't important."

She turned on her high heel. At first he thought she was blowing him off, but then she came back. "I hope she knows how lucky she is," she said and slapped the phone into his hand.

He had to call Ethan at Mary's house first to get Joy's cell phone number. "What happened?" Ethan demanded. "Joy was a mess when she left here."

"What time was that?"

"Ten-ish. She should be home now. Ty's in the ER until eleven in case you're wondering."

"I wasn't going to ask you that, Ethan," Jeremy said. "Right now I'm borrowing someone's phone, but I'll call you tomorrow."

He hung up so he could call Joy. The phone rang a few times then went to voicemail. It was sitting on the bottom of her new Marc Jacobs bag, underneath her cashmere scarf and gloves that muted the sound of the ring. She'd been sitting by herself in that big house, thinking about everything Jeremy had said and wishing he would call her back. It was shortly after 10:00 p.m. on the way home when she'd swallowed her pride and called his phone. At 11:24 she gave up and went to bed, thinking he was on the airplane.

When she didn't pick up the phone, he didn't leave her a voicemail, but he did send her a text message: *Do you give yet Joy? Cuz I do. I give. J.*

The bartender allowed Jeremy to hold onto her cell phone while he had another drink in the event Joy texted him back or called. "What's her name?" she asked and sighed when he told her. "I figured it would be something beautiful and unique. So, how'd you meet her?"

He wiped the Jack Daniels off his mouth with the back of his hand. "When we were three-years-old I saw her playing in her yard and squeezed under the fence. I've loved her ever since."

His words drew a long silent stare from the bartender. Her business was waiting on men, listening to their stories and their heartaches, flirting with them enough to get good tips but not enough to bring on their advances unless they were someone like the guy sitting in front of her. But never in her life had she heard such words come from a man.

"This one's on me," she told him and filled his glass. "So, did you fly out here to see her?"

"Not exactly. I came home because my dad died." She offered her condolences and Jeremy realized she was the first person to do so. "Thank you," he said sincerely. To the world, Bob might have been a kind neighbor, but to Jeremy he was his father, his role model, the person with whom, aside from Joy, he'd shared the most meaningful relationship of his life.

After reflecting on it the bartender added, "I really do hope things work out, because it sounds like they're meant to, but…" She took a few seconds to get up the nerve. "I could give you my phone number in case they don't."

He stared into the amber liquid in the glass. "I live in L.A. now," he said. "I'm not coming back here unless it's to be with her. But thanks for asking. You're a nice person."

The bartender wasn't sure whether to be injured or flattered. It was an unusual statement—*you're a nice person*. Most men made comments about her smile or her legs. "So are you," she replied. "It almost makes me wish we didn't meet. Now I'll be wishing all guys were like you."

Addiction is a form of possession. Something foreign enters and takes over the person's free will. Jeremy was caught in its grip…and he knew it. "Be happy they're not," he said as he pulled his wallet out to pay her. "My head's not on right."

Joy never saw the text message that he sent. Due to a reception glitch, it didn't arrive until 11:29, the same time Ty was digging through her bag for keys so he could move the Mercedes into the garage. The text was sent from a number he didn't recognize, but from the letter "J", he knew that it was Jeremy. It was Ty's suspicion that he texted her regularly. In truth, it was the first time he'd ever done it. To Ty what it came down to was *do I make a big deal out of this or do I pretend it never happened*? He stared at the message, but couldn't understand its meaning in context to a relationship. For him it was an easy decision. He hit delete.

CHAPTER TWENTY FOUR
Mr. Hyde

He was on the beach in Plymouth, lying on the sand with Joy. The sound of surf was in his ears and frigid water was rolling rhythmically over their feet. Snow was falling, touching down lightly on his face, but it wasn't cold. He opened his eyes and realized that they were flower petals falling, not snowflakes. The thought of how much she would love them brought a smile to his lips, but then there were too many and they were coming so quickly that he was afraid they might be buried. He reached for her, but she wasn't there. The petals were falling faster, swirling like snowflakes in a blizzard. On his knees, he searched for her with his hands in the piles of petals, but it was fruitless. She was nowhere and the heaps were so deep now that even the ocean was no longer visible. His heart was crashing against his ribs as he ran through the white landscape in search of her. "Joy!" he screamed in anguish.

And woke himself up.

The woman lounging in the recliner next to the couch, her short hair dyed black as a crow, looked horrified. Jeremy's hair was wet with sweat and his body was shaking so much that he was nearly convulsing. He wiped at his eyes with his hands before he reached for the Jack Daniels on the table and took a drink as he swung his legs over the side of the couch.

"Who's Joy?" the woman asked icily and Jeremy jerked his head toward the sound of her name. He took another drink, though, before he answered.

"My wife," he said.

His feet hit the floor and he slid his jeans on before he headed to the door, still holding the bottle in one hand and his Harley Davidson t-shirt in the other. He turned back before he turned the doorknob. "Look I...can't do this anymore," he told the woman watching him.

There was no real connection between them, even though they'd known each other for a month. He barely spoke. She'd found him passed out on the beach near her apartment and taken him as a gift from God. Never had she seen such beautiful eyes, and he was sweet and soft-spoken.

It didn't take long to realize that there was something wrong with him, though, something more than the drinking problem that was evident by the bottle that almost never left his hand. He had the haunted look of a war veteran. When he muttered those last words from the doorway she presumed he was talking about their relationship, whatever that was, but she'd presumed wrongly. He was referring to something much bigger than that. She shrugged her shoulders—*no big loss*—and he walked out.

Jeremy wandered onto the beach, sliding his Oakley's on to block the blinding sunlight. He'd been getting migraines for over a year now, since he'd started using alcohol again, but in his mind it was since Bob's death and his latest separation from Joy. He associated the headaches with grief, not addiction. The migraines came nearly every day. But it didn't matter to him anymore. Nothing mattered, not the grief, the headaches, the scratched sunglasses or the waves he was watching but could no longer ride. Not even the Jack Daniels in his hand.

In his wallet he had exactly two hundred dollars. That was all he had left. His business, his apartment, his bike, even his boards were all gone. That's why he'd called Jeff back in December and told him not to come out this year. He didn't want him to know how far he'd fallen. It hadn't taken long— one year and four months—to lose everything he'd worked for years to gain. There used to be a nice little nest egg tucked aside so he'd have something to start a life with Joy when the day finally came, but once he'd started drinking again he'd lost control of his business. It didn't matter anyway, he reminded himself, because that day—the one he'd been waiting for— wasn't coming.

Jeremy pulled the stone arrowhead on the leather cord out of his pocket. He'd been carrying it for almost twelve years. It was the only thing he still owned that he couldn't bear to leave behind. In the back pocket of his jeans, there was an envelope addressed to Jeff with three stamps on it so that all he'd have to do is remember to drop it in a mailbox by the end of the day. His thumb stroked the rough stone before it went back in his pocket. Not yet. He couldn't let go of it yet.

When the bottle was empty, he started walking. En route to a local bar where he'd drank too many times to count, he passed a homeless guy on the sidewalk. Back when he was still sober and in AA, he used to walk by homeless people and say to himself *but for the grace of God, there go I*. The guy was passed out and didn't know Jeremy had stopped to look at him. *There I am*, he thought this time. *It's like looking in a fucking mirror*. The man's hands were shaking even in his unconscious state, and his face was just as red from the alcohol as his own. Around his head and shoulders, Jeremy could see a cloudy gray, smoke-like, energy. Instinctively, he laid his hands on the homeless person's chest. There was an illness in the man's heart that would soon take him from the physical world, regardless of Jeremy's actions, but the body is not the only aspect of human beings that can be healed. His mind and emotions were sick, as well.

"Hey man, you all right?" Jeremy asked when the guy's bright green eyes popped open.

Jeremy tried to hold his breath inconspicuously while the homeless person stammered out an answer, because the stench from his mouth was overpowering. Jeremy gave him half the money in his wallet before he walked away and left the guy alone with his misery. He couldn't give it all away because today he'd need to be seriously sedated to carry through with his plan.

It was 2:31 a.m. Pacific time when the two Native American men convened on the train track near Long Beach, California. Although they were as visible to each other as any other people would be while engaged in conversation with a friend, they were not visible to most human beings still contained inside a physical body. Some with a clairvoyant ability might have caught a glimpse of their forms, and others might've felt their presence, but none could be completely aware of the two men and their conversation unless they, too, were in spirit form.

"Get through to him," Moonhawk pleaded.

"I've tried," Running Deer responded. "You know I've tried, relentlessly. He's closed his channel. There's nothing I can do."

"It's because of the alcohol—the alcohol blocked the channel."

"That's self-will. I warned Elia before he followed her here that I wouldn't override his will."

"He couldn't have known it would be like this."

"That's why we have guides, for counsel. We both told him to choose a different mother."

"But compassion, Running Deer. Surely you can grant him compassion and intervene."

Running Deer's black eyes silently assessed his friend. They had a history that ran deeper than the Earth's oceans. They'd traveled together as friends, brothers, confidantes, and even served as each other's spirit guides. Moonhawk sighed. "Forgive me—he's my brother. It hurts me to see it."

"Then look away. Be with Kalli. This is the path he's chosen. God gave him free will. It's not for us to take it back. When you think it's all gone wrong, remember how much he's grown during this lifetime, how much deeper he's learned to love."

In the distance on the track they could make out the shadowy figure of Jeremy, his bare feet staggering beneath him. He stopped where they were standing as if he was aware of them, but he wasn't. It was they who knew where his journey would end. He placed an empty Jack Daniels bottle on the track and his hands reached for his knees as a sob escaped him. Moonhawk moved closer and placed an unnoticed hand on his shoulder.

"I'm right here," he said, but Jeremy couldn't hear him. Moonhawk's arms encircled Jeremy, and he allowed his energy to completely enfold him. "Elia, try to listen. I'm here with you." Jeremy broke down and cried, not because he heard Moonhawk, but because he thought he was alone.

"It's too late for that. You have to leave," Running Deer said sternly. "Be with Kalli."

"She's sleeping. I can see her." He could view Joy remotely from where he was standing next to Jeremy, three thousand miles away.

"She might feel the impact."

The words startled Moonhawk. He hadn't thought of that, how tightly their energies were connected. It wouldn't be the first time they'd felt each other's pain. "You'll bring him over?"

"Yes, of course," Running Deer reassured him. "I'll bring him home."

The train's headlights were already approaching when Moonhawk hugged his brother goodbye. He'd see him again soon, but never again in the physical form known as Jeremy Blake. He turned his eyes one last time to Running Deer, and then he was gone.

A bright light was glaring in her face and her body jerked violently as pain ripped through her head and chest. Joy blinked her eyelids open, trying to bear the sunlight invading through the blinds. Before she saw it with her eyes, she could have sworn the glare was coming from headlights.

"What happened?" she asked out loud, but she was alone.

Ty was at the hospital. As she trudged to the bathroom, she had the feeling of impending doom and couldn't identify the cause. She quickly rehashed the events of the evening before. Everything had been fine, ordinary, when she went to bed and read a novel before giving herself over to sleep. Maybe a detail in the story had tangled itself into her subconscious mind, and manifested in a nightmare. But never before had she awakened in pain from a dream. It exited her body almost immediately, but now she was aware of a strange emptiness in its place.

The light pouring in through the windows downstairs was bright too, bouncing off a fresh layer of snow. It was March, and still there was no reprieve. She was tired of waiting to cast off the cold and feel reborn like the crocuses pushing through the frozen earth. The clock over the stove indicated it was only 5:42 a.m. She was never awake at this hour. Once she'd toasted an English muffin and poured a cup of coffee, she curled up on the couch to watch a movie she'd rented from Netflix, *13 Conversations About One Thing*.

It was the hardest day of Jeff Cosgrove's life, the day he received the call on his cell phone from Belinda Blake that his best friend had committed suicide by throwing himself in front of a train. He'd lived through his mother's diagnosis of breast cancer when he was only twelve years old and her death when he was fourteen, and he'd managed to survive and even stay sober when his father died prematurely of a heart attack. But Jeremy's death had blindsided him, caught him utterly by surprise. It was 11:35 a.m. Eastern time when he received the news.

Now it was almost an hour later and he was driving to Joy's house to carry the message to her. He had promised Jeremy's mother that he would, but he was nauseous and trembling from the shock. His stomach gurgled as he pulled into the driveway of her home on Dragonfly Lane and threw the Mustang into park. He felt so sick that he wasn't sure his legs could carry him inside, but they had to. If he didn't tell Joy, Belinda would. And Joy still hated Belinda.

He stepped out of the car and breathed in the brisk air. It helped to clear his brain. But then he caught sight of Joy, standing in the doorway watching him approach. She was dressed in sweatpants and a t-shirt and with her blonde hair falling on her shoulders, she looked just like she had in high school, despite the fact that she'd be thirty soon. But what created a photographic image in his mind was the expression on her face. She looked thrilled to see him. He couldn't return the warm smile and had to look down at his work boots crunching through the snow while she held the door open. It had been more than a year since they'd seen each other, at her father's funeral.

Jeff had never been inside her home, though he'd driven past it with Jeremy. The foyer had a cathedral ceiling and no furniture blocking the view of the spiral staircase. In the first five-second sweep, his eyes took in Joy's surroundings that were so different than the home she'd grown up in. The house didn't feel cold, but empty in some inexplicable way, and then right as her arms reached for him, he understood. She was lonely. It was her loneliness that was filling up that wide-open foyer.

"I've missed you, Jeff," she said as his arms held her close, but he couldn't hide the fact that his body was shaking and he still couldn't meet her eyes. "What's wrong?" she asked.

He had to wrench the words out of his throat. There was a Persian carpet under his feet, and he focused on one little detail, a gold leaf, while he coached himself. "It's Jeremy," he managed to say but his voice was hoarse, as if even his throat was protesting the conversation.

Joy took his hand. "Is he hurt? Did he crash his motorcycle?" she gasped.

He shook his head and she exhaled relief. Jeff realized his error and had to fix it. "I mean, there was an accident, but not on his...not on his motorcycle." She groaned, and Jeff held her waist with his free hand. "This is the hardest thing I've ever had to say," he admitted.

"Where is he?" She squeezed his hand so hard it hurt. "Tell me where he is, Jeff!"

"He died, Joy. He got hit by a train. They...the police...they said he did it on purpose."

A train. Headlights.

Her initial reaction—in the first few seconds—was vaguely what Jeff expected. She dropped her face into her hands, processing what he'd said. But then she met his eyes intensely and shook her head. "That's not right," she argued. "He wouldn't do that. He promised me. He said he'd come back when I called him, and Jeremy always keeps his promises."

She moved over to the glass storm door. Gazing out onto Jeff's Mustang in the driveway, she was remembering the last time it was parked there. It was after Lily's wedding, when Jeremy had driven her home. The memory of that night was crystal clear, how she hadn't wanted to kiss him goodbye and let him go back to L.A., but how she'd felt that there wasn't a choice.

The smallest of storms was brewing, a tiny black sphere born from rage and pain growing in her solar plexus. She stayed perfectly still, feeling it move upward into her chest,where it caught fire as if someone had saturated her heart with lighter fluid and tossed a match on it. She could feel it writhing around, this pain that was moving like a serpent inside her, throbbing with Jeff's words, *Jeremy died, he died, he died.* It moved upward into her throat, trying to find its way out, but she was mute and there was no escape. Her arms moved above her head in some kind of ancient dance to force the monster out. But it was there, too, in her arms and hands, traveling like arsenic through her bloodstream. She summoned all the despair inside her and tried to thrust it out as she brought her arms back down again.

To Jeff it looked like this: Joy stared silently through the storm door for a prolonged moment. She was in shock, he presumed, and fixated on a neighbor who was walking her Irish setter past the yard. When Joy lifted her arms, he thought she was greeting or gesturing to the woman, but then she did something odd: she clasped her hands together above her head before she did the most unexpected and horrific thing he'd ever witnessed. She thrust both arms downward through the storm door. After that, it was all a blur of shattered glass and blood, and someone was screaming but it wasn't Joy. It was the neighbor—hysterical over what she'd happened to see.

Jeff dragged Joy away from the jagged edges hovering like a shark's teeth. She was completely still, more like a mannequin than a woman. He wrapped his shirt around the ten-inch gash on her right forearm while he shouted to the neighbor to call 911. Her hands and left arm were bleeding too, but the blood was oozing from those wounds, not spurting like a fountain.

"Come back, J-Jeremy," she was sobbing.

Jeff pulled her onto his lap on the floor with the thousands of glass shards surrounding them. When the ambulance pulled up, followed closely by a police cruiser, it must have looked like the scene of a murder; the blood that had shot out through the broken door reddened the freshly fallen snow on the steps, and Joy was hyperventilating in Jeff's arms.

"She can't breathe," he told the two paramedics who raced up the driveway to assist. "I've been putting pressure on her arm, but she's lost a lot of blood."

"What happened?" a police officer asked Jeff.

"It was an accident." Joy clung to Jeff when the paramedics tried to coax her onto the stretcher. "It's okay," he told her. "I'll go with you." she let go and they moved her into the ambulance. The cop was still watching Jeff. "Look, she got some bad news and… can I go? I want to ride with her."

"Go ahead," the officer said, but he pulled out a small pad of paper. "What's your name?"

"Jeffrey Cosgrove. I live right down the street."

"Cosgrove Construction, right?"

"Right," Jeff answered and crawled into the back of the ambulance next to Joy. He yelled up front to the driver, "You better call the hospital and give her husband the heads up."

"Who's her husband?" the other paramedic asked, the one who was monitoring her blood pressure that was dangerously low.

"Ty Connors."

"You mean Dr. Connors, the emergency room physician?" he asked.

"That would be the one," Jeff said and dropped his head onto the palm of his hand, unknowingly leaving a smudge of blood on his forehead that looked like war paint. His eyes fell on his white t-shirt that was drenched with blood, then shifted to Joy whose face was so white it looked completely drained of it. She was like a discarded doll with her lifeless blue eyes focused on nothing at all. He called out her name several times. She didn't even blink.

The paramedic had a compassionate eye on them. "Listen," he said softly, confidentially. "The person that made the 911 call…she said Mrs. Connors did this on purpose."

"She didn't understand," Jeff countered. He glanced at Joy—no sign of life. "Is there anyone you couldn't imagine living without for the rest of your life, say they died unexpectedly?"

"Sure. My twin sister," the guy answered. "I figure we'll pass over about the same time."

"That's what this is," Jeff told him. "When she got word that he was gone, I think something inside her was looking for the exit."

CHAPTER TWENTY FIVE
Promises Kept

He was in the emergency room, his forehead resting like dead weight on the metal safety bars of Joy's bed, when he could have sworn he felt a hand on his shoulder. Jeff lifted his head and looked around. There was no one in the room, but Joy was stirring restlessly in the bed. "Jeremy," she called out, and it knocked the breath out of him.

"It's Jeff, Joy," he voiced softly and took her hand in both of his. Her arms were ghastly, the smooth white skin stitched together like Frankenstein's face. As she moved toward consciousness, her face could have been a child's with her clear blue eyes and small mouth shaped like a doll's. Jeff could still see her in his mind's eye when she was a little girl, stepping onto the school bus clutching Jeremy's hand and staring defiantly at the rest of the kids, daring them to challenge her. The memory forced him to swallow to choke back tears.

"He was here a minute ago," she said. Neither of them was paying attention to Ty, who'd entered quietly and was watching the interaction ten feet from the end of the bed.

"Who?" Jeff mustered.

"Jeremy. He had the most beautiful blue light around him."

Ty heard the comment and stepped forward. "Are you in pain, Joy?" he asked.

"I can barely feel my arms, but my chest feels like my heart exploded inside of me. Got anything to make that go away?"

"I called Ethan," he said as if he hadn't heard her. "He's on his way."

"Don't let him tell my mom and Lily that Jeremy killed himself," she pleaded. "We don't know if it's true."

"Why else would he have been on the train tracks?"

"How am I supposed to know, Ty? I wasn't there, remember?"

Ty took a few steps away as if her energy had pushed him and picked up the chart at the foot of her bed. "I didn't mean to upset you," he murmured.

"My mother thinks of him as her son—you never understood that," she snapped.

Ty made a notation in her chart, increasing her sedative dose, before he left the room.

Jeff took Joy's hand again. "You were a good friend to me," she said to him. "I'm sorry I wasn't a good friend to you. That last day at the Rexham house—"

He quickly interrupted her. "Hey Joy, let's do this some other time, all right? We've both got too much on our plates right now to be worried about stupid shit."

She closed her eyes, but every time she'd start to fall asleep, she'd see a flash of blinding light, like a train was bearing down on her. "I keep seeing the train," she said out loud. "It woke me up, you know, when it happened."

Jeff started to ask what she meant when a nurse came in to give her the sedative. "Your brother's in the hallway," she announced.

Ethan walked briskly into the room, his energy a tangible mixture of fear and grief. His serious dark eyes absorbed his sister who was nearly as white as her bed sheets. He kissed her forehead before he acknowledged Jeff. They weren't friends anymore, even though they'd known each other forever. Ethan's union with Hannah had changed that, but now their connection to Jeremy trumped that painful romantic history. "I'm sorry," Ethan offered and embraced him roughly, like guys do. "I can't fuckin' believe it."

Jeff moved his feet nervously. His face was flushed again and his breath was irregular. He was fighting back tears and didn't want to lose that battle in front of Ethan. He gave Joy a quick kiss and promised to return the next day before he bolted.

Ethan and Joy watched each other wordlessly. In the hallway, chaos loomed as doctors and nurses worked to save other people's lives. But Jeremy's was already lost and no one could change that.

240

"Move over," Ethan commanded. He shed his boots and climbed into the bed with his baby sister. She had to stay on her back so her arms wouldn't be further injured, but with Ethan lying on his side, she managed to nestle her head under his chin. The familiar scent of motor oil on his skin was comforting. She felt safe enough to let sleep have its way with her.

While he held onto her, Ethan thought about what he'd learned. He only believed that Jeremy had taken his own life because during recent conversations it was obvious that alcoholism and depression had gained the upper hand. When he'd passed the news on to Mary, it'd knocked her legs right out from under her. She was so distraught that he'd insisted she stay at home with Lily, and now he was glad he had. Seeing Joy torn to shreds like she'd been swallowed up by a vicious machine was almost more than he could bear. She looked like she was eleven again, clinging to that cigarette carton after Jeremy was taken away.

"It's not your fault," she suddenly said, but her eyes were still closed. "I should have asked you to come back." Her face was animated like she was conversing with someone, but her breath was slow and steady. She appeared to be asleep. "Forgive me. Please forgive me, Jeremy."

Hearing his name startled Ethan. He didn't know if Joy was awake or asleep, and Ty had mentioned to him in the hallway that Joy's primary care physician had requested a psychiatric evaluation due to the possible suicide attempt. Ethan jerked her shoulder until she opened her eyes with a gasp— he'd startled the breath out of her. "Joy, you okay?" he asked.

At first, it appeared she was going to reprimand him, but then her expression softened, prompted by the concern she saw on his face. It had been a long time since she'd felt that kind of closeness to her brother; it was like being a kid again when he was already a teenager and strong enough to lift her into his arms. "I'm fine," she assured him and tucked her head back under his chin.

When Jeff exited Joy's room, his only intent was to get out of that stifling building that smelled like sickness and death. He needed to be alone before the grief burst out of him. Through the glass doors in the lobby, he could already see outside when he heard someone behind him call his name. It was Ty, he knew, before he turned around. *Brother, you look like shit*—that was his first thought when his eyes scanned Ty's face. *Back when you were king of the high school, I bet you never dreamed you'd have to live through something like this*—that was his second one, but he kept it to himself. "You all right?" he asked instead.

"I'm not sure."

It was the most honest statement to leave Ty's mouth in years. He'd always told himself that Joy chose him because they were perfectly suited for each other and that the other man she openly pined for could never satisfy her needs. How could someone with a less than average IQ, who couldn't even manage to graduate from high school, maintain a relationship with a woman like Joy? But there was no denying that Jeremy had kept a hold on her all those years. Now he was dead…and he still had a hold on her.

"Thanks for getting her here," Ty offered. "Joy would have died if we hadn't stopped the bleeding. But I need to know if she meant to hurt herself, Jeff. Did she give any indication beforehand?"

"No. Honestly, it was eerie how quiet she was. She didn't react at all. Jeremy told me how she'd shut down sometimes, but I'm sure you know about that."

"I don't. When it comes to my wife, I feel like I've been the one living on the west coast."

At first Jeff didn't respond. He was trying to imagine what it must feel like to be Ty. The guy had gone out and conquered the world, done everything but slain a dragon, but he couldn't compete. Jeff pondered that— what Ty could have done differently to change his situation with Joy. *Not a Goddamned thing*, he concluded. "From what Jeremy told me, it started when he went into foster care," he offered. "They'd never been apart before that."

"And she reacted badly?"

"I'd say that's an understatement. I know she stopped making art while he was gone."

Ty looked away. "She doesn't draw at all now. She hasn't since we got married."

In his mind's eye, Jeff could see the walls in the Rexham house covered with her pencil sketches. Jeremy had insisted on hanging every single one of them. "Jeremy mentioned that a couple of years ago—that he was worried she might not be drawing or painting."

"Why didn't he ask her about it?"

The word *disconnect* was pulsating like an alarm clock in Jeff's brain. "Because they weren't talking." He pictured Joy standing in the massive foyer of their home with loneliness clinging to her like a child. And meanwhile Ty was stitching up patients, saving other people's lives but not having the slightest clue about his own. "Listen man, after Jeremy left for California, Joy wouldn't forgive him. She didn't talk to him again until Lily's wedding."

"Jeremy wasn't at Lily's wedding," Ty countered.

"Yeah, he was. You missed it—look, I'm probably saying too much."

Ty nodded his head thoughtfully. "One last thing—Joy won't be attending any services."

"I doubt there will be any. He wanted to be cremated. The thing is—and you're going to love this—Joy knows the place he wanted his ashes to be released. He wanted her to do it."

Ty's pager went off. "About the ashes, hold onto them. Don't mention it to Joy yet. When she's recovered, then she can deal with it. Fair enough?"

Jeff nodded because he agreed with the plan, but the words Ty chose, *the ashes,* made it sound like Jeremy was an inanimate object, not his best friend and a person who'd taken his own life. As he walked away, he wondered if Ty had any idea how aloof he came across to people.

The sun bouncing off car hoods in the parking lot was beckoning to him. Light shining on metal had always meant good things to Jeff: riding his dirt bike or his quad, and driving his Mustang in the spring and summer when it seemed to float through the streets of Marshfield. He was in such a hurry to escape the confines of the hospital that he had forgotten his car was still in Joy's driveway. His eyes lingered on Jeremy's name on the contact list of his cell phone. The fact that he had died still felt surreal, like he was about to be jarred awake any minute to the realization that the whole day had been a bad dream. Jeff closed his eyes and stroked his brow. He'd have to call someone for a ride who knew better than to stop at a package store. He speed dialed his brother, Chris, and spilled his guts about wanting to drink before he found himself caught in the same trap as his best friend.

"Do me a favor," he added. "Grab me a pack of butts on the way."

It was a startling image that met Chris' eyes when he pulled up. Jeff had blood on his face and his t-shirt was completely discolored by it. "I'll take you to a meeting," Chris offered.

Jeff shook his head. "No, later. I need to do something first. You got the cigarettes?"

"They're in the glove box. You sure about that? It's been, what, two years?"

"Today it's either Winstons or Wild Turkey." Jeff opened the car door. He couldn't wait to get the God damned cigarette in his mouth. "You can go back to work. I'm all right."

"You don't look all right. Besides, the work day's already over."

"Really?" Jeff gasped. On this strange day, time didn't seem to apply, like in dreams when it doesn't matter what day or time or season, only that something significant is happening. He inhaled as much smoke as his lungs would allow, and then stuck his head out the open window like a dog, letting the wind blow away the tears he couldn't fight any more, like raindrops off a windshield.

For a panic-stricken moment after they arrived in Joy's driveway, Jeff thought he'd lost the keys to his car, but then he saw them in the ignition, and the door was unlocked. Normally he'd never make such a mistake, not with his 'Stang. In the driver's seat of his own car, he located a CD that Jeremy had given him for his last birthday. It was *Light Grenades* by Incubus, his favorite band. One of the songs kept circling his mind and he needed to hear it, even though he knew every word, just like he needed to go to the sea wall at Brant Rock, even though he could see it perfectly in his mind's eye. It was a place as familiar to him as his own back yard, but it was the presence of the place that he needed to feel.

Just fucking let go, he told himself and broke down right there in Joy and Ty's driveway with his forehead on the steering wheel. All day he'd been telling himself that he could wait until he got to the beach, to the place where he'd feel all their childhood spirits still lingering together by the ocean. But he couldn't. He couldn't make it that far. Jeff looked around through the windshield to make sure he was alone and had a sudden realization. He'd never been so alone in his life. "How did we all end up so fucking alone?" he said out loud and wiped his tears away with his hands before he threw the Mustang into reverse.

The CD was still in his hand. He slid it into the player, hit the button to track 5 and listened respectfully to the vocalist all the way down Sea Street until he arrived at the spot where he and Joy had gotten stoned together that first day. It was almost the exact place where Jeremy had fallen off the sea wall. "You can't leave without me!" Joy had screamed. That night it had seemed possible that her pleas had delivered him from death. *Not this time* Jeff realized, and his breath caught in his throat again.

He put his jacket on and zipped it over his bloody t-shirt so he wouldn't look like the kind of person mothers drag their children away from, before he took his seat on the cold concrete wall. Jeff let his legs hang over the edge like he used to do as a child when his mom would walk him down with Chris. He thought if he was very, very still and very, very quiet, he might hear the voices of his childhood swept into the wind like a skin he'd unwillingly shed. He lay down on his back and tried to imagine Joy's head touching his while they talked and laughed about stupid things that didn't matter worth shit but had created a lasting impression anyway.

It was the friendship. That was the part that had left a mark on him, changed him, like every person he'd come to love. Every one of them had been carved into who he was, some deeper than others—like Jeremy—but all of them permanent. The thought reminded him of the totem poles he'd learned about as a child, where every mark symbolized something. Jeremy would like that analogy, he realized, Jeremy and his love of all things native. He wondered where his arrowhead was as he watched the seagulls soar above him. Their effortless movement reminded Jeff of something else about his friend. He had sworn that he used to leave his body and fly while he was sleeping. *That's called dreaming*, he'd teased, but Jeremy had argued that unlike a dream, he could control it. He'd said that sometimes he'd go to Joy's house and move up the stairs to the last bedroom at the end of the hall where he could see her sleeping in her bed, and return to his body knowing she was safe.

Jeremy had claimed there was something innate in him, like a GPS that could lead him to wherever he wanted to be, which was usually wherever Joy was. Jeff used to give him shit about that—his spiritual TomTom—but now he was wondering if there was any truth in it. Maybe he'd ask Joy where her bedroom was located. Jeremy had been absolutely certain that he was going to live forever; he said his spirit guide had told him so. Jeff sat up again and looked around, for the second time making sure he was alone, not because he was crying this time but because there was some crap he needed to get off his chest, and at that moment he believed Jeremy would hear him.

"You suck for leaving like that!" he shouted, even though he'd intended to keep his voice low so he wouldn't look like a madman to people driving by. "What the fuck did you think would happen to the rest of us?"

The anger and hurt were mixed together like an explosive concoction he'd stirred up in chemistry class, making him heave the words out. "But I guess by now you're feeling like shit because of what happened to Joy so I'll shut up. You should know, though, that I'm really fucked up about this. I'll try to help her, but you know how she is. You're the only one that's ever frigging good enough for Joy."

That was all he could summon. *Now what?* There was no point in going to his house. The family home hung like an albatross around his neck, a constant reminder that he had no family of his own to fill up all those empty rooms. Every night he'd blast the stereo to shatter the silence. On second thought, he knew exactly what to do. He got back in his Mustang and cranked Incubus all the way to Chris' house so he could take in an AA meeting.

CHAPTER TWENTY SIX
Twin Feathers

Hey sweetheart, she heard and someone kissed her forehead. She had been dreaming and the voice startled her out of it. It sounded like Jeremy. The recollection of his death tugged the corners of her mouth into a frown and her eyelids blinked back tears. *Shh, don't cry. Everything's okay. I love you and I won't leave you.*

Joy opened her eyes. No one else was in the room. She pushed the button and a squat woman in scrubs shuffled in. "Is everything all right?" the nurse asked.

"Was someone in here a minute ago? I thought I heard..."

The nurse's face took on a familiar expression, the one that revealed her inner musings over dealing with a psychiatric patient. "We don't allow visitors at this hour," she replied. "But your husband called. He took the day off so he can bring you home after breakfast."

"Are you sure you heard him right? Ty never takes a day off."

"Apparently he does now. He said he took tomorrow off too."

Joy stared at the woman blankly. She was one out of four nurses that had taken care of her for the past three days, and every single one of them had made a point of telling her how lucky she was to be married to *Dr. Connors*. Apparently he was the crush of the nursing squad.

"How are your arms feeling today?" the nurse asked.

"Like hell," Joy complained.

"That means they're healing." The nurse took a closer look to make sure there were no signs of infection. I'll get you something for the pain, but wait for your breakfast to take it so you don't upset your stomach." At the door she turned back. "Mrs. Connors, the medications could be making you dream more."

Joy smiled tightly. "It was Jeremy," she said softly once the woman was gone. She wanted him to know that she knew. "You kept your promise," she whispered. "You came back."

The nurse returned and handed her a cup with pills, and the nurse's aide had just placed her breakfast in front of her when Ty entered exuberantly, carrying a dozen red roses.

"Good morning ladies," he offered cheerfully. After a quick kiss on Joy's cheek he tucked the roses in the crux of her arm. The nurse and the aide quickly exited the room. "Your color's better. You probably heard that we're discharging you. Why don't we go home and get you cleaned up and then go out for lunch or take a ride down the Cape?"

She was speechless. It had been years since she and Ty had spent an entire day together. It felt almost too intimate to look in his eyes. So instead she looked down at the roses, and that drew her eyes to the massacre splattered across her arms.

"Joy," Ty gently prodded. "I want to change whatever I can to make life better for you. I want you to be happy. I don't always know what it is you need, but if you'd just tell me…"

She couldn't lift her eyes from the roses. "Ty, the thing that's broken is broken in me. Our relationship is broken too, but maybe for the same reason. I'm not sure."

Joy removed the silver dome from her breakfast plate. Blueberry pancakes with powdered sugar—was that someone's idea of a joke?

"I don't think it matters why it's broken," Ty declared. "What matters is whether or not we're willing to fix it, and I am. You're the only woman I've ever wanted to have a life with."

"Maybe you're selling yourself short," she replied and cut into the pancakes. "Apparently half the nurses here are in love with you."

He reached for her hand, the one that wasn't forking pancakes into her mouth. "I don't see it that way," he said. "I've never once regretted my decision to marry you."

Joy's eyes were filling with tears and the familiar choking sensation was returning to her throat because she couldn't say the same was true for her. She'd regretted it from the moment she'd said her vows in front of that huge crowd. The visual the thought created of standing up with Ty in that grand white church brought back the painful conversation she'd had with Jeremy on the beach. *You're my wife and you always have been.*

"I don't know, Ty," she stammered. "It's really nice what you said, but I just don't know."

"Joy, I want you to know that I'm sorry Jeremy died. Maybe I can help you deal with it."

She took a couple more bites of food while she thought it over. "Do you know the worst thing about death? Separation. Separation is hell."

Ty hesitantly moved into speaking mode. "Well, death is the end of life."

"No, it isn't," Joy replied.

"It is," Ty argued. "Do you know how many people I've seen die?"

She snorted. "You've seen bodies die, Ty, not people. That doesn't mean they're gone. Jeremy has always been good at vanishing acts, but he always comes back."

"Not this time."

"You're wrong about that. I understand why you think you're right, but you couldn't be more wrong. You don't know him like I do. He would never leave me, not forever."

That silenced him. He helped her get dressed and brush her teeth before he pushed her in a wheelchair down to the ground floor. It was a beautiful day. Somehow that made it more painful walking out into it. The exuberance of the birds in the trees near the parking lot made Joy miss Jeremy's presence in the world. If he were here, would they fly closer?

The thought triggered her recollection of the mourning dove feather, so as soon as they arrived home she went on a mission to find it. The urge was gripping her to caress her face with it, the same way she'd comforted herself in his absence as a child. There were several cardboard boxes in the basement that her mom had brought over the summer before. Mary had set out to remove Bob's clothes from the closet, but by the end of that weekend, the other bedrooms had been cleaned out, while Bob's stuff still hung in their closet. She could live without the clothes, she'd told her kids, but not the smell of Bob that still clung to them.

Tucked away in the first box, Joy found old portraits rolled in a cylinder tube. There was one of Jeremy on the seawall wearing his fringe jacket, and it made her weep to see it. She'd never considered herself the artist he'd always thought she was, but that day she'd captured the shyness in his face over being drawn publicly, the grinning lips that said *do whatever you want with me* tempered by bashful eyes that pleaded *but get it over with quickly*.

She got to the bottom of the last box. It wasn't there. "How could I have lost it?" she said out loud. "How could I have been so careless?"

"Joy?" Ty called out as he moved down the stairs and found her sitting cross-legged next to the empty boxes. "Are you all right?"

She only moved her shoulders a little bit. She felt devastated, but she could never express to Ty that she'd lost something so valuable that its absence made Jeremy seem even more absent.

"What is it you're looking for?" he asked.

"A feather," she replied and waited for his reaction. Ty was a caring person, but he wasn't Jeremy; he would never understand the importance of twin feathers.

He crouched next to her. "It has nostalgic value?"

"Jeremy gave it to me the day he was taken away. He has the matching one." When she realized what she'd said, her chest heaved again. *Where was it now?*

Ty placed both hands gingerly on her knees. "The day he went to a foster home," he noted. "Maybe when you feel up to it, you can tell me about that."

She met his eyes and nodded. Then she handed him the portrait she'd drawn of Jeremy when they were nineteen. It was the first time he'd seen her art. He unrolled it and let his eyes take their time with it. "You're an artist," he said proudly. "Why haven't you let yourself be an artist?"

"I don't know," she cried. "Because it hurt too much, I guess." Art had always been an expression of what she loved. *After Jeremy left, how could she bear painting him, even though she had photographic recollection of every line of his face? And how could she now?*

Ty reached to embrace her and she let him. "Come on," he said, "I have something to show you." He carried the portrait upstairs and led her into the office that housed the antique desk Bob had helped to carry into the house on the day his illness had been thrown into the light. Stacks of drawing paper and colored pencils were piled on it. "At the hospital, Jeff told me that Jeremy asked him if you were drawing or painting. He was concerned that you might not be."

"He was?"

Ty nodded. "To be honest, it used to bother me when I found out he knew things about you that I don't. But the last couple of days I've been thinking a lot, and I finally figured out that if a guy who's been living in another state for ten years—"

"Eight and a half."

"Okay, but regardless if he knows you better than I do, then it's at least partially my fault."

"And mine," she admitted. "I never let you know me the way Jeremy does. I can't promise I'll change that because I don't know if I can, but I will try. My mom used to say we were like Siamese twins separated at birth. It's still the best description I can think of."

"Big shoes to fill," Ty remarked.

She smacked her lips. "Please don't try," she advised. "I'll only resent it."

⁂

Grief is a changeling creature. It moves like mercury, silently and insidiously, then, without warning it shifts and becomes something more reckless like an ocean wave. Lunch with Ty was quiet and enjoyable. Then en route to Mary's house, Joy could feel the anguish being born again. Every place her eyes fell recalled Jeremy. It takes practice for the mind to understand that someone who has always been there no longer is. Even then, it sometimes spits the information back out like a defective computer. A guy in a black leather jacket pulled up beside them on his motorcycle and for a full thirty seconds Joy was absolutely certain it was Jeremy. She was about to bang on the window when he turned his head. And he was just some guy on a motorcycle, not Jeremy at all.

Ty had given her a pain killer that she'd washed down with her latte so by the time she stepped out of the Mercedes at her mom's house she wasn't in physical pain, but her legs felt funny, like they weren't completely solid underneath her. Lily's beat up Camaro was in the driveway with the car seat jammed into the backseat. Chloe McCormack had been born in July, six months after her cousin Maria was born to Ethan and Hannah, and both babies had already proven to be a powerful ointment for the gushing wound created by Bob's death. Even now, walking toward the front door on her woozy legs, Joy was anticipating holding Chloe. She was a beautiful imp with clear blue eyes like Lily's and Eddie's thick black hair.

"Chloe," she cooed as she entered the house. The nine-month-old took it as a game and scampered to the other side of the coffee table. Mary grasped her waist from behind and lifted her into Joy's arms. "How are you, Mom?" she asked over Chloe's tiny shoulder.

"I've been better. I finally walked down to see Belinda. I was feeling guilty thinking of her all alone in that house but she had friends with her, people from her AA group."

"That's good I guess," Joy said and set the wiggling Chloe free.

The skin around Mary's eyes had a bruise-like quality to them as if she hadn't slept in days and her small frame looked swallowed in one of Bob's old sweatshirts. "Jeff stopped by. He said Jeremy wanted you to take his ashes somewhere. Apparently you know the place?"

"I do?" Joy gasped.

"Mary, please," Ty interjected.

Joy's mom leaned back in her seat like she was done talking, but Lily picked up where she left off as she entered from the kitchen, testing the temperature of bottled milk on her forearm. "You guys always had secret places," she said to pacify Joy. "It'll come to you."

"I know it," Joy suddenly blurted and smiled with satisfaction. "It's the beach in Plymouth, the place I gave him the arrowhead. He said it would be a good place..." The smile faded as his words came back to her. *A good place to die.*

"Jeff has the arrowhead," Lily informed her. "It came in the mail this morning. It was Jeremy's handwriting...on the envelope."

The significance of her words took a minute to sink in. Jeremy mailed it before he died. So his death was premeditated. "Was there a note?" she asked.

"No. But maybe that's a good thing." Lily picked up Chloe who was reaching for her now that she'd eyed the bottle. "Jeff said you can have the arrowhead if you want it."

She shook her head. "No, I think Jeff should wear it now." Ty looked like he was trying to find an exit but couldn't quite fathom one. "You don't have to stick around," Joy told him. "We have a lot to talk about, and I might even take a nap here."

"I can drive her home after dinner," Lily offered.

Once Ty was gone, Joy turned her eyes to her mother. There was something she'd wanted to ask when they were discussing the arrowhead, and she knew Mary had picked up on it.

"It's in my room," she said, and Joy bee-lined to the jewelry box she'd made out of a cigar box and beach shells for a Mother's Day gift in fourth grade. And there it was—the silver charm bracelet that Jeremy had given her on her eighteenth birthday. The day he'd left for California she'd flung it across the kitchen and Mary had safely stashed it away. With a sigh of relief, she clasped it on her wrist and returned to the living room.

"You're wearing it?" her mother gasped. "How do you think Ty will feel about that?"

"Mom!" Lily hissed.

"This bracelet has nothing to do with Ty," Joy stated flatly.

"It has everything to do with Ty because he's your husband," Mary responded.

"I think you're wrong," Joy rebutted. "I think love is bigger than that."

"You're supposed to love the man you married," her mother said sharply.

"But I do love Ty. He's a wonderful person and my closest friend. Do I love him the way I love Jeremy? No, I don't, but so what? I never lied to him—or to Jeremy—about that."

Joy pivoted and retreated to her old bedroom. It was so inviting getting into the twin-sized bed and thinking about all the nights she'd spent there with Jeremy. Her breath was slowing down as she edged toward sleep, but then a tiny sound, a tinkling of metal, caught her attention and she felt a tug on her bracelet. Her first thought was that it was her mother trying to take it off. "Don't," she mumbled. And then she felt something else, like a feather brushing across her forehead. What was it? It shifted, and soon the sensation was lingering around her lips, dancing as if it were an electric current. It was some kind of energy moving like fingers across the top of her hair now and making it feel like she'd slid across a carpeted floor in her socks.

Suddenly she had the awareness that Jeremy was lying beside her. She could *feel* him, not his body, but his presence. And, strangely, it wasn't shocking or frightening. It felt natural. She closed her eyes with a sense of peace, and fell asleep feeling like she was in his embrace.

It was later in the evening when something even more miraculous occurred. She was opening the door to Lily's Camaro to go home when something on the driveway near her feet caught her eye.

"What'd you lose something?" Lily asked. She was buckling Chloe into the car seat.

"No," Joy replied. "I found something."

It was a mourning dove feather with a coffee-colored spot like a thumbprint and a white tip exactly like hers and Jeremy's, and it was lying right at her feet as if it were waiting for her to stumble upon it. To anyone else, it would have been a ratty old bird feather, but to her it was a message from Jeremy. She brought it to her face and caressed her forehead with it.

"Inseparable," her lips murmured.

CHAPTER TWENTY SEVEN
Love Will Find a Way

It was June before Joy felt strong enough to carry Jeremy's ashes to the beach in Plymouth. It would be a day of firsts since his death; riding in Jeff's Mustang, seeing the box that contained Jeremy's ashes, and visiting the beach she hadn't glimpsed since they'd broken up. She awakened nauseous and with adrenalin already streaming through her blood.

Sitting cross-legged on a stretch of light in the sun room, she gazed at the portrait of Jeremy that she'd found in the basement. There were more portraits leaning against the walls, some of him and others of every member of her family. Ty had brought them all to be framed. In the pencil sketch of Jeremy his hair was so long that it grazed his shoulders. "I loved your hair like that," she said out loud. She'd developed the habit of conversing with him as if he were right beside her. He was, but she couldn't see him.

At the moment Jeremy had gained enough awareness to understand what had happened to him and to grasp the bigger picture—all the implications involved in the fact that he had prematurely ended his life—he sped to Joy and stayed with her. Even in the beginning, when Running Deer and Moonhawk tried to convince him to take time to heal, he'd rebelled against their counsel and did his grieving by her side. He was in mourning for his own loss and for hers, and for the life they would have had together if he hadn't lost perspective. He stood vigil, watching Moonhawk send her healing energy and wishing he were well enough to do the same.

The couple had walked a similar path once before. As Standing Bear, he'd also exited prematurely. But during that lifetime Moonhawk had traveled with them and he remained after Standing Bear's death. That had been the key. He'd helped them to communicate and to feel each other's energies.

The phone rang and Joy jumped.

It was Jeff calling to inform her that he was in the driveway. *Should he bring the box of ashes into the house?* He'd once been a person who carried a bit of laughter in his voice; a giggle could spill out with the slightest prompt. But now he sounded worn out and distrustful, like he was expecting someone else to throw themselves in front of a train or through a glass door. Anything can happen to human beings, Jeff had come to realize. They can be afflicted with cancer and die at the age of forty two even if they have two sons to raise, or drop dead from a heart attack with no warning whatsoever; they can be possessed by addiction and allow a train to annihilate their body, or grieve so deeply that inflicting hundreds of wounds with shattered glass looks like an escape.

"Here we go," Jeff said out loud after he'd hung up the phone and reached for the box riding in the car beside him like a passenger. "So bro, if there's another side to life and I see you when I get there, just for the record you owe me one." It was in his hands, but he wasn't looking at the box containing what used to be the body of his best friend. He was talking to a photograph of Jeremy that he kept in his visor. He had taken the picture four or five years before when they'd driven Jeremy's bike to Santa Barbara. His blue eyes were squinting in the bright sunlight and his fake leather jacket was zipped up to his chin, a cup of Starbucks espresso in his hand. Some things the guy just couldn't live without. The thought leaped over from espresso to Jack Daniels, and Jeff sighed as he stepped out of the car.

"That's it?" Joy asked as soon as he entered. "How could his whole body be inside there?"

"This is what Belinda gave me," he shot back defensively and handed it to her.

"I can't believe he's in this box. He's not really in this box, is he?"

Her breath became irregular, and Jeff had to fight the urge to drag her away from the storm door. She wasn't crying, but she hadn't been crying the day she'd thrust her arms through the glass either. Today she was wearing a t-shirt, and her arms looked even worse without the stitches. Ty wanted her to see a plastic surgeon, but so far she'd dug in her heels.

"For what it's worth, Jeremy would agree with you," Jeff said. "He used to say his body was like a car for his spirit to move around in while he was on Earth."

It was worth a lot. She kissed his cheek. "It was a beautiful body though, wasn't it?" spilled out of her, and Jeff laughed a little bit.

He noticed her eyes on the photo as soon as they were belted into the Mustang and slid it out of the visor. "I was with him the day he bought that coat," he told her. "He liked it because it wasn't made out of animal skins but was still thick enough to protect him on his bike. He said he didn't believe in killing animals because he could see God in them."

He could see God in them. Joy let her head fall back on the head-rest.

Jeff's dark brown eyes stayed on her face as long as he could allow them to without driving into a tree. "Pass me a cigarette, would ya?" he asked. He hadn't even tried to give them up yet. He figured if his life ended as randomly as everyone else's, he'd quit smoking and get squashed by a car the next day. More than three months had passed since Jeremy's suicide, and he was still having nightmares about it. Some days he'd obsess over it until his limbs felt like they were made of pins and needles. Nothing was back to normal, and he was beginning to suspect nothing would ever be normal again.

"He was pretty smart for someone who wasn't supposed to be," he offered in follow up to the God comment.

"What do you mean?" Joy challenged and gave him a glare reminiscent of the prosecutor that time he got arrested in high school for carrying a dime bag of weed.

"Well, you know…" he started cautiously, "'cause he had that disability."

"No, he didn't," Joy argued.

Jesus Christ, he'd definitely ventured down the wrong path. He inhaled smoke, which bought him a few seconds to think. "Maybe I'm wrong," he muttered. He wasn't and he knew it, but he'd rather be wrong than right and pinned down like a butterfly on a page.

"What kind of disability?" she asked, and Jeff literally squirmed in his seat.

"From Belinda drinking while she was pregnant—that's why he was born too soon and it was hard for him to learn stuff. Something syndrome."

"You don't mean fetal alcohol syndrome?"

"Yep, that's it."

"No. Jeremy *did not* have fetal alcohol syndrome. How could he have run a business?"

"He had an accountant. Jeremy was a good mechanic and people liked him. They trusted him with their bikes. That's why he did so well, not 'cause he was good with numbers."

Since he'd received the call from Joy that she was ready to carry the ashes to the beach, Jeff had been worried about this day. But his concern had been focused on whether Joy was ready to deal with the reality of Jeremy's body burned to ashes. He'd suspected her refusal to see a plastic surgeon was based on her desire to carry the scars of Jeremy's death as a living reminder of his annihilation by the train. He no longer had a body, but she could wear the scars for him. And that disturbed him. But what Jeff hadn't expected was that she would challenge him as if they were on different teams.

"When did he tell you that?" she asked, "after he left for California, or before?"

"I really don't know," he sighed. "I've known for a long time. It never made a difference."

"It makes a difference to me," she said softly, but didn't turn her face to look at him. She was slumped in the bucket seat, gazing at the sky through the window.

Romantic love was something that Jeff could never get his arms around. The only time he'd been in love was with Hannah, and that had backfired so painfully that it was still hard to think about. But to him, Jeremy and Joy had always been so natural together, as if they were born out of the same flesh, so they understood each other in ways other people couldn't hope to. He'd give anything to have a partner like that, scrap his whole life and start from scratch if he had to. But here was Joy holding what was left of Jeremy in her hands and focusing on the most insignificant details.

"I pushed him, Jeff," she suddenly said. "I must have made life so hard for him."

"What do you mean?"

"I screamed at him for dropping out of high school. I called him names. I thought he was lazy. I looked down on you guys for building houses. I looked down on him for working on motorcycles. I don't know who the fuck I thought I was."

Jeff reached for her hand and held it the rest of the way to the beach. *Smart people are so complicated*, he thought. He'd been average his entire life, and for once he was glad for that. Grief was agonizing enough without analyzing every word that had ever been said. God fucking damn, he'd rather get hit by a train himself than be in Joy's shoes. When they pulled into the pea stone parking lot, there were two other cars already parked there. They shared a glance, both thinking it could pose a problem. Some mom with her little kids probably wouldn't take kindly to them scattering the ashes of a dead body in their midst.

"Look, the wild roses are in bloom," Joy mentioned a few minutes later as they descended the wide path that led to the ocean.

She sat on the first step with the wooden box on her lap and Jeff sat beside her, holding one of the blossoms between his fingers. It was a beautiful image, Jeff's callused hand cupping the silky pink petals, one of those contrasts that make life feel excruciatingly fragile and therefore even more precious.

"I've got a jackknife in the car so we can bring some home," Jeff offered. "You sure you're up for this?"

"I feel like throwing up, but I can do it," she assured him. "Let's go."

On the beach a group of teenagers were sprawled on a blanket drinking Mike's Hard Lemonade with Nirvana's *Smells like Teen Spirit* playing from their IPod dock. They watched anxiously as Jeff and Joy approached—were they busted? Consumed with their own world, they didn't even notice the box.

"If they knew our history, they wouldn't be so nervous," Jeff whispered.

"Of course the Hanson cops probably said the same thing after we drove off," Joy replied and Jeff smiled at her insight.

"So, how do you want to do this?" he asked. "Should we put the ashes in the water or…?"

"Jeremy loved this whole place: the ocean, the sky, the cliffs, the tide pools. I want to hold him in my hands and open them so the wind takes him to all those places." Jeff looked taken aback by her statement. "But you don't have to," she added.

"No, I want to, but I feel kinda like I'm in the way."

"You're not. We were both his best friends in different ways. We should do this together. But first there's something I need to ask you, Jeff." She took a long, deep breath. "If I die before you, will you bring me here and, you know, do the same thing? I want to be where Jeremy is. When I die, wherever he is, that's where I want to be."

Friendship is a curious thing. No one can predict when it begins where it's going to lead. It's one big leap of faith. There was no way of knowing when Jeff walked past Fairview Lane during his senior year of high school and saw Jeremy on his motorcycle that they'd be like brothers for the next twelve years. It was just a *hey man, you want a ride to school?* followed by a nod of his head, and that interaction changed the course of their lives. Or when he asked Joy to dance with him at the prom as she walked away in that smoky blue dress that was cut all the way down to her ass—he never even expected her to say *yes* never mind become the kind of friend who would ask him to scatter her ashes when she died. It was more like playing a lottery ticket. He'd taken a chance because he'd believed there was nothing at stake, other than a *no freak, I would never dance with you*, and he'd heard that before anyway.

He nodded his head at her imploring eyes. Of course he'd scatter her ashes. Of course he'd bring her to wherever Jeremy was. She was his friend and he couldn't imagine a circumstance that could change that.

Led Zeppelin's *The Ocean* was playing on the teenagers' IPod as Joy took the lid off the box and dug her hand in. "It seems right that the Zeppelin song's playing," Jeff noted and took some ashes.

"Yeah, I didn't think of that," Joy replied. She slowly opened her fingers and let the wind blow the ashes. Some of them were carried upward toward the cliffs, but not all of them made it that far. The heavier ones came to rest on the sand. "Your turn," she said softly.

"Hey, brother," Jeff said, "I hope where you are there's Zeppelin playing…"

I'm right here beside you; I hear what you hear, Jeremy answered, but no one could hear him. His words were like the ashes from his body, untraceable in the ocean breeze.

Joy grinned through her tears. She liked this game. "And yellow cake with chocolate frosting." She took more ashes, threw both arms out and spun, opening her hand while she rotated. A few of the ashes briefly took flight; others landed in the water.

"Good friends to hang with. And Harleys," Jeff said and let go of some more.

I've got all the friends I need Jeremy sent out, his words lost again to the wind.

"Angels to take care of you," Joy cried.

My angel is right here. You're my angel.

"Sunny days, killer waves, and a McTavish fireball."

"What's that?"

"His surfboard. You should have seen him on it," Jeff said.

"Yeah, I should have," she agreed and spun again letting the ashes go. "Bonfires on sandy beaches, sea glass and starfish." A few of the ashes were swept away toward the ocean but changed direction before they arrived and fell instead in a small tide-pool.

Jeff held the box out so the wind would lift the last ashes from it and set it down. "Peace out bro. We'll always love you," he said. He lost control of his emotions and walked away.

Joy plopped down on the sand like a ragdoll and brushed the ashes from her hand. Jeremy sat beside her with his hip against hers. A laughing gull ventured closer. Unlike Joy, the bird could see him so Jeremy reached his hand out to it. The sea bird passed through it just like Joy's hip had passed through his when he nestled against it. The density of their bodies was so different that they could not make contact. He could feel Joy's spirit with his own; it was her physical body that he couldn't connect with.

To say that Jeremy's existence was painful would be an understatement. His own will had led to a disastrous result, and now here he was beside Joy, exactly where he wanted to be, but powerless to comfort her or even reassure her of his existence. He could feel her grief, riding like a monster on her shoulders. She pulled her hair back from her face and her blue sea glass earrings were glimmering in the sun, like Caribbean water. Jeremy knew she'd bought them because the sea glass reminded her of their childhood days collecting it. They gave him an idea.

He focused his energy on one of the earrings and pushed it from her ear. It landed on the crux of her leg and hip, startling her. *I love you*, he was saying, but she couldn't hear him. Then he had another thought. He'd caught her attention with the earring, but she wasn't making the connection yet. Maybe he could manipulate the teenager's radio. Joy's forehead was resting on her knees and she was stroking the sea glass earring with one hand, deep in thought. Was she wondering if he'd pushed the earring out?

The Tesla song started to play, but at first Joy didn't notice it. *It's gonna take a little time. Time is sure to mend your broken heart.* She looked up and turned her head toward the teenagers. *Love will find a way. So look around, open your eyes.* Then she noticed the laughing gull only inches away—closer to her than a bird had ever come…unless Jeremy was present.

"Jeremy?" she suddenly said.

I'm here, Joy. His fingers reached for her face. They moved through it, leaving behind a trail of static electricity. The desire to embrace her was overwhelming, but there was an invisible wall preventing it. He felt like weeping until he saw her bring her fingertips to her face where his had just been. She'd felt him. There were tears spilling down her cheeks, but she was happy, not sad; he could see it in her eyes.

"Jeremy, I know you're here," she stated calmly, then caught Jeff in her peripheral vision.

"Are you okay?" he asked as soon as he reached her.

She nodded. Jeff knelt beside her and pulled her into his strong arms. She wrapped her arms around his neck and watched her tears leave a path down his bare back.

"I'm glad you're wearing the arrowhead," she told him as they stood up. "It looks right on you. When we were teenagers I used to think you looked Native American." He smiled at her remark and reached for her hand before they climbed the stairs. "You don't think Jeremy would mind me holding your hand, do you?" she asked.

Jeff laughed. "No, 'cause we'll never be more than friends. He straightened me out on that when we were still in high school." Joy smiled at the picture his words created in her mind. "Tell you the truth I'd give just about anything to have what you guys had."

"Me, too," she murmured. "Jeff…" She hesitated, unsure of whether or not to proceed. "This might sound strange but…I think Jeremy's still here. A couple minutes ago I felt him."

"What do you mean?"

"I mean his spirit. There was this song we liked by Tesla—"

"*Love Song.* That's what it's called. Jeremy had it programmed into his cell phone so that when you'd call him that song would play."

265

His comment made her gasp. It also reinforced her belief that Jeremy was nearby so she told him about the sea glass earring falling out for no apparent reason and how Jeremy had always loved blue sea glass. Then she told him that the Tesla song had played right after it.

"Huh," Jeff mumbled with no intonation in his voice. "Might be a weird coincidence. Let's get the jackknife and cut you some roses." She followed him up the incline toward the car, feeling a little put off by his response, but before they reached the Mustang, he suddenly asked, "At your house on Dragonfly Lane is your bedroom upstairs, the last one at the end of the hall?"

"Yeah, why?" she replied.

"Just...Jeremy said so." Jeff unlocked the doors with the key chain gadget. Joy's eyes remained fixed on him as he reached into the glove compartment for the jackknife and tossed her the keys so she could start the car and get the AC going while he retrieved the roses.

"Jeremy was never inside my house," Joy countered.

"I know." Jeff walked away after that and Joy climbed into the Mustang, still thinking about what he'd said and wondering how Jeremy knew where her bedroom was situated. She turned the key to start the ignition. *Love is all around you. Love is knocking outside your door* came out of the speakers. A sound erupted out of her—a hybrid between a laugh and a scream.

"Jeff!" she shouted through the open window and he ran up the hill, pink roses in hand. "Listen!" She cranked the volume on the stereo.

When he realized it was the Tesla song playing again Jeff threw his head back and laughed. "Isn't that just like Jeremy," he said when he reached her. "Having to prove me wrong?"

CHAPTER TWENTY EIGHT

Inseparable

Joy believed with all her heart that Jeremy was near her, but still what she was about to pursue was unnerving. She was in Lily's Camaro, it was a hot Sunday in July, and the air conditioner was broken. The stereo that had a higher retail value than the car was cranking classic rock, the only music Lily listened to, and they were on their way to see a medium perform.

Joy had agreed to go with her after promising she would not rat her out to Eddie. Lily was unsure how Eddie's Catholic upbringing would affect his view on what she thought of as *the supernatural*. They had also decided not to breathe a word to their mother unless the medium turned out to be legitimate. Mary's grief still wasn't appeasing. The only times she seemed like her old self was when the three grandchildren were near, Chloe, Robbie and his little sister Maria (who looked so much like Hannah she might have been one of those dolls made with specific instructions to resemble the new owner).

"There's nothing to be scared of," Lily said as she veered off the exit to the tune of Molly Hatchet's *Flirtin' with Disaster*.

"I didn't say I was scared," Joy countered.

"I've known you for thirty years. I know when you're scared."

"Well, what if it's creepy or something, like a séance?"

"If it is, we'll leave." Lily steered the Camaro into the parking lot of a brick building identified by a sign as *The Inner Life Healing Center* and parked next to two elderly ladies exiting their Cadillac. "See, don't they look normal?" Lily pointed out as Joy checked her reflection in the rearview. Her hair was plastered to her forehead with sweat.

"They look like two widows who have a double date with their dead husbands," she said.

"That's a terrible thing to say!" Lily scolded and the shock in her voice made her sister laugh.

"Check out the dresses…and the hand bags," Joy whispered as they walked behind the old women across the parking lot toward the entrance. "And oh my God, the heels!"

"Shut up!" Lily hissed.

Joy giggled. "I was only noting the fact that they're wearing date clothes."

"That could be us someday."

"God, no; I would never wear those shoes," Joy joked. "Not even for a date with my dead husband."

"We'll see who's laughing on the way out. And don't get the giggles inside there, Joy, because when you start, I do too, and I'm always the one who can't stop."

"I won't," Joy assured her as they stepped inside the building. "I'm too scared to laugh."

The old ladies both dropped twenty-dollar bills into a wicker basket at the entrance of a small lecture hall where about fifty metal fold-up chairs had been placed in rows. "Twenty dollars to talk to the dead," Joy remarked. "That's a good deal, isn't it?"

"I'll happily pay twenty dollars to hear from Daddy," Lily snapped. "Wouldn't you pay twenty dollars to talk to Jeremy?"

"I'd slit my throat to talk to Jeremy," she replied. The sharp pinch she received on her arm caught her by surprise. "Ow, Lily!" she fussed. "I was only kidding."

"Then you have a sick sense of humor." It was hard for Joy to hold her head high after that reprimand, and her lips kept curling into a pout. Lily took advantage of her atypical remorse and dragged her to the front row. Shortly after they were seated, a middle-aged woman in a simple blouse and slacks moved to the podium. *Surely she's not the medium*, Joy thought. There was no apparent difference between her and everyone else in the room.

Had she been able see the drama going on behind the scenes, she would not have questioned the medium's capabilities. Hundreds of people in spirit, drawn there because of the rare opportunity to get a message through to a loved one were waiting for their chance. To those human beings attuned to its feeling, the air was thick and active with spirit energy. Others could make out the flash of various colored lights that were representative of the sum total of the soul's evolution, in Jeremy's case an electric blue, the same color as Joy's sea glass earrings.

"Good afternoon," the woman at the podium said. "My name is Ruth Lydin and I am what is usually referred to as a *medium* or a *channel*. Basically that means I'm an instrument your loved ones in spirit can use to reach you. Let's not keep them waiting." She had been in many rooms like this before, had seen the nervous, yet excited, faces of those who had braved meeting a medium for what they believed was a slight possibility of hearing from a loved one who had passed over to the spirit side of life. It was her responsibility, she believed, to show the audience what she had discovered, that life does indeed continue after physical death.

There were only two people ahead of them, a brother and sister in their thirties, present in hopes of hearing from their mother who had died of ovarian cancer. The medium described a woman on "the mother's side of the family", nearing sixty who had passed from a painful disease in her abdomen, something that caused her to lose a remarkable amount of weight and become bedbound. She didn't say "this is your mother" or "this person had ovarian cancer", but she was close. Consider that the medium was receiving information from a person existing on a different plane and her descriptive comments could be considered a home run.

The medium stated, "This lady says you're arguing over something that you think matters to her, but it doesn't. It's in regard to the family home." Her son admitted that they had been squabbling over whether or not to sell it. They needed the money, but his sister thought their mother would not approve of the home leaving the family. The message brought them peace. They could sell the house without any more contention. And their mother could rest assured that her children—if not completely convinced—at least had an inkling that she had not extinguished like a candle.

Messages from spirit, though unique to each individual, tend to share common themes. The person in spirit form might mention specific events or interests, likes or dislikes. Mostly that is for identification purposes. But the actual messages, when honed down for content, are usually one of the following: *I love you*; *Thank you*; *Please forgive me*; *I forgive you* or *Don't grieve for me—I'm still here*. They are universal messages—the same kinds of things we often think about when someone we love dies. We might whisper the words out loud as a kind of prayer, hoping the person who died can somehow hear us. They can, and are often whispering the same.

Lily greeted the medium with a smile. Immediately the woman made a statement that made both Joy and her gasp. "There are two men here with you, a father and son." Again, a skeptic could have claimed that she was wrong, and technically she was, but what better way could she have described Bob and Jeremy? "The older man has a hand on each of your shoulders. Usually when someone is touching you it tells me you belong to them somehow. Is your father in spirit?"

"Yes," Joy answered, coaching herself to sound calm.

"This man had trouble breathing before he passed," Ruth said. "I'm asking him to step back because I feel tightness in my lungs but he doesn't want to. He's stubborn and eager to talk to you. Yes, that's better." (She was talking to Bob.) "Your father worked with his hands? They're calloused."

"That's right," Joy affirmed.

"Is there a Marie in your family?" the medium asked.

"Mary," Joy quickly spit out. "Do you mean Mary?"

"Does she wear his shirts?"

The women acknowledged that she did, nearly every day. "He wants you to tell her that he's fine. He's saying, *Sweetheart*—did he call her sweetheart?" Joy and Lily, crying now, both nodded. *"It's time to stop grieving."* She appeared finished then added, *"Kiss the babies*. He wants you to kiss the babies for him." Lily burst into tears and dropped out of the interaction.

The medium took a breath then focused her eyes on Joy's. "The younger man is so close that he's actually moving in and out of you…like a twin…but he's not. This is a lover, right? A soul mate. You're inseparable, he says. He's waiting here—this part is important. He needs you to know that he won't leave without you." Tears were spilling from Joy's eyes, dripping from her jaw. Still, she held the woman's gaze. "This man's eyes are remarkably blue and he has an endearing smile. Oh, there's a dog with him. Do you have a dog in spirit?" Joy shook her head. "It has a scrunched face, like a pug."

"Henri!" Lily hissed in Joy's ear.

"Oh, yes we do." Joy corrected. "It's a French bulldog we grew up with."

"The little dog was waiting for him when he passed over. Your friend says it still follows him. One last thing; he's offering you flowers. I don't know what they're called, but they're white."

"They're lilacs," Joy muttered and held her breath to prevent a sob from escaping.

After all the readings were finished, Joy quickly approached the medium. Her head was still spinning with the messages she'd received. "How do people learn to do this?" she asked.

"I read books on spirit communication, and I learned how to meditate," Ruth explained. "That was the key." Jeremy had said the same thing, that meditation helped him hear Running Deer, *his spirit guide*. It was like snapping the last piece in a puzzle. "To open your channel," the medium said, "you have to be dedicated. Focus on daily meditation and ask your spirit guide for help. Yours is Native American—we call them Indian guides. I caught a glimpse of him."

Life is a spiritual journey. It took Jeremy's death for Joy to understand that. And intelligence isn't everything it's cracked up to be. All her life she'd touted that card, reminded herself and everyone else that she was the brightest of the bright, the most capable of human beings. She could have chosen to do many things with her life, but what had she actually done? Not much on her own. So far most of the accomplishments in her life were really Ty's accomplishments.

But Jeremy had been dealt an entirely different hand. When they were children he'd told her that he weighed only two pounds when he was born. She'd never questioned the reason for that until Jeff disclosed the fetal alcohol syndrome. Then she'd Googled it and discovered that low birth weight is common in infants whose mothers ingest alcohol during pregnancy. She'd also found out that newborns with fetal alcohol syndrome (sometimes referred to as "FAS"), often have vision difficulties, which explained the need for Jeremy to wear glasses as a child and contacts later in life. Many FAS babies are born mentally retarded and have facial abnormalities, while others, who are not as severely affected, develop more slowly and have difficulty learning. But perhaps the most heartbreaking part of the research was discovering that FAS children often have an inherited propensity to drink alcohol.

Lying on his chest under the weeping willow tree that first night together after the prom, Jeremy had tried to tell her that alcohol affected him differently than other people—like Belinda he'd said. Still, she had encouraged him to drink because she hadn't understood. To her it was nothing more than a fun thing to do, no more dangerous than riding his motorcycle. She had no way of knowing that handing Jeremy a bottle of tequila was like feeding him poison. And she'd left him alone with the illness that, according to Jeff, was responsible for him ending him life.

Jeremy's death and her discoveries about him since were the most humbling experiences of Joy's life. She'd pushed him to be something he wasn't capable of and refused to acknowledge his many accomplishments. She'd resented his success, his business, his motorcycle, his surfboard, even California—*everything* that got to be a part of his new life. She now understood that his decision to leave for the West Coast was a matter of self-preservation. It was a difficult thing to come to terms with, the fact that he'd left without her because she was part of the problem.

Upon reflection, this insight led to a greater awareness: that she was part of the problem with her family relationships, too. In order to heal them she would have to make a conscious effort to focus only on her own shortcomings and not on her perception of theirs.

Sitting cross-legged in the sunroom, she gazed at Jeremy's nineteen year old face that she had immortalized on paper. "I'm proud of you," she finally said, "for how you lived your life. I thought I was the smart one, but only my brain was smarter than yours because that's how I was born. If you'll help me now, I want to learn. And please forgive me, Jeremy, for not understanding sooner."

If Joy were capable of it at that point in time, she would have heard in response, *You're judging yourself too harshly. You're forgetting all the times you stood up for me, the love you gave me, the times you made me feel strong enough and smart enough to do all the things I wouldn't have tried without your faith in me.* He brushed his fingers made of light across her cheek that was also made of energy but of a much denser design until he had her attention. To Joy it felt like a spider dragging its web across her skin. She smiled seemingly at no one. It's an act of faith to love someone who no longer has a body. You have to trust your own intuition and the love the person had for you, because the eyes are not a fine enough instrument to verify their existence in your surroundings. You have to know it and act on it.

"Remember when we were little and you used to follow me everywhere?" Joy said out loud. "It'll have to be like that now. You'll have to follow me, Jeremy, because I can't see you but I know you can see me. We need to buy some books so we can open my channel." It was unfortunate that she couldn't see him, the relief and excitement that swept his face.

Jeremy moved up the stairs—in much the same way he had done when he used to leave his body during sleep—following Joy so she could dress for the shopping trip. He stayed by her side perpetually, whether she was awake or asleep, alone or with others. Every word she whispered he caught and every vibration that left her spirit he felt.

273

Joy would be surprised in her grief and regret to realize that her love for Jeremy that was constantly vibrating from her was helping him to heal. And as he healed his own love sped back to her as an offering of the same, a way to heal her hurt and anguish. They were two points on the same circular wave of energy that moved continuously between them like an electric current.

Every night Jeremy practiced talking to her even before she was aware of it. Once she was under the covers he'd touch her hand and say in her ear *you are my love*. Sometimes she appeared to notice the sensations on her skin, but she'd never responded to his words. The day she visited the bookstore, he did the same thing he had done for months, but this time her lips quietly mimicked his words. "You are my love," she whispered and her eyes opened.

Jeremy turned to Moonhawk who stood behind him, like a vigilant soldier. "She'll hear it as a rhythm," he told Jeremy. "Say it as if you're beating it with a drumstick, sharp and quick."

"YOU-ARE-MY-LOVE." His face was near hers, passing through it, though, not making the contact he so badly wanted. Static electricity danced on her lips and Joy scratched at the itchy sensation it caused. It reminded her of the way Jeremy never moved his mouth away from hers like Ty did when he spoke so she could feel the vibration of his words.

She'd noticed the difference the first night they'd spent together in her bed, when he'd asked her to teach him how to touch her. It hadn't taken long for Jeremy to become an expert. *You should insure those fingers* she'd told him once. *They're worth millions.* "God fucking damn," she said out loud at the visual of herself writhing like a wild animal under his hand.

Jeremy looked to Moonhawk for insight. He had access to her thoughts because he was her spirit guide. "She's remembering you making love to her and missing it," he said simply.

Joy fell asleep without noticing any other contact. Ty tiptoed into the room after the News ended, never guessing that another man was kneeling beside his sleeping wife and holding her hand that dangled over the side of the bed. Jeremy watched and envied him, this man who was completely unaware of his presence. It was an odd scenario. The two men envied each other for what each of them lacked. What Ty desired most was Joy's love that still flowed to Jeremy, but Ty had the one thing Jeremy did not, a body to love her with.

The nights they shared had gone by too quickly. Why hadn't he stayed awake just one of those nights to memorize what her skin felt like on his fingertips, to do nothing more than focus on the shape of her body pressed into his belly? He'd give it all the time in the universe now…now that it was too late to kiss her delicate fingers and graze her eyelashes with his lips. All those nights sleep had seduced him away from the attention he could have given her. What he wouldn't give—years of that life—to make love to her one more time.

He listened to the sound of her breath, that was as near as it was when he was in flesh and imagined how he would do things differently if he had one more day to walk by her side. "It would be easier if you would advance to your true form," Moonhawk constantly reminded him, but he wasn't ready to be Elia again. He would remain Jeremy until Joy was Kalli.

Jeremy understood that, like every other soul, he would pass through a life review. He wasn't afraid because he knew it would not be a verdict of Heaven or Hell, but rather kind counsel by guides and loved ones to help him understand why things happened the way they did. It was designed as a tool for evolutionary growth. If he were to leave temporarily and focus only on himself, he could gain more understanding. He could return to the greater soul that he was, Elia, who'd lived enough lives to know that mistakes are part of the evolutionary process and not worthy of self-condemnation. But he was not willing to do that.

"I'm right here waiting for you, Joy," he spoke into the darkness. To him, his voice was the same as it had always been, right down to the timbre, but to Joy and Ty it was nonexistent.

CHAPTER TWENTY NINE
The Spirit World

The feeling was nothing less than euphoric, his eyes every bit as blue as she remembered. She was sitting on the grass...somewhere...facing Jeremy with her legs stretched over his and he was holding her hand. As he leaned in closer his lips curled into a grin. There was such clarity to his face, to the colors, to the flawless texture of his skin and the whiteness of his teeth. "What is this place?" she asked. A small laugh escaped him as his eyes scanned the fields of flowers and mountains in the distance. "Home," he said and stroked her face with the back of his fingers, sending sensations through her entire body that felt like lovemaking. Several of his shirt buttons were undone and she could see the arrowhead resting against his chest. He slid a ring unceremoniously onto her finger. It was a band made of a pale yellow glasslike substance, not metal—like a moon beam, Joy thought, and he smiled in response. "Does this mean we're getting married?" she asked him playfully. "We're already married," he replied.

The alarm went off and reality shifted. The interaction was so lucid that it didn't feel at all like a dream, but it must have been—because the ring wasn't on her finger. After breakfast she took time to meditate as had become her practice. She always invited her Indian guide and Jeremy to be present, and already she'd experienced a couple of breakthroughs. The now-familiar spider web-like sensation on her cheeks and eyelashes, lips and extremities, was more prevalent during meditation. And lately, she'd noticed a tingling sensation in the center of her forehead, which she had read marked the opening of her third eye chakra and the ability to see clairvoyantly.

This time, something entirely new happened. She saw lights behind her closed eyes, white lights alternating with blue ones. As always, she concluded the meditation by thanking her spirit guide. A feeling of respect was growing for this man whom she could not yet see or hear. She could feel his presence and his support. As she rose to her feet, she saw a small blue light in her peripheral vision. Throughout the day she glimpsed the light often, and surmised correctly that it was Jeremy. His presence in her surroundings was nothing new. It was her ability to see him that had changed.

Her first stop of the day was at a nursery. She was on a mission to create a garden. Since she'd started meditating, her eye was more often drawn to beauty; the sleekness of a cat's fur and the inky blackness of the night sky were captivating. The day before, some tiger lilies in the neighborhood had captured her attention. It was the deep orange color of the flowers that had given birth to the idea of creating a garden.

Jeremy's birthday was coming up and she wanted to plant a lilac bush in his memory, but at the nursery she was instead drawn to a white hydrangea tree. She felt an emotional connection to the tree that she couldn't explain. Nonetheless, she bought it as the centerpiece of her new garden and chose all white annuals to plant around it. When Ty's car pulled into the driveway, it was early evening and Joy had just planted her last impatien. He appeared exhausted from his shift at the hospital as he took a seat beside her on the front steps. And he had quite a story to tell.

An emergency room physician has to be a sort of jack-of-all-trades. During one shift the doctor might see a dozen people with various types of abdominal pain. The causes can range from indigestion to viral infection to an inflamed or ruptured appendix.

Never in his career had Ty seen a patient with a ruptured abdominal aortic aneurysm. Once or twice he'd suspected an abdominal aneurysm and many times he'd ordered tests to rule it out, even though he was almost certain something else was causing the pain. He'd done this for one simple reason: because an aneurysm about to burst is a life-threatening condition. Saving a patient with an aneurysm that'd already ruptured was next to impossible. Ty knew the signs and symptoms and he knew what to do—call in a vascular surgeon, and in the interim, deal with the code situation because invariably once there's a rupture the patient is in code status due to blood loss. That day while Joy meditated, Ty put theory to practice.

The call came through from the paramedic at 9:10 a.m. en route to the emergency room. Reportedly, the patient had been complaining of severe abdominal pain that radiated to his back when he arrived at his job, the local Sunoco Station where he pumped gas, right before he collapsed. The paramedic was having difficulty reading his blood pressure and that piece of information combined with the patient's complaints alerted Ty to the possibility of a ruptured abdominal aortic aneurysm. By the time the patient arrived, he'd assembled the code team and arranged for a bedside ultrasound. Ty was a born leader, calm and level-headed in the face of chaos, a good thinker under pressure. And that morning when thirty four year old Emanuel Rodriquez was wheeled into the emergency room in shock, Ty was under pressure. His actions and the instructions he gave to the code team would determine whether the man lived or died.

First, he intubated the patient because he wasn't breathing on his own, then he shouted orders for medications to restore his blood pressure. An ultrasound revealed free fluid in the abdomen, exactly what Ty was looking for. He was sure it was blood, the result of a rupture. The surgeon was en route and would arrive any minute. Ty's objective was to stabilize the patient so that he could withstand surgery.

A blood test showed a staggeringly low hematocrit, which further supported his theory that the man was hemorrhaging internally. He ordered blood transfusions to replace the lost blood. Still, the patient had to be resuscitated twice. "Listen to me!" Ty yelled at the unconscious man on the table. "You have to hang in there. Come on, you can do this!" If it was a matter of sheer will Ty would force the guy back to life, even if it meant pouring his own life force into him.

Once the patient was adequately stabilized and the baton was passed off to the surgeon, he told the head nurse he needed a minute and headed for the doctors' lounge. Ty had seen many people die, but he'd never felt quite so responsible for the outcome. This wasn't someone who had been failing due to a serious illness or an elderly person who'd collapsed suddenly of a heart attack. This patient was a man very close to his own age, who had arisen that morning thinking it was a typical day, and headed out to work without realizing a crucial piece of equipment in his body, one invisible to the eye, was about to malfunction and cause his entire system to shut down.

He swallowed a glass of water and sat down for a minute to catch his breath before he headed back to the emergency room where he knew other patients were waiting to be evaluated. There was probably quite a backlog, due to the time spent on Emanuel Rodriquez, the unlucky man whose aortic artery had torn for some unfathomable reason and was likely going to die that day despite surgical intervention. *If Joy were here she'd say a prayer,* he thought before he pulled the curtain back to examine his next patient, an eight-year-old who had fallen off her bike, but he couldn't see the sense in that. He'd seen too much sickness and death to be spiritual or even optimistic. And a patient with a ruptured abdominal aortic aneurysm? It would take a whole flock of angels to save that guy.

The rest of the day felt like someone had poured concrete in his shoes and it had hardened there, stiff and heavy. At 7:15 that evening the emergency room was adequately in the hands of another physician and Ty was headed out the door when he had a second thought and walked to the Critical Care Unit to find out what had happened to Emanuel Rodriquez. His expectation was that he'd passed away during surgery or shortly thereafter. In the hallway of the CCU he walked right past the surgeon before he realized it was him.

"Steve," he shouted at his back and the surgeon turned to face him.

"Quite a case we shared today," Dr. Steve Feldman said as he extended his hand.

Ty exhaled loudly. "That's why I'm here actually. Did he make it through surgery?"

"Oh yeah. He made it through all right."

"No kidding?" Ty stammered. "Was it a rupture like we suspected?" The surgeon nodded his head, a boyish grin still lingering on his lips. "He was flat line a little while ago," Ty added.

"I know," Dr. Feldman agreed, "but he's alive and talking about it now. See for yourself."

When Ty pulled back the curtain, what his intelligent eyes took in was Emanuel Rodriquez seemingly asleep on the hospital bed. He stared at him for a long moment, half-expecting to find some piece of evidence that he was in the final moments of his life. But there was no longer anything to indicate that. He picked up the chart at the foot of the bed and his eyes performed their expert analysis. Blood pressure: normal; heart rate: normal; hematocrit: nearly normal. His eyes blinked at the information. The man was a medical marvel, one whose story he would tell to interns someday, but not for the reasons he was thinking in that moment. It was because of what Emanuel Rodriquez was about to say. Ty put the chart back and realized the patient was awake and watching him through sleepy eyes.

"You're the guy," he said groggily. "You were there."

"In the ER?" Ty responded. "Yeah, I was there all right."

"I died, you know," the patient said. "I died and floated right out of my body."

Twice the man's heart had stopped beating and needed to be electrically stimulated, that much was true. It was the second half of his statement that Ty was wrestling with in his analytical brain. "It probably felt that way," he said. "We used a lot of medication."

"No, you don't understand." The patient's voice was hoarse as if it were difficult for him to speak—from the insertion of the endotracheal tube.

"Take it easy," Ty suggested. "I don't know if you realize what you've been through—"

"I saw my mom," burst out of the patient. "She died when I was nine. I saw her and she gave me a hug." His eyes spilled tears. "She—she said, 'not yet Manny. You gotta go back.' So I did."

280

"Wow, nice dream," Ty asserted.

"I haven't been hugged by my mother in twenty five years. It was no dream. I saw you. You put a tube down my throat, right? I watched you do it. You were telling everyone what to do, and you were talking to me, too. You said *hang in there—you can do this*."

When he walked out of the hospital that day Ty looked like *he'd* just survived a trauma. What Emanuel Rodriquez had said to him was supportive of Joy's new perspective on life—that it was bigger than the physical body. Ty had listened respectfully to her when she shared her "spiritual" experiences, but his brain had disabled them a piece at a time without revealing it to her. She was grieving; that was the core of Joy's experiences. Jeremy's death piled on top of her father's had been more than her mind could grasp, and so it had created an avenue that she could live with, a sort of fantasy realm in which her dead father and former lover could continue to exist. Ty had not seen any point in voicing his analysis. It would create another wall between them, and besides, why take away something that was giving her comfort?

As he turned the key to start his Mercedes he thought about the mechanics of it. As far as he could figure, a car operated similarly to a human body. The engine was like the heart of the car, a crucial organ, the vehicle's computer like the brain. Both ran on fuel and both excreted waste. Ty took comfort in such concrete information, and in the ability to analyze it. When other people turned to religion for explanations, he thought they were doing so out of ignorance, because they did not sufficiently understand the workings of the human body, which to him was amazing enough without having to believe it was created by a supreme force.

But if what Emanuel Rodriquez said to him was even remotely true—the part about watching him place the endotracheal tube—then something else had to exist, not God necessarily, but a human spirit that could live independent of a physical body. The man's eyes were closed—he was *unconscious*. The one thing Ty felt absolutely sure of was that the patient had not seen the occurrence with his eyes. So then, how had he seen it? And how had he seen *him* to recognize him? The part about visiting his dead mother Ty dismissed as a dream or hallucination. But the visual aspect…how could he neatly categorize that?

It was twilight by the time he arrived home, Joy's favorite time of day, when the sky was brimmed with gold like the physical world was in alignment with the spiritual one. After he finished telling her the story of Emanuel Rodriquez, the man who didn't die despite the odds stacked against him, Ty asked her why she'd planted the garden.

She replied, "Because I want to bring as much beauty and light into the world as I can."

It was a staggering statement, particularly coming from his wife.

"You're like a whole new Joy," he finally responded. *One I barely recognize* he thought, but didn't voice.

"New Joy?" she repeated slowly, measuring the words. "I like the sound of that."

Ty smiled but didn't comment. His shape against the darkening sky looked twenty years older than it was. He had given of himself quite literally to save the life of Emanuel Rodriquez, a man he didn't know existed before 9:10 that morning.

"You're a light worker, you know," Joy said.

Ty looked over at her and noticed that her fingernails were packed with dirt. The woman he'd married never would have allowed her manicure to be ruined by planting flowers. Then again, the Joy he'd married had never looked quite as…joyful…as she did at that moment.

"What do you mean?" he asked. He'd never heard the term "light worker".

"There are people here for the purpose of helping others stay on their spirit path. They're called light workers, and you're one of them. That guy would be dead right now if it weren't for you, and he's not supposed to be dead yet. His work here isn't done."

"Do you believe that, Joy, the whole story about his mother and everything?"

His questioning reminded her of the conversation she'd had with Jeremy on the beach on his eighteenth birthday. Now she understood where Jeremy had been coming from. And Ty was now where she used to be—considering the possibility of another realm of existence, but not entirely swallowing it. So she repeated what Jeremy had told her. "I don't question it, Ty. I know it's real."

CHAPTER THIRTY
The Orange Tree

Joy's mediumship ability developed rapidly. She was determined to open her channel, so she meditated with a fierce dedication, always remembering to ask for help and to thank her spirit guide afterward. The fact that she had two teachers, Moonhawk and Jeremy, strengthened her cause, particularly given the fact that they had both helped her develop once before.

Years of practice in a different lifetime was the reason her lips sometimes mimicked the words Jeremy spoke to her as he sat beside her bed. It was basically the same concept as a three-year-old that picks up a musical instrument and inexplicably knows how to play it. Although Joy sensed that Jeremy was near her and could feel the energy of his touch, she had very little awareness that she was repeating or channeling his words. Her ability to hear clairaudiently, however, was progressing steadily during meditation. So far, she had been able to decipher a number of words including Moonhawk's name and Jeremy's phrase, *my love*.

Her first visual breakthrough was a newfound ability to see auras. It wasn't at all what she had expected. She couldn't walk up to people and say *blue, green, pink* or whatever color light was encircling them. Her proficiency was far more random than strategic. The first time it happened she was attending a dinner with Ty at a local country club to celebrate the opening of a new hospital wing. She was listening to the Chief of Surgery speak from the podium when she suddenly noticed a yellowish-green light radiating two to three feet off his entire body. It was particularly noticeable around his head and shoulders. After that, the phenomenon occurred more often, usually when she wasn't too near the person and when the room wasn't overly bright. Soon she was seeing Ty's aura nearly every day. It was a soft shade of green, which made perfect sense to her because she had read that a green aura is indicative of a person possessing healing abilities.

She shared her experiences with Lily and her mother, but with Ty she was careful in what she revealed. Although his mind had opened somewhat since the near-death experience he'd witnessed, the possibility of life continuing after physical death made him wary of her spiritual pursuits. He understood now that Joy was pursuing Jeremy, even though he was no longer in flesh. It made him wonder: *If I were the one who died prematurely, would she be pursuing me?* And he was never comfortable with the answer his brain spit back out at him. Joy had never pursued him. She had only given in to his pursuit of her when Jeremy was absent…like now. But that was the big question, wasn't it, his mind would taunt, *is he absent now or isn't he?*

It was late—close to 11:30—on a Sunday night when he received his answer. The house was silent when he returned from work and most of the lights were off. He made his way quietly up the stairs, not wanting to disturb his wife's sleep, and was walking down the hallway toward their bedroom when he heard her voice. Later he would look back and ask himself what it was that made him realize something was amiss. After all, the simplest explanation would have been that she was talking on the telephone with her mother, a daily occurrence since they'd mended the relationship. "Say it again," Ty heard her say, and he knew what was happening even before he heard her next words. "Jeremy, please say it again. I can't understand you."

Ty had never heard the word *clairaudience*. No one had told him that some people can communicate with those in the spirit realm, and even if they had, he would have disregarded it as fiction because it was not part of reality as he understood it. But as he stood in the doorway listening to the elation in his wife's voice, he knew it was because she was somehow communing with Jeremy. The man had been run down by a train, and still they'd found a way to be together. He had come back to be with Joy. And she'd welcomed him with open arms. It wasn't his body that she loved after all. It was something much bigger than that. The concept was dizzying.

"What are you doing?" Joy suddenly asked. She'd spotted him in the doorway.

"I have no idea anymore," he answered.

Ty walked past her and into the bathroom, turned on the shower and hoped Joy would be sleeping by the time he got out. He kept wondering how many nights Jeremy had been in their bedroom. Was he there when they made love? Did he wonder why they didn't do it more often, or did he know the answer to that too? Was *he* the reason and was that new, since his death, or had he always been the reason?

By the time he was dried off, Joy was asleep but still he couldn't bring himself to share a bed with her. For the first time in their married life, he retired in the guest room. He laid awake thinking, and when he finally closed his eyes he knew what he needed to do.

He awakened before the sun rose and packed a bag. He threw on jeans and a Holy Cross sweatshirt and went downstairs to make coffee, not expecting his wife to arise for another hour or two. But she had noticed his absence from the bed and followed him down the stairs.

"What's the matter Ty?" she said to his back.

He pushed the button on the coffee pot and closed his eyes to gather his nerve before he turned to face her. His voice was shaky when he said, "I heard you last night." Joy pinched her eyebrows together and took a step toward him. "Talking to Jeremy. I heard you say his name."

"Oh."

"Joy, sit down," he said and even though he was hurt and angry, his hand gestured politely to the kitchen table. She cinched the belt of her robe and took a seat. "I want to ask you a few questions and I need you to be honest." She nodded her assent, but tears were clouding her vision. "Is he here? I'm not asking if you hope he is or anything that could fall under imagination. In a concrete way, is Jeremy here in this house?"

Joy bit her bottom lip and nodded again. She couldn't bring herself to look at him. But his next question drew her eyes immediately to his. "Can you ask him to leave?"

"No," she whimpered. "Ty, please don't ask me that."

He sat across from her at the table. "Because you love him?" came out with a sigh.

"Why are you doing this?" she cried. "I never lied to you about that."

"If you loved each other so much, why didn't you marry him?"

"It's really complicated. Again, I've told you a lot of it already. I was only twenty-one when Jeremy left for California. I was very immature. I didn't know how to handle it."

Ty stood up and poured them coffee. Joy collapsed onto the table, her face resting on the cold glass top. "Have you ever regretted it?" he inquired from the other side of the room.

She exhaled a grumble. "Do you really want an answer?"

"You just gave me one," he muttered and placed the mug in front of her. She was praying the conversation was over when he said, "One more question—this is the really important one." Her limbs grew weak. "If you were married to Jeremy, would you have his children?"

"Oh my God, Ty," she exclaimed. "That's not fair."

There was absolutely nothing in the universe she could think of that would wound Ty more than the three letter word about to escape her lips. Her throat was so sticky from nerves she wasn't sure she could get it out. But she didn't have to. All she had to do was look in his eyes, and he knew the truth. "Yeah, I thought so," he said before he stood up and walked away.

When he returned he had the travel bag with him. If he'd struck her across the face it couldn't have shocked her more than seeing the bag in his hand. "You're not leaving, Ty…you're n-not…" She lost her breath and cupped her hands over her nose and mouth.

He stooped down in front of her, and everything she had ever loved about him was right there on his face: kindness and sincerity in his expression, all mixed together with a sharp intelligence in his eyes. He had never been anything but good to her, but she couldn't pull out one argument to convince him to stay. She couldn't even convince herself that it would be fair to try.

"It's not that I don't love you, Joy," Ty said gently. "But I can't be married to you because you already have that with someone else." He pressed his lips to her forehead and his fingers combed her hair before he stood up. "I'll call you in a couple days," he said as he walked away.

Since she'd started reading metaphysical books, she had been introduced to the concept that no human being is ever truly alone. It is an illusion created by our own limited senses. She learned that at least one main guide is present at all times. Various other spirit guides step in to lend assistance at various points along the person's path, depending on their needs, and on goals set forth before they were born. Friends and family members who have passed over also check in often and some, like Jeremy, rarely leave our sides. Joy knew all this as she sat at the kitchen table sobbing into her hands. She could even feel the static electricity moving over the hair on the crown of her head—Jeremy reminding her of his presence. But despite the knowledge and the reassurances, at least on some level, she couldn't help feeling like she was now alone.

A few days later, when Ty showed up to retrieve the rest of his clothes, she was purposefully at the supermarket with Lily and Chloe so she didn't have to watch him do it. They'd returned home and Joy was unpacking the groceries when Lily called her out to the sun-room.

Sitting in a patch of sunshine was one solitary plant with gold foil wrapped around its base. It looked like a small tree, and as Joy stepped closer, she noticed there were tiny oranges on it about an inch in diameter. She sighed as she bent down beside the orange tree and read the card: *To help with your new joy.* The words made her burst into tears. Her high-pitched sob startled Chloe. She belted out a wail and a tiny orange that she'd been chewing.

"How'd you get that in your mouth so fast?" Lily scolded, but the toddler-almost- choking-on-an-orange crisis had created a diversion. Joy stopped crying and gave Chloe a hug. "Only Ty," she said with a laugh, "would leave a gift for someone he just dumped."

It smelled like sweat, the floors were scratched, and the paint was peeling off the walls, but Joy could see past all that. She hoped Jeff could, too. What she focused on when she stood in the middle of the shop was the skyline outside its windows, the seagulls and the beachgoers walking by with their fold-up chairs. Salty ocean air drifted in through the windows, just like it used to flow into her bedroom on Fairview Lane. But Jeff wasn't there to value the aesthetics of the place. He was helping her decide if the building was structurally sound and a good investment.

It stood alone, like a two story house, and was old but in a great location, at the tip of Brant Rock, next to the restaurant she'd sworn off on Jeremy's eighteenth birthday because of the flirtatious waitress. Joy had been practicing yoga there since the prior summer. Now it was spring again, and her instructor had recently informed her that the class would likely end soon because the building was for sale. The instructor's words planted a seed in her brain to purchase the building and use the downstairs as a combined art gallery and women's center. She could invite the yoga instructor to continue her classes and find a teacher for a REIKI healing class. She might even start a meditation group for developing mediumship abilities.

File cabinets were crammed into the upstairs level that had been used as office space. There was no air conditioning and the windows that looked out over the Atlantic Ocean were too small for such a spectacular view. The floors were linoleum tiles, and dark, 70's style paneling covered the walls. In Joy's mind, all these deficiencies were stripped away. With some work, it could be a studio apartment for her to live in. From there, she could keep it all within her sight—the sandy beach and the seawall, her beloved sea birds, and the indigo water that turned green close to shore. *Home.*

Ty offered to buy her out of her share of the house, which would provide the cash she needed to purchase the property. Now it was all resting on Jeff's experience and judgment. She was gazing out over the water, imagining white curtains blowing in the breeze, when she heard his work boots running up the stairs. "How much do you like this place?" he asked, as his eyes slowly appraised the space.

"Honestly, I love it, Jeff."

He rubbed the whiskers on his chin for dramatic effect while his eyes continued to take in the room an inch at a time. One side of his mouth crept into a grin. "Me, too," he said.

"Really?" Joy exclaimed and leaped into his arms. "Will you help me with it?"

He swung her, lifting her feet off the ground. "You know I will," he said then added as her toes touched the floor, "Hey, know what I like most about you? Even though you're all grown up, you're not really that grown up." Joy laughed. It was the best compliment she'd received in years.

Jeff accompanied her to the real estate office to make the offer on the building, and the next day Joy received the telephone call confirming that it had been accepted by the seller. It was the start of a whirlwind. Ty wrote the check without involving his divorce attorney, who later called the decision reckless and foolish. Joy, on the other hand, was so impressed by his willingness to help her establish a new life that she not only signed the deed to the house on Dragonfly Lane over to him, but also promised that she had no intention of seeking alimony, even though her attorney was determined to demand it. Ty was her oldest living friend and she had no intention of harming him in any way or creating conflict between them. Besides, it was time she learned to live independently.

Jeff handled all the renovations. He knocked the wall down between the two downstairs rooms, stripped and polished the wood floors, and replaced the two small windows with a large bay window. The entire Sanders family gathered to paint the interior a periwinkle blue, and when that was completed, Joy added slick white trim to match the milk glass on the new light fixtures. Finally, she added a large colorful rug to the art gallery. Joy brought some of her own drawings and paintings in, but she didn't place all of them in the gallery area for sale. Most she hung them in the learning center where they could serve as constant reminders of the people she loved. There were portraits of every member of her Sanders family, as well as Jeremy and Ty, and even Moonhawk and Standing Bear whom she sometimes glimpsed during meditations and in dreams.

The orange tree, that had grown a good six inches already, was placed strategically in the bay window where it could receive plenty of sunlight and could be seen by passerby. Joy had taken a curious liking to the orange tree. Her ability to keep it alive had both surprised and pleased her. Because Ty had given it to her when he'd exited her life as her spouse, it was a reminder that love can continue even when it changes. An astute observer might have noted her connection to the tree. The sign hanging on the front door read *Orange Blossoms*, the name of her new business.

The business was more fun than work. Every day Joy painted, practiced yoga and meditated, and every day she socialized with different people. She wasn't making much money, but she didn't need much. Mary volunteered to be the receptionist and soon she was participating in the classes, as well. When Lily threw her natural marketing talents into the mix, the Sanders women became a force. On weekends they played together too. Every Friday night Joy and Mary babysat Robbie, Maria and Chloe so their parents could go out to dinner or to a movie. And every Sunday morning the whole Sanders clan had breakfast together at the family home on Fairview Lane.

By the fall Jeff had completed the renovations to the apartment upstairs, and Joy exuberantly moved into it. With all her new female companions, Jeff remained her closest friend. Most days he'd stop by to see her on his way home from work, and they'd often have dinner together. The women at her shop would tease Joy about her cute "boyfriend", but he was never that. They shared an intimacy that Joy didn't share with anyone else; still she kept the line in the sand carefully drawn.

Every night when she crawled into bed, she spoke to Jeremy who, she knew, had been by her side the entire day. Her clairaudience was well developed. Although she couldn't understand everything he said, sometimes she could if he spoke slowly and in short phrases. All the while she could feel his energy mingling with hers, but there was no physical body to touch.

"I miss your skin," or "I miss your chest on mine," she'd complain and then laugh at herself for how ridiculous it sounded. She had his *soul*, his very being. Why did she need his body?

"I miss it, too," he'd say.

"When I die, will I be able to kiss you again?" she asked him one night.

"Yes, when you *pass to spirit*. You'll never die."

"Tell me what it's like—Heaven."

"It's everything we want. Heaven is a word people use to describe the way they think life should be. It's different for everyone."

"Say it again. Heaven is what we want?"

"We create it." She nodded, having picked up the word *create* this time. "There's something new…a surprise."

"Did you say *surprise*?"

Jeremy grinned. Joy was thirty-one years old, but to him she still looked like a little girl awaiting a happy ending to a bedtime story. "Orange trees," he said, "in our yard."

"Orange trees? You said *orange trees*. Did you plant them?"

He chuckled. She couldn't hear it, though sometimes she picked up on the vibration of it and asked *are you laughing* and he would confess that he was. "I manifested them. Manifest. Manifest…with my thoughts. I manifested the orange trees."

"You made them," she said simply. "You could be there now…in Heaven. Why aren't you?"

"It's not Heaven without you," he said only once, but the expression around her mouth grew serious as if she understood. "I can hold your hand," he offered and knew she heard him correctly because she removed it from under the covers and laid it on her belly.

"Two can be like one holding hands," she said and smiled coyly in the direction of where she thought he was.

Jeremy turned to Moonhawk, his eyes begging the question *do you remember*? Moonhawk laid a reassuring hand on his shoulder. He remembered every moment of Joy's life. He hadn't missed a single one.

"Remember I told you about the monkeys in our yard? They love the orange trees."

"Monkeys?"

"The monkeys…love…the orange trees."

Joy smiled. She was imagining them, the small monkeys he had told her about with the black shiny eyes. "Tell me more about the monkeys."

"You say *let me see*, and they show you their teeth. It makes you laugh. What's wrong?"

"I miss them. I don't remember them, but I miss them. That doesn't make sense."

"When we miss someone, we miss them with our soul, not our mind. The soul remembers everything. Close your eyes," Jeremy coaxed, "and I'll tell you about our home. There's a little cottage with the most magnificent garden—"

"A garden?" Joy interrupted. "You mean our white garden?"

"Yes, our white garden. And in the woods nearby there are animals." Her eyes opened at the word *animals*. "Close your eyes," he said again. "You don't need your eyes to see."

"Are they dangerous?"

His hand stroked her hair and her face relaxed at the familiar sensation. "No, sweetheart. Nothing can hurt you in Heaven. The animals are our friends."

She'd heard only the word *friends*. "We know them?" He answered *yes*, but she didn't hear it. "Do we, Jeremy, even wild animals?"

"Yes. There are white lions more beautiful than you can imagine." The last thing he said so fascinated her that she didn't ask any more questions, even though she caught only the last four words. She wanted to fall asleep imagining it. "Sometimes they let you ride on their backs."

CHAPTER THIRTY ONE
A Love with no Lines

The orange tree had grown another foot during the year and a half that'd passed since Joy last saw Ty, on the day they stood up in front of the judge at the Plymouth Probate and Family Court to obtain a divorce. It was during the summer of 2010, a sweltering Wednesday in July that he ventured into *Orange Blossoms* for the first time. Joy saw him enter and her heart fell into her stomach. Her life with him seemed eons ago, even though less than three years had passed since their separation. She was leading a group of women in a guided meditation at the conclusion of her mediumship development class, so she held her hand up, fingers spread, to signal *give me five minutes*.

An interesting occurrence had transpired during the class. One of the women in the group had seen Standing Bear clairvoyantly. Occasionally, when Joy communicated with Jeremy he shifted into Standing Bear and told her about the life they shared, which she usually became aware of by his altered speech pattern. His sentences were not fluid like Jeremy's and he didn't like to answer questions directly. He was playful, though. Once, during meditation, she caught a glimpse of him with his face painted black and white. The paint didn't mask the handsomeness of his face, but it was the endearing smile he broke into that took her breath away. "Are you always so beautiful?" she'd asked. "To you," he'd replied, and there was satisfaction in his words.

The concept was fascinating. Joy visualized the soul as a cut diamond with each side representing a personality from a prior life. She never asked about their other lifetimes together because she thought too much information would be overwhelming, but the life they shared as Native Americans—*Indians*, Standing Bear always insisted—felt close and familiar.

Jeremy had carried so much of Standing Bear's character into his personality that she shared a familiarity with him from the start. The dislike of shoes, the arrowhead and his long hair, his respect for all living creatures and an understanding of the Great Spirit's presence throughout them all were lessons learned during that prior life. When Madeleine, the young clairvoyant, saw him standing behind Joy, she did a remarkable job of describing him, right down to the two feathers in his hair.

"We all have a love story," Joy told her. "I'm just lucky enough to know mine."

When the guided meditation was over and the women were clearing out, she approached Ty and gave him a hug. As he stepped back, his fingers tugged on his short hair, a nervous habit that his ex-wife immediately recognized. "This is harder than I thought it would be—" he started.

"I already know about your wedding this weekend if that's what you're anxious about," she kindly offered.

"Lily…?"

"Of course," Joy laughed. "It's okay, Ty. I'm happy for you. I want you to have a good life."

He smiled his relief, and she offered to give him a tour. They began in the gallery where he stopped to look at a portrait of a little girl with black hair and enormous blue eyes. "That's Chloe," Joy told him when she realized he didn't recognize her. It upset him to realize that she was no longer a toddler, so Joy led him into the learning center where most of the portraits were familiar to his eyes. He was the one who'd had them framed. There was even one of him sitting at the kitchen table in their old house on Dragonfly Lane reading a newspaper. She'd used a green pencil to color around him…which was the way she saw him, as a kind soul and a natural healer.

"You made me look like a nice guy," he observed.

"Ty, you *are* a nice guy. I only draw what I see." She could now take Jeremy's childhood advice and look for a person's "light" as an indication of character.

"That's arguable," he countered. "Nice guys don't usually walk out on their wives."

"You did what you thought was right, and I respect that."

She embraced him and he held tightly to her waist. "I'm so sorry, Joy," he said in her ear.

"I'm sorry, too, but I'm grateful that I had you in my life. Thanks for always being there."

"Can we be friends?" Ty asked.

She smiled. "Of course! We always have been friends, haven't we?"

After a thoughtful pause he said, "I guess that's what we were all along."

"Maybe we all place too much importance on labels," Joy suggested.

"Well, whatever we are, I'll always be here if you need me."

"I know," she said, and meant it.

Before Ty left that Wednesday afternoon, he offered her the walnut desk that she'd fallen in love with a decade earlier in an antique store on the Plymouth waterfront, the same one her father had carried into the new house the day his illness was recognized. That night Ethan picked it up in his truck and left it next to the current desk at *Orange Blossoms* that still held papers and office equipment. When Joy ventured down the stairs on Thursday morning, her first task was to clear off the old steel desk and move the walnut desk into its place. But the steel desk was heavier than she'd realized.

She brought a blanket down from upstairs and laid it on the wood floor so she wouldn't ruin Jeff's beautiful handiwork. There was no chance she could carry the desk by herself, but she could push it. It was situated on a small elevation in the corner of the gallery, about four inches high. Maybe, she thought, if she could push the old desk to the edge of the step there would be enough room to squeeze the antique desk past it and Jeff could remove the old one at the end of his work day. Joy used her whole body to give the desk a shove first on one side and then on the other. The second shove was over-calculated and the corner slipped off the edge of the step.

It was a reflex reaction. Joy threw herself in front of the desk, thinking she could stop it from plummeting and ruining the floors. The heavy steel desk slammed into her left shin, causing her to cry out in pain, but she managed to prevent the rest of her body from being crushed by it. It left a deep gouge in the floor, though, and there was a golf-ball sized red mass where the desk had struck her shin. She held onto the oak railing that Jeff had carved by hand, up the stairs to her apartment where she put ice on her leg until she felt emotionally stable enough to call him. She heard his voice on the phone and cried anyway. "I'm on my way," he said and hung up.

Once he arrived, Jeff did what he always did, made her feel loved and protected. He set her up on the couch with pillows propped under her leg and gave her Ibuprofen. When she refused to be carted off to the emergency room, he went downstairs and left a note for Mary and Lily.

"You can go to work," Joy told him when he returned. "My mom will check on me."

"I'd rather stay," he replied and reached for the remote control.

"It's only a bruise, Jeff."

"I know," he agreed. "Now move over, would ya?"

She lifted her torso so she was no longer taking up the entire couch. Jeff sat down in the empty space and Joy put her head down on his lap. It was an unusual relationship they shared. He was like her partner, but he wasn't. Sometimes she'd even curl up in his arms if she needed to be held, but she'd never kissed him on the mouth and she wouldn't allow herself to imagine what it would be like to make love to him.

By evening, the injury was still throbbing and red, and felt warm to touch. Jeff was concerned and tried to convince her to call Ty. "He's getting married the day after tomorrow," Joy countered. "His fiancée might think I'm interfering."

"Then we should go to the ER."

"It's not an emergency, Jeff," she argued. "People don't die from leg injuries. If it's not better by Monday I'll see my regular doctor."

The next day Joy went back to work, but she was wearing yoga pants so no one could see that the injury was turning a deep shade of reddish-purple. She took Ibuprofen and did what she did with everything else in life that she didn't want to deal with—ignored it.

Jeff called her on Friday to inform her that the pedestal sink and claw foot tub they'd ordered for her bathroom had arrived. He'd install them over the weekend if she could live without running water. That was an easy fix—she could stay at her mom's house. Lily insisted on sleeping at the family home, too, and bringing Chloe so they could have a girls' sleepover. When they closed *Orange Blossoms* on Saturday, Jeff was already upstairs working. Joy hobbled up the stairs to grab her overnight bag and found him on his hands and knees in the bathroom with dust in his hair from the holes he'd drilled in the wall.

"What is it?" he asked without lifting his head because he could feel her watching him.

"I was just wondering what you'll look like as an old man."

"Why's that?"

"Because you have that white dust in your hair. Think we'll still be friends when we're old?"

"I'm pretty sure of it," he stated.

"I think so, too. Will you be okay here by yourself tonight?"

"Have a good time," Jeff replied. "I'll see you soon enough. If you girls do anything wild, I want to hear about it." She crouched down and grazed his face with her fingers. "More dust?" he asked.

"No." His dark eyes looked back at hers until she turned them away. Joy reached for her bag and walked out to the living room before she turned back and stuck her head in the bathroom doorway. "Hey Jeff, thanks for everything. I love you a lot, you know."

"What're you taking off for Mexico or something?" he teased.

"No, I just had the urge to tell you that."

"I love you, too," he yelled after she was out of sight. He knew she heard him, though, because her footsteps became silent momentarily before she trotted down the stairs like a horse. *Her leg must be feeling better*, he thought. It wasn't, but she was doing a good job of ignoring it.

An hour later Ethan and Robbie showed up at the Sanders' residence in direct violation of the "girls only" sleepover rule, but they had three large pizzas in their possession, which gained their entry.

"Where's Maria?" four-year-old Chloe demanded the second she saw them. Her cousin Maria was her favorite person on the planet.

"Sorry, beauty," Ethan said as he scooped her into his arms. "Maria's at her other Grandma's house."

"How come you're here then?"

"Because we wanted to crash the party," he whispered confidentially.

"You wanted to *what*?" Chloe wrinkled her nose at him like he was talking nonsense.

"We've never been to a sleepover," Robbie stated seriously.

Robbie was eight years old. He looked like Ethan and Bob, and walked like Ethan and Bob, but the words that came from his mouth were very different from the other Sanders' men. And he was easily bruised. The fact that the girls were having an exclusive party had hurt his feelings, which was the reason Ethan hatched the plan to "crash it". Although he didn't always understand his sensitive child, Ethan made great efforts to appease him. He was the dad that his own dad had taught him through example to be: loving, accepting and loyal regardless of the circumstance.

"The only thing better than a girls' sleepover is a girl-boy sleepover," Lily giggled, and her brother chastised her with his serious eyes.

After dinner they set up a Monopoly game and played in pairs. Joy claimed her mom as a partner, which drew from her siblings taunts of *Why, because you're the baby?* Finally, Joy could laugh it off. Later Ethan fell asleep in the recliner, and Mary covered him with a blanket.

"It's like looking at Daddy, isn't it?" Lily suggested, and the women smiled their agreement.

Robbie crawled into his sleeping bag next to his father and fell asleep within minutes. It took much longer to coax Chloe to sleep in Ethan's old room with the promise that her mother would soon join her. The women wanted to have tea together as they still managed to do most days, but Joy had only taken a sip when she announced that she was heading to bed. "I'm not feeling well, like I'm getting a cold," she told her mom and Lily. "It's kind of hard to catch my breath."

"Are you sure you're okay?" Mary asked.

"I just need a good night's sleep. I love you, Mom," she said and hugged her, then Lily.

"Good night, Joy," Lily said. "I'll go to your house with you in the morning to see the new bathroom. I'm planning on using that tub, you know."

"Okay," Joy agreed as she stepped into the living room to give her sleeping brother a kiss. "I love you," she whispered to Ethan then turned back to Lily. "But I want to leave early to bring Jeff coffee. Knowing him, he'll be working before the sun is up."

"That Jeff—what a sweetheart," Lily remarked. She was always trying to convince Joy to see him as more than a friend.

"*I know*, Lily. See you in the morning."

It was close to 1:30 a.m. and Joy was asleep when she became aware of a tingling sensation throughout her body. *I know what this is*, she thought. Several women in her mediumship group had shared with her their experiences in astral projection, which is when the spirit exits the body, but stays attached to it by what is known as a silver cord. As long as the cord remains attached, she'd read, a spirit can travel the Earth or into spirit realms and return safely. But once the cord is severed, physical death occurs, and the spirit can no longer return to the body.

The women in Joy's group had described a tingling sensation when the spirit first begins to disengage, and it was that feeling that captured her attention, but then it shifted so it felt like an earthquake erupting in her solar plexus and spreading throughout her entire body. She thought she was awake and paying attention, but she was actually unconscious. The leg injury had developed a blood clot deep inside a vein. The clot had broken loose and traveled to her lung. Her body was dying, but she didn't know it. She heard a pop and then she was floating—hovering above her unconscious body—and she thought she heard Jeremy's voice.

"I'm right here," he was saying. "Joy," he said patiently, and this time she was sure it was him. She could make out the dim outline of a man standing beside the bed. It was as if she were viewing his reflection in a pool of water. His image was fluctuating, but eventually it stilled and his face became as clear as it had been to her when she'd last seen him inhabiting a body, the day of her father's funeral in Jeff's Mustang.

"Jeremy!" she cried out.

His lips and his eyes were smiling, and his arms were reaching for her. "Come here sweetheart," he coaxed. "Come into my arms. I'll carry you home."

"I'm sorry I slammed the door on you," she blurted as soon as she was enfolded in his embrace. Seeing him had brought her back to that moment, the day he left for California for the last time and their bitter parting from each other. She hugged him around his neck and her fingers played with his hair. It was long again, like it had been when they were teenagers.

"There's nothing to be sorry for," Jeremy told her, but she didn't hear him say it. It was odd, like she somehow understood his thought without him expressing it. "Telepathy," he said out loud this time. "We can communicate either way."

The extraordinary content of his message, combined with the fact that she was holding him in her arms, *touching* him, suddenly startled her. "What do you mean go home?" she asked. She'd been so elated by his presence that briefly she'd believed he was somehow coming back to her, not the other way around.

"Something's gone wrong in your body," he explained. "It's called a pulmonary embolism—a blood clot in your lung. You can come home with me now."

"You mean I'm dying?" she gasped.

"No, sweetheart." He kissed her and his mouth was warm and soft, just like it always was. "There's no such thing. You'll never die." She peeked over at the bed, where strangely she could see herself under the covers, her eyes closed as if in sleep. "Look at *this* body," he suggested and held her hands in front of her face. They were a perfect replica of the ones she knew so well, that were now lying lifelessly on top of the sheets. "There's nothing to be afraid of. You accomplished everything you set out to do, and you did a terrific job. I'm so proud of you."

There seemed like many arguments could be made against his statement. She didn't feel like she'd done a good job; she had thought there would be plenty of time, until she was an old woman, to get things right. And how could this be death? It wasn't at all what she had imagined and been intimidated by her entire life. It was only a moment—a transitory moment— like so many others she'd experienced. It was more like tiptoeing from one room into another.

"Think of your relationships with the family," Jeremy suggested. "You healed all the old wounds. You were there when they needed you." His hand was in her hair, stroking it while he spoke to her. "But if you want to stay longer you can. It's up to you."

"How—isn't my body dead?"

"No, not yet. If you decide to stay we'll help you. Do you know what intuition is? It's when someone in spirit alerts you of something. Your mother will check on you and call an ambulance. Later she'll say it was intuition. You won't remember any of it, not even seeing me. You'll awaken in a hospital."

"But my mother's sound asleep."

"Take a look," Jeremy suggested, and somehow she could see her mother asleep in her bed, as if the house had no interior walls. Bob was lying beside her with his arm around her waist…like he always used to. *He'll wake her* Jeremy told her without telling her at all.

302

"Daddy?" Joy exclaimed and Bob looked over. She saw the laugh lines around his eyes when he smiled at her, but his hair was pure brown again with no gray in it, and when he approached her with his arms open wide to embrace her he wasn't limping. Joy threw her arms around her father who now looked the same age as her, and she could smell the wood chips in his hair. A thousand things were said in that moment, but not one of them out loud.

We've all missed you so much.

I've been right here the whole time.

You have granddaughters and they're so beautiful and smart…

I know, Joy, I know. I know everything that's happened with all of you.

It was with reluctance that Joy turned away from him and back to Jeremy. She couldn't stay. She wanted to, but she couldn't. His lips parted when he picked up her thought and his eyebrows tugged together in a question: *Why not?*

"I can't leave my mother."

"Your mom knows you're with me. She has more faith than you realize, and she'll use that to help people who are grieving—you can't see it yet, but there's a purpose. She and Lily will take over your business. There are women who need their help, women who have lost children."

Joy shook her head. "That would be too much for her."

"Do you remember what you said when Madeleine saw me as Standing Bear, *that everyone has a love story?* Your mom has your dad, like you have me. He won't leave her."

"What about Jeff? He can't be left alone."

"He won't be." Jeremy held her hands and she noticed how solid they felt. "Let me show you."

Instantaneously they were in a large hall like a VFW. About a hundred people were sitting in rows of fold-up chairs. A young guy was standing at a podium and boisterously telling them some kind of tale. Near the exit two women were sitting together at a plywood table drinking coffee out of

Styrofoam cups. One of the women, the brunette, turned her head and Joy realized it was Belinda.

"It's an AA meeting," Jeremy told her. The younger woman was crying and confiding in Jeremy's mother. As the words penetrated, Joy realized there was a little girl playing on the floor near their feet. "Recycling at its best," he added.

"What do you mean?"

"Belinda's turning her mistakes into wisdom. And because she's using it to help someone else, her own spirit is growing."

"Who's that person she's talking to?"

"Another alcoholic trying to get sober. See the little girl? Because of Belinda, she won't grow up the way I did. Belinda's going to sponsor her mother and help her stay sober. It's beautiful, isn't it, what human beings are capable of?"

Joy was silent. Belinda had been the villain in her lifetime. She had met no one whom she believed capable of greater atrocities, but she couldn't deny the truth of Jeremy's words. Maybe Belinda's addiction and turnaround had served a purpose after all.

"I thought you were going to show me something about Jeff," she said.

"I am," Jeremy softly countered. "The woman Belinda's helping is Jeff's wife. He doesn't know it; he doesn't even know her yet, but he's going to marry her."

"How could you know that it if they don't even know each other?"

"Because events start occurring long before people are able to see them. If human beings were more in tune with their spirits, they'd feel what's coming, like animals do before an earthquake. Jeff and his wife have been moving toward each other for quite some time."

"And you've been watching?"

Jeremy nodded with a playful smirk. "Her daughter is only three years old. Jeff's going to be her dad. When we get home, I'll introduce you to the person who's going to be their son. Jeff will finally have what he's wanted all along, his own family."

"This must be a dream," Joy said with a laugh "All of this can't be true."

"It is true. We're all connected, so once we're free of our bodies we can see and feel each other's experiences. All life is created from the same energy that takes various forms but is part of the same consciousness. That's why every act of violence is a display of ignorance—it's impossible to harm others without harming ourselves. You'll understand more soon."

This wasn't the same Jeremy she'd grown up with, Joy realized. He was, but he wasn't because he was no longer disabled by the fetal alcohol syndrome. He was downright articulate now. Joy watched the woman crying to Belinda and thought about how lucky she'd be to have Jeff in her life. *I'll never get to see him as an old man*, she thought. Earlier that same day, when she'd watched him work at her house, she'd imagined herself growing old beside him.

"I'll miss him so much," she mumbled.

Jeremy squeezed her hand. "I miss him, too, even when I'm standing right beside him. But one day he'll come home. And we'll be waiting."

Joy's eyes were still on Jeff's future wife. She had Jeremy now, everything she had ever wanted, so why should she feel envious? Because Jeff had been *her* friend, that was why. He had been loyal to *her* all these years. She was happy for him that he would finally have a real lover, but now she couldn't be part of his life at all. She would only be part of his past.

"That's not true, Joy," Jeremy countered. "Jeff loves you. He'll carry you with him. It doesn't make a difference whether you're in a body or not. Love is much bigger than that."

She understood. It was like loving Jeremy and Ty at the same time but in completely different ways. There weren't lines that couldn't be drawn outside of like in a coloring book —someone dies and you stop loving them; you marry someone and stop loving everyone else. Come to think of it, there didn't seem to be as many lines as people had always tried to tell her there were.

"They're all man-made. It's like looking at the Earth from space. There are no lines between countries. People create the concept of ownership because it makes them feel safe, but it's not real."

"Jeff isn't what you are to me," Joy clarified. "I don't want you to misunderstand."

Jeremy listened without interruption, a trait he had carried over from his Cherokee culture, before he spoke. "If you ever have the opportunity to love someone else, take it. Love is a direct connection with God, the Great Spirit. I'll never ask you to explain or apologize for it."

What he was offering her was something very different than any kind of relationship Joy had heard of, a love with no lines. It was almost more than she could fathom, but still his words resonated as truth. "You're the only one," she said, "that I can't be without."

"We're never apart for long," he explained. "If one of us passes over, the other always follows. What happened with your arms the day I passed over was you trying to break free. But when it was pointed out to you that your other relationships still needed work, you reconsidered."

"I didn't know I was trying to die. And when I hurt my leg, I didn't know then either."

Jeremy nodded. "I don't mean suicide. It's not the mind that makes the decision; it's the soul. Think about your last interactions with the people you love."

"I told Ethan I loved him."

"And Jeff…because part of you knew you were leaving."

Joy pondered his words. She had already made the decision without knowing it. "I'm ready to stay with you," she conceded.

"I know," he said softly and took her hand.

Like Sea Birds

A tragedy can be seen two ways, from the outside or the inside. It's a matter of perspective. To Joy's family and friends her death was a horrific shock, too difficult to accept. She had been young and in perfect health. To their eyes, she still had a long life ahead of her that they had expected to be a part of. But to Joy and Jeremy, it was the happy ending to another chapter of their still unfolding story. They were together, which was the most they could hope for.

As they lingered on the cliffs in Plymouth that he loved so much, she could see the little boy version of Jeremy still alive in his eyes and his grin. His face was ageless now, unscathed by pain or heartache. No disease or human condition weighed him down. He was, at last, a true free spirit. Joy slid her fingers through his, drawing comfort from his presence. Today they'd bid farewell to their family and return home. They were waiting for them to arrive so they could do so. She knew Jeff would lead the way, like she had asked him to.

From where they were standing, she could see the fish swimming in the ocean, the eyes of the seagulls as they passed over the water in search of them, and the ridge of water where the waves formed in between the two. Her visual acuity, now that she was free from her body, was mesmerizing. Colors were deeper, images sharper, and if she needed to see something better she simply moved closer to it instantaneously. It wasn't running or flying, but something in between, a simpler sort of movement made possible by her own will. It was the *ease* of mobility that had initially taken her by surprise. Jeremy had compared it to swimming with clothes on, and then stripping them off and suddenly feeling like a seal, sleek and smooth in the water.

Joy remembered it well, the sensation of total freedom that came from existence without the added girth of a physical body, even though she could not yet recall everything about her prior incarnations and their spirit home. The feeling of freedom was so deeply embedded in her that it had resurfaced many times during her lifetime: on the motorcycle with Jeremy, dancing with her friends, running on the beach, and throwing herself off the sea wall. During those moments, she recalled without realizing it, the pure pleasure of existence as a liberated spirit. That was the pull inside her that had felt so familiar and enticing. It was a sort of soul remembering.

Hazy images of home had been coming to her, and Jeremy had explained that her lack of complete recall was due to the intense memories from her most recent lifetime that still needed to be reviewed with Moonhawk's assistance. Once that occurred, she would have full recollection. Still, as they waited, she prodded him for information about it. "Take a look," he suggested.

"How?"

"Tell yourself you want to see it. It's accomplished by focusing your will, like everything else."

She was silent for a prolonged moment while she practiced remotely viewing their home in the spirit realm. "The flowers!" she suddenly exclaimed and he laughed.

"Our white garden," he said serenely.

"Yes," came out of her with a breathy sigh.

"Do you remember it?" he asked hesitantly.

"I've *dreamed* of it. There's a hydrangea tree like the one I planted for you."

"That's our favorite place to sit. Can you see the cottage?"

"No. Wait, yes…beyond the garden. It's white, too, like the flowers."

He smiled at her comment. "You'd be surprised how much is white."

"But why? Is everything in Heaven white?"

"No," he laughed. "Only in our Heaven. We create what we love, and you love white."

"I'm closer to the door now, so close that I think I could reach out and open it."

"See the honeysuckle growing beside it? It's from our last lifetime. You insisted on it," he concluded with a shrug, "now turn the door knob and go inside."

She focused, and somehow her hand that she could now see extending in front of her was able to turn the knob and push the door open. And inside was their home. In an instant she remembered it right down to the details, the plank floors, the flickering candles on the mantel over a roaring fire and the white flower blossoms carefully arranged in glass vases—they had reproduced those vases based on ones they'd had in Italy. *Italy...Italy*.

"Remember Venice?" she asked and he burst out laughing.

"How could I forget Venice? You were adored by everyone because of that voice of yours—you were an opera singer. I had to fight for your attention."

"But you won out in the end," Joy said.

"In the end I always do. Go to the windows and look out."

It took Joy a moment to re-acclimate to the cottage after the conversation and the images of Italy that were flashing before her like pictures in a slideshow. Once she did, she let out a gasp. "The monkeys!" she gushed. "Can I play with them?"

"Sweetheart," he breathed, "you can do anything you want."

In her mind's eye like a meditation journey, she burst through the door and startled the monkeys. They peered at her from the treetops until she invited them down. "Jeremy!" she yelled. "The orange trees! Look at all the orange trees!"

There were white blossoms covering the trees, and their fragrance was exactly like the ones on the tree Ty had given her. The trees were abundant with fruit, too. The monkeys were eating it. She sat on the ground and let them climb on her. They were chattering, and somehow she understood what they were saying. They were playfully echoing her phrase *the orange trees!*

She shifted her focus and was immediately beside Jeremy again looking out over the magnificent Atlantic Ocean. "It's Heaven. Everything here is Heaven too, isn't that right?"

He agreed without saying a word, then gestured with his hand toward their family walking down the path toward the beach. Mary was arm in arm with Lily with Hannah and Eddie close behind. Ethan was leading the way and holding the box of ashes in his hands, his face pale. How strange, Joy thought, that what had once been her body was now in that box in her brother's hands. She felt no attachment to it or sorrow over its loss, *like a snake that's shed its skin* Jeremy silently pointed out. Her sorrow was instead directed toward Ethan and the grief she knew he would shoulder alone. When she saw Jeff walking behind her family with Chloe on his shoulders and Robbie and Maria on either side she nearly sobbed. It surprised her, the amount of pain she was still capable of feeling.

"We never stop being human," Jeremy said. "We never stop feeling emotion."

The group stopped walking once they were all on the beach, and looked around aimlessly, considering where to release the ashes. Watching them, Joy suddenly became aware that Robbie was looking straight at them. Jeremy waved and Robbie actually returned the gesture.

"He can see us?" Joy gasped.

"For now. You'd be surprised how many of our abilities are lost due to the fear and confusion of adults. But Robbie has your mom and Lily. He has a better chance than most. Listen."

On the beach they could hear Mary ask him, "Who are you waving to?"

"Uncle Jeremy," he answered casually. "He's standing on the cliff with Aunt Joy."

Mary and Lily both pivoted and turned their eyes upward to the dramatic cliffs that bordered the beach, toward the place where Joy and Jeremy were jumping up and down and waving their arms frantically. "I can't see them," Mary finally sighed.

Robbie took her hand. "But they can see you," he advised. "Wave, Grandma." So she did, and it made Joy weep to witness it. Jeremy held onto her while she moved against him and into him, their spirit bodies meshing together. They were like one being, but she could still feel her own hair, separate from his, being tugged at by the wind.

"I remember that," she told him. "I remember talking to you when I couldn't see you or hear you, when only my intuition knew you were there."

"Loving someone is always an act of faith," he said quietly, "in the physical world, at least. Think about it—no one can see inside another person's heart or brain. They can't read their feelings or thoughts. It's all based on what we believe to be true, not on what we know."

Joy weighed his words and what she came to conclude was that human beings are braver creatures than she'd ever realized. To venture forth from a place of pure love and safety, where other people's intentions are as transparent as rain-water, and into a world where absolutely nothing is certain takes tremendous courage and trust.

"Let's get closer so they can feel our presence," Jeremy suggested. "Remember those sea birds you used to like? We're just like them now." She turned her face away from their family on the beach below and toward him, her eyes fixed on his. He held her hands securely and with a quick grin stepped off the edge of the cliff.

THE END

311

Acknowledgements:

There are not enough words to express my appreciation for the life I have that is made whole, happy and creative on a daily basis because of my family and friends. That having been said, there are a handful of people that I need to recognize for their support in the expression of this story:

Edan, Jillian and Ayala. In the midst of this tumultuous experience called life, you are invariably my safe haven, my home. For your constant love and acceptance I am forever grateful.

Allison Mulvey. You bring an objective, critical and often brilliant eye to the editing process. Thank you for reading this manuscript numerous times and for your suggestions that made it a better book.

My cousin and fellow author, Mary Rowen. Your copyediting in the eleventh hour gave this manuscript its final tightening before publication. I appreciate your time, valuable skill, insight and support.

Kim Robinson Range, my friend and loyal advocate. Thank you for everything you do for my work and for your faith in me. It means more to me than you know.

My "readers", Martha Ready Murphy, Julie Mulvey, Christine Ives, Althea Lachicotte, Marianne Maloney Cipullo, Jeanne Gorman Hickey, Shirley Avery and Kara Welstead. I am grateful not only for your feedback, but for your precious time, sharp eyes, endless encouragement and last but certainly not least—friendship.

Amber Tanderes, young graphic designer extraordinaire. Thank you for everything you brought to this book—your talent, time and enthusiasm. Your graphics made the words more beautiful.

Members of the band Tesla: Jeff Keith, Brian Wheat, Frank Hannon, Troy Luccketta, Dave Rude, and their Creative Director, Adam Wolf, at pigFACTORY USA. Thank you so very much for allowing me to use your inspired lyrics as the voice of Jeremy reaching over to his lover from the other side of life.

Maureen Hancock, psychic medium, spiritual healer, "God Squad" member, and all around wonderful human being. I am honored that you took time out of your busy and very important work to read my novel. Thank you for your lovely comments and for your support. A big thank you also goes out to my friend Bob Hancock for making the introduction.

If you are looking to connect with your spirit loved ones, please visit Maureen's website: www.maureenhancock.com. You can find her on Facebook, as well.

With all the love and light that I can radiate,

Kathleen

About the Author

Kathleen Ready Dayan is the author of *L.A. Ice*, a personal though fictional novel about drug addiction, and children's book *Cape Cod Bear*.

In a Garden White is her second novel. It arose out of her interest in the metaphysical and her own experiences with spirit communication.

A native of Massachusetts, she lives with her family and Boston terrier in Plymouth.

Made in the USA
Charleston, SC
26 May 2013